12

Kelvin V.A Allison & Lisa Hutchinson

This novel is dedicated to each other,
and the power of love and friendship
K & L

Chapter One

"Wow"

Turning his head from where he had been staring up at the house that he had driven over three hundred miles to see, Richard Miles studied his friend, chuckling as he saw her throw him an uneasy glance then look back at the building. For a moment longer he studied his best friend in silence then he raised an eyebrow, "So, was that a good wow or a bad wow?"

Myra chuckled, head shaking as she dragged her eyes from the house and met his gaze once more, a lopsided smile upon her face as if she was in a state of shock, "Did you see this place before you bought it?"

Richard nodded, smiling at her words and she let out a long whistle, head shaking, "Well, Mr big shot author, it looks like you are now the proud owner of the Amityville house of horror"

He laughed at her words, the sound loud in the quiet of the grey November afternoon, and somewhere in the grounds of the house a crow cawed back as if irritated by his sudden outburst.

Beside him, Myra chuckled, head shaking so that the curly brown hair that was hanging below the rim on the thick pink woollen hat she was wearing swung slightly, "Upsetting the neighbours already"

He grinned, turning to look back at the house that he had purchased just days before, his grey eyes drifting over the exterior of his new home, taking in the stone steps that led to the large front door under the porch. Time lost all meaning as he studied the large house in more detail. The building was old, built in 1640 by all accounts by a Swedish family arriving in England from a colony in Virginia, though little more than that was lost on Richard, his knowledge of architecture barely enough to fill a postcard, but he knew that despite its age, the building appeared to be in great condition. The first of the five levels were hidden below ground, his only knowledge of that level's existence having come from the print outs that real estate agents had given him when he had expressed an interest in the property, back in July. Closing his eyes, he imagined how the cellar level might look, his authors imagination conjuring up an image of the writer's study that he had been planning for years. Smiling to himself, he opened his eyes once more and raised them to study the ground floor of the property, the smile slipping from his bearded features as he studied the wide front door, painted black like an open mouth awaiting him. Groaning inwardly as he pushed the thought aside, Richard raised his eyes to the first floor, frowning at a broken wooden shutter that hung haphazardly from one of the windows, then moved on to the second floor. His smile reappeared as he noticed that the wooden cladding on the rest of the front of the property appeared to be in relatively good condition here apart from the flaking black paint that covered the majority of the old building. Glancing back at Myra, Richard shook his head slightly in bewilderment as he saw that she was still studying the house with a look of shock, then turned his attention to the roof of the property, and the two small turrets that jutted skyward from the middle section of that level. The information he had received from the real agents had stated this was effectively one large room, while the turrets themselves had apparently served as viewing posts for the property's original owner's centuries before. Frowning, Richard turned his attention away from the old building and glanced back over his shoulder, his brow furrowing once more as he chewed his bottom lip. Behind him and Myra, the grounds of the property stretched away for nearly fifty metres before reaching the stone wall which bordered the property on all sides, and the large metal gate through which they had driven. The grounds within the wall were a mismatch of tall skeletal trees, robbed of their finery by the autumn, and thickly overgrown bushes and weeds, which lined the wide gravel driveway. Beyond the walls on the southern side of the house, sat a narrow road and then a large green area around which the houses of the small village of Evenfield clustered, like travellers around a campfire, huddling together for safety, while the rolling green hills that made up County Durham hemmed them in on the south, east and north, and the start of the Northern Pennines loomed in the west, their higher reaches covered in snow. Frowning, Richard turned his head to the left, his nose wrinkling as he stared at the overgrown cemetery that sat there in the distance by some bushes. For long moments, he studied the shapes of the tombstones, his frown becoming a grin as he imagined bodies pushing themselves from the ground, his imagination running wild once more, his enjoyment fuelled by the horror on Myra's face when he had told her that his new home included an old cemetery on the long drive up from Portsmouth. Then he turned his head to the right, looking past Myra back at the house, his eyes drifting once more to the twin turrets, his heart skipping a beat as his imagination briefly turned what was clearly an old net curtain into something nefarious. Releasing the shaky breath that he was holding, he was about to turn away when he realised that he couldn't, some morbid part of his mind forcing him to stay staring up at the small rectangle of dirty glass, stained with dust and bird excrement as if he were in some trance. His stomach knotted, his free hand clenching beside him as he suddenly pictured a pale face sliding into view on the other side of the window, their hands pressed desperately to the glass, their lips moving silently, mouthing his name, "Richard!"

"Richard!" he jerked as Myra raised her voice, turning slightly towards him, an amused expression upon her features. Swallowing against the tightness in his throat, the author forced a smile, knowing as he did so that he had failed to convey his intended expression with any success. For a moment, his best friend stayed silent and then frowned, her smile slipping as she raised a hand to his bearded right cheek, her eyes locked to his, "Are you OK?"

"Sure" he nodded, trying to smile once more, this time with more success, "I was daydreaming"

"Daydreaming?" she gave a smile, "More like you are having a panic over how scary the place looks!"

He chuckled, his earlier dread fading away on the autumn breeze, the face he had imagined in the window forgotten, "Am I that transparent?"

"Yes" the answer came honestly with no malice.

"Touché" Richard feigned insult, then eyed his best friend with amusement, "She's not that scary is she...are you still going to come and live with me?"

"Oh darling, of course" she turned to glance back at the building, and then stepped dramatically into his arms, laughing aloud, his encircling her waist as she spoke once more, their closeness more like that of a couple than friends, "This place is so us!"

"Broken down, rotten and in need of repair?"

"Hush fool" she bumped back into him slightly with her hip as she stepped away, "Or the marriage between us is off!"

Laughing, Richard shook his head, "You couldn't handle being married to me, it's why nature made us best friends...I'm too frisky for you"

She laughed, turning to face him, "Frisky?"

"Yes...frisky...problem?"

"Not for me" she smiled mischievously, "I just didn't know anyone still used that word except for people who named cat food"

Richard nodded sagely, "I am very wise"

"Yes, you are" she nodded, then raised a perfectly sculpted eyebrow, "So?"

"So?"

She groaned, rolling her eyes, "Are you glad that you've brought the Amityville House of Horror?"

"This house?"

"Duh" she sent him a look that warned he was nearing the end of her patience, "Yes, this house"

"Oh" he feigned innocence, and turned back to study it once more, being sure not to let his gaze drift back to the tower windows, "I'm sure it's great...Norman Bates and his mother seemed to enjoy living here!"

"Wrong movie, that was Psycho not Amityville"
Richard grinned, throwing her a wink, "Right. But
yeah. I'm glad I bought it...although I nearly changed
my mind because it does look scary"
Her laugh was rich, "But you write horror novels"
He shrugged, "You know what I am like"
"A big girl's blouse?" she teased, shaking her head
again, "I can never get my head around how someone
that writes such disturbing horror as you do, is
scared of places that look a bit gloomy"
Richard grinned again, "Which is why I will outlive
you should we ever encounter any ghosts!"
"Oh my God, that's awful!" Myra laughed aloud.
A comfortable silence descended over the pair, until
finally with a groan, she sent him a weary glance,
"What is the time now? Is it one PM yet?"
"Long gone" Richard stated, "The guy should have
been here with the keys half an hour ago"
Myra frowned, "I wonder where they are?"
"Maybe the house ate them" Richard cast a look at the
building that seemed to be watching them intently.
Myra sent him a scowl, "And their car?"
"Maybe" he nodded, "Old buildings get hungry!"
"Dickhead"
"We have established this..." Richard pointed out.
Chuckling, Myra smiled broadly, "Are you sure this is
the right property? Maybe there is a really nice

building made out of smiles and unicorn farts that we are meant to be at instead!"

"Sorry" he shook his head, "This is the place, The Sanderson House, Evenfield"

She nodded at his words, then frowned suddenly, brow furrowing, "You never told me how much you paid for this place...a couple of million?"

"Five hundred thousand"

"Shut up" she eyed him in disbelief, her head turning to study the grounds and the house before looking back at him, "No way you got this for half a million"

He shrugged, smiling at her, "I did, apparently it's been empty for a couple of years, and no-one has been interested in it because of the maid"

"The maid?"

"Yeah, she comes with the house, it was in the agreement set out by the village council that she keeps her position"

"Oh my God!" she spun to face him again, "You get a maid as well...for half a million?"

Richard nodded, "Maybe she is some busty redhead with bad taste in older bearded men"

"Your type exactly" Myra teased, and he nodded.

"I might be forced to marry her"

Myra gave a sneer, suddenly serious, "Just make sure she isn't after your money dude, you know how daft you are when it comes to spending"

He nodded, staying silent as he studied her intently, wondering briefly how she would react when she found out that this was the first time that he had seen Sanderson House in person, chuckling as he imagined her complete shock. She was going to be furious. Myra was good to him, the best friend that he could ever remember having in the forty years of his life, but she worried about him way too much.

For the past decade he had already carved out a name for himself as the newest British horror author, earning himself a huge following in his genre but thanks to a TV serialisation of one of his novels, the show having won several viewer's choice awards on both sides of the Atlantic and being picked up for a second season, he was a household name worldwide.

Realising that she was still studying him intently, Richard threw her a wink, "Don't worry, if any women do make a move on me, I'll tell them that you are my dangerously unhinged lover"

"Twat" she laughed, and he nodded back at her.

"I know, as if we could ever be lovers!"

As she laughed and swung a half-hearted kick at him, he stepped to the side and turned, his eyes studying their reflections in the passenger window of his beloved brown Toyota Hilux.

Myra was the same height as he, but he was broader by far, while she was athletic and strong, her large chest and her attractive features, framed by her dark brown hair, belying the fact that she was nearly forty. Smiling, he met his own gaze in the reflection of his car window, taking in his grey eyes set with crow's feet and his thick brown beard flecked with iron, giving him the appearance of his much-hated father. "I'll never be you, not ever" he muttered under his breath, low enough that Myra didn't hear his words. Movement in his peripheral vision as he gazed at his reflection, made him tense, his stomach lurching as he saw a pale hand reach for his shoulder, the vague image of someone dressed in black moving in quickly behind him. Cursing, Richard spun around, the speed of his turn sending him crashing off balance into the side of his car beside a confused Myra, his eyes wide as he frantically searched for the person that he thought he had seen standing close in behind him. "Dude?" Myra asked in concern, "What?"

"I thought I saw…" his words trailed off as they both turned their heads to watch as a Jaguar drove into view through the open gate of the property, the gravel crunching beneath its expensive tyres.

Chapter Two

Jonty Beaumont was late, but he didn't care.

Throwing his Jaguar XJS around a tight curve in the road, narrowly avoiding a collision with a wide lorry that was coming the other way, he laughed aloud, his amusement heightened by the brief glimpse of the lorry drivers shocked face as he swerved away.

That and the drugs in his system.

His laughter died in his throat though as he turned yet another corner, his left foot slamming down on the brakes as he saw the red sign flash in the distance, warning him he was going way too fast.

Cursing, his mood darkening, Jonty forced himself to meet the speed limit, his blue eyes glaring angrily as he passed a sign that read; 'Welcome to Cockwood, please drive responsibly'.

Hands drumming on the leather steering wheel, he meandered his way through the village, throwing black looks at anyone that dared to glance his way, knowing that they would be able to hear his music blaring despite the fact that the windows of the scarlet vehicle were closed fully due to the weather.

"Fucking peasants" he screwed his nose up as he drove past the village post office, his gaze drifting over a small group of women that were stood around some pushchairs, chatting amiably together.

Then suddenly, the few houses and the one street of shops were gone, and another sign thanked him for driving slowly and respecting the village.

Laughing once more, he put his foot down, the horsepower of the vintage car throwing the vehicle down the road at breakneck speed and he gave a smirk, "Fuck you Cockwood"

The minutes dragged by as he sped along, heedless to traffic that might be coming his way, knowing from his previous visits to the old Sanderson House that the roads were often quiet in this part of Durham. Not that it would have changed his driving had it been busy. He had always been this way.

Born into the Wiltshire Beaumont's, Jonty had grown up a spoiled and petulant child despite his fathers attempts to raise him otherwise, the man's efforts thwarted at every turn by Jonty's overbearing mother, who had worshipped their only son with a love that had bordered on incestuous mania.

Despairing of her influence, his father had sent Jonty to Halcott Academy, the seat of the nations finest future leaders and influencers, hoping that his former school would save the boy from himself. At the elite Halcott, Jonty found that his family name combined with his good looks, quick wit and natural athleticism quickly earned him both the grudging respect and bitter enmity of both his peers and tutors.

He had been tipped for the top, much to the disapproval of many, and his future had seemed certain. Yet unfortunately Jonty was as cruel and vindictive as he was talented, and a prank of a sexual nature upon a rival led the boy to take his own life in embarrassment and shame, and the young Beaumont had found himself expelled from his new home. Returning to his furious father, Jonty had sought the protection of his mother but by that time she had swapped her affection for him to that of gin, spending her days in a barely coherent fugue state.

Admonished and shamed, Jonty had been sent to stay with his maternal uncle in Durham, until such time as he had matured enough to return, taking a position at the widow's exclusive branch of property agents.

Yet despite this vast change of circumstance, Jonty had still thrived, worming his way into the good books of his uncle, and rising quickly through the business until he was virtually indispensable to the elderly man, who had no children of his own.

Yes, as always there were complaints about the way he spoke to some customers and members of staff that he viewed beneath him, but in Jonty's opinion it was just the sour grapes of lesser men and women, determined to destroy him, just like those at Halcott, his culpability in the death of his fellow student never having occurred to him for the briefest of moments.

People were there to be used and discarded.

A disposable never ending supply of peasants.

He chuckled cruelly as he thought suddenly of the new young receptionist that he had taken to bed two nights before, a hand rising to scratch at his clean shaven cheek, a smile creasing his flawless features as he pictured taking her again. Taking her. Using her. Just like he had with countless colleagues and customers, his attentions not limited to women.

He grimaced as an image of the young Indian Ranjit, that had recently started working for the company came to his head, recalling how he had taken the effeminate man roughly over his uncles desk, calling him all manner of derogatory slurs, only to angrily threaten the man the next day when he had dared to presume Jonty was gay.

His top lip curled as he drove, head shaking.

How dare he.

He wasn't gay. Not he. No never. Not ever.

Sex was just sex. A fuck was a fuck.

That's all there was too it.

He frowned suddenly, wondering if the person that he was handing the keys of the Sanderson House to was going to be a male or a female, his imagination starting to run away with him as he chuckled.

After being on the books for what had seemed years, a buyer had suddenly appeared for the old building, and the talk in the office was that it had been purchased by a famous author or director and no-one knew if it would be the mysterious celebrity receiving the keys to the house or to one of their assistants. Yet eager to take the opportunity to rub shoulders, and possibly genitalia, with someone famous, Jonty had talked his uncle into letting him hand the keys over, much to the disapproval of Lydia, the woman who had made the sale. He had laughed aloud as he had seen the look of hurt and pain in the middle-aged woman's eyes as she had found out the news, mirroring the look she had worn when Jonty had used her and cast her aside shortly after joining his uncles firm nearly a decade before, the memory of it bringing a broad smile to his face as he reached the outskirts of Evenfield and slowed his vehicle once more, knowing from his previous visits that the road into the village turned a sharp curve to the right. And there it was suddenly; The Sanderson House, the property and its vast grounds dominating the eastern side of the old village, visible even above the high stone wall that ran the length of its perimeter. Gripping the wheel tighter, Jonty gave a sneer of disgust as he considered how cheaply the estate had been sold for, head shaking in disbelief at the half a million pound price tag, his sudden anger fuelled as he considered his several attempts over the last few years to talk his uncle into purchasing the land, flattening the house and building expensive homes for those seeking the Durham hills for a retreat.

Yet each time his uncle had turned his suggestion down, pointing out that the company were simply handling the sale for the village who owned the deeds to the land and the house, and who had set out strict rules regarding who be allowed to purchase it, these stringent criteria having ruined every sale until now. Nearly snarling now, Jonty studied the wall to his right, knowing that the entrance was coming up, head shaking as he considered the villages bizarre set of demands; the new owner must have no children, they must be a single male, and they must agree to keep the housekeeper on to work within the house.

Yet despite these rules, the house had finally sold, even though rumours abounded the office that the place was haunted, his uncle swearing the woman involved in the sale to secrecy regarding the matter. Haunted.

Jonty chuckled at the thought, eyes turning to study the roof of the house above the wall as he drove, his head shaking at the possibility. Ghost were not real. They were the crutch of the simple-minded fool who was scared of the strange noise in the dark, and a tool for the parent trying to scare their child into not leaving their bedrooms late at night. Nothing more.

Haunted indeed. How ridiculous.

The entrance suddenly loomed large to his right, and cursing, Jonty braked hard and turned the wheel sharply, steering his vehicle through the large stone gate columns, and past the large metal gate, his brow furrowing as he saw the three figures standing beside the large brown 4x4 that was parked near the house.

"What is this, a fucking gangbang?" he sneered, then chuckled, feeling himself harden slightly as he considered the sudden thought of such an act. Following the driveway, he turned the music down, the sudden sound of the gravel crunching beneath the wheels of his vehicle making him cringe, cursing as bits bounced off the door panels, and cursing under his breath he glanced at the trio, studying the broad bearded man and woman who stood beside him, then frowned at the old woman in black who stood behind the pair, steel grey hair pulled back from her face.

"Oh wonderful" Jonty grimaced, "They've brought the fucking grandmother with them"

Trying to keep his temper under control, he pulled the car up beside the brown vehicle, and clambered out, hands brushing down his expensive suit as he closed the door and cast an appraising look over his reflection, smirking at the handsome man with the blonde hair who stared arrogantly back at him. Satisfied that he looked as good as he felt, Jonty rounded the vehicles, open hand towards the bearded man, "Good afternoon, I'm…"

"Late?" the man smiled back, taking the offered hand and shaking it firmly in his own, his grey eyes bright. Forcing himself to not react, Jonty nodded, holding to the hand that had taken his, "You have my apologies…I was held up…bloody tractors think they own the road…these farmers think…"

"My father was a farmer" the bearded man nodded, releasing his hand, the smile still bright amid his beard but the light was no longer in his eyes.

For long moments, Jonty held the gaze of the older and shorter man, angered that he did not seen in the slight intimidated by the property agent as many other such men were, a sudden desire to punch the bearded man washing over him with the strength of a tsunami, nearly washing him away in a sea of anger. Somehow though he stayed afloat, and blinking, he turned his gaze upon the woman that stood alongside the infuriating man, a shot of arousal coursing through him as he saw how attractive she was.

"Hello" he turned a smile upon her, and she grinned, casting a quick glance at the bearded man beside her before taking his hand, and nodding back at Jonty.

"Afternoon"

Resisting the urge to stare as he noticed the swell on the front of her coat, fighting an image of her unfastening the zipper to expose her large tits, he turned away from her towards the old woman, only to grunt in confusion as he found that she had gone. For a moment, he turned his head about the area then glanced towards the front of the house, thinking for a second that she had entered the building only to remember that he still had the keys safely tucked within his suit breast pocket. Didn't he?

Blinking, he raised his right hand, stomach knotting as he felt the hardness of the keys there, the words of his colleagues stating that the old house was haunted returning to him in a rush. No, that was ridiculous.

"Are you OK?" the bearded man's voice dragged his attention back towards him, anger rising in him once again as he saw the smile on the man's lips, "Have you lost something?"

"Your companion" Jonty stated, hating the way that his voice came out sounding young and unsure, "The older woman in black with the silver hair"

"What?" there was confusion in the eyes of the bearded man, coupled with something else.

Fear?

"There's no-one with us" the woman stated, frowning as Jonty turned to face her, then she smiled a finger pointing at his chest as she nodded, "Ah...nice try"

"Nice try?" he repeated her words, glancing at the bearded author for help but the man was still studying him in silence, the look of fear still in his eyes, and fighting feelings that he didn't comprehend, Jonty turned back to the woman and shook his head in confusion, "I don't quite understand"

She chuckled, nodding, "You are trying to scare us right...what with Richard being a horror author?"

Time seemed to stand still as Jonty held her gaze, his tongue wetting his dry lips, and then he gave a forced smile, forcing a laugh of his own as he pointed back at her, "I nearly had you!"

She laughed, and he joined in, his unease lifting as he considered what he had seen, his pragmatic mind telling him that it had been a shadow, turned into something more by the coke in his system. Yet as he turned to look back at the author, he felt his stomach knot in dread as he found the man glancing about nervously, a hand rubbing the back of his neck.

"Are we going in or not?" the voice of the woman asked, and turning, he saw her smile at him over her shoulder as she began to walk towards the front door, a lusty smirk creasing his lips as his blue eyes dropped to study her firm arse as it swayed ahead of him in her tight blue jeans, the last traces of dread chased away by his returning sense of arousal.

Chapter Three

As the woman reached the front door of the building, she turned and stepped aside, smiling at Jonty as he approached, and grinning back, he moved to stand beside her in the overhang of the house, enjoying their close proximity. She smiled again, dimples appearing on her cheeks as she looked up at him, and he inside Jonty celebration bells began to ring. She was his, all he needed was some time to get her alone. She suddenly turned away from him, looking back at the bearded man, "Are you coming or not...what are you waiting for?"

Turning his head, Jonty frowned, initially irritated that the woman's attention had left him but then troubled as he saw the author staring about slowly as if in a daze, the voice of the woman loud beside him as she called out once more, "You need to go in first, it's your house!"

"And you are...his sister?" Jonty asked, smiling as she turned her attention back upon him again, her head shaking as she gave a throaty chuckle and grinned.

"No, I'm his best friend...his only friend"

"I didn't catch your name just now" Jonty smiled, extending his hand once more, gripping gently to hers as she took it, "I'm Jonty...Jonty Beaumont"

"Myra"

"Myra" he repeated, still holding her hand, "Nice"

She chuckled again, head shaking, and then took her hand, turning to smile at the author as he joined them in the porch, "Are you OK Richard?"

The bearded man forced a smile at her, his broad shoulders shrugging slightly as he scratched at his left cheek, "Yeah, I thought I saw something"

Myra laughed, glancing at Jonty and then back at her friend, "It wasn't the old woman was it?"

The Property Agent laughed at her words, his eyes drifting to meet those of the author, then suddenly felt as if he had a million spiders crawling through his hair as he saw the fear in the mans grey orbs, and he quickly looked away, hands fumbling the keys as he withdrew them from his shirt pocket to reach out.

"Here you go" he passed them to the bearded man, suddenly inexplicably scared to meet the author's gaze, hating himself for his irrational weakness.

Stepping back as the author took the keys from him and stepped towards the door, Jonty watched the man raise them to the lock upon the front door, insert them and then turn his hand, pushing with the other. As the large door clicked open, and the author took a step forward, opening it wide before him, Jonty took a step away, holding his breath in dread, his eyes narrowing as he stared into the interior of house, then flinched as something touched the nape of his neck, featherlight and fleeting. Cursing, he stepped quickly forwards, spinning about to find that there was nothing there, his internal monologue chastising him almost immediately, '*Of course there's nothing there you fool. What did you expect?*'

"Everything OK there?" the deep voice of the bearded author had Jonty turning to face him as he stood just inside the property, one hand holding the door wide, the woman beside him, both studying him intently.

"Yeah, of course" the trademark shit-eating grin was instantly back in place as he nodded at them.

"Well" the author gave what looked like a forced smile, "Would you like to come in and see the place...it'll be the first time for us all"

"Are you joking?" Myra turned her gaze upon her friend, eyes wide as she stepped closer, "You told me that you had been here and seen the place!"

The author shrugged, chuckling, "I lied...relax"

"Relax?" she gave a shake of her head, a hand reaching up to drag the woollen hat free, her long dark brown hair pooling about her features, "I seriously worry about you Richard!"

The authors laugh was rich, "And its appreciated"

They both suddenly seemed to remember that Jonty was standing in the doorway watching them and the author raised an eyebrow at him, gesturing with a hand, "Are you coming in?"

"I really don't know if I have time" Jonty winced, eyes peering beyond the author into the gloom of the property, then raised an arm before his face, feigning checking his expensive watch, fighting the irrational fear that was coursing through him like wildfire.

"Please" Myra rolled her eyes, smiling, "Until we know that this loon hasn't purchased a house full of drunken rapist tramps, join us...it'd be good to have a man with us"

"Hey, what am I?" Richard sent her a look of mock hurt, head shaking, "Chopped liver?"

"No" she told him, "But chopped liver is what we could end up as if there *are* some weirdos here. At least with Jonty here we'll be extra safe"

With that she turned and smiled at Jonty, her apparent need for his protection turning the spark of his attraction for the woman into an inferno, and he smirked, his fear gone, "How can I say no to a lady"

His head shaking, Richard gave his female friend a grin and stepped aside, gesturing for the younger man to join them both, "Then you'd best come in, Sir Knight"

A half an hour later, Jonty was bored.

The tour of the five floor property had been long, and dull, the house appearing to be fully furnished within and maintained to a high standard to match the appearance of the outside of the property, and as they had traversed its long corridors, the woman Myra, had clung to her best friends arm as if she had forgotten that Jonty Beaumont even existed anymore. "Bitch" he muttered under his breath for the tenth time as she turned away from a window at the other end of the attic, following the author back down the stairs, and sighing heavily, Jonty made to follow then froze as his mobile phone rang. He flinched, cursed and nearly slid on the wooden floor of the attic, the shuffling of his feet drawing concerned glances from the others as they turned to stare at him curiously. "It's fine, it's the office" he raised a hand, smiling with less enthusiasm than before, after all, the keys were handed over and it looked like a fuck wasn't on the cards. What reason was there to remain anything more than civil to the pair? It was time for him to go. "We'll be downstairs" the author sent him a nod, and with that the pair of them were gone front sight, the sound of them descending the narrow wooden staircase to the second floor followed by an angry gesture from Jonty. For a moment longer, he let his phone ring and then he cursed once more as he saw the name illuminated on his phone, a slide of his thumb answering it, "What do you want?"

"I'm telling your uncle everything" the voice of Ranjit answered, the tone thick with fear, and Jonty could picture the effeminate man shaking on the other end of the call, "The way you treated me was...wrong...I want your uncle to know"

"You ridiculous little man" Jonty sneered, head shaking, "How dare you threaten me, do you really think my uncle is going to believe you?"

There was a moments silence and then the younger man spoke once more, "Then I'll tell the police"

"Wait!" the cold shaft of fear stabbed into Jonty's gut, his voice lowering as he snarled into the phone, his body twisting on the spot, "Why the police!"

"The things you did to me...! "Ranjit gave a sob.

"Now just you wait!" Jonty snapped, "What we did was one hundred per cent consensual!"

"The things?" the Indian sobbed, "You can't even say the words can you, you monster!"

"Sex!" Jonty snapped, panicking now, "The sex between us was consensual...we both wanted it!"

There was a moment silence and then the voice of Ranjit returned, the grief gone, replaced by amusement, "Yes it was...and now I have you on tape saying it...have you heard of blackmail, Jonty? I think your uncle will believe what we did now!"

"He wont care!" Jonty felt sick, head shaking.

"No...on his desk...beside the picture of his dead wife...oh I think he'll care!" Ranjit was laughing, "We need to talk, I want reparation, or I am going to tell your uncle everything!"

"You fucking little bastard!" Jonty's voice was an almost feral snarl, "You fucking Paki poof!"

The phone went dead.

"Hello!" Jonty spun about in the attic, mind reeling in dread as he considered what had just happened. Then with a curse he was hurtling down the stairs towards the second floor, heels catching upon the red and gold carpet as he reached it. With another curse, he fell to his hands and knees, his phone slipping from his fingers to rest upon the edge of the top step.

"Jonty"

He turned his head, a look of surprise creeping onto his features as he saw Myra standing at the entrance to one of the rooms on this floor, a bedroom, her head tilted to one side as she studied him, smiling softly. For a moment, he stayed where he was, a jolt of lust striking through him as he saw she had removed her coat and was wearing just her tight jeans and what looked like a grey sweat-shirt, the material stretching out over her large chest, and then he pushed himself to his feet, "Hello again"

She smiled as he moved over to stand before her, his brow furrowing, "I thought you had gone downstairs with your bearded friend"

"No" she shook her head, her eyes looking into his as she reached out to rest a hand upon his right shoulder, "I thought I'd wait here and surprise you"

"Oh?" he raised an eyebrow, smirking as she stared into her big brown eyes, "Surprise me?"

Without another word, she released him and stepped back into the bedroom, her left hand reaching up to slowly drag down the zipper upon her sweat-shirt, her eyes locked to his own, as she licked her lips. Grinning, his troubles with Ranjit all but forgotten in the wake of his growing lust, Jonty leaned against the door frame, watching as the dark-haired woman spread the two sides wide to reveal that she was wearing just an ivory coloured bra beneath, the material doing little to contain the large breasts within. With a deft manoeuvre, the sweat-shirt was down and off her arms, and in her just her bra and jeans, she sat down upon one side of the rooms large double bed, turning to beckon him with a finger. Grinning, Jonty turned and cast a look back along the corridor and then towards the stairs, ensuring that they were not about to be disturbed and then he moved over to stand before her, hands reaching down for her breasts only to frown as she grabbed at his wrists, her head shaking as she released them and began to unfasten the front of his trousers, "This first"

Heart in his mouth he lowered his gaze, watching as she spread the front of his trousers wide and dragged down the elastic of his jockey shorts, a shudder coursing through him as he felt her ice cool hands wrap about his hardness, her fingers sliding as she looked up into his eyes, a smile on her face, "What do you want me to do with this?"

"Suck it" he grunted, his usual dominance showing itself, as he reached out with a hand to the back of her head, pushing her towards him, then he was groaning as he felt her mouth sheathe him, sliding deep then dragging at him as she pulled back, his eyes closing as she repeated the movement, moaning in pleasure.

Legs threatening to buckle beneath him, Jonty opened his eyes and turned his head away from the busty woman that was working away at him, watching her in the mirror of a high wardrobe. Then he turned to the left, looking out of the window at a pair of huge oak trees that grew behind the house, dominating the area there. As he stared, the bearded figure of the author came into view, hands on his hips as he stared up at the giant trees, head shaking as he turned to speak to someone, the woman Myra stepping into view, her own face turned up to study the trees.

The realisation of what he was seeing sent a shard of ice through his bowels and snapping his head down, he stared in disbelief at the black haired woman that

was bobbing her head back and forth on his engorged cock, moaning aloud, her fingers holding him still. "What the fuck!" his voice was high, whiny, a sob of terror escaping him as the woman suddenly looked up at him, her thin features and hook nose the face of a stranger, excitement in her eyes as she looked up at him, mouth sliding, spittle connecting her to him. "Get the fuck away from me!" he pushed at her, a curse of terror escaping him as she sat back and he saw her fully, her thin form clad in dirty brown clothes, her coarse chuckle like nails in his ears. "Bastard!" the voice of a man suddenly snarled in his ear, and Jonty spun about, head shaking in disbelief as he saw the ruddy faced man that stood in the corner dressed in similar clothes to the woman upon the bed, his large hands thick with dirt, a bush of black hair atop his head, large sideburns nearly meeting upon his big chin, resembling the serial killer Fred West. For a moment, the large man glared at him angrily, and then with a roar like a wounded beast he charged forwards, hands reaching out. Despite his muscular, athletic form, his years of bullying weaker men had earned him no skill in fighting, and faced with real danger, Jonty fled the room, hands desperately trying to put away his rapidly retreating penis, his heart racing.
He reached the top of the stairs unharmed and

paused, head turning back to stare at the doorway through which he had just fled, ears straining for any sound of pursuit, brow furrowing as he realised that there was none. Grimacing, he gave a shake of his head and turned towards the stairs, right hand reaching for the wooden banister then screamed in raw terror at the overweight red-faced bald man that he found standing there where no-one had been moments before, the strangers body clad from head to toe in black, a cross upon a leather thong about his fat neck. As Jonty screamed, the man reached for him, his words an almost incoherent, *"Foul fornicator!"* In terror Jonty stepped back, his foot almost slipping upon the stair and desperately he jerked his other foot about quickly, taking his weight upon that. The mobile phone that he had previously dropped slipped from beneath his foot, and suddenly he was flying, his body lurching over the wooden banister, falling headfirst into the void down between the stairs. Screaming, he tried to stop himself, his right shoulder catching upon the rim of the first -floor landing, his arm breaking in several places, the collar bone cracking with an audible crunch and then the ground floor hallway rushed up to meet him,
As he lay there dying, choking on his own blood, the sudden sound of footsteps on the wooden floor heralding the arrival of Richard and Myra, Jonty

turned his head sideways, and stared with rapidly
fading vision at the little boy in the grey old fashioned
nightshirt who was sat nearby watching him, a cold
smile on its pale face, toying with a knife in its hands.

Chapter Four

"So"

"So?" Richard looked up from his cup of coffee, meeting the gaze of his best friend as she sat beside him at the large dining table in the kitchen of Sanderson House. For a moment they held each other's gaze in silence, then one of Myra's eyebrow rose in question and he gave a chuckle, head shaking slowly, "It's too early for guessing games"

She sighed, "How are you feeling?"

"Hungry" a smirk formed amid his beard, "You?"

She ignored his question, eyes narrowing, "You know full well that I wasn't enquiring as to your health Rich, how do you feel about yesterday?"

"Yesterday?"

"Yeah" she gestured with an arm towards the direction of the foyer of the house, "You do remember that a guy died out there yesterday?"

"Oh that"

She eyed him curiously, "Are you OK, Rich?"

He gave a smile, but he knew it didn't reach his eyes, his broad shoulder shrugging, "I guess...I mean what can I do...sell the house? I haven't even lived her twenty-four hours yet"

Myra nodded, "What do you think happened?"

Richard winced, shrugging, "I wish I knew"

She grimaced, "How the Hell did he fall down the middle of the stairwell?"

"Maybe he was looking down at the ground floor and slipped?" Richard offered and Myra nodded.

"Yeah, what else can it have been?"

As his best friend raised her cup of coffee to her lips and blew upon the hot liquid, the author sat back on the wooden chair that, along with the table had come with the house, his mind drifting back to the awful moment the previous afternoon that he and Myra had heard the scream of terror. At the time the pair had been at the rear of the property, staring up in amazement at the two huge oaks that grew there, the thick branches on the sides nearest each other having grown together so that it looked like the ancient trees resembled two giant old men holding hands.

They had begun to turn towards the house, chatting about God knows what, when the scream had sounded from within, loud and shrill, the hairs on the back of Richards neck rising as he recalled how utterly terrified the man had sounded. Without a word, they had both begun running back towards the house, entering through the large overgrown greenhouse that was built onto the rear of the property, the pair freezing and exchanging glances as the scream had sounded once more, and then they were off once more, charging in through into the kitchen in which they were now sat, a curse of shock escaping Myra as the sound of something heavy hitting the ground had sounded from the hallway. Seconds later they had been standing staring down at Jonty, Richard reaching out to take Myra's hand as they had backed from the growing pool of blood in which the young man had lain like a human island amid a red sea, arms and legs bent at angles which nature had never imagined in her wildest dreams. As Myra had cursed, her hands dragging her mobile phone out of her pocket and begun desperately trying to call an ambulance, Richard had edged around the body of the younger man, cringing as he had studied his broken features, his nose all but flattened, one cheekbone looking like it had caved in, his lips thick with blood. Yet despite the gore and ruin of the man's features, his blue eyes had seemed to shine as they stared out ahead of him as if he had seen something in his last moments, his formerly handsome features locked in a mask of terror. Vaguely aware of Myra giving someone on the end of the phone the address of his new home, Richard had turned to look at her, head shaking slowly, "I think he's beyond an ambulance"

She had cursed, apologised to the person on the phone and then shouted out once more, "What's this village called?"

"Evenfield" Richard's voice had been surprisingly calm as he had dropped to a crouch, just feet from the body, aware of Myra repeating his words, then he turned his head to study the wall that the unfortunate man appeared to be staring at, "What are you looking at I wonder?"

Richard had flinched as air rushed past his face, skin scrawling as what had sounded like a child's footsteps had rushed from the hallway past him, and on shaky legs, he had risen and stared about curiously, then moved to the open doorway at the end of the hallway, peering at the furnished room within. A long deep red leather sofa dominated one wall, its back, legs and arm rests dark wood, and three armchairs upholstered the same way were dotted about the large, low coffee table that sat in its centre. Frowning, Richard had turned his head, studying the pair of high dark wood bookcases, against the far wall of the room, the rich greenery of a couple of large rubber plants on two separate small tables breaking up the gloomy aura that the dark wood and red leather sofas had given the room, then he had sighed, hands rubbing at his tired eyes.

"Richard?" Myra had asked, her footsteps sounding as she had moved across the hallway to join him at the doorway, her phone conversation over, and turning to her, he had sighed and forced a weary smile.

"Are they on their way?"

She had nodded, glancing past him at the room he had been studying, "What are you doing?"

"Nothing" he had chuckled, the sound coming out forced and before she could ask another question, he had taken her hand and led her out of the front door to await the ambulance crew for to arrive.

Less than two hours later, the body was gone, taken away by the paramedics to God knows where, and the police that had arrived with them had left as well after taking a statement from both him and Myra, They had spent the night together at the Premier Inn that he had booked for them both in Durham, twenty miles from his new home, and as they had done many times before, as friends, huddled beneath the duvet, Myra resting her head on his chest as she had snored, her body warm against his as he had laid there with his eyes clasped tightly shut, not wanting to open them and see the dread terrors that his authors imagination was already beginning to conjure. For a moment, he had considered rising from the bed and taking one of the tablets that his doctor had prescribed for when he began to have one of his episodes, but that would have meant leaving the safety of the bed, his memories of his childhood and the monsters his mind had created returning to him.

No, far safer to stay where he was with Myra. Somehow, heart hammering in his chest like when he had been a terrified child on his fathers farm, hiding beneath the covers, he had fallen asleep, waking to the sound of his best friend groaning as she had sat up beside him the next morning as the autumn sunlight shone through the window, and after a cold and tasteless McDonalds breakfast, the pair of them had returned back to the sprawling Sanderson House.

"What are you going to do with all the furniture in this place?" the voice of Myra dragged him suddenly from his memories and glancing up he found her sitting at the table watching him, her coffee cup clasped between her hands as she waited for a reply.

"I don't know" he gave a shake of his head, a lopsided grin on his face, "I hadn't realised that it was going to be furnished, the first removal van arrives today with my belongings"

She laughed at his words, then winced, "So, how do you feel about sleeping here tonight?"

Richard shrugged, trying to act unconcerned, his stomach knotting as he raised his coffee to his lips, the accident replaying in his head again.

He could almost hear the screams of terror.

Screams. Plural.

"Wait" he lowered his coffee cup, brow furrowing as he stared at Myra, "He screamed twice"

"What?" she sent him a confused look, "Who?"

"Who do you think?" he sighed, "Jonty…the guy, from yesterday…he screamed twice"

"Did he?" she raised an eyebrow, "I don't recall"

Richard nodded, feeling sick, "Yeah, but why?"

"Why what?"

"Why scream twice?"

For a moment, Myra held his gaze without speaking, a frown on her face and then she shrugged, "The guy was falling…he was scared"

Richard swallowed the tightness in his throat, "There was a pause…he screamed…we ran in from the back garden, through the conservatory…then he screamed again…why?"

She gave a weary smile, "I expect you'd scream if you fell over the top banister…its natural"

"But why the pause?" Richard placed his cup down, wanting to conceal how much his hands were shaking, "Its quicker to fall from the top of the stairs to the ground than it is for us to run in from out the back surely?"

"I don't know" she seemed unconcerned by his words, "Maybe the first scream was him falling over the banister, and the second was when he hit the floor?"

"No…there was a scream…we made it to the conservatory and he screamed again…then there wasn't the sound of him hitting the ground until we reached the kitchen!"

Long moments drifted by as they stared at each other, her features slightly paler as he raised an eyebrow, "What made him scream first?"

They both jerked in shock, Richard lurching to his feet and spilling what remained of his coffee as the door to the hallway suddenly opened behind them, and eyes wide they turned, watching in confusion as a thin woman strode past them and placed a plastic carrier bag upon the worktop beside the large rectangle sink. Exchanging glances with Myra, Richard sat back down on his chair, watching as the woman removed her coat, placed it over the back of an empty chair and then began to fill the kettle. Stunned, the author studied the woman intently, her lean form carrying an aura of power despite the fact that she was stick thin, her bobbed hair iron grey, her form clad in a blue knitted cardigan and a pair of black slacks. For a moment he let her potter about, then he gave a cough, trying to politely attract her attention, only to wince as she turned towards him, her features matronly, her voice thick with a northern accent, "Is there a problem, Mr Miles?"

"Oh" he winced, head shaking, thrown by the fact that she knew his name, "Er, no…no problem"

She studied him for a moment as if she expected him

to change his mind, then returned her attention to the kettle, humming as she retrieved a cup from the wooden cupboard by her knees, her voice reaching back to him, "Would you like another cup Mr Miles?"

"Oh, no, not thank you"

She gave a barely perceptible nod, "And the girl...would she like another?"

"No" Myra answered before Richard could speak, amusement on her features at the old woman's referral to Myra as a girl, "The girl is fine thank you very much"

"As you wish" the old woman continued to hum, her narrow shoulders appearing to sway slightly and eyes wide, Richard looked at his best friend, lips silently moving as he gestured at the old woman. 'Who is this?'

'Ask' she mouthed back, trying not to laugh.

Taking a deep breath, Richard cleared his throat, wincing once more as the woman turned to eye him with a matronly look, "Are you sure there isn't something amiss, Mr Miles?"

"Well..." he began, face screwing up, "I...er..."

"He wants to know who you are" Myra interrupted him, drawing a withering glance from the old woman in the dark blue cardigan, her lips twisting together.

"Does he?"

"Yeah" Richard's admission had her turning back towards him, "Sorry, but who exactly are you?"

"I am Ms Sanderson" she gave him a nod, then turned back to study the kettle as it began to boil, her voice continuing, "I was led to believe that you were aware that my continued employment was part of you buying Sanderson House..."

"Ah" the author clicked his fingers, watching as she began to pour water into her cup, "The maid"

"Maid, cook, housekeeper...whichever term makes you feel most at ease Mr Miles" the old woman returned to the plastic bag that she had carried in, retrieving a carton of milk, the faint trace of a smile creasing her thin lips as she nodded at him, "You may call me Margaret"

"OK" he smiled back, relaxing slightly as she turned away and continued making her drink, "I wasn't sure when you would want to start?"

"Start Mr Miles?"

"Please, its Richard, and this is my friend Myra"

She nodded at his words, repeating the gesture to his best friend and then frowned, "I like to come every day and give the house a clean, a house this size needs constant care or it becomes a mess"

"Right" he nodded, frowning, "And I pay you?"

"Oh good heavens no" she turned to look at him,

shock on her features, "I am paid by the village"

"Oh" he glanced at Myra, then back at her, "The village pay you to clean my house?"

"Indeed Sir…it is how it has always been, and how it will continue to remain"

"Wait a minute" Myra sent her a frown, "Your surname is the same name as the house"

Something unreadable crossed over the old woman's face, an expression so quick that Richard wasn't sure he had really seen it, her voice slightly tighter as she nodded, "Indeed, this house was built by my ancestors long ago"

There was a silence as she stood there, regarding them both, a look of infinite sadness reaching her eyes and then she seemed to snap out of it, turning back to her drink, "If I may have this hot drink first, sir, I will begin my chores for the day"

"Sure" Richard nodded, giving up on getting her to use his first name, "Take your time, like I say I really wasn't expecting you for a few days, especially after what happened here yesterday"

She nodded at him, turning to study the author with her steaming cup in her hands, "I assume you are referring to the handsome young man with the blond hair and the blue eyes"

"Yeah" he nodded, not surprised that the news of the death had spread around the village but surprised by how accurate the details had been, and was about to speak again when he saw her staring past him at the far side of the kitchen, the muscles in her cheeks tensing as if she were trying not to react to something, "Are you OK?"

"Yes, Sir" her smile didn't reached her eyes as she turned back to face him, "Never better"

Chapter Five

Several hours later, Richard was standing at the front door of the Sanderson House, a hand raising to wave at the driver and crew of the removal lorry as they pulled out of the gateway. Smiling, he waited until they were gone and then turned, the expression slipping as he saw the large hallway of the house full with packing boxes and pieces of furniture from his large house in Portsmouth, "Oh for fuck sake"

A polite cough from nearby made him turn, wincing as he saw Myra and Margaret standing in the doorway of the large sitting room, each holding a cup in their hands as they watched him, a frown upon the lined face of the older woman, a broad grin on the face of his best friend as she shook her head, "Do you have to swear so much?"

Sighing heavily, he shook his head, directing his reply to the housekeeper who he realised had coughed when he had sworn, "I'm sorry, I wasn't expecting to have to store everything in the hallway...its going to make things difficult until I can get rid of the older stuff and fit mine in"

He tensed at the sudden sharp intake of breath from the old woman, what little colour had been in her cheeks seeming to fade as she shook her head, "Get rid...some of this furniture has been in the house since I was a child Mr Miles"

"Oh" Richard nodded, not sure what she was expecting of him, but not wanting to offend the old woman on the first day of their acquaintance.

"Hey you don't need to make any decisions today right?" Myra stepped out into the hallway to stand before him, winking as she spoke, throwing him the lifeline that he so desperately needed in that moment.

"No, you're right" he nodded, glancing past her to smile at the old woman, seeing the concern lift from her like an almost visible cloud, "Hey, I might like some of the stuff better than my own!"

Smiling at him, Myra winked again then turned to look at the housekeeper, "Have you really been at this house since you were a kid, Margaret?"

The old woman nodded, her features lighting up with a smile, her eyes seeming to sparkle and Richard realised that in her youth she must have be quite striking, "Oh yes, my mother worked here for the village and various owners, and before her my grandparents did the same job"

Myra chuckled, "I bet you've seen some things"

"Such as?" the smile faded from the face of the old woman, her tone suddenly defensive, her voice cold.

"Oh, nothing in particular" Myra glanced at Richard and then back at the older woman, head shaking, "It's just a phrase isn't it?"

"Is it?" Margaret seemed to have tensed, her eyes

flitting about the hallway and the furniture and boxes that were stacked there, her head shaking as she turned back to Richard, "Right, I must be getting on with my chores, with all these boxes the house will be getting dustier by the minute"

"Are you OK?" Richard asked as she left the doorway of the sitting room and began to move past them on route to the kitchen, "If we have offended you in any way then I…"

"I am fine Mr Miles" she continued on, her tone no longer conversational, "But I am very busy, I am sure you understand that"

"Of course" he nodded, a sad smile on his bearded features as he watched until she had entered the kitchen, and then turned to look at Myra, "I think we have upset the old girl"

"How?" Myra asked, confusion on her face.

"I don't know but she obviously feels very strongly about this place" he shrugged, "Have you seen how she glances about all the time as if she is seeing things? I thought at first that she was a bit…you know…mad…but I think she is just caught up in memories"

Myra nodded at him, then smirked as she glanced at the huge jumble of boxes and furniture, "So, any more removal vans coming today?"

"No thank God, but there is tomorrow"

Myra laughed at his words and he groaned, shaking his head as he turned and stared at the crowded hallway, wondering where on Earth he was going to put everything when it turned up.

"Hey do you fancy a walk?" her voice dragged his attention back on her and he nodded, smiling.

"Sure...lets go meet the rest of the locals"

Minutes later, after shouting through to the old woman that they were heading into the village, the pair left the Sanderson House wrapped in their coats, Myra sporting her pink woollen hat once more.

Side by side, they left the gate of the property, made their way over the road outside, and then began to head across the village green to the semi-circle of village buildings that surrounded it, Richard frowning as he had realised for the first time just how small a place Evenfield was, each of the buildings built from light beige quarry stone. Starting on the left sat the village post office, a small hardware store beside that, then a few houses, a larger building that had the words Village Hall emblazoned across its doors.

There was a road that angled past the village hall, leading to what looked like a small crop of houses, smoke coming from their chimneys, and then on the other side of the road sat what looked like a food shop, a larger building, bigger than even the village hall, then a few more homes and finally a small church, facing the post office across the village green. They had paused for a moment, exchanging glances and Myra had frowned, "Well, that seems odd"

"What?" he had sent her a grin, "What's odd?"

"There's no pub"

He gave a laugh, about to point out that she really needed to get a handle on her drinking when he realised that she was right, his brow furrowing.

"Seems a bit odd for a place like this" Myra frowned, turning her head about, her confused expression drawing a fresh smile from Richard as he studied her.

"Expert on Durham villages, are you?"

"No, but you know what I mean"

And he did.

In the forty years of his life he had never passed through any village anywhere that hadn't had at least one public house, often the centre of the community, yet Evenfield seemed to have none to call its own.

"Maybe that's it" she gestured to the large building beside the food shop, "It looks closed"

"It's got no sign or anything" Richard shook his head, hurrying to catch up as she began to walk towards the building, her interest piqued, her strides quick. From the sky above them there came an ominous rumble, and casting an uncertain glance up at the dark clouds that seemed to be gathering above the small village, Richard winced, "I think its going to start raining"

"Yeah" Myra nodded, clearly not listening, her eyes focused on the building that they were approaching and sighing, Richard continued after her, his head turning about, stomach knotting as he saw a man standing in the door of the post office watching them intently, an elderly couple appearing at the window of the hardware store, their heads also turned towards him and Myra, one man pointing a finger. "Shit" he muttered, stomach lurching as in the windows of the houses, curtains began to twitch, and a trio of figures emerged from the village hall to watch them, "This is like the Wicker Man"

"There!" he glanced back at his friend as she hurried across the little road that followed the arc of shops and homes, joining the main road past Sanderson House at both ends, and gritting his teeth, he hurried to catch up with her as she stood on the other pavement, looking up at the tall wooden beam that rose up in front of the large building, towering over the pair of them, backlit by the grey autumn sky. Frowning, Richard stared up at the wooden beam in confusion, the frame of a square at its top, his brow furrowing as he studied a single piece of link chain that was hanging from the underneath of the top part of the square, "What's that?"

"What is missing from there?" Myra sent him a smile, her eyes drifting back to study the beam.

The author shrugged, "I don't know...what?"

"A pub sign" she glanced back at him, "Look, the chain for it is still hanging up there"

For a moment, he nodded, staring at the chain and then sent her a smile, "And your point is?"

Groaning, she turned to him, "This used to be a pub...or an Inn or whatever they used to call them...I wonder why they don't have one now?"

"Drink you are after is it?" the deep voice asked, and cursing, Myra spun about to move beside Richard, the pair of them standing, staring at the large middle-aged man that stood watching them from the door of the shop beside them, ginger hair bushy and the white apron that he wore bulging over his stomach.

"Hi" Richard nodded at him, stepping forward, his right hand extending in greeting, "I've j..."

"Just moved in to the Sanderson House" the large man finished for him, a hand like a paw wrapping the authors as he shook it, a smile spreading across his features, "I'm George...George Wolf"

"George" Richard nodded, feeling awkward as the man continued to hold to his hand, "I'm Richard Miles, and this is Myra"

At his introduction, George Wolf released his hand and turned an appraising stare upon his best friend, eyes narrowing as he addressed Richard, "And she is what...your daughter?"

The author laughed, confused as to why everyone assumed she was younger than him, "She's my friend"

The shopkeeper gave a nod, his eyes still resting upon a smiling Myra, "A friend...and will you be living at Sanderson House with Mr Miles?"

As she opened her mouth to give a confirmation, Richard laughed once more, suddenly desperate to not reveal that she would be, unsure why, "No, she is staying with me while I move in, a week, no more...you know, just so I have a friendly face"

The big man turned to glance at him then, his red cheeked features splitting into a broad grin as he laughed, "That's a relief...there's few things in life as depressing as a man who has to share his home, do yourself a favour and keep it that way lad!"

"Lad?" Myra sent Richard an amused look, and he rolled his eyes, then glanced up, groaning as above the them the dark clouds finally opened, and a heavy rain began to fall upon Evenfield.

Chapter Six

"Well, that could have gone better" Myra stated as they walked back between the gateposts and into the grounds of Sanderson House just twenty minutes later, the pair of them completely soaked to the skin. As the rain had begun to fall, George Wolf had thrown them both a wink, shaken the hand of Richard once more, and hurried back inside his shop, shouting to them to be sure to shop local, leaving the pair exchanging amused glances as they had walked away. Bending into the rain, stunned by how cold the temperature of it was, they had made their way left along the crescent that made up the front of the village, passing by the town hall, the hardware shop and the post office, nodding at the villagers who still stood studying them as if they had two heads each, then turned to head back across the village green. Richard turned to throw her a smile, nudging her with an elbow as they walked side by side, "At least George was friendly"

"To you"

Richard grinned, "He was nice to you"

"Eventually" she sent him a sideways look and he frowned, realising that she was being serious.

"Hey, what's wrong?"

She paused, turning to face him in the overhang before the front door, a hand dragging her wet woollen hat from her head, "This place is weird"

He nodded, "It's a village"

"Oh, that explains everything" the trace of a smile appeared on her attractive features, as she raised a hand to wipe the raindrops away, and Richard sighed, suddenly extremely concerned for his best friend. "Are you OK, or not?"

She shrugged, made a non-committal face and shook her head, "Its weird, like yeah George was fine with me but only when you lied and told him that I wasn't going to be staying here...and why did you do that?"

"I don't know" he winced, being one hundred per cent honest, "It just felt like the right thing to do"

"So you realised that he was being weird"

"I guess" the author nodded, "But it wasn't like a conscious thought, more like a sudden feeling"

She shook her head, her smile grim, "And did you see the looks on the faces of the rest of them when they were looking at me...it's like they haven't seen a woman before!"

"Maybe they've just never seen one as attractive as you" Richard grinned, wiggling his eyebrows, "Maybe you have upset all the women because they know now there's a new woman in the village and they are scared they will lose their husbands to the dark-haired temptress!"

Myra laughed at his words, punching him softly in the right shoulder, "Dick head!"

"I'm being serious!" he grinned at her, pointing back in the direction of the village, "I bet that as we speak poor George Wolf is being read the riot attack my Mrs Wolf...she's probably called Winifred or something..."

"Winifred Wolf!" Myra was in hysterics, her eyes wet with laughter, head shaking, "You are a bloody idiot!"

Still smiling, he leaned back against the wall behind him, nodding, "I am...it's been proven"

"Time and time again" she chuckled back at him.

A comfortable silence descended upon them as they stood there, the heavy patter of the rain on the gravel loud beside them and then he smiled once more, "Listen, I don't care what the village of the damned think. You are my best friend; this is my house and I decide what happens in it!"

Without warning, she stepped forward and hugged him, drawing a laugh from the author, his head shaking as she stepped back, "Right, now that is that drama out of the way can we go in?"

Laughing, she nodded and he stepped past her, inserting his key into the lock and turning it, pushing the large wooden door open wide before him.

For a moment he groaned as he saw the huge pile of

furniture and boxes, having momentarily forgotten they were cluttering up his hallway then he turned to watch as Myra nudged him with an elbow, "Fancy coming in to the living room and playing cards?"

He nodded, and she made to step past him, "I'll go make us a cup of tea first!"

"No" he stopped her, winking, "You've had a stressful day, you go sit down, I'll make the tea"

"Cheers wifey" she grinned, poking her tongue out at him and as she headed through into the living room and laughing, Richard turned and made his way to the kitchen, only to pause, hand on the handle as he heard two voices from speaking beyond the door. Frowning, he leaned closer, wondering if perhaps he was imagining things but no, there were definitely two voices, one calm and insistent, barely audible through the wood of the door and then came the voice of Ms Sanderson, sounding as if she was trying to control her anger, "...and I told you that Mr Miles is a busy man!"

There was a brief silence, and then the other voice sounded, that of a young woman, "I don't want to cause problems, I just want to let him know about the history of the house...he has a right to know, doesn't he?"

"Perhaps" came the reply from the elderly woman, weariness sounding in her voice, "But not yet...leave the man be...for pity's sake!"

"Please" the younger woman replied, her tone still conversational despite her words, "I am asking first out of respect for you and what you do here at Sanderson House...it's a thankless job"

"Your respect is appreciated, as is how little of a nuisance you make of yourself" the reply came from the housekeeper, "However, I bid you leave the poor man alone"

"I don't have to ask for your permission to see him...if I want to, I will"

"Cherry!" the voice of Ms Sanderson was ice cold, and Richard could imagine the stern look upon her angular features, "Do not do this..."

Sighing heavily, the author turned the handle and pushed the door open, striding into the kitchen, a broad smile upon his face as he glanced from the young woman with the blue hair that was standing beside the large wooden table, her face turning towards him as he entered, and then he met the gaze of Ms Sanderson as she turned to look at him in shock, "Ah, Sir, can I fetch you anything...a cup of tea perhaps?"

He smiled, nodding, "Well, I was coming to make some tea yes but...

"Nonsense" she spun to face the counter, hands dragging a cup from the cupboard, "What is the point of having me here if you have to make your own cup of tea...I'm not doing anything else after all, just enjoying my own company"

Richard laughed at her words, throwing the blue haired young woman a confused look, getting one back in return, as he glanced back at the elderly woman, "Are you going to introduce me to your friend...I heard you from the hallway, I don't mind meeting new people, its fine"

At the kitchen worktop, Ms Sanderson stiffened, her hands stopping fussing with the cups, her face half turning towards him, "My friend?"

He nodded, glancing back at the blue-haired woman to find her watching him with a curious smile upon her features, a wave of attraction coursing through the author as he studied her, then glanced back to find the old woman standing watching him with a bemused look upon her features, "Mr Miles...Sir..."

"Look, I really appreciate you looking out for me but its fine," he waved a hand at her, smiling broadly as turned back to the other woman, "Cherry was it?"

She nodded a confirmation, her deep brown eyes flicking to meet those of the elderly housekeeper before she met his gaze, and Richard chuckled, "I'd love to learn more about this place"

"Well, Margaret is right" the voice of the young woman was soft, rich with the same accent that George Wolf and Ms Sanderson had but with an almost musical lilt to it, "You are still moving in, let's give it a couple of days and if you'd like to see me again, I will come back"

"OK" he nodded, confused by the deep sense of disappointment he felt as he realised she was about to leave, then he forced a smile, "Sure that'd be great"

"That's settled then" she took a step towards the kitchen door and he moved with her, smiling still. "Come on, I'll walk you out"

"Out?" she frowned, then chuckled, "Right, sorry"

"Some of us men have manners" he laughed then cringed, head shaking, "Sorry that sounded...I don't know...I'm not being creepy"

"Creepy?"

"Oh God" he gave a laugh, head shaking, "Ignore me"

Smiling, the young woman cast a final glance at Ms Sanderson and then stepped past him as he opened the kitchen door into the hallway, following him past the huge pile of furniture, a laugh escaping her, "You have a lot of stuff"

"This is just half of it" he grinned, nodding as he reached the front door and opened it wide, "I've got so much stuff I could stay here forever"

The young woman winced at his words, and he raised an eyebrow, "Did I say something wrong?"

"No" she stepped past him, turning back to face him in the overhang of the doorway, the heavy rain still falling upon Evenfield loud once more, a sudden sadness on her face, "Thank you for seeing me, Mr Miles...it means a lot"

"Richard" he smiled broadly and she gave a shake of her head, a sudden laugh escaping the young woman.

"What?" the author found himself grinning at her.

For a moment, she stayed silent then she shook her head, still smiling, "You are a peculiar man, Richard"

He chuckled, "I'll take that as a compliment"

"Hey, where's the cups of tea?"

Richard turned at the sound of Myra's voice, cringing as he realised she was about to tease him for flirting, and glanced back at the young woman only to find that she had gone, no doubt having headed out into the rain before he could embarrass himself more.

"What on Earth are you doing at the door?" Myra moved alongside him, an arm slipping about his waist in that familiar manner they shared, "Eh?"

For a second he considered telling her about Cherry but then he changed his mind, knowing that she would be like a dog with a bone, and winked at her, "I was enjoying the fresh air"

As she gave him a look of confusion, he shut the door and gestured for her to follow, "Come on, you can help me with the tea"

Chapter Seven

"And how did you sleep last night, Mr Miles?"

"Eh?" Richard looked up from the newspaper that was spread out on his lap, smiling as he found Ms Sanderson watching from the doorway to the large sitting room where he was relaxing the next morning. She smiled, stepping inside the room, "How was your first night in your new home?"

"Good" he nodded, then folded up the newspaper and placed it upon the coffee table, gesturing for Ms Sanderson to sit down, "Take a break"

The elderly woman eyed him in confusion for a moment, smiling as if she were unsure if he were joking and then shook her head, "Well, I'm not sure if I have the time, the kitchen needs..."

"Please, Margaret" Richard chuckled, "It's fine"

"As you wish" she moved to the closest of the large leather bound armchairs and slowly lowered herself down to perch upon the edge, brow furrowing as if such an act was strange to her and the author gave a sad smile as he realised that a lifetime of serving wealthy people had no doubt instilled a sense of servitude in her that she found her to dismiss.

He waited until she was as settled as it looked like she was going to get and then he smiled, "So, my first night was good, much to my surprise"

"Oh?" she raised a silver eyebrow, the thin line of her lips pressing together tightly for a moment before she continued, "What had you expected?"

He shrugged, feeling suddenly stupid, "Ah nothing, I am just being daft"

"Humour me" she smiled softly, nodding as she spoke as if that simple act would encourage him to do so.

For long moments, he sat there his bottom lip caught between his teeth as he studied the woman, wondering just how much he could tell her without her thinking that he was as mad as other people had during his forty years. Everyone but Myra that was.

"Well?" she raised an eyebrow again and then he sighed heavily, throwing his hands up slightly before gripping to his knees, head shaking as he chuckled.

"Ghosts"

"Oh?" that single word once more, yet each time it left her lips it sounded as if she had asked him a question, and smiling like an idiot, he waved a hand at her.

"Yeah, I know, the famous horror novelist is scared of ghosts and ghoulies"

Yet instead of looking even the least bit amused by his words, Ms Sanderson nodded once more, her voice tight as she spoke, "And did you see any ghosts during the night, Mr Miles?"

"What?" he gave a laugh that came out sounding like a choke, brow furrowing as he held her gaze.

"Did any of the residents of Sanderson House bother you…at all?" Ms Sanderson asked him, voice soft. Throat tight, he gave a shake of his head, the hairs rising upon his arms as he watched her give a nod, relaxing somewhat and then he leaned forwards, "Are you telling me this place is…"

"Haunted?" she finished, her lips twisting into a humourless smile, "Yes Mr Miles, dreadfully so. It always has been, since long before my time"

On the large leather sofa, Richard nodded, unsure what to do with the information that she had just given him, stomach knotting as she spoke again, "You see them don't you Mr Miles…ghosts"

"I don't understand…" he began, head shaking and she nodded at him, a warm smile on her face.

"Yes, that much was obvious from the very first moment that we met, yet I was unsure how attuned you were to their presence"

"I think you are mistaken" he tried to smile, reaching into the breast pocket of the brown and white lumberjack shirt that he was wearing, dragging out the small bottle of pills, "I have episodes, I…see things…its why I take these"

She nodded, her eyes studying the small plastic bottle that he was holding with a look like he was handling dog faeces, and then she met his gaze once more, "Ah, the shelter of the rational mind…who gave you these…a doctor?"

"Yes, a specialist…like I said, I have these episodes where I see things that aren't there…my agent says its good for the novels but…"

"Things or people?"

He winced, and she nodded as if that was all the answer that she needed, "And how long have you been having these…episodes?"

"Since I was a boy…I think my earliest memory of them was when I was about four" his voice was monotone, eyes peering into the past as he spoke, "I was in the bedroom at the farm…"

"Your home?"

"Yes" he gave a nod, his voice barely more than a whisper, "I told my mother that there was a lady in the wardrobe…with black hair…she…I…"

"Your mother?" the voice of Ms Sanderson came to him as if from a distance, "Not your father?"

He flinched at her words, hearing the angry drunken shouts of the man that had given him life, a pin prick of fear rising in his heart as he recalled the large, angry bull of a man who had helped to make his childhood a living Hell, "No, it made him angry"

He tensed as Ms Sanderson nodded, the sudden movement jarring him into looking back at her as she spoke, "What did your mother say?"

"Say?"

"About the woman in the wardrobe"

He swallowed the tightness in his throat, his palms rubbing on the thighs of his jeans, "She told me there was no-one there"

"But there was wasn't there a woman" it wasn't a question, "What did she do to you, this woman?"

He tried to stand as a sob suddenly escaped him, head shaking, "She...I...she would watch me...all the time...bath-time...mealtimes...while I lay in bed...she would stand and watch me..."

"And?"

"That was enough" he snapped, jerking his head towards the elderly woman, then winced as he realised he had almost shouted, "I...I'm sorry"

She stayed silent for a moment, her head tilting to one side as she studied him, and then she gave a sad smile, "And so they medicated you...and kept you quiet...but it doesn't work does it"

Another statement.

"No"

"Ghosts exist, you aren't insane, you are gifted...or cursed...it's a cross that we must bear"

"We?" he studied her intently, "You?"

"Yes" her voice was tight once more, "Since I was a girl, my mother said it was a gift, my father tried to beat it out of me, fearing what would happen when I came to work here"

Richard winced, "What did happen?"

She gave a shrug, her narrow shoulders barely moving but it was as if it had taken every ounce of her energy, "I survived, Mr Miles"

A heavy silence descended upon the room, the minutes drifting out for what seemed like hours and then she nodded, "Have you seen anything during your time here?"

He made a face, remembering the moment out the front of the house two days before, "I thought I saw a figure in black standing behind me in the reflection in the car window"

"Agnes" Ms Sanderson grimaced, head nodding.

"Agnes?" he felt physically sick, "Who is she?"

"All in good time, Mr Miles...and others?"

"There's a child"

She nodded, "There is...and?"

The author shook his head, "No others"

She frowned then nodded, "Tell me about Myra"

At the mention of the dark-haired, Richard gave a smile, "She's my best friend"

"Have you known her long?"

"Since I was a child" he nodded, his mood darkening as he thought of those dark times once more, "She lived on the next farm...we spent all our time together...she keeps me sane"

The elderly woman nodded, smiling, "She seems very important to you"

"She is" he shrugged, the truth of the woman's words striking a chord within him, "I don't know what I'd do without her"

The housekeeper smiled once more then raised an eyebrow, "Where is she?"

"Upstairs" he chuckled, "Asleep when I left her"

The elderly woman sat for a moment longer and then sighed, rising to her feet with a fluid motion, "Back to work it is…but remember that I am here to talk, should you need to do so"

"Thank you" he smiled, watching as she moved to the door and then rose himself, "Wait a moment"

"Mr Miles?" she turned to face him at the door.

"That woman that was here yesterday…Cherry"

Ms Sanderson nodded, "My granddaughter"

"Oh" he winced, "I wasn't aware"

The elderly woman raised an eyebrow, "Sir?"

"I was just wondering do you know how I might contact her?" he stumbled, wincing as he spoke, realising how bad it sounded, "I mean, to learn about the house…"

The housekeeper held his gaze in for a moment before turning to walk away, her voice reaching back to him, "She is always about Mr Miles, its just a matter of catching her at the right time"

Chapter Eight

Standing in the living room, staring at the doorway where Ms Sanderson had just been standing, Richard listened to the sound of her shoes on the floor of the hallway as she walked away, his brow furrowing as he considered everything she had just related to him.

Sanderson House was haunted.

And she believed that he could see ghosts, Hell, she had been the one who had suggested it.

Not only that but she apparently did too.

A cold place opened up in the pit of his stomach as an image of the woman with the black hair suddenly returned to him, and he let out a shaky gasp, hands reaching instantly for the breast pocket of his shirt where his bottle of pills were waiting ready for him.

Then he froze, eyes narrowing as he stared down at the floor. If the old housekeeper was right and everything that he had always thought that he had imagined was real, the pills wouldn't help at all.

All they would do is make him sleepy and happy.

He had spent far too long in that state.

But if he didn't take the pills, he would see *them*.

The ones that had always tried to talk to him throughout his life, despite every figure of authority that he had ever known telling him that it was all just a part of his fractured psyche, the brains efforts to protect him from the horror of his childhood, that singular dark moment that he could not remember but which never left his mind. Grimacing, he took a shaky breath, seeming to watch the child version of himself from above as he raced into the barn upon their farm, hands dragging at the rungs of the old ladder as he climbed up into the hay loft and ran along the edge, then froze as he stared down at the area at the back of the barn, his stomach knotting in dread, a scream of raw unbridled terror escaping him as he stared down and saw…saw…

Saw what?

What had he seen that had damaged him so?

Forcing himself to focus, Richard blinked, took a deep breath and nearly fell to the side before righting himself, his hand rising to the pocket containing the pills, only to drop away again, his head shaking. Letting out a shaky breath, he bent at the waist, hands resting on his knees and then straightened again, heading towards the door on shaky legs.

He needed Myra; she would know what to do.

She always did. The one constant in his life.

Cursing as he entered the hallway and nearly fell over a collection of boxes from the delivery the day before, the author skirted through the furniture and reached the stairs, pausing as he stared down at the spot where Jonty had died, then tilted his head back to look up the stairs, pondering the young man's death.

He screamed in shock as he saw the pale face staring back down at him through the wooden railings of the second floor far above, and cursing, he staggered back and fell heavily against a wardrobe that had been delivered from his home in Portsmouth. Wincing as he suddenly pictured the black haired woman that had hid within the wardrobe in his childhood, he pushed himself forwards and away from it sprawling on all fours upon the wide stairs as he turned to stare back at it in dread, heart racing. Yet there was no fiend from his past there to haunt him as she always had, her features hidden by the hair that had always hung down past her features. Of course there wasn't.

This was a different house with different ghosts.

Great. Wonderful.

Sighing heavily, Richard tilted his head back, staring up into the features of the pale little boy, surprised to find that the face was still there, pale white hands holding to the railings as it stared down at him, a humourless smile upon his face. Without giving it rational thought, Richard began to climb the stairs towards the first floor, turning at the halfway point and looked up once more to find that the boy was still watching him, a cold sweat washing over him as he heard a giggle floating down the stairs to meet him.

He froze for a moment, unsure what he was actually intending to do, fear touching him in a sudden wave.

This child, this boy, was a ghost.

Ms Sanderson had said as much.

Yet here he was climbing the stairs to see him.

But far better to meet this ghostly boy than meet the black garbed figure that he had glimpsed reaching for him outside the house days before. He shuddered as he recalled her the brief reflection of the figure behind him in the window of his car, then cursed and stopped walking as he recalled the unfortunate estate agent asking him and Myra where the old woman had gone. Had he seen her too?

Who else could he have meant if not?

What had the elderly housekeeper called her?

Angela? Agnetha? No, Agnes.

That was it.

Who was she and why was she here at the house?

For that matter why was the boy at the house?

Had the pair of them died here years before?

Without giving it conscious thought, he was moving once more, climbing the stairs to the first floor and then continuing up to the half way landing of the stairs to the second floor, heart hammering in his chest like a jackhammer as he turned to meet the gaze of the little boy in the nightshirt that was watching back through the wooden balustrade.

Time seemed to lose all meaning as they held each other's gaze in silence and then somehow, much to his surprise, the author found the ability to speak, his voice a whisper as if he were afraid that he would scare the child, "Hey…I'm Richard"

The smile on the face of the boy grew wider, and he released his grip upon the railings, and rose to his bare feet, a hand gesturing for Richard to follow him as he backed along the second floor, out of sight.

"Wait!" the author winced, climbing cautiously to the top of the stairs then peering around into the wide hallway, his stomach knotting as he found the child halfway along its length, past several of the bedroom doors, hand still beckoning to him. Pausing, face screwing up in dread, the author nodded and began to slowly follow the boy, nervously glancing at the open doorways as he passed them by, his hands shaking at his sides, then turned back to find that the ghost of the strange little boy had vanished.

"What the fuck?" he muttered, then cringed as he heard his name voiced from somewhere behind him, not spoken as such, but breathed heavily, "Richard"

Heart in his mouth, he turned, eyes widening as he saw the familiar figure of the estate agent Jonty standing beside one of the open doors to the bedrooms, a look of utter mania in his eyes as he stood between a large, brutish looking man and an angular, stick thin woman with long black hair.

"Help me" the estate agents lips moved as he stared at the author but no sound came out, and chuckling, the woman leaned heavily against him, hands stroking his chest and lower as she turned to stare at Richard, a sexual hunger in her expression, while the man took a step towards him, growling angrily, their bodies clad in brown clothes from a bygone era.

"No!" Richard shook his head, his steps taking him over near the balustrade and the drop to the stairs, stomach knotting as he began to edge past the couple, wincing as he saw Jonty's expression of raw terror. The childish chuckle made Richard turn back towards the top of the stairs, a moan of raw terror escaping the author as he saw the boy in the nightshirt standing there smiling coldly back at him, what looked like a small knife clasped tightly in a hand "Whoa!" the author raised his hands, eyes locked to that tiny blade, his head shaking in dread as the boy took several quick steps towards him, knife raised. Then suddenly Ms Sanderson was there before him, her right hand sweeping out before her in an arc, what looked like a handful of sand striking the ghostly child across its pale face. With a scream that had Richard dropping to his knees in dread, the child vanished, and in disbelief, the author turned to watch as the elderly woman took a step towards the couple that stood with Jonty, her voice angry, "Enough, be gone this instance!"

For a moment, they lingered, the features of the man and woman twisted in hatred, the estate agents in terror, and then the three of them were gone, fading away as if they had never been.

Chapter Nine

 "Jesus fucking Christ!" Richard somehow made it to his feet, a shaking hand grasping at the wooden railing atop the balustrade beside him, eyes wide as he stared first at the doorway where the trio had been and then back at where he had last seen the ghostly boy with the blade. For a moment longer he stared at the space and then he turned his head, flinching at the movement beside him, then relaxed as he saw Ms Sanderson there, here brow furrowed as she turned to glance at him, "Are you well?"

The author nodded, his throat tight, as he gestured to the doorway, "Who were they!"

"The couple?" the voice of the old woman was tight as she turned her face in the direction that Richard was pointing, "Clemence Stoke and Elias Crumb…The Witch and The Devil"

"The witch and…what?" Richard winced, his stomach twisting into a tight knot within him.

Ms Sanderson stayed silent, her eyes upon the doorway still, and then she nodded, "Aye, a pair of murderers most foul with names to suit them!"

Blinking, Richard released a shaky breath, "That was the estate agent with them…I mean…his…"

"His ghost" she nodded, her features grim, "Indeed it was, the young man was killed here and so here he will remain forever"

"Killed?" Richard sent her a look of utter shock.

"Indeed Mr Miles" her reply was calm, measured, as if she had been waiting for the moment to speak these words, "There have been many deaths at Sanderson House, none of which have been accidents. The presence of Clemence and Elias with him would suggest that they had some part in the unfortunate young man's death"

As he stared back at her in disbelief, she stepped away towards the top of the stairs, gesturing for him to follow her, "Come along now Sir, I have banished them for now, but they will return"

"Banished them?" he sent her a confused look, recalling the dust she had swept at the ghost of the boy, "What did you throw at the boy?"

"Salt" she was several steps down the stairs, gesturing with a tilt of her head for him to follow her and nodding he did as she had bid, moving down to stand beside her on the wooden steps of the stairs. Grimacing, Ms Sanderson studied the floor above them for a moment longer and then without warning began to descend once more, her tone matronly as she sent him a scowl, "You are incredibly lucky that Frances didn't hurt you"

"Frances?"

"Frances Goodnestone" her voice was grim, the

colour gone from her features, "Known as The Black Sheep, the bane of the Goodnestone family…one of the most malevolent of the Twelve…you were lucky"

"The Twelve?" he gaped at her in disbelief, eyes wide as he shook his head, "Are you telling me that there are twelve ghosts in this house!"

Her chuckle was without humour, "Of course not"

He breathed a sigh of relief, then winced as she continued, "There are dozens upon dozens of ghosts at Sanderson House, their numbers swell with each death that happens on these grounds"

"Like with Jonty" Richard's voice was a whisper.

She nodded, "Like with Jonty"

"So, who are the Twelv…" his words trailed off to a whimper as they reached the landing of the first floor, steps slowing as he saw the three figures that stood waiting there staring at them as they passed by.

"Pay them no heed" the hissed voice of Ms Sanderson urged him, and he nodded weakly, feeling like a child walking past the school yard bullies, his eyes inadvertently drifting towards them despite his efforts to the contrary, a cold sweat bathing him.

Nearest to the stairs stood the largest man that Richard had ever seen in person, his powerfully built frame standing at easily over six and a half feet tall, his shoulders impossibly wide, his square jawed features blank as they stared back at Richard, the mans body clad in what looked like brown woollen breeches and a dirty homespun cotton shirt which might have once been white but was now stained with dirt and dark stains. As Richard moved past the huge man, his eyes slipped to the woman that stood several feet back, confusion striking him as he saw her watching him with the trace of a smile upon her attractive features, her fair hair pulled back from her features in a tight ponytail, her full, wholesome figure threatening to escape from the low cut beige bodice that she wore above a long brown dress that reached the floor. As he stared at the woman, she lowered her head slightly, glancing up at him almost shyly through her eyelashes, a hand rising to trace the bare skin of her neck and despite himself Richard groaned. Then screamed in terror as the third figure stepped quickly past the woman, its stick thin form clad in black and white checked pantaloons and tunic, white ruffs at each wrist and ankle, and a similarly coloured conical hat atop its head. Cursing, heart hammering in his chest, Richard toppled into the wooden balustrade and fell forward to his knees, watching in dread as the clown skittered closer, its movements disjointed and angular, its white grease painted features split with a black toothed smile that its wide scarlet lips couldn't conceal. The clown stopped just feet before him, dropping down to a crouch as it held his gaze and with a snort like the bull it resembled, the huge man moved to join it, the laughter of the woman sounding as she did stepped alongside them. "Up Mr Miles" Ms Sanderson was suddenly at his side once more, a bony hand reaching down to hook under his left armpit, urging him to his feet as she spoke again, disdain in her voice, "They cannot hurt you and they know it"

Head spinning, he nodded, forcing himself to avoid looking at the trio of ghosts as he stood once more, and headed for the stairs, shame touching him like fire as he realised suddenly that he hadn't waited for the elderly housekeeper to move down with him. Five steps below, he paused and turned, watching as she joined him, then allowed his gaze to drift back towards the trio, surprised to find that only the huge man remained, his square-jawed features still blank as he watched them, his shoulders rising and falling as if he were about to launch into a violent rage. "Mr Miles!" he snapped his head to the side as he realised that Ms Sanderson was addressing him, her right hand linking through his left arm as she continued onwards down the stairs, leading him. "I'm sorry" he breathed, hating how scared he sounded, his head shaking for a moment and then he felt his heart skip a beat as he recalled his original reason for heading upstairs, "I...oh my God! Myra!"

"Mr Miles!" Ms Sanderson snapped at him as he tried to free himself from her grip, "Calm please!"

"No" he shook his head, trying to head back up the stairs but the old woman was gripping to him with both hands and he was afraid he would hurt her, "I need to get upstairs to Myra!"

"She isn't there!"

"What?" Richard threw her a look of confusion.

For a moment, the elderly woman studied him in silence, hands still gripping to his, and then she gave a sigh, "I was coming to find you…to tell you that she was downstairs…look…she is there by the furniture in the lobby!"

The author frowned, head shaking as he turned his eyes upon the horde of furniture and boxes, scanning them for a sign of his friend, his lips moving, "Myra…" And then there she was, stepping around the edge of the large wardrobe that he had collided with on his way up the stairs, a cup of tea in her hands, a smile on her face as she looked at him, "Hey, what's wrong!" Choking back a sob of relief, he made to move down the stairs, and this time the housekeeper let him go. Reaching the lobby he threw his arms about his childhood friend, hugging her tight as she returned the embrace with one hand, her chuckle soft in his ear, "What's up you daft sod?"

Sighing, he released her and stepped back, turning to

study Ms Sanderson as she stood on the stairs, hands clasped before her waist, a sad smile upon her wizened features as she watched him in silence.

Then he nodded, voice grim, "Tell us everything"

Ms Sanderson smiled, but it didn't seem to reach her eyes, "As you wish"

Chapter Ten

"This house was built by my ancestors, the Sanderson's, hence it's name" the voice of the elderly housekeeper was tense as she sat across the large wooden table from Richard, a steaming cup of tea resting there between her wrinkled old hands.

The author nodded at her words, then frowned, "Why can't you tell me in front of Myra?"

She grimaced, head shaking, "As I told you Mr Miles, I am willing to tell you, and you alone"

"But..."

"My decision is final" she started to rise and he sighed heavily, gesturing for her to sit down back down.

"Fine, fine...go on"

She sat for a moment as if expecting him to change his mind and then gave a nod, "Originally, the Sanderson's were from Sweden, as our family name might imply, but in April, 1612, the head of the family, Haller Sanderson, took his child bride Ingrid and their two infant sons, Abram and Larens with them across the Atlantic to the New World. The boys were three years old at the time according to family legend, and the family settled into the new Colony of Virginia in Jamestown, one hundred and fifty miles or so up the coast from the island of Roanoke, with the wealth that Haller had accumulated back home in Sweden"

"Roanoke" Richard muttered, frowning at her words and she nodded, drinking deeply from her cup before placing it back down and continuing with her story. "Indeed, unlike the unfortunate Roanoke settlement however, the Colony of Virginia was a success. Initially there were the troubles of the Starving Times in the winter of 1610, plus the wars with the Powhatan tribe and illness but they persevered and got past them. My ancestors, led by Haller, arrived after this time, and quickly immersed themselves in the burgeoning tobacco industry, quickly becoming rich, and influential"

"I don't understand" he interrupted, "What the Hell were the starving times?"

The old woman grimaced, "I am no student of history but I believe there was a shortage of food and the colony turned to cannibalism after they had eaten all of the animals...including the rats"

The author winced, head shaking and the old woman gave a cold smile, "People will survive at all odds, it is in our nature to do so"

He nodded at her words, feeling uncomfortable under her gaze and she gave an almost bitter chuckle, "We are able to convince ourselves of pretty much anything if it means that we can continue living"

Grimacing, he nodded, watching as she lowered her gaze, studying her cup for a moment before meeting his gaze once more, "In the spring of 1640, Haller and his sons, now in their early thirties, each married with children, boarded a ship for England with a large quantity of their servants and friends, arriving here in County Durham in early June of that year"

"What about his wife?" Richard raised an eyebrow.

"Dead by that time" she stated simply, "Killed in one of several attacks by the Powhatan tribe"

Wincing, the author nodded, "Sorry, go on"

"With the wealth accumulated in America, Haller purchased the land upon which Evenfield now sits, becoming its landowner and having this very house built for he and his family to live in. However, he was in his late sixties by this time and he would not live to see its completion, Abram and Larens instead taking over his duties, splitting the responsibility between them both, with the more physical Abrams focusing upon the protection and law of the growing village, inhabited by workers that they had brought back with them from the American colony, and Larens becoming the villages spiritual leader"

"Like a priest?" Richard asked and she smiled, her head shaking as she held his curious gaze.

"Of a sort, but not the type you might expect. You see in America, Larens had become fascinated with the people of the Patawomeck tribe, enemies of the Powhatan's that had killed his mother when he was but a boy, and he brought a lot of their beliefs back to England with him"

"Like a witch doctor?"

She shrugged, frail shoulders lifting and falling with what looked like supreme effort, "I do not know, what I do know is that he was fascinated with the afterlife and with the natural world"

There was a heavy silence as she sat looking back at Richard, and he shook his head, "I don't see what any of this has to do with the ghosts"

"It was November 1645 when it happened" her voice was a hushed whisper, her eyes narrowing as she spoke, and fighting the shudder that threatened to shake him apart, Rich nodded at her, brow furrowing. "What was it?"

She blinked at his question, "Abram's had a daughter, Ingrid, named for her grandmother, with a shock of golden hair. In that November, she went missing while out in the village, a bad time of year to be lost out in the cold of Durham. Naturally, Abram's searched for her, taking with him a group of reliable men from the village, including Chaqit, a Patowomeck tribesman that they had brought with them from America with whom Abram's had formed a strong friendship. Chaqit tracked the girl's footsteps to the remote Jackman farm, ten miles from the village, and the source of much of the areas beef and cattle"

"Go on" Richard nodded at her, wincing slightly.

"Well, the owner of the farm and his wife were nowhere to be seen" Ms Sanderson stated, a strange look upon her features, "But they found their son James…a huge, hulking brute of a man, slow-witted and dull, with the raw strength of a bull…he claimed to have no knowledge of the whereabouts of young Ingrid, blaming the blood upon the tunic and breeches he wore upon the cattle that he had slaughtered that morning"

"Oh God" Richard blinked, "He killed her"

The elderly housekeeper nodded, her features grim, "While Abram's talked with the large man, the tribesman, Chaqit, searched the farm, and found the unfortunate young girl upon a metal hook in one of the barns, violated and bloody, and he cried blue murder! Upon hearing the cries of Chaqit, Abram's knew that his beloved daughter was dead and drew his flintlock pistol, ordering James Jackman to stand down. Instead, the huge man attacked the group with a hammer, slaying seven of their number despite taking shots from muskets and pistols, until finally Abram and Chaqit were able to subdue him, and bring him back to Evenfield and this house"

"Holy fuck!" the author muttered, picturing the violent scene in his head, then let out a gasp, "Oh God…that was him on the landing!"

89

Ms Sanderson nodded, her face grim, "It was, James Jackman, The Butcher. Once subdued, Abram and Chaqit searched the farm, discovering the remains of his parents in a room of the house, the flesh gone from their bones, but their skulls crushed, as well as twenty-three other skeletons"

"Oh God" Richard cursed, his stomach knotting in dread, "What happened next?"

"James Jackman was found guilty, not only of the murders of his parents, and the twenty-three unidentified but also of poor Ingrid and the seven men that had accompanied Abrams to the farm, and sentenced to hang until he was dead"

"Thirty-three murders!" Richard was astounded, his head shaking slowly, "How is it I have never heard of him before now?"

"No-one has" Ms Sanderson grimaced, "Abram's was furious and feared that in some way the monster would escape punishment, and so the trial was held here at Sanderson House, with Larens as the judge, a jury comprised of villagers, and with Abram's as executioner"

"Whoa" Richard gave a surprised chuckle, "That's hardly an impartial trial is it...the uncle of one of his victims is the judge and the jury were no doubt friends and family of the seven men!"

"I am just telling you facts as I know them...he was tried in secret, and his fate and crimes became and stayed a village secret" Ms Sanderson stated.

"Shit" Richard winced, "I don't know what to say"

"He was the first of The Twelve" the elderly woman said the words with an almost reverence, wincing as she spoke, "After that, Abram's would seek out killers in the area, and bring them back here to be tried and hung...then when he was too old, his son took over, then his son, and so on"

"And the village kept the secret?" he asked, a look of astonishment on his face, "Seriously?"

"Of course" Ms Sanderson nodded, "You have to remember that my family had housed and fed them, given them jobs, protected them even"

Richard nodded at her words, sensing the defensive tone in the old woman's voice, then he frowned, "How many were executed here?"

She shrugged, "The executions ceased in 1899, but up to that time I would say around eight hundred, some of my ancestors were more efficient than others"

"Eight hundred!" the author was on his feet, eyes wide as he stared down at the old woman, stunned by her calm manner, "Eight hundred?"

"Perhaps more" she nodded, sipping her tea.

With a heavy sigh, he dropped back down onto his chair, hands rubbing at his eyes for a moment before he met the gaze of Ms Sanderson again.

"I still don't understand what The Twelve are!"

She nodded at his words, "The Twelve are the foulest of the foul, those who have killed more than any other of the killers executed here"

"Here?" Richard blinked, suddenly realising that she had said several times, "Here where?"

She gestured with a hand, "From the twins"

"The twins?" he frowned for a moment then nodded, "You mean the two huge oak trees"

"I do" the old woman nodded, "Each of those that my family have found guilty have been hung from those trees, their spirits eternally bound to the oaks by the ceremonies that Larens and Abram had learned from Chaqit and his people"

"Bound to the trees" Richard repeated her words, head shaking as he considered what she had said, his head turning as if he could see through the wall, "But if the spirits are bound to the trees then how are they in the house?"

Ms Sanderson gave a heavy sigh, "I do not know for certain; family lore says that the ghosts did not begin to show themselves within the house until the early nineteenth century. My great uncle believed that the roots of the trees had spread beneath the foundations of this house and across the estate, enabling the spirits to move about"

As Richard nodded, considering her words, Ms Sanderson rose from the table, placing her cup in the sink, then turned to face him, drawing a curious look from the author, "So why not just get rid of the trees"

Standing against the kitchen worktop it was if he had threatened to murder Ms Sanderson, her face twisting in dread, her head shaking, "No!"

"Why not?" he shrugged, "It makes sense surely?"

"The spirits are only bound to the trees while they live…if the trees are ever destroyed the spirits that inhabit this house and grounds will be free to take their revenge upon the village"

Letting out a shaky sigh, Richard nodded his head slowly, "So if we keep the trees safe it's only this house and grounds that can be bothered by this Twelve…and I bought it…go me!"

Ms Sanderson winced, and he winced, "What?"

"There is something else…even if the trees are healthy, the moment that the last descendant of the Sanderson family dies or spends longer than three days away from the house, the ghosts will be free"

"Oh my God" he shook his head, "So, we need to keep your granddaughter safe from harm?"

She flinched at his words, the colour draining from her features at the mention of her granddaughter then turned her head as a knocking sounded at the front door, accompanied by a scream of agony.

Chapter Eleven

"Myra!" Richard was up and moving at once, Ms Sanderson close behind him, as he entered the hallway, and began edging his way through the furniture and boxes towards the front door.

"Myra!" he shouted once more, glancing up the stairs, panic touching him, then snapped his head back around as the banging sounded on the door once more, followed by another scream and what sounded like a man talking to someone in a deep bass voice.

"It's not her!" Ms Sanderson stated, moving alongside him as he paused several feet from the door, his stomach knotting as he stared at it in sudden dread.

"The ghosts?" Richard turned to throw her a look of sudden concern and she shook her head in reply.

"No, the ghosts cannot harm people yet"

"What?" he sent her a look of confusion, "But you said that they killed the estate agent, and that I was lucky that Frances had not harmed me!"

"No, Mr Miles…I said that Clemence and Elias had played a part in his death, and I feared that Frances might have caused you to have an accident" she turned her head as the banging sounded again, and without another word she stepped forwards and opened the door. Instantly she took a step back, a gasp of shock escaping the usually stoic old woman and feeling sick, Richard stepped alongside her, his eyes widening as he saw the two men in the porch. For a moment, the author stood there staring at the two men, mind reeling as he tried to work out what was happening, his nose wrinkling at the copper stench of the blood that they appeared to be drenched in as one laid limp across the others lap. "Help us!" the man at the back of the pair gave a sob of shock, his bearded features twisted in abject terror, both of his hands clasped to the bloody severed right wrist of his companion as the thin man leaned back against his, his features pale despite the fresh blood that was upon them. Cursing in concern, suddenly galvanised into action by the sheer terror in the mans voice, Richard reached down, hands frantically unbuttoning his belt as he rushed forwards, his stomach lurching as he nearly slipped in blood as he dragged it free. Gritting his teeth in an effort not to gag as blood pumped rhythmically from the severed wrist, he dropped down beside the conscious man, slipped his looped belt over the end of the limb, pulling tight as he met the gaze of the conscious man, "How did this happen...who are you?" "Johnsons" the bearded man gave a nod, his voice sounding for all the world like he was about to pass out at any moment like his badly wounded friend, and Richard frowned as he finished fastening the belt about the limb, only to suddenly notice the removal van in the driveway, and the insignia upon the men's beige overalls. It was his second furniture delivery.

"You were here yesterday!" Richard nodded, as he eased the unconscious man from his friends lap to lay upon the tiled floor of the porch, recognising the bearded man from the day before, and the other nodded a confirmation, then glanced at his colleague. "Will Keith be OK?"

"I don't know, we need to keep the pressure on, and something to cover the wrist" the author stated, "We need to stop him bleeding out"

"How about this?" the bearded man dragged a handkerchief from his pocket, "Will it do?"

"Better than nothing" Richard nodded, releasing the pressure upon the belt as the bearded man folded the handkerchief double thickness and then wrapped it over the end of his colleague's bloody stump, the author securing it with the belt once more, grimacing as the material began to darken, "We need to get him inside and phone an ambulance"

"Excuse me, Mr Miles" Ms Sanderson stepped from the door of the house, her voice tense, and turning his head, he saw her give a barely perceptible shake of her head, "I think he would be safer if left out here"

"What?" the bearded man glanced from her to Richard, features twisted in confusion, "I don't…"

"She's right" the author nodded, "We are probably best not to move him...Ms Sanderson can you fetch him some blankets...and get Myra"

She nodded, stepping back towards the door, "I will phone for an ambulance too Mr Miles"

With that she was gone, and gritting his teeth, Richard turned back to the bearded man, "What happened to him?"

"I don't know" he shook his head, eyes wide in his face, "I was heading for the door to let you know we were here...Keith was opening up the back of the van...then he shouted in shock, and I heard the back of the van slam shut, and he started screaming"

"It slammed on him?" Richard grimaced, "How does that even happen?"

"It shouldn't" the man shook his head, "Me and Keith have been working together for years, and he's good at his job...he's not careless!"

"The...woman" Richard felt the hairs rise on his neck as the badly wounded man suddenly spoke, having regained consciousness without them noticing, voice barely more than a whisper, "She...startled...me"

"What's that Keith, mate?" the bearded man moved to kneel beside him, leaning closer, "I didn't hear you"

"Woman...in...black" the man's bloody lips barely moved but it was almost as if he had shouted in Richards ear, the author releasing a shaky breath.

"He's delirious" the bearded removal man knelt up straight, meeting Richard's face across his friend as the man passed out once more, "Poor bastard...do you think he'll live...he's got kids!"

"I honestly don't know..." Richard's words trailed off as he caught movement in his peripheral vision, towards the removal van and supressing a shudder, he turned his face round towards it, the sudden, almost overwhelming desire to scream in terror rushing through him unchecked as he saw the pale features of an old woman with iron grey hair staring back at him from beside the large vehicle, just half of her face visible. Snapping his face away, Richard took a deep steadying breath, glancing up as he realised that the bearded man was talking to him, "How long do you think the ambulance is going to take?"

"It took over an hour the other day" the author stated, the winced as the man shot him a look of confusion. "How often do you have accidents here?"

Richard ignored his question, half turning his face towards the van once more, the breath leaving him in a rush as he saw the woman was closer now, standing fully in sight before the cab of the van, her body clad in an old black dress. As he stared across at her she suddenly gave a sickly smile which seemed to spread from ear to ear, her thin arms reaching before her as if she were sleepwalking, long bony fish-white fingers wiggling in the air before her, and then she began to walk towards where he was knelt, one slow step after the other, legs rising high as if she were a child creeping up on someone, and it was all Richard could do to not to scream and run away to hide in terror. Because this was Agnes.

The old ghost that Ms Sanderson had mentioned earlier in the living room and one of The Twelve.

The deadliest of all of the ghosts on the estate.

"You OK mate?"

Richard snapped his face towards the bearded man, trying to smile as he saw the concern on the others face only to fail miserably, "I...we..."

"What?" the man shook his head, features twisting in confusion and Richard nearly sobbed as he saw the figure of Agnes creep into view behind the bearded man, still walking in that strange, childlike way, the hairs rising on his neck as he heard the soft sing-song hum that was coming from her as she approached.

"Holy Mary Mother of God" Richard muttered, eyes not leaving the blanched features of the ghost of the old woman, his right hand rising before him to cross himself, his Catholic upbringing returning to him in a heady rush although he hadn't used it in decades.

Yet Agnes seemed unperturbed by his sudden plea for salvation to a God that he had not addressed since the death of his mother in his late teenage years, and grimacing, the author stared in dread as it drew even nearer, its hands reaching out to rest upon the shoulders of the bearded man before him, long dirty nails stroking over the material of his beige overalls. Before Richard, the kneeling bearded removals man gave an involuntary shudder and stretched his neck forward, while behind him, Agnes seemed to chuckle and then give a sigh of pleasure, her hands stroking over the skin of the man's neck as she stared into the authors eyes, his bladder threatening to loosen in terror as she suddenly began to sing, her voice high and scratchy;

"Three blind mice. Three blind mice.
See how they run. See how they run.
They all ran after the farmer's wife,
Who cut off their tails with a carving knife,
Did you ever see such a sight in your life,
As three blind mice?"

As she finished, she snarled hungrily and bared her teeth, head dropping as if to bite into the side of the removals man's throat and Richard screamed in terror, reaching quickly over the unconscious man to grasp at the other's overalls, and drag him forwards and out harm's way.

"What the fuck are you doing you mad man!" the bearded removal man fought the authors hands from his body, head shaking as he rose quickly and backed away, a finger rising to point at Richard, "Keep back...I wont tell you again!"

The author nodded, both embarrassment and anger coursing through him as he glanced from the angry man, eyes searching for the ghost of the old woman, but there was nothing to see. Agnes was gone.

Chapter Twelve

"Do you want to tell me what you were doing while I was out there getting covered in the blood of some random removals man?" Richard stood in the doorway of the living room, a frown on his features as he stared at his best friend as she lay upon the sofa, her long hair pooled about her pale features, her eyes half closed, "Well?"

"I feel weird" she stated, her voice strained, and shaking his head, the author moved over to her.

"Like weird as in ill?"

"I don't know" she shrugged weakly, a hand rising to touch her own forehead, "I'm so cold"

Richard grimaced, concern touching him as he sat down on the edge of the sofa that she was sprawled upon, "I wasn't sure where you had got to...there was a man with no hand...and..."

His words trailed off and Myra nodded, "Is that where all the blood is from?"

"Yeah" he nodded, "I need to go and change"

"What happened?" she tried to sit up, groaned and lay back down, the hand returning to her forehead, eyes half closed as she looked at him, "Is it sorted now?"

The author sighed heavily, nodding once more, his stomach twisting as he considered the morning that he had endured so far already; the encounters with several of The Twelve upstairs, Ms Sanderson's revelations about the house that he had sunk half a million pounds into, and then the near death of the removal man and Agnes. He let out a shaky breath as he pictured the ghost, the memory of the nursery rhyme that she had sung making him feel queasy, and on the sofa, Myra raised an eyebrow, "Tell me"

He winced, head shaking as he told her about the accident that the man had suffered, and of how he and the mans colleague had stopped him from bleeding to death on the front porch. As she had stared back at him in shock, he winced once more, recalling how as the ambulance had arrived and loaded the man into it, his colleague had opened the removal van's rear and retrieved his severed hand, which the paramedics had taken with them before speeding off to hospital. Then, after a cup of tea for them both made by Ms Sanderson, and several phone calls to hospital and the removal company to appraise them of the situation, Richard had finally helped the remaining removal man unload the rest of the furniture. That man had left moments before, heading straight to Durham hospital to see his colleague, and with a moment to relax, as if he could ever do such a thing now he knew the history of the house, Richard had begun looking for Myra, Ms Sanderson having not seen her several hours.

Forcing himself to focus, he frowned down at his friend, "So you have been here all the time?"

She nodded, then shrugged, "I guess"

"You guess?" Richard eyed her in confusion.

"Yeah, I can't remember"

"You can't remember?" he repeated her words, his own hand rising to touch her forehead, "You feel cold, you might be coming down with flu"

"Maybe" she gave a non-committal shrug, sighing. For several moments he sat there watching as she closed her eyes, and then he shook his head, smiling in confusion, "You really didn't hear me or the other two men shouting?"

"No" her eyes stayed shut, "I told you"

"We were just out there" he gestured with an arm, frowning, "Were you asleep?"

She shrugged again, her eyes opening to stare up into his, "I don't think so, it's just like there's nothing there…like amnesia"

"OK" the author nodded, "What's the last thing that you remember before I came in here?"

She frowned, thinking for a moment, then, "We were outside the kitchen, Margaret said that she would tell you everything you wanted to know but that I had to wait outside"

"OK" the author raised an eyebrow, "That's it?"

"Yeah"

"That was several hours ago" he eyed her curiously, head shaking, "Have you been here since then?"

"I told you, I don't remember" there was a touch of irritation in her voice that Richard knew from past experience not to push. She was getting angry.

He blinked, head shaking as he tried to snatch the fleeting memory that had reared its head, images of a child Myra shouting angrily at him flashing past.

He blinked at the voice of his best friend, lowering his gaze to find her studying him intently, "Are you OK?"

"Sorry, I was trying to remember something"

Myra nodded at his words, "Do you want to talk about it...you went all weird"

Richard laughed, head shaking, "It was nothing"

"OK" she nodded, eyes narrowing, "So what did Margaret tell you in the kitchen?"

Richard caught the inside of his cheek between his back teeth as he studied her, for some reason unsure as to whether he should tell her the truth, and then he sighed, "She said that Sanderson House and it's grounds are haunted"

On the sofa, Myra stared at him for a moment and then she chuckled softly, nodding as she spoke, "Nice, OK, what did she really say?"

"That's what she said" Richard held her gaze.

Myra grinned, "Was she when you laughed?"

Sitting on the edge of the sofa, Richard winced and Myra gave a groan, rolling her eyes, "Oh don't tell me she has got you buying into it!"

"I've seen them" the words left him in a hushed whisper and Myra gave a shake of her head as if she wasn't sure she had heard what he'd said correctly. "Say that again"

"I've seen them" there was more resolve in his voice now, his head nodding as he spoke, "On the first day we were here I thought I saw someone beside me outside...in the reflection of my car window, remember that estate agent asked about the old woman...that was her...Agnes!"

Myra's grin was broad, "They have names?"

"What?" he eyed her as if she were mad, "Of course they have names...I only know a few of them...Agnes, Clemence, Elias...James Jackman...and...damn, I cant remember the name of the little boy!"

"So, there are a few ghosts then?" Myra asked as she sat up, "How many exactly?"

He shrugged, "Over eight hundred...but there are a certain twelve that are the most dangerous!"

"Right, and why are they here?"

"They were all executed here"

"By who?" She raised an eyebrow, still smiling.

"Ms Sanderson's family"

On the sofa Myra stared back at him in silence for a moment and then nodded, her smile no longer as bright, "Is this the plot for your next book…are you trying it out on me…is that what this is?"

"What?"

"Because it's good" she nodded, "I like it, that bit about the twelve makes it sound like Thirteen Ghosts so you may want to change that number to a diff…"

"What are you talking about?" he rose to his feet, head shaking as he stared at her, "This is real!"

She nodded, "Have you taken your pills today?"

"Fuck the pills" he shouted, anger coursing through him but on the sofa, Myra didn't seem fazed by his outburst other than by smiling sadly up at him.

"Your doctor said you need to take them when you see stuff…remember…we talked about how important it is that you look after your health!"

"Fuck him…fuck the pills" Richard snapped, taking a step away from her, "I know what I saw…a man has just lost a hand because of Agnes scaring him…the estate agent…Jonty…he died because of one of them!"

"What?" she rose to face him, "That's insane"

"That's insane or I'm insane?" his voice dropped to a whisper, his head shaking as he stared at her.

"Hey, I never said that!"

"You didn't need to" he took a step back towards the door, head shaking again, "I'm not mad Myra…I know what I saw…I saw Jonty…upstairs!"

Before him, Myra folded her arms across her chest, anger in her eyes and then she strode past him, out into the lobby of the house that was even more cluttered than that morning, her head shaking as she headed for the stairs and Richard grimaced, "Wait, you cant go up there alone!"

"Why?" she paused halfway up the first flight, her head turning to look back at him, "Because of the ghosts right? Trust me Richard, I'll be fine"

"Myra!" he shook his head, watching as she turned the midway landing and began to climb up once more without looking back, "Myra!"

But she was gone. Leaving him alone once more.

Chapter Thirteen

"She thinks I am insane!" Richard stormed into the kitchen, shaking his head at Ms Sanderson as she turned from where she was making a drink to face him, "I told her about the ghosts, and she thinks I am truly and utterly insane!"

"Who thinks you are insane?" the soft voice made him turn to the left, wincing in embarrassment as he saw the familiar figure of Cherry seated at the table.

"Myra" he stated, cringing as she frowned and glanced over at her grandmother for an explanation.

"Myra is Mr Miles'…friend" the elderly woman told her, nodding as she spoke as if it explained everything, and Richard shook his head quickly.

"No, see that makes it sound sordid when you say it like that" he told the housekeeper then glanced at the younger woman, "She's my best friend, we have been inseparable since we were kids"

"Oh" Cherry nodded, casting another glance at her grandmother before meeting his gaze again, "And you have brought her to Sanderson House?"

"Yeah, she's going to be staying with me"

Once more the young woman glanced at her grandmother and Richard frowned, glancing at Ms Sanderson, "Is there a problem?"

"A problem?" she shook her head, smiling as she moved to the table, placing a hot drink down upon its surface before seating herself, and holding the cup between the palms of her hands, warming them.

"Are you not having a tea?" Richard glanced at Cherry, "I can make you one if you like?"

"No" she shook her head quickly, "I can't..."

"Can't?" he gave a confused chuckle, "Why not?"

At his question, the blue-haired woman winced and looked at her Grandmother and frowning, the author followed the glance, watching as his housekeeper met his gaze, nodding as she spoke, a smile on her face.

"Alas, Cherry is one of these vegans...she doesn't drink milk of the cow variety"

"Really?" Richard turned to look back at the women, making a face of confusion as he found her gaze lingering on her grandmother before meeting his again, "Are sure you don't want a black coffee?"

"No" she answered him, perhaps a little too quickly, and he raised an eyebrow curiously, an uneasy feeling settling about him as he studied her intently.

"When did you get here? I didn't see you come in"

"She has just arrived" the housekeeper answered for her, drawing his gaze, "I believe you were in the living room with Myra when I let her in"

"Right" he nodded, chewing the inside of his cheek as he studied her, then sighed heavily. For a moment he looked down at the floor, hands rising to rub at his eyes and then glanced up as Ms Sanderson spoke.

111

"Where did you learn how to do that, if you don't mind me asking?"

"Eh?" he shook his head, "Do what?"

"You saved that man's life" she explained with a smile, "Were it not for your quick thinking, he might have bled to death on the doorstep"

He paused for a moment, brow furrowing as he stared back at her, and then shrugged, "My novels, I do a lot of research...I've had a couple of characters suffer similar injuries...I needed to know how to make it sound convincing...I guess I learned without actually trying"

She nodded, then frowned as he groaned, and gave a humourless chuckle, "What is it Mr Miles?"

"My belt" he pointed to his waist, beginning to laugh hysterically, "I didn't get it back"

As the housekeeper exchanged glances with her granddaughter, Richard gave a sigh, his laughter fading away and then he nodded, "And I saw her"

"Her?" Cherry asked, "You saw who?"

He studied her for a moment and then glanced at Ms Sanderson, "Does she know about them?"

"The ghosts?" the elderly woman winced, "Aye, she has a better understanding than most"

"Oh?" Richard glanced at the blue-haired woman. The corners of her mouth twitched in the promise of a smile, "Who did you see?"

"Agnes" just saying the name made his throat feel like it was beginning to swell up, "Outside"

Ms Sanderson raised an eyebrow, "I didn't see her…"

"You had gone inside…to phone the ambulance"

"What did she do?" the voice of Cherry drew Richard's attention back to her, the author feeling himself drown a little in the depth of her brown eyes as he stared at her, forcing himself to focus properly.

"I…she…she crept up behind the removal guy that was helping me…and she began to sing"

"Three Blind Mice" the young woman nodded.

"Yes!" he nearly cried out, nodding frantically as he took a step towards her, "How do you know?"

She studied him for a moment in silence, her gaze drifting towards her grandmother before she looked back at him and swallowed, then gave a nod of resignation, "Because that was the song she was singing the day she killed my mother"

At her words, Ms Sanderson made a strange noise of pain in the back of her throat, and Richard glanced back at her in concern, turning to face her as she raised a hand to her face as she sat at the table, "Ms Sanderson…can I help?"

For a moment she stayed still, grieving silently and then she raised her face to meet his, anger upon her lined features, "Lilith…Cherry's mother was my daughter…my only child"

"Oh, I am so sorry" he winced, head shaking, then turned to glance back at Cherry only to find her gone. Eyes wide he stepped towards where she had been sitting, then turned back towards where his housekeeper stood watching him, "Where…"

"The Twins, sir" Ms Sanderson smiled sadly, nodding as she spoke, "She will be at the Twins"

"Hey"

The blue-haired young woman turned from where she was standing looking up at the two huge old oak trees, to watch as he approached her, his hands thrust deep into the pockets of the red and black chequered padded lumberjack coat that he was wearing, the cream fleece collar turned up about his neck. For a moment she studied him in silence, her own body clad in a coat that she hadn't been wearing in the kitchen, a grey beanie pulled down about her features. Then she gave a faint smile, "Let me guess, you're a lumberjack and you're OK?"

He laughed at her words, taken by surprise by her sudden joke and he nodded, "Yeah, I sleep all night and I work all day"

This time she laughed with him, features seeming to light up as he stepped alongside her before the trees. Nearly a minute drifted by as they stood there side by side, staring up at the large trees that towered over them both, the trunks of each of them easily as wide as a car, their thick branches visible through the rust covered leaves that still clung to the trees with impressive determination while their brethren littered the ground beneath like fallen soldiers. Taking a deep breath, Richard turned his face from the trees, a hand rising to scratch his beard as he studied the woman beside him, noticing for the first time she had a ring in her bottom lip, "Did it hurt?"

She half turned, eyes narrowing as she sent him a weary look, "When I fell from heaven?"

His laugh was part embarrassment, part genuine humour, "What…no…I meant the lip ring!"

She winced, a hand rising to clasp to the side of her face as she rolled her eyes, "I am so sorry"

"It's fine"

"No" she shook her head, "I thought it was…"

"What?"

"You know?"

He frowned, then chuckled, "A chat up line?"

She sent him a look of mock offence, "Thank you very much for laughing"

He grinned, "I take it you get chatted up a lot"

"Not enough" she smiled, "Not any more…you?"

Richards laugh was loud, his head shaking, "No"

A comfortable silence settled over them once more, one of Cherry's hands rising to toy with the ring in her lip as if his mention of it had made her suddenly aware of its existence and then she sighed, "I'm sorry for just now"

"Just now?"

She nodded, "Leaving the kitchen"

"Oh" he smiled, shrugging, "It's fine...although I am beginning to think you might be a ghost"

"What" she turned to stare at him, muscles tightening in her cheeks, "What do you mean by that?"

He chuckled, "You move so quietly...that's twice you have vanished on me now"

She winced at his words, "How did you find me?"

"Ms Sand...your grandmother" he nodded, "She said you would be out here...listen, if I had known about Agnes and your...mother...I..."

"It's OK" she nodded at him, forcing a smile, "It was a long time ago...it's fine honestly"

He nodded, turning his gaze back upon the trees then followed her gesture as she pointed to a worn spot on the large branch to their left on the larger of the two oaks, "That's her branch"

"Her?"

"Agnes" there was anger in the voice of Cherry, and letting out a low whistle, Richard looked from the branch to her and then back to the tree once more. "How do you know that?"

"The family journal" she nodded as if that answered

everything, "Each of the executioners in my family left records of who they executed, why, and from which branch they were hung. If you were to get closer each of the thicker branches is inscribed with a letter of the alphabet…Agnes was branch F"
Stunned, the author nodded, eyes travelling across the length of the branch, then focusing as she pointed with an arm, "Where it meets the trunk, see it?"
Grimacing, he took a step closer, shuddering as he saw the letter carved into the bark, no more than a couple of inches high. Then he turned to look at the young woman, "What did she do?"

Chapter Fourteen

She stared back at him for a long moment, her head tilting to one side as she studied him intently, and then she nodded, "OK, let's walk, and I'll tell you"

As she turned away from the trees and began to walk along the back of the grounds of the estate that he was now the owner of, Richard turned his head, staring out across the open ground beyond the waist high wall that bordered the rear of the property, eyes drifting over the hills and open country that lay in that direction. When he had been looking for a new place to live, seeking an escape to the countryside he had originally been intending to stay in the South where he had spent his forty years, yet upon seeing pictures of the grounds surrounding Sanderson House he had known instantly that he had to come.

"It's beautiful isn't it?" Cherry turned to throw him a smile, having seen the direction that he was glancing in and he nodded back at her, smiling as he spoke.

"It is, I love it here"

She grinned at his words, and he turned away from her, frowning as he stared up at the huge house to their right, surprised at how much bigger it looked from this direction. For a moment, he let his gaze drift over the windows facing them then he gave a sigh, head shaking, "It's a shame about this old place"

"A shame?" she looked wounded, "In what way?"

"The ghosts" he gave a soft chuckle, "I have no idea how I am going to be able to live here knowing that they are all over the place"

The young woman nodded, the pair of them walking on for several steps before she spoke again, "You know they can't hurt you?"

He stopped walking and she followed suit, turning to watch him as he shook his head, "That's what your grandmother said but Agnes made that man lose his hand...and you said..."

"My mother" she nodded, smiling sadly, "Yeah, Agnes was responsible, but indirectly...it sounds like that's what happened with the removal guy"

He winced, nodding, and they began walking once more, shoulder to shoulder, the author pulling his collar tighter about his face as fine spots of rain began to fall, "So, Agnes..."

Beside him Cherry sighed, nodding, "The Cook"

"The Cook?" he grimaced, "I'm not sure I want to know what she did after all now"

Cherry nodded at his words, and he sighed, "No, I don't want to know...but I need to know"

The blue-haired young woman gave a tight smile and shrugged, "Where to start...Agnes Rand lived in a village three miles from here called Capley...she was executed here in May 1782 by my ancestor James

Sanderson for her crimes"

He winced, "What did she do?"

Cherry stopped walking once more, turning to face him, a hand rising to brush a strand of blue hair that had slipped from beneath her hat away from her face, "She killed children...little girls"

"What?" he felt sick, head spinning, "Really?"

She nodded at him, "She was apparently something of a character in her own village where she ran a small shop selling pies and meat treats in pastry"

"Oh God, no"

Eyes locked to his, Cherry continued, "She would leave the children of Capley alone, and venture off into the countryside, on the pretence of gathering herbs and vegetables, accompanied by her son who in todays terms would be classed as special needs. Most times, they would find a sheep, or catch rabbits or wood pigeons...but sometimes, just sometimes, they would happen across a young girl playing by itself"

Richard released a shaky breath, and Cherry nodded at him, "Yeah, apparently old Agnes had a taste for little girls...she said that the belly fat from them was the sweetest of meats"

Suddenly giddy, Richard bent at the waist, hands on his knees as he fought the urge to vomit, nearly a minute passing before he found the strength to straighten once more and nod at Cherry, "Go on...I need to know the rest"

"When they did happen across a child, Agnes would creep towards them, doing a silly walk and dance, singing rhymes to set them at ease"

Richard shuddered as he recalled the way that she had been walking up behind the removal man, her high scratchy voice singing in his ear, and forcing himself to focus, he nodded at Cherry, urging her to continue, "Then her son, Giles, would subdue the girl, and place her in a sack, then carry her unconscious back to Capley, bound and gagged in case they awoke. On the occasion that they did, Agnes would tell people she had a lamb or piglet in the sack, and that good pies were to come. Then once back in the shop, she would kill the girls, drain their blood for sausages, and use their flesh for her pies"

"Sweet Jesus" Richard felt sick, "How many?"

"Seventeen that she admitted to" Cherry nodded, wincing, "She made a mistake when a grieving parent happened to pass through Capley, and found Giles playing with a rag doll that had gone missing with their daughter a year before"

"What happened?"

"A search was made of her shop, bones were found, and an angry mob, probably mortified that they had been tricked into becoming cannibals besieged her shop. Giles was beaten to death by the angry crowd, and Agnes was about to suffer the same fate when James Sanderson arrived with his men to take her into their custody"

The author nodded, "And she was brought here to be tried and executed"

"She was" Cherry confirmed, turning to glance back at the tree, "Apparently at the end she was quite vocal about what she had done, claiming that she wanted to punish the parents of healthy children who let them wander unprotected while she was left with a dullard for a child"

Richard blinked, head shaking, "She wanted to punish them...by eating their children?"

"Oh Agnes never ate her own pies" Cherry gave a humourless chuckle, "She however was quite content to let her neighbours in Capley do so, a punishment she claimed for their taunts of her child for his inadequacies"

Long moments drifted by as she finished talking, and then Richard shook his head, "I really don't know what to say to that...what a monster"

"She was" Cherry nodded, then shrugged, "But if you keep your wits about you then she can't hurt you...none of The Twelve can"

"And like I said they have managed to kill the estate agent two days ago and nearly killed a removal man this morning..."

"By suddenly scaring them I would imagine" she gave a knowing nod, "Just like how Agnes killed my mother when I was a child"

Richard held her gaze, not daring to speak as she continued, knowing that such a moment must be hard to talk about, "Mum was carrying me downstairs in her arms...we got to the top of the first landing and then..."

"Agnes"

She nodded, her features strained, "She rushed at us from one of the bedrooms, reaching for me and mum flinched away from her and we fell over the banister to the lobby"

"Fucking Hell" Richard was unable to stop the curse escaping his lips, "How old were you?"

"Five" she nodded, "But I can remember it clearly. We were laying on the floor and Agnes began to creep down towards us, step by step, singing that fucking rhyme...then grandmother found us, and Agnes vanished. She thinks that Agnes wanted me"

Lowering his gaze to the ground at his feet, unable to bear the pain on her face any longer, Richard gave a heavy sigh, and then met her gaze again, forcing a sad smile, "It's a miracle you didn't die as well"

The muscles tightened in her cheeks at his words, and he winced, "I'm sorry, I didn't mean any offence...I mean...shit...I'm sorry"

"It's fine" she gave a weak smile, "It's not your fault…it's theirs…you just have to remember that they will take any opportunity to scare you…it's the only power that they have"

"So, I basically have to prepare myself for being jump scared at any opportunity?" he gave her an amused look, "I don't think my anxiety can take that…I'll be dead within the week. I have no idea how the previous owners managed it!"

She made a face and he raised an eyebrow in question, "What?"

"Hasn't my grandmother told you about them?"

He shook his head, then cursed as the faint rain upon them began to grow heavier, "You tell me"

For a moment she seemed uncertain, and he gave a smile, "Please…I need help with this"

"They both died…heart attacks…within days of each other. Grandmother found them"

"Fuck" Richard turned to look through the rain at the house, then back at her, "When was this?"

She shrugged, "Ten years ago…no-one has lived here since…the village pay grandmother to stay here and keep it liveable…and there are conditions that the new owner must adhere to…no children, in case it provokes Agnes or Frances…"

"The child ghost?"

She nodded, "Yes, and no women in case it causes Elias to cause problems"

"Elias…is he the one with the woman?"

Cherry nodded, "Yeah, he's an absolute lunatic"

Richard grimaced, "Well, he's in the right house"

Chapter Fifteen

Above them, thunder rumbled ominously among the dark clouds, and without warning the downpour came, hammering down upon them. As Richard cursed, and glanced up at the clouds, Cherry gave a chuckle, "Get in before you catch your death of cold"

He grinned, a hand wiping rain from his bearded features as they headed back towards the house, barely visible through the torrential rain, "I am going to need a hot shower after this...wait...does this place have showers...or just baths?"

Her chuckle was rich, "There are showers in a couple bathrooms on the second floor I believe"

He grunted at her words and she threw him a glance as they rounded the side of the house, heading for the front porch, "What's the matter?"

He forced a smile, "The thought of taking a shower and having one of The Twelve appear"

She nodded in understanding, turning to face him as they stepped into the protective shelter of the porch. "Still, I need to get out of these clothes, I've probably got the removal guys blood all over my coat...a hot shower it is" he shrugged, surprised that he was able to make light of his terrifying situation, and then he shrugged, gesturing to the door, "Are you coming?"

"For a shower?" Cherry raised an eyebrow, smiling.

"What?" the author swallowed the sudden tightness

in his throat, his cheeks flushing with colour beneath his beard, "No, I meant are you coming into the house not the shower...I don't want a shower with you!"

"Thanks" she fixed him with an offended look.

He winced, shaking his head, "I didn't mean I wouldn't want to have a shower with you!"

"So you do want to have a hot shower with me?"

"Wait...no, I mean I would...not that you are asking, I mean that what I meant...look...I"

His words trailed off as she gave a laugh, her head shaking as he met her gaze, "It's OK, I'm joking...I knew what you meant!"

The author sighed, smiling awkwardly and she took a step back out into the heavy rain, winking at him as she turned to walk away, "Have fun"

Shaking his head, he watched her go until she had vanished amid the heavy rain, a deep sense of loss washing over him as he finally lost sight of her.

He hesitated a moment longer, perhaps hoping that she would return, and then sighing, he turned and entered the house and shutting the door behind him. Removing his coat, he was about to hang it up when he caught sight of the blood upon his chequered shirt and cursing, he turned his coat over, relieved to find that no blood had stained it. Hanging it back upon the coat stand beside the door, he turned and stared up the stairs, his stomach knotting as he considered climbing them, knowing that any of the ghosts could appear at any moment, unsure if he could do it.

How could he live in a building full of ghosts?

Agreed, they couldn't hurt him themselves, but they could still cause him to have fatal accidents.

And all possibly because the roots of the trees had spread under the house in every single direction.

Sighing, he imagined how the place must have been to live in before the roots had passed under the foundations, recalling Ms Sanderson's claims that the house had not always been haunted by The Twelve.

Wait. Not always been haunted. The roots.

Eyes widening as a thought occurred to him, he turned on his heel, hurrying through to the kitchen where his housekeeper was cleaning the worktops, humming softly to herself, "Margaret...do the roots go right under the house...I mean completely under?"

She turned to face him, a confused smile upon her features, "Why, I'm sure I don't know, Sir"

Damn.

"OK" he nodded, a finger rising to tap his lips for a moment before he pointed at her, a fresh idea forming, "You see the ghosts right?"

She nodded and he raised an eyebrow, "Are there any rooms or areas of the house they never enter?"

The elderly woman frowned, thoughtful for a moment before nodding, "Aye, there are a few"

"Which ones are they?"

"The rooms?"

He nodded and she shrugged, "The bedrooms and bathrooms at the Eastern edge of the house on the second floor, the main bathroom and bedroom on the first floor and the large sitting room that you have been using recently"

Turning as if he could see through the walls of the house, Richard nodded, then looked back at her, "And they are all above one another, right?"

"They are"

Without another word, he stepped away from her, turning and leaving the kitchen, eyes staring down at the floor of the hallway. He turned his head as Ms Sanderson joined him, "Mr Miles?"

"The basement" he pointed down at the floor, a lopsided smile on his face as he studied her, "Is there a lot of ghost activity beneath the sitting room?"

She thought for a moment, then, "No"

He clicked his fingers, a broad smile spreading across his face as he began to turn slowly about, staring at the floor beneath their feet, "It is the roots...I think your great uncle was right!"

"Mr Miles" she shook her head, "I am not sure I follow you...what about the roots?"

Grinning at her, he began to back away until his back was at the entrance to the sitting room with the leather sofas, "You told me that when this house was originally built there were no ghosts reported within it...but as the centuries passed they were seen more and more...remember?"

She nodded, "Of course"

"Right" he pointed at her, "And your great uncle claimed that it was because the roots were beginning to grow under the foundations allowing them to travel through the house above"

Once more she gave a nod, "That's right"

"But in the rooms on this side of the house the ghosts aren't seen...that means that the roots might not have grown this far under the foundations...in time they might but not yet!"

At his words, Ms Sanderson raised her gaze, staring up at the ceiling overhead, then down at the floor, her brow furrowing as she met the author's gaze once more, "Are you telling me that they can't reach this side of the house?"

"Maybe" he nodded, grinning as he took a step towards her, "And you know what that means?"

"Go on" she raised an eyebrow, clearly intrigued.

"That I can have a shower in peace" the smile slipping from his face as he turned to study the wide stairs beyond his piled high furniture, "All I need to do now is figure out how to get to one of those bathrooms without having a heart attack"

Chapter Sixteen

"Fifteen...sixteen...seventeen..." eyes clamped shut tightly, Richard took a deep breath his right foot reaching out in front of him instead of rising upwards for another step, hoping that he hadn't miscounted and was about to trip onto his face. He sighed in relief as his leading foot came down on the floor the same height as his left, and he quickly took two steps forward to take him away from the top of the stairs, his left hand reaching out to touch the wall beside him with shaky fingertips, his breathing slowing.

"Mr Miles" the voice of the elderly woman suddenly travelled up to him from the bottom of the stairs where he had left her, "Are you sure this is wise?"

He grimaced, trying to fight away the panic her sudden voice had sent crashing through him like an out of control car, his senses jangling. Then he released a shaky breath, eyes still closed, "I'm fine...and yeah, I have no other choice"

There was a grunt of disapproval from the bottom of the stairs and the voice of the housekeeper sounded once more, "Well, you could just walk upstairs with your eyes open instead of...whatever this is"

He sighed, "This is me finding a way to live in the house without getting killed by the ghosts"

"I thought I made it clear that they cannot harm you Mr Miles" the voice of the old woman returned, a weary tone in her voice as if he were some naughty child not paying attention to her and she his nanny. "Yeah" he gave a nod, his voice little more than a whisper, "Tell that to Jonty and your daughter"

"What was that?" her voice sounded closer than before and he cringed in dread, both startled and concerned that she might have heard his flippant comments regarding her daughter's untimely death. "Nothing" he half turned, "Where are you? I told you to stay down in the lobby"

Another weary sigh, "I *was* coming to help you"

"No" he waved his right hand, not knowing if she was far enough up the stairs to see the gesture, "I need to do this on my own"

"I still don't see what you aim to achieve" Ms Sanderson didn't try to hide the irritation in her voice, "You could fall and hurt yourself!"

Richard nodded, knowing she was right but then shrugged, "If all the ghosts can do to hurt me is jump scare me then I need to find a way round that...if it means I have to walk around like Matt Murdoch until I find a better way then I will!"

"Who?"

"Matt Murdoch...Daredevil" he stated, realising that he was wasting his breath, "Never mind. I am at the first floor...you said go left, right?"

"No, just left"

The author took a deep breath at her confusion, forcing himself to stay calm, "OK, sure...but left"

"Yes Mr Miles, that is what I said"

"And how many doors do I pass before I reach the safe area?" he cringed at his wording, hoping that he wasn't mistaken about the roots and their reach.

"Three doors along, on the left hand side, I did tell you this before you headed up the stairs"

Fighting the urge to make a sarcastic comment, he stepped into the hallway, and turned to his left, his left hand staying in contact with the wall as he began to move along it with steady steps, his mind racing as he tried to picture the hallway from his memory.

On his first night here the previous night, God it seemed so long ago now, he and Myra had shared a bed in one of the bedrooms on the first floor.

Yet the second floor was still largely unexplored by him apart from when he had looked about it on their arrival and when he had climbed it following the child ghost of The Twelve earlier that morning.

At the memory, Richard froze, his heart skipping a beat as he imagined the members of The Twelve that he had already encountered, standing watching him.

But if he was right, by closing his eyes, he had removed the small amount of power they had.

He cursed as what felt like the featherlight touch of something swept over the back of his neck, his body lurching forward several steps in absolute terror. Heart hammering in his chest, he stepped closer to the wall that his left hand had been touching and turned to face outwards, his eyes still clamped shut together as he considered what might have touched his neck, images of the way Agnes has stroked the throat of the removal man, making him shudder, returning to him in a sudden maddening rush.

Oh God. Was she here now?

How many times had he felt that in his life.

What if each time he had ever felt that way was because some random ghost had touched him? Shaking his head, a hand rising to clasp his forehead, he turned once more, left hand touching the wall as he began moving then froze almost instantly as he felt the ridge of a door frame. Taking a deep breath, he began moving once more, letting his fingers drop past the frame onto the door and then bump up the other side once more, tracing their way past the frame and onto the wall, continuing his journey.

He reached the second door and passed it, his pace quickening as the featherlight touch came upon his neck once more, and he gave a shake of his head, trying not to think about which of The Twelve it might be, if it was any of them at all, "Fuck off!"

After all, he had seen Clemence and Elias, the boy Frances, the clown, the busty blonde woman, the hulking James Jackman, and Agnes...but that still left another five that he had no knowledge of whatsoever. He paused as he reached the third doorway, turning his body as his fingers traced their way down to the handle, then froze, brow furrowing in confusion.

He had asked Ms Sanderson how many doors he had to pass to reach the area they thought might be safe from the ghosts. She had replied something about three doors on the left side of the long hallway.

But did that mean that he had to go past three doors on the left side or was the third door safe?

Fuck. Shit.

What had her words been exactly?

Grimacing, he turned the handle and pushed, hearing the door creak open before him, and hands outstretched, he felt his way through into the room, his breathing coming in ragged gasps as he closed the door behind him, and stepped back to lean upon it. For long moments, he stood there in silence, his head starting to ache from constantly keeping his eyes shut, and then with a heavy sigh, he lifted his right eyelid a fraction, peering ahead of him, finding that he was in what looked like a study. Slowly turning his head, his other eye gradually opening, he glanced about the room, taking in the antique wooden writing

desk in the corner facing the door, a chaise lounge upholstered with a deep crimson material, and several book cases, their shelves filled to overflowing with old tomes. Frowning, he stepped closer, bending slightly as he traced a finger over the spines of the books, his lips moving silently as he repeated the names of authors he had never heard before, soon realising that every one of the books all seemed to be regarding the study of the paranormal in some way. "Well, this is the right library for this place" he straightened, a soft chuckle escaping his lips, then screamed in terror as he saw the thin man in the black frock coat and trousers that was sat upon the chaise longue watching him, a small black bow tie stark against the crisp white of his shirt, his black hair oiled down across his head. Groaning in terror, Richard backed slowly away towards the door, head shaking as the man rose to his feet before him, a finger rising to push the tiny round pair of spectacles that it wore further back up along his nose, thin lips twisting as it stepped towards him, the voice as cold as the rain outside, "*You have a fever...come here*"
"How about no" the author shook his head, stomach knotting as the ghost raised its right hand before it's body, what looked like a straight razor held in it.
"*You have a fever*" the figure repeated, its thin lips drawing back in an almost skeletal smile to reveal a

perfect set of teeth, "*Let me bleed you!*"

Cursing, Richard clasped his eyes shut and wrenched open the door behind him, trying to hurriedly back away from the ghost he had seen, then cursed and spun to the side as his right shoulder didn't clear the door frame in time. Off balance, he spun into the hallway, hands reaching to stop his fall as he fell to his knees, then cursed once more as he realised that he now had no idea where he was in the slightest. Finding his way to a wall would be no trouble but which wall was it going to be? Was he facing one of the two long sides or had he even been turned around so that if he walked forward he would pass right the way back down the corridor?

Sighing, he sat back up on his knees, and then rose to his feet, grimacing as he knew that he had no choice other than to open his eyes wide once more.

Cursing once, he did just that, then fell back as something in front of his swept at his face, the floor of the hallway stopping him hard as he landed upon his back, pain shooting through his upper body.

Blinking past the pain, he watched as the ghost that he had just encountered in the room took another step towards him, that skeletal smile still wide as it raised the straight razor again, "*You have a fever!*"

Movement behind the well-dressed ghost made Richard snap his head towards it, stomach lurching as he saw the clown from that morning suddenly shambling towards them at high speed, cackling insanely, the lumbering figure of James Jackman taking shape beyond it far off in the distance.

With shock, the author suddenly realised that he was almost at the end of the long corridor in the direction that he had been heading, his tumble having sent him towards his ultimate goal, and forcing himself to rise, he hurried towards the door he had been intending to enter, not pausing to look back at the nightmares following behind.

Chapter Seventeen

Rushing inside the room, Richard slammed the door behind him and then backed away, his eyes opening slowly as he stared at the door, heart pounding in his chest as it if were alive and trying to free itself from the bony cage of his ribs. He gasped as his legs bumped the edge of the bed that sat in the room and sat down hard on the mattress, his hands resting palms down, his mouth dry as he stared at the door ahead of him.

The author lost all sense of time as he sat there, waiting for one of the three ghosts that had had just seen to either walk through the door or materialize in the room and prove that he had been wrong, yet nothing happened, and the quiet was unnerving.

He had recognised the shambling clown from earlier that morning although he had yet to discover both its name and the reason that it was there, and he had of course recognised the huge James Jackman as he had stalked towards him but the man in the suit had been someone new. Yet who was he?

His comments about having a fever implied that he had perhaps been a doctor, and the offer to *bleed* Richard and the style of suit that he had been wearing made it look as though he were from the Victorian era or from sometime around that time. Rising to his feet, he took a step towards the door, his courage having returned slightly as he raised his voice, "So, are any of you coming in?"

As he had expected there was no reply and he gave a nod, smiling, "I'll take that as a no then"

Turning away from the door, his eyes seemingly reluctant to leave its wooden surface, the author surveyed the room that he had found himself in, his gaze drifting across the dark wood furniture before settling upon the large bed, a wry smile creasing his bearded features, "Hey, I'm Richard...you are going to be seeing a lot of me"

Chuckling, he raised his hands to his cheeks, head shaking slowly, "I'm going fucking insane"

Lowering his hands to his hips, he turned once more, focusing upon the door on the other side of the room to where he was standing, "And where do you lead too, I wonder?"

Stepping closer, he reached out, his fingers turning the handle and pushing forward, his stomach knotting as it swung slowly open to reveal a large bathroom. For long moments, the author studied the huge tub, then let his gaze fall on the walk in shower that was built against the far wall, a chuckle escaping his lips as he unbuttoned his bloodstained shirt, and stepped into the bathroom, a hand reaching in to his breast pocket to retrieve his bottle of pills. Opening a medicine cabinet that was hanging on the wall to the right of the door, Richard placed his bottle of pills inside then turned to back at the shower, "Hello...I was looking for you"

Five minutes later, he was standing beneath the rushing hot water, hands reaching up to run back through his short brown hair, eyes closed as he groaned aloud, "Now this is what it's all about!" Opening his eyes, he reached out a hand, collecting the bar of soap that was resting upon the small shelf built into the wall, placed there by Ms Sanderson the moment she had heard that the old house was getting a new owner, just like the towels he had found folded on the back of the toilet upon entering the bathroom. Rubbing the soap against the palm of his other hand, he worked up a lather and then proceeded to work it over his body, cursing himself as he always did as his hands rubbed over his slight paunch, nostalgic for the days when he had attended a gym regularly and worked out. Sighing heavily, he glanced down at himself, eyes travelling over the curve of his stomach, shaking his head once more as he began to wash his groin, "Someone's put a roof over the toy shop" What a joke. As if anyone would find him even remotely sexually attractive in his current state. He frowned, wondering when he'd last been on a date, nodding as he recalled the brown-haired librarian that his publishing agent had set him up with, then cringed as he recalled her personality.

Carrie. That had been her name.

He cringed as he recalled how angry she had been when he had tried to end it after their one and only date, screaming down the phone at him in anger.

Jesus Christ. Was that all he could attract? Psychopaths and crazies?

Surely the law of averaged meant that his wealth and name should be making women swoon at his feet if nothing else did. He grinned at the thought, knowing that such a relationship was the last thing he wanted. Raising his hands, he began to rub the soap into his beard, and over his face, his mind continuing down the road that he had set it on, his brow furrowing as he realised that the fault for his solitude was his.

He spent too much time alone writing, pushing what he had always assumed was the product of his mental illness out onto the paper, never having considered what he was seeing was anything but his imagination. Not until he had come to Sanderson House.

Sighing, the author stepped further under the shower head, letting the force of the hot rushing water begin to clean the soap away from his face and beard, a smile creasing his features as he recalled how much of an idiot he had made himself with Cherry earlier.

As if he would ever have had the courage to ask her come upstairs and share a hot shower with him. The smile slipped from his features as he suddenly had an image of her stepping naked into the shower with him, his throat tightening with the image and what might follow, and then shaking his head, he rubbed his hands over his features, then reached out with a hand and turned the shower switch off. Feeling stupid, he opened the door of the shower and stepped out onto the bathmat, his head shaking as he reached for the towel that was waiting for him on the toilet lid. As if someone that was as attractive as Cherry could ever be remotely interested in someone that looked like he did in his current condition. What was she? Twenty three…twenty four? Sixteen years his junior if she was a single day.

"Fucking idiot" he muttered, rubbing the towel over his face, and then wrapping it about his waist he gave his feet another wipe on the mat and headed for the bedroom beyond the door. He cursed as he opened it and saw the figure on the bed, head to toe sideways so they were facing him as he entered, "Fuck!"

"What's the matter?" Myra asked, amusement upon her face, "Think I was one of your ghosts?"

"Yeah" he nodded, shaking his head as he tried to calm his heart rate back down, "That's exactly what I thought you were"

"Well?" she raised an eyebrow, a smile growing on her full lips, "Have you seen any more?"

He caught the inside of his right cheek between his back teeth, fighting the urge to give her a sarcastic reply, "Ghosts? Yeah, I have actually"

She grinned, swinging her legs around to sit up on the bottom of the bed, watching as he moved to stand several feet away, "And? Tell me"

"Tell you what?" he stepped back into the bathroom, grabbing up a smaller towel and began to dry his beard and face once more, before throwing it back onto the toilet seat and turning to face his friend, "So you can mock me again...is that why?"

She smiled, "I wasn't mocking you"

"Weren't you?" he sent her a disbelieving look, then frowned, "Where have you been?"

She shrugged, "I was asleep, I didn't hear you come in...I just woke up and heard the shower"

Richard blinked, head shaking, "What?"

"I was asleep, I didn't hear you come in"

For several moments he stared back at her in silence and then he frowned, "You weren't here"

"What?" she gave a chuckle, head shaking, "I was"

"No" he eyed her in confusion, "I came rushing in here because...well, never mind, but I came in and you weren't here...I would have seen you!"

"You were probably too busy being spooked by your

ghosts" she gave a laugh, and he grimaced at her.
"Myra!"

"Richie" she gave an almost childlike giggle, her head
shaking once more, and he cringed as he felt the hairs
rise upon the back of his neck at her choice of words.

"What?" she eyed him in confusion, "What now?"

"Why did you call me that?"

"Call you what?" she looked at him as if he were
insane, her mouth twisting as she made a face of
confusion, "You are starting to worry me"

"You called me Richie...like when we were kids"

She blinked, "Did I? When?"

"Just now" he stated, his voice strained, "Where were
you really Myra?"

He stepped back as she surged to her feet, her voice
thick with anger, a hand pointing behind her, "I told
you I was here...in this bed...asleep!"

"No, this room was empty" he shook his head.

"Then why did I just wake up here?" she shouted,
taking a step towards him and flinching he took a
step back, hands rising defensively before him.

"Calm down, Myra!"

"Why?" she snarled, head shaking, "Why the sudden
interest in what I do..."

"What?" he winced, "What does that mean?"

She glared at him for a moment, eyes flashing
dangerously and then she shrugged, "Ever since we

came here we hardly speak...you keep leaving me by myself and I can't remember anything...it's this place Richard...it's pulling us apart!"

He shook his head, "What does that mean?"

"We've only been here a couple of days and it's like you don't think about me anymore...we are drifting apart Richard...I can feel it!"

"Hey" he stepped forwards, arms wrapping about her as she dragged her into an embrace, his right hand brushing over her back, "That will never happen...we will always be together!"

She leaned back at his words, looking him in the eyes, "Do you promise...really?"

He nodded, "Not even death can keep us apart"

Chapter Eighteen

"Are you awake?" Richard asked some time later as the pair of them lay upon the rooms large bed, she dressed and he just wearing the underwear and jeans that he had taken off before getting in the shower. They had talked at length, he reassuring her that he wasn't going to be abandoning her any time soon, why would he after a lifetime of friendship, and she finally confessing that she had been experiencing bouts of amnesia for decades, almost the entirety of their friendship something that had left him troubled. They had nearly argued once more, Richard offering to pay to get her checked out by a doctor, and she as usual, saying that it wasn't his job to support her. Eventually they had fallen into a comfortable silence, her head resting upon his arm about her shoulder, he gently stroking her back in circles of decreasing and increasing sizes, until he had noticed something above the bottom of the bed he hadn't seen before. When she didn't respond, he turned his face to look at her, frowning as he saw that she was asleep, and reaching out with his other hand he placed it upon her forehead, concern touching him once more as he felt how cold her skin was. Carefully so as not to wake her, Richard dragged his arm out from beneath his head, then sat up, watching as she rolled on her side.

Rising, he lifted the side of the duvet that he had been laying upon and folded it over Myra, then stepped back and studied her, wondering what he would ever do if she wasn't there in his life. Then, frowning once more, he raised his eyes to what he had noticed while he was lying down, eyes narrowing in curiosity as he studied it. It appeared to be a hatch, square in shape and roughly three feet across, the narrow gap between it and the actual ceiling, having been mainly covered in paint so that he had not noticed it at first. Now that he knew it was there however the hatch stuck out like a sore thumb, his eyes easily able to trace it's outline even where paint was covering it. It was obviously an entrance to the attic, but he hadn't noticed it when he had been up there the day of their arrival. Was it sealed from within?

Maybe it was an old part of the house and had been closed off due to no longer being needed anymore. Turning suddenly, the author scanned the room, inspiration touching him as he saw the large chest of drawers beside the entrance to the bathroom, just feet away from where he stood. Without hesitating, he stepped over to the chest of drawers, and grasped at its sides, dragging back with all his might only for it to hardly move. Cursing, he moved to one end, grabbed it once more and tried to shift it to the side, managing to move it at least a foot so that it was sticking out from the wall at a forty-five-degree angle. Stepping back, he glanced up at the hatch in the ceiling once more, realising that if he moved the other end of the chest of drawers it would be directly underneath it. Nodding, he moved to the end of the chest of drawers still touching the wall and began to drag it out so that it was straight, then moved around to clamber up onto the bed. For a moment, he stepped from side to side, off balance but then he stepped from the bed onto the wide top of the chest of drawers and turned to look back at Myra as she lay under the duvet, snoring softly as he studied her.

He frowned then, considering her claim that she had been fast asleep in the bed when he had come staggering in, pursued by the trio of ghosts.

She hadn't. He was one hundred per cent sure.

Which meant that she must have entered the room after he had got into the shower and fallen asleep, but why couldn't she remember that? How ill was she? During the research of his third novel, he had studied the horror of early-onset Alzheimer's disease, and learned how awful it could be to everyone involved. Was that what was happening with Myra?

Feeling sick at the thought of losing her, he released a shaky breath and raised his eyes once more, staring up at the hatch which was directly above him now.

149

Raising his arms, he placed his hands upon the hatch, brow furrowing as he pushed upwards only to find that nothing happened at all. Grunting, refusing to be beaten, he pushed harder, the chest of drawers creaking beneath his bare feet as he shifted position, his voice strained as he cursed, "Come on you fuck..." With a crack, the hatch moved, one side of it rising higher than the other as it folder upwards and changing position, the author pushed on that edge, watching with astonishment as it swung upwards and out of sight with a deep dull thud.

Wincing, he turned his face back towards Myra, fully expecting her to be sat up and staring at him in confusion, demanding to know what he thought he was doing on top of a chest of drawers half-dressed but to his surprise she was still asleep on the bed. Smirking, head shaking, he turned back to the now open hatch above him and looked up, an eyebrow rising as he saw that somehow the area above him that he could see was dimly illuminated, dust motes dancing lazily in the strands of light above him. Reaching up with his hands, his curiosity piqued, Richard tried to haul himself up, only succeeding in raising his head above the entrance to the hatch before he groaned and lowered himself back down once more, hands rising to rub at the muscles of the opposite arms. For a moment, he stood staring about the room, seeking something that he could use as a step then he grinned, clambering down from his perch to stand before a small bookcase in the far corner of the room. Bending, he picked out the handful of books upon it, placing them down upon the floor before picking up the surprisingly heavy bit of furniture and carrying it to the chest of drawers. Sliding it atop his initial perch, Richard climbed back onto the bed, then carefully stepped back onto the top of the chest of drawers, a smile creasing his bearded features as he imagined what the newspaper headlines would say if he were to topple off and break his neck – *Best-selling Horror author found dead in haunted house. Coroner rules it a case of utter stupidity. Friends are not surprised.*

Shaking his head, he cast another glance at Myra and then reached up with his hands to grab at the rib of the hatch, his right foot rising to gingerly use the second shelf of the bookcase as a step, relieved to discover that it took his weight easily. Pulling with his arms, he raised his left foot to stand upon the second shelf of the old bookcase, smiling in triumph as his head and shoulders cleared the hatch once more.

"Well fuck me" he muttered, head turning slowly as he studied the dimly lit room in which the hatch exited, eyes taking in the old fashioned writing desk and the chair before it, the walls either side lined with sheaths of paper and scrolls, the smell of dust heavy in the small area. Lifting his eyes from the desk, Richard stared at the small window in the slanted roof, grey light coming through the dirty pane. Raising his right foot to another shelf, the author pushed with his arms and gave a little jump, boosting himself up to sit on the edge of the hatch, head turning once more as he gave a broad smile. This had clearly once been someone's private study, a place where the owner had perhaps come for solace or contemplation in complete solitude and quiet.

But why had it been closed off?

Had whoever had painted over the hatch known of its presence? How could they not have done?

Frowning, Richard leaned back, swinging his legs up into the small room, and then carefully rose, pleased to find there was enough headroom for him to do so easily without cracking his skull off the sloping roof above. Stepping past the hatch, casting a glance at the room he had left behind, Richard moved to the desk and stared down at the contents upon it, a smile creasing his features as he saw the quill resting upon its weathered surface alongside a grey rectangle metal wrapped in string with the end exposed. Frowning, he reached down, raising the item before his face, smiling once more as he realised that it was an early pencil, just a piece of graphite wrapped in string to make holding it easier. Shaking his head, he placed it back down and retrieved the quill, chuckling as he turned it before his eyes, "Well look at you"

For a writer it was like finding a goldmine.

Placing it back upon the desk, Richard turned, studying the shelves to his left for several moments, excitement coursing through him as he imagined what might be upon the scrolls and papers, then raised an eyebrow as he noticed a small leather pouch amongst them, several small wooden beads attached to the front by what looked like twine. Reaching out, he picked it up, hefting the weight of the bag in the palm of his right hand, the fingers of his left hand moving towards the top of the bag where it was sealed with more cord, "And what might you be?"

He froze as the sound of a soft chuckle suddenly sounded from his right, and heart in his mouth, he turned his face, a grimace creasing his face as he stared at the wall beside him, ears straining.

For long moments there was nothing except the sound of his haggard breathing, and raising his free hand, he wiped the sweat from his brow, his head shaking slowly as he glanced up at the small window, telling himself that it was just the wind.

Yeah, because the wind chuckles. Get real.

He gave a low moan of dread as the chuckle came once more, louder this time, and taking a shaky breath, the author stepped closer to the wall. Beyond it was the rest of the attic, he was sure.

So, what the fuck was chuckling?

Stepping back, he glanced at the wall before him, his eyes travelling across its surface intently, searching for any holes that he might be able to look through, grimacing as he noticed one to his left at waist height, level with the open hatch to the bedroom below. Placing the small bag that he had found in a front pocket of his jeans, Richard moved to the hole and dropped crouched before it, his hands resting upon the dusty old wall either side. As the chuckle sounded again, he groaned, then he leaned forwards, his left eye closing as he placed his right eye against the hole which was no larger in size than a one-pound coin. For a moment he saw nothing but darkness and he blinked, thinking that there was something obstructing his vision before realising that there was no light on in the attic on the other side of the wall. Grimacing, he strained his eye, glancing about as best as he could, his vision gradually growing accustomed to the darkness beyond, and then he frowned as he noticed a lighter patch of darkness amid the blackness, "What the Hell is…"

The ghost of the clown came shambling out of the

darkness of the attic towards him as if it was sprinting, chuckling insanely, hands reaching for him as he crouched on the other side of the false wall. With a scream born of pure terror, Richard pushed himself quickly back away from the hole, the heels of his bare feet catching upon the rim of the hatch, refusing to budge any further and he fell backwards. His scream turned to a grunt, as the lip of the hatch entrance cracked him across the back of the head, his vision wavering then he was falling, crashing down across the bookcase that stood atop the large chest of drawers. Barely conscious, he turned his head, staring down at the floor as he wobbled precariously, the realisation that he was about to break bones washing over him with disturbing calmness.

Then he toppled sideways and fell the other way. With a grunt, he bounced upon the top of the bed several times and then rolled from it to the floor, cursing in shock and pain as he landed heavily. Long minutes dragged past as he lay there on the carpet, his left hand clasped to the back of his head, his eyes locked to the hatch as if expecting the clown to follow him through into the room to attack him. Yet the clown never came as he knew it couldn't. He had been right about this room. He was safe. Groaning, he sat up, the fingers of his left hand leaving the back of his head to raise before his face and he sighed as he realised there was no blood on them. Thank God for small mercies at least.

Gritting his teeth, he managed to stand, leaning heavily upon the top of the bed as he fought the wave of dizziness coursing through his body, then he cursed in dread as he realised that Myra was gone.

Chapter Nineteen

"Myra!" he wrenched open the door of the bedroom, grimacing as he stared at the long corridor ahead of him, head turning as he searched in vain for a sign of his best friend. Cursing, he glanced back at the room behind him, then up at the hatch, then stepped over to where he had placed his clothes before getting into the shower, dragging his socks and shoes back on. Lifting the shirt, he paused, realising the futility of having washed only to put dirty clothes back on, then he was sliding his arms into the sleeves and fastening the buttons as he headed for the door. He paused once more as he reached the threshold of the hallway, glancing down at the floor, then studied the area ahead, knowing that somewhere out there the ghosts were waiting to scare him, just like the clown had. Grimacing, he glanced up at the ceiling overhead, his right hand rising to gently touch the small lump on the back of his head where he had struck it on the hatch lip, wincing as he did so, his eyes watering. "Bastards" he took a step forward, eyes drifting to the edge of the corridor on the right where the stairs began, the wooden balustrade lining that section showing where the stairs where, then he glanced about once more, head shaking, "Ah fuck this" Without another word he began to run, for possibly the first time in over a decade, arms pumping at his sides as he charged down the hallway, shouting in a mixture of fear and anger, refusing to be a victim. This was his house. His. Not theirs.

He'd spent half a million pounds on it and there was no way he was going to spend it being a prisoner any longer. Fuck The Twelve. Fuck them all.

His shout turned to a whimper as something moved in his peripheral vision, and he turned his head as he ran past, stomach knotting as he saw a powerfully built man with long black hair and an unkempt beard rushing for him, a long handled axe clasped in his dirty fingers, the voice of the ghost little more than a snarl, "*Heathen!*"

Wincing as he saw the axe swinging in at him, Richard charged on, hoping against hope that Ms Sanderson and her granddaughter hadn't been wrong about them being unable to hurt living people, then he cursed as the black robed figure of an overweight man with a red face appeared in front of him, features twisted in hatred as it pointed at him, "*Fornicator!*"

Too late to avoid the figure, Richard charged into it, arms rising before his face out of instinct to protect him from the collision with the fat man, only to gasp in shock as he passed out the other side, his body feeling as if he'd just had a bucket of cold water thrown over him, "Fuck, fuck, shit, fuck!"

Off balance, he fell to one knee, then rose quickly, casting a glance back at the hallway behind him, his bowels turning to water as he saw that there were seven figures there following him; the fat man, the wild man, the doctor, the couple Clemence and Elias, James Jackman; The Butcher, and then there he was at the back, weaving through the others as it charged along the hallway, laughing aloud, hands reaching.

"That fucking clown!" Richard gave a shout that was half snarl and half terrified whimper, as he staggered towards the top of the staircase, and then down them. He paused to look back as he reached the midway landing, cursing as the ghost of the boy, Frances, appeared just steps above him, "Shit!"

Half slipping, he hurried down the last steps to the lobby, backing away as the boy followed him, then turned as Ms Sanderson appeared from the kitchen doorway, "What is the commotion!"

"Myra!" Richard took a step towards her quickly, his head shaking, "She's gone…again!"

The old woman held his gaze in silence for a moment, her brow furrowing then she shook her head, "Come into the kitchen, let us talk"

"Have you seen her?" he asked, a quick glance over his shoulder showing that the ghost of the child had vanished, then he met the gaze of the old woman again, "Please, she's not well"

The housekeeper sighed, "Mr Miles…"

"I asked you a question" he snapped, anger coursing through him, "Have you seen her?"

The muscles in her cheeks tightened at his outburst, but she stood her ground, holding his gaze in silence.

"Fuck!" he shouted in frustration, hands clasping at his head as he spun on the spot, then headed towards the open door of the living room, weaving among the furniture that had been delivered, "Myra…Myra are you in there?"

Hands grasping either side of the door frame as he reached the room, he looked inside, shaking his head as he found it empty then turned back to find Ms Sanderson watching him with a sad smile upon her features, "Please Mr Miles…she's gone"

"Gone?" he stepped towards her, "Gone where?"

The old woman winced, "Please, listen to me"

Head shaking, he stared back at the old in shock and confusion, "Where is she…the village?"

Ms Sanderson winced, "You have to let her go"

"Let her go…what do you mean?" he stepped towards the coat rack, snatching up his jacket then glanced back at the old woman, "I'm sorry for shouting at you but I need to find her!"

Without another word, he opened the front door, cursing as what felt like sheet of heavy rain blew in at him, his right hand raising to wipe his face.

"Where are you going?" Ms Sanderson snapped, head shaking as she reached the open doorway, her hands dragging her cardigan tighter about her frail form as the wind blew in at her, concern in her eyes as she met his gaze, "Please, its almost dark...this a storm, you can't go out there!"

He shook his head at her as he stepped out into the rain, the wet gravel crunching beneath his feet as he left the porch, his voice almost lost to the wind as he replied, "I don't have a choice...she's all I have!"

"Mr Miles!" there was panic in her voice as she called out, a hand holding to the door frame as she stepped out under the porch, "Richard!"

He froze at her sudden use of his Christian name, realising how much it must have taken the old woman to do so, then he forced a smile, "Don't worry, I'll be back as soon as I can"

Chapter Twenty

Head bent against the heavy wind that was whipping the rain against him, Richard hurried past his car parked on the long driveway, headed for the metal gate between the two large gateposts then froze as something suddenly moved somewhere off to his left. Turning in that direction, he leaned forward peering through the rain, head moving as he tried to spot what it was that he had seen, his heart racing. Grimacing, he wiped his face free of rain once more, and cast a glance back at the large house, relieved to find that Ms Sanderson had finally gone back inside. Turning back to begin walking towards the gate once more he screamed, flinching suddenly as Agnes Rand charged at him out of the rain, long nails reaching for him and with a curse, he fell back, feet tangling, to land heavily upon the gravel path. His scream off shock was cut off as he grunted in pain, his already injured head bouncing off the floor, and instinctively he rolled to his front, gasping in pain as something sharp jabbed him in the thigh. Jerking his groin away from the ground and the sudden pain, he thrust his hand into the front pocket of his jeans and withdrew the small bag he had found in the attic, eyes widening as he saw what looked like a tooth sticking through it.

The sudden scratchy voice of Agnes above him, made him roll to his back once more, both his hands held before him defensively as he cursed in pure terror. For a moment, the twisted features of the child killer stared down at him in a mixture of amusement and hatred, her fingers reaching for him even though she must have known that she could not touch him physically, only to suddenly freeze, her hands recoiling away from him as if burnt, her eyes locked to the small bag as she screamed in raw terror.

And just like that she faded away.

Heart hammering in his chest, blinking at the rain that was falling into his bearded features, Richard rolled to his knees, his eyes drifting to study the small bag that he was holding in his right hand, his thumb brushing over the bleached piece of bone, tooth or claw that was sticking out from the split material. What the Hell was it? And why had Agnes Rand been so terrified of it that she had fled away from it? Shaking his head, he clasped it in his hand and began to move once more, opening the large metal gate and passing out through the gateposts. Hurrying across the small road onto the village green, he shivered as the rain suddenly seemed to increase in strength, his clothes and coat already soaked through to the skin. Hurrying along, he slipped on the wet grass, muddied his jeans and was up once more, moving more carefully now, his eyes scanning the area for any sign of Myra, but it was almost impossible to see through the heavy downpour. Feeling suddenly weak, he bent at the waist, hands resting on his knees as he fought to catch his breath, then straightened, hands cupping to his mouth as he called out, "Myra!"

Yet there was no sound but the wind and rain. Cursing aloud, he turned to his left, making out the distant shapes of the first of the buildings on that side; the post office and the hardware store, and he took a couple of steps towards them, then turned as he spied a light through the falling rain at the bottom of the slope. Turning, he began to hurry towards it, slipping twice more but each time he was up instantly and hurrying on through the fading light. Abruptly the large shape of what Myra had believed was a former country pub appeared out of the rain before him and he slowed, head turning to study the light which he realised was the convenience store owned by George Wolf. Angling his route towards it, he crossed the small road and staggered to the door of the shop, pushing it wide open, the young couple behind the counter cursing and gasping in shock as they saw him standing there, caked in mud and rain. Rising a hand to wipe his face, he paused as he saw his muddy fingers and sighed, glancing back at the couple as the man stepped around the counter to eye him in concern, "Can I help you?"

"I'm looking for my friend" he managed to gasp, the exertions of his race through the heavy rain seeming to settle about him like a shroud, "A woman…nearly forty but she looks a lot younger…dark brown hair…she's called Myra"

The man glanced at his companion and then back at Richard, "We've seen no-one like that…fact hardly anyone's been in all afternoon what with this rain"

"Damn" Richard stepped back to the open door, turning to look out at the heavy rain then glanced back at the man moved to stand beside him, peering out at the storm that was besieging Evenfield.

"Looks like its here for the night"

Richard nodded, not really listening and the man continued, "So, where'd you lose your friend? Are you passing through?"

The author shook his head, meeting the gaze of the curious man, "No, I've just moved here"

"You are the man who has brought the big house!" the young woman stated suddenly, moving further along behind the counter, "The famous author"

"Oh" the man beside Richard nodded in sudden understanding, then frowned, "So this friend, have you got a photo or something? "

"No, I don't" Richard shook his head, glancing back out into the rain then clicked his fingers and turned back to the couple as an idea suddenly occurred to him, "Is George here?"

The man blinked, head shaking, "Who?"

"George...George Wolf" Richard stated, frowning as the man gave a sudden curse of shock and grimaced.

"What's wrong?" the author glanced from the grim features of the man to find the woman staring at her companion in shock, "What is it?"

"How do you know George?" the woman asked, her voice strained, and turning away from the pale features of the man beside him, Richard forced a smile as he took a step closer over to the counter.

"I met him yesterday...outside, me and Myra were looking at the big building next door and he came over to speak with us"

"John?" the woman glanced away from Richard to her companion and frowning in confusion, the author followed her gaze, tensing as he saw the grim expression now upon the face of the young man.

"What's going on?" Richard shook his head, sighing heavily, "Is George OK?"

"My dad's dead...seven years this winter" the voice of the man named John was thick with barely controlled emotion, his head shaking as he stared at Richard.

"What?" Richard blinked, staring at the man in disbelief as he began to move back around the counter to stand alongside the woman, one of her arms reaching comfortingly about his waist.

"We haven't seen your friend" the woman gave a shake of her head, her smile apologetic, "I'm sorry...please will you leave us be now"

"Look, I don't understand..."

"Out!" the man suddenly erupted in a rage, hands pressing against the counter as if he intended to clamber over it, tears in his eyes and Richard backed out of the shop, hands raised defensively before him. "I'm sorry..."

Within the shop, the man suddenly rounded the counter, the woman dragging back on his jumper, screaming for him to calm down, and cursing, Richard backed away from the doorway in dread, wincing as instead of attacking him the man slammed the door, the closed sign appearing amid the postcard ads upon its window. Heart racing, Richard moved back onto the village green, mind reeling as he tried to make sense of what had just happened in the shop.

"Richard?"

He turned, hope taking flight within him as he heard the female voice suddenly call his name over the rain, a dim shape forming in the darkness that had fallen during the brief period that he had been within the interior of the small shop, "Myra?"

Then he was off again, running through the rain.

Chapter Twenty One

"Myra!" he charged onwards, a forearm clearing his features from rain, feet almost sliding in the mud but then, there she was, straight ahead of him in the darkness of the night, hurrying towards him.

"Richard!"

"Cherry?" he slowed, a turmoil of emotions washing over him; joy at seeing his new friend but sadness to discover that it hadn't been Myra calling out to him.

"What are you doing?" the blue haired woman was suddenly there before him, her hands grasping to his arms, "You shouldn't be out in this storm"

"Myra" he felt suddenly weak, "She's gone"

Cherry held his gaze for a moment, attractive features streaked with rain, and then she gave a shake of her head, forcing a smile, "Maybe she has found her way back to Sanderson House"

He lifted his gaze to stare up the green, unable to see his new home through the storm, and he shook his head, "No, she isn't there, I can feel it"

"Richard"

"She's left me" he shook his head, fighting the wave of emotion that surged through him, "I wasn't giving her enough attention...she's gone"

The blue-haired woman held his gaze in silence, her eyes searching his face and then she stepped forward, pulling him into an embrace, his head dropping to rest upon her shoulder as she stroked his back, "We need to get you out of the rain"

"I can't go back there" he raised his head to stare off into the darkness, "Not yet, not without her"

"You can't stay here out in this rain" she shook her head, releasing him to step back and meet his gaze once more, "You need to get under cover"

"I told you" he shook his head, "I can't go back there yet...I need to be out of that house! It's like there is so much going on I can't even think!"

"The church" she pointed, a hand rising to point at the vague shape amid the darkness, "I know a place there where you will be dry, come on"

Frowning, Richard let her take him by the hand, the pair of them traipsing across the muddy village green until they reached the small road once more, and the church appeared out of the darkness ahead of them, a low old stone wall rimming the building perimeter in all directions. As they reached the lychgate built into the wall, Cherry hurried under it and beckoned for Richard to join her as she sat on one of the narrow wooden benches that was built into its structure. Nodding, he did so, dropping down to sit beside her, his eyes staring out at the heavily falling rain for a moment before turning to meet her gaze, "I cant get my head around all of this...it's insane"

"It?" she raised an eyebrow, "The ghosts?"

"Yeah" he nodded, sighing, "That and the fact that your ancestors went round executing people and covering the whole thing up with this village"

She winced and he shook his head, "I'm not blaming you...fuck, I'm not even blaming them...I guess what they did was a good thing but shit..."

She looked down at the ground as he studied her, her eyes turning to glance at the church and he followed her gaze, "What is this place?"

She gave an uncertain chuckle, turning back to meet his gaze, "It's a church..."

Much to his surprise he found the ability to laugh softly, "I know...but your grandmother told me that the villagers of Evenfield had all followed the religion that one of the original brothers..."

"Larens"

He nodded, "Yeah, him, had brought back from America...some sort of Native American faith?"

Cherry studied him for a moment, nodding slowly then, "This place was built around the late nineteenth century...once my descendants had lost their sway over the village"

"Lost their sway?" he blinked, studying her intently as he gave a shake of his head, "What does that mean?"

The young woman held his gaze for what seemed an eternity before she shook her head, "There's lots you need to know before that, that's the end of the story"

He grimaced, nodding, "I guess"

Nearly a minute drifted by as they stared at each other in the near darkness off the lychgate, the rain hammering down heavily upon its wooden roof, then she nodded, "Have you seen them all...The Twelve?"

"No" he shook his head, grimacing as he pictured the newest of the ghosts that he had encountered since seeing her before his shower, "But I have seen three more...a man in a suit, a man with a beard and an axe and a fat man with a red face"

She nodded knowingly at him, "The Fever, The Vessel and The Penitent Man"

"Good God" he grimaced, "I know which one the Fever was...he offered to bleed me"

Cherry nodded at his words, "Just as he did to twenty-three women who he was trusted to care for at the County Durham Lunatic Asylum, slicing their wrists with a straight razor so it appeared as if they had somehow taken their own lives"

"Twenty-three?" Richard winced in shock and then frowned at her, "Where was the asylum?"

"Far Winterton, near the town of Sedgefield" she told him, "About fifteen miles from here...it closed in the early nineties I think"

"When did your family...you know?"

"The asylum opened in 1858 and by 1860 he was on

the Twins...my great, great, great grandfather Britt hung him. He was the last executioner"

Richard winced, "You call him The Fever...what was his real name?"

"Dr Edwin Bennet"

The author repeated the name, shaking his head slowly and then raised an eyebrow, "And the other two that I saw for the first time today?"

"The man with the axe is William Haggarty, The Vessel...he was executed in 1666 for his crimes"

"Which were?"

"He killed priests, monks, nuns...I don't know how many" she winced, "My ancestors found out, and he was hunted down and captured by Abram, the first executioner and Chaqit, the tribesman...then brought here to hang"

"Why did he do it?" Richard asked, picturing the angry features of the man that he had seen with his long beard and hair, almost foaming at the mouth as he had swung his axe, "Was he mad?"

She shrugged, "Most likely, the records claim that he believed he was the Vessel of the archangel Michael, sent to England in the wake of the Bubonic Plague and the great Fire of London to punish fake holy men and women for their sins and their failure to save God's faithful"

Richard cursed under his breath, rising to his feet,

eyes drifting to stare into the churchyard for several moments before he looked back to find her studying him with a strange look upon her features, "And The Penitent Man?"

"Father Ambrose Dewitt" she grimaced, her mouth twisting in disgust, "A rapist and killer of young men and boys in the area around the village of Ramshort, sating his lust on their bodies before blaming them for his sins, and killing them in a rage, strangling them to death"

"How many?"

"Fifteen that he admitted to"

Richard grimaced, then gave a grim smile, "It's a shame he didn't run into the Vessel"

Cherry matched his expression, her head shaking slowly, "Alas, Father Dewitt was executed in 1840, nearly two hundred years later"

"Shame" he repeated, moving to sit back down next to the young woman, a comfortable silence descending upon the pair for a moment before he turned to look at her, "Thank you"

"What for?" she seemed genuinely perplexed.

"For this…for giving me answers…for coming out in the middle of a storm to find me" he smiled, the expression slipping as he raised an eyebrow as he studied her, "How did you know I was out?"

"What?" she shook her head, smiling awkwardly.

"How did you know that I was out in the storm?"
The blue-haired woman blinked at his words, her head shaking, "Why do you have to go and make things difficult Richard?"

"Difficult?" he gave a confused chuckle, "Am I?"
She nodded, forcing a smile, "Just accept that I am here to help you and go with it, please"

"I am" he eyed her in confusion, "I told you that I appreciate your help...have I offended you?"

"No" she rose to her feet, head shaking as she stared down at him, "But things aren't always how they seem...people aren't what they seem"

"Myra?" he asked, suddenly defensive as he rose to his feet, "Is that who you mean?"

Cherry caught her lip between her teeth, head shaking once more, "That's not what I meant"

He grimaced, taking a step back, "Why are you and your Grandmother so against her? You haven't even met her!"

The blue-haired young woman winced, "She isn't good for you Richard...it's not healthy"

"Healthy?" he stepped back out under the heavy rain, shuddering slightly as it fell on him, "She's my best friend...men and women can be friends without sex being involved!"

For long moments, Cherry stared back at him in silence as he stood beneath the heavy rain, a sad look upon her features as she shook her head, "You're not listening to me!"

"No" he turned to walk away, "I'm not!"

Chapter Twenty Two

Head spinning, mind racing, Richard stormed back across the road onto the village green, leaving the church lychgate behind him, the shouts of Cherry gradually fading on the wind. He was angry, his attraction towards the blue-haired woman blurred by the fact that she seemed to have some kind of problem with Myra. She had claimed that she hadn't then gone on to say that their friendship was unhealthy for him. Was she jealous? Could that be it? He laughed bitterly as he pushed the thought away, ashamed of his arrogance. Of course, she wasn't.

He was an out of shape middle-aged man.

Why would she be!

No, there was something about Myra that both she and her grandmother seemed to dislike. But what? What had his friend done to earn their anger and apparent distrust? Just like George had seemed to dislike her when they had met him yesterday.

No, he shook his head, feeling nauseous.

George Wolf was dead.

A ghost. Like the others.

How had he not realised this?

But then ghosts were not like they were portrayed in the movies and on the television, transparent and ethereal. In the real world they looked no different than any other person did. Yes, there were some that were clearly dead and carried the injuries that had taken their lives and others still stood out from the usual by their attire but other than that they looked like people. He knew that it hadn't been his fault for his failure to realise that the jovial George Wolf was no longer one of the living, but that didn't stop the embarrassment and shame he felt as he considered how he had just stood in the shop and told the young man that he had recently seen his dead father.

Groaning, Richard stopped walking as he reached the small road which separated the village green from the entrance to Sanderson House and its grounds, and sighing heavily, he turned back to stare at Evenfield. It was lost to him now, obscured by the darkness and the rain but he let his gaze drift slowly over what the buildings he knew was there, regret touching him again as he glanced in the direction of the small shop and then let his gaze settle upon where he knew the church sat amid the darkness.

He had left Cherry there after she had ventured out into the storm to make sure that he was OK.

What was wrong with him?

Cursing, he started walking back down the slope towards it, intent on apologising to Cherry and making sure that she got back to Sanderson House or her own home safely, then froze as he heard what sounded like a mournful sob off to his left in the dark.

Stomach tight with sudden dread, he turned towards it, eyes narrowing as he tried to see who it was that had made the noise, his voice tense as he called out, "Cherry…Myra…who is that?"

The sob came again, louder and closer than before and he cringed, the hairs rising on his neck as he suddenly realised that it sounded like a young child. *Oh God.*

Grimacing, trying to appear brave, he shook his head, addressing the young male ghost from the house, "If that's you Frances, you can fuck off!"

There came no answer save for another sob, and head shaking, the author took a step towards the sound, "Hey…are you hurt?"

"Help me…please" the pained sob of a young girl replied and cursing, he moved towards it, then winced as it sobbed again, realising that he had passed the young girl in the darkness and rain.

Turning to his left, he hurried back several steps, gasping in concern as the girl sobbed again and he realised that he had been about to step on her.

Wincing, he dropped down to kneel beside her, ignoring the cold patch that spread through the knees of his jeans as the wet mud soaked through, brow furrowing as he studied the pale face looking up at him, her young features twisted in pain, "What are you doing out in this storm?"

She gave a half-sob, then tilted her chin back to face him, a resilience in her eyes as if she didn't want to show weakness in front of him, her long brown hair hanging about her face, "I'm lost…I can't remember"
He blinked, recognition touching him suddenly, his head shaking, "Are you from the village?"
"The farm" she gestured with a hand, dark eyes locked to his, "It's dark and I can't find my way"
Richard grimaced, nodding, "Are you hurt?"
"My throat feels funny, and my right leg hurts"
"You are probably on the way to catching your death of cold" he sent her a smile which had no effect whatsoever in bringing one to the face of the child, and the author winced. What the Hell was she doing out in the storm on her own anyway?
What was she? Ten…eleven at the oldest.
Grimacing, suddenly furious with the young girl's parents, he raised an eyebrow, "Can you walk?"
She nodded, beginning to force herself up before he could ask if she needed help, her fingers clasping to the hand that he had been extending to help her to her feet, "Can I go home now?"
Richard nodded down at her as she looked up at him, her face the only visible part of her that he could discern in the darkness, "Sure, but we will have to go to my house first…the big house over the road…my housekeeper will know which farm you mean, she

might even know your parents"

The girl stopped walking, still holding his hand and he stopped with her, "What is it?"

"You ain't one of them bad men are you?"

"What?" he blinked, head shaking, "What...no!"

She shook her head, eyeing him, "Are you sure?"

"Yeah" he winced, trying to let go of her hand, suddenly realising how inappropriate it might look if anyone from the village were to somehow see them, but she held on tight to his fingers, staring at him. Without warning, the girl began walking once more, the pair of them reaching the small road once more, Richard glancing down at the girl in curiosity, "What's your name?"

"Miriam"

"Miriam" he nodded, smiling sideways at her.

"Yes, I hate it" she gave a soft chuckle as they reached the gateposts of his property and he nodded at her then suddenly froze, glancing about in concern at the darkness within the walls bordering his estate.

"What is it, Richard?" she asked, her voice little more than a whisper and he grimaced, unsure if he should be telling the young girl about the ghosts that were probably waiting somewhere in the darkness ahead.

"Nothing" he lied, hoping against hope that Agnes didn't make a sudden appearance, then reached into his pocket with his free hand to withdraw the leather pouch, still unsure what it was but hoping that it would somehow deter the ghost of the murderous old woman until he could get the girl into the house.

In the house. With the other ghosts.

Cursing, he led her into the grounds, moving quicker now as the shape of the house came into sight as he passed his car, and then they were under the porch, Richard reaching for the door only to freeze as something suddenly occurred to him, "How did you know my name?"

Her soft chuckle had the hairs rising upon the back of his neck, "Silly Richie"

"What?" he closed his eyes, every muscle in his body seeming to cramp up as he tensed in sudden dread. For long moments he stood there, his forehead lowering to press against the door, and then with what felt like a supreme effort he turned the handle and pushed it wide open before him. Heart in his mouth, he turned in the doorway, eyes downcast to the floor, a sob escaping him as he saw the feet of the young girl before him, the left wearing a soaking wet turquoise and pink sock, the right clad in a muddy baseball boot, the dirty long laces trailing behind it. Hot tears stinging his bearded cheeks, he slowly raised his gaze up the girl's body, choking back a sob as he saw her badly broken left leg, the bone visible beneath her pale skin as her legs extended out of the grimy denim shorts she was wearing. Head shaking, he continued rising his gaze, his broad shoulders sagging as his eyes travelled up over the familiar Care Bear tee shirt, and then higher. His heart broke as he saw the purple and blue contusions that covered her throat in the shape of finger-marks, her neck bent at an angle that he hadn't previously seen in the darkness of the storm. As if in a dream, he lifted his head that final few inches, staring back into the bruised features of his childhood best friend, noting the blood around her left nostril and the bruising around her right eye, the orb itself filled with blood, as she stared out from amid her long brown hair, his voice breaking as he sobbed, "Myra...no...no...!"

The ghost opened her mouth to smile, her front teeth missing, "You never could say Miriam"

Chapter Twenty Three

Richard was scared.

No, that was something of an understatement.

Fear was usually the governing emotion where anything involving his father was concerned.

This was different. This time he was terrified.

He had been enjoying the summer sun, sitting in the back yard of the family farm at a small table, happy to be outside of the house, the family dog on his lap. Then his father had returned from the fields, furious because the timing belt had broken upon the tractor he had been using and the sight of his son doing anything other than chores had been like a red rag to an enraged bull. With a roar of anger he had charged at Richard, a sweep of a burly arm turning over the table that he had been sitting at, and then he had felt his bladder loosen in terror as the big man had grabbed his shirt, the man's anger growing as he had seen that his son had wet himself. The first back-handed slap had sent Richard tumbling to the yard floor, the second throwing him back down as he had started to rise, and knowing from experience that to keep getting up would only make things worse he had clenched his teeth and laid there, waiting for the his father to remove his belt and beat him.

The scream of agony as the first lash had struck him, catching him across his shoulders, was tore from his

lungs as the pain spread across him in a stripe of fire, and through tear filled eyes, he had fought not to sob. Hope had taken flight within him as he had heard his mothers voice, pleading with her husband to leave him be, that hope fading as he had heard his fathers angry voice and knew that he would turn on her next. So he had started to rise, knowing that it would draw his fathers anger back upon him, the lash of the belt second slater confirming it, the nearly unintelligible curses of the barrel chested man accompanying each strike and Richard had released that this was it.
He was going to die.
Then, just as he had expected another strike to land, he had heard his father grunt in shock and pain, and looking back, he had seen him bent at the waist, a hand clasped tight to his forehead. Blinking in shock, his father had bent, a large hand collecting a round stone from the ground by his feet then straightened once more, head turning about to search for his attacker, his top lip snarling, "Little cunt!"
Wincing past his pain, Richard had turned his head then stared in disbelief as had seen his best friend Myra standing on the wall beside the machinery shed, her features defiant as she stood there in her denim shorts and Care bear tee shirt, a handful of stones in her left hand, her right clasped tight to another as she brought her arm back, "Leave Richie alone!"

"Go on, get out of here now!" his father had roared, a finger rising to point at her, his purple features twisting in anger, "You…get away…get of my land!" He grunted as her arm whipped out, the stone hitting him on the forehead, rocking him back several steps, his eyes rolling. For a second, he looked ready to fall, but then somehow, he got his legs under him, his right arm casting the belt aside as he gave a bellow of rage and charged in the direction of the girl, "Go on, get out of here!"

"Run Myra" Richard had screamed in concern for the young girl as she turned and ran, his voice almost falsetto as he had struggled to his feet. His father had paused, glancing back at him, red faced, and Richard had winced, fearing the worst but then the man had charged off in pursuit of Myra, roaring like a bear.

He was back racing for the barn near the edge of their property, bordering with that owned by Myra's parents, his hands dragging at the rungs of the old ladder. Clambering up into the hay loft of the almost derelict barn, he made his way through the gloomy interior, knowing from experience where the planks beneath his feet were old and rotten. He reached the centre and turned in a circle, his hushed voice calling out to Myra, scanning the darkness for his friend.

He tensed at the gasping noise from his left, over near the edge of the loft, and trying to keep calm, knowing his best friend's fondness for jumping out on him, he moved slowly towards the sound.

Dropping down to his stomach, Richard slid forwards, trying not to smile as he peered over the edge of the hay loft into the back of the bar where all manner of old and broken machinery was stored, then frowned, his features screwing up as he tried to work out what he was seeing.

As the true horror of the scene below unfolded, he pushed himself back, face pressing down on the boards of the hay loft for several seconds, his eyes filled with tears, and then he pushed himself forwards once more, being careful to not be seen by his father as the man sat on an old oil drum.

Richard squeezed his eyes shut, hot tears running down his face, small fists forming so hard that his nails cut into the palms of his hands as he fought to stop from screaming in heartache. Then, only when he was sure that he was in control did he open his eyes once more, his gaze drifting to the broken and bent form of Myra as she lay upon a tarpaulin in front of the farmer, her left leg bent at an awful angle, her neck bent so that she seemed to be looking up at Richard, one of her wide eyes blood red, tongue poking from her mouth as if she were panting for air.

And that was when he finally screamed.

With a groan, Richard opened his eyes, blinking in confusion as he found himself lying upon the floor, his legs protruding from the front door of Sanderson House. Wincing, he pushed himself up on one arm, staring out through the open door at the heavy rain for a moment before lowering his gaze back down to study the thick tartan blanket that was upon him.
"I thought it best to keep you warm" the soft voice of Ms Sanderson made him flinch and turn, eyes widening as he found the elderly woman sitting upon one of the chairs from the table in the kitchen, her frail form wearing a coat and hat, a steaming cup clasped in her wrinkled hands, "How do you feel?"
For a moment, he held her gaze in silence then he winced, his heart feeling like it was tearing, "Myra"
The old housekeeper nodded, a sad smile on her face as she held his gaze, "Yes, Mr Miles...I am so sorry"
He winced, stunned by her calm, "You knew?"
Again, she nodded, raising her cup to sip at its contents before lowering it once more, "I did"
He grimaced, head shaking as he rose to his knees then his feet, staring down at the old woman, "And you didn't think to tell me?"
"Oh but I did" her smile was not unkind, her voice

matter of fact, "Several times, but you would not listen to me. I know that burden"

He opened his mouth to argue, to say that she was wrong, but he could remember now, he knew the truth, there was no hiding it from himself anymore. Myra was gone. She had been for thirty years.

"How did she die?"

Richard glanced back at her at the question, blinking for a moment before the old woman continued, hands gesturing to her own throat, "The bruising…"

"The bruising" he shook his head, mind reeling as he held her gaze, his throat tightening with emotion, "You have seen her that way?"

She gave him another sad smile, "My dear that is the only way that I have seen her…from that first day when I met you in the kitchen, and there she was, a sad little girl standing right beside you"

"No" he shook his head, remembering that she had referred to Myra as a girl, hysteria threatening to wash over him, suddenly doubting what he could remember. Hadn't he fallen from the hatch in the bedroom and hit his head? That was it. He was concussed and imagining this entire thing, "She was my age…grown up…she drank tea…she had a phone!"

"What is her phone number?"

He blinked, "Sorry?"

"Her number" the old woman smiled, taking what

appeared to be an old Nokia from her coat pocket, her hand reaching out for him to take it, "Phone her" Grimacing, he took the phone from the old woman, punching in Myra's phone number and pressed dial, then flinched as within the pocket of his coat, his own mobile phone began to ring. With a shaking hand, he withdrew it, holding it up as he answered it, "Hello" He flinched as he heard his voice on the old woman's phone, his stomach lurching, "No"

"I am sorry Mr Miles"

"No" he shook his head, passing the elderly woman her phone, "She called the ambulance when the estate agent fell to his death!"

Ms Sanderson nodded, "Have you phoned anyone since arriving at Sanderson House Mr Miles?"

He frowned, head shaking, "No"

"Who did you ring last?"

Casting her a confused look, he opened the call log on his phone, a curse escaping him as he shook his head in confusion, "That's not possible…I didn't phone 999…it was Myra…it wasn't me!"

She stayed silent, holding his gaze and he clicked his fingers, pointing at her, "Why do I see her as an adult…if she is dead and you see a child then why am I seeing an adult? For that matter Jonty spoke to her…he spoke to her before he died!"

"And he saw her as a woman?"

Richard frowned, casting his mind back, "Yes, I think so…how do you explain that?"

She gave a shrug, "The mind is a powerful tool Mr Miles. You and I share the gift. The heart sees what it wants to see Mr Miles, poor young Myra has aged as you imagine she would, and her spirit has gone with the change. She has aged because you made her, and with the power of you gift and the supernatural energy of this estate I believe this Jonty tapped into what it was you were seeing"

"So why did you see her as a girl?"

Ms Sanderson chuckled softly, "I have been doing this a lot longer than you, my dear, my gift was obviously able to see through the deception you'd created"

Richard grimaced, "This isn't right…why is she here…she isn't one of those executed here!"

The old woman studied him intently for a moment, sipping her tea once more and then she nodded, "Well, that's simple, you brought her with you"

"What?"

"I told you that you have powers…the ability to see the dead. Myra has attached herself to you decades ago, attracted by your grief, bonded by your love. The poor thing probably doesn't know she isn't alive"

Richard grimaced, "So why now…why is she changing…just now…I saw her…as she was"

"Ah" Ms Sanderson nodded, "And that explains why I found you passed out in the doorway"

"Well?"

She shrugged once more, "This house has so much activity Mr Miles that it drains the likes of us...The Twelve, and the others that linger here sap us like sponges, leeching our spiritual energy from us with each passing second...perhaps that left nothing for you to retain your hold on Myra"

He blinked at her words, "She's gone...for good?"

"Perhaps" the old woman rose, "Now come, we both deserve a fresh cup of tea"

Richard raised an eyebrow, "Really...now?"

Her smile was business-like, "Especially now"

Chapter Twenty Four

"You still haven't told me how she died"

The soft voice of Ms Sanderson dragged Richards face away from where he had been staring at the old wooden surface of the dinner table, a hand rising to clear the tears from his eyes as he met her questioning gaze, "She...my father...he strangled her in a rage...I...we...were just ten years old"

She made a face, her eyes flashing with anger as she stared down at her hot drink, her voice angry, "Angry men and their angry ways"

He frowned at her words but didn't push her, his hand raising his cup of tea to his lips, and he swallowed slowly, letting the drink slowly warm through his body, the rain soaked clothes that he wore having made him begin to shiver violently.

Across the table, Ms Sanderson shook her head and began to rise, "You need to get out of those clothes Mr Miles before you catch your death"

He chuckled, surprised that he still could, "You sound like Cherry"

"Oh?" she sent him a guarded look, "How so?"

"She told me the same thing when I saw her out in the storm..." his words trailed off as he remembered that he had been intending to return to Cherry when he had heard the pained gasps of Myra...the young Myra.

"What is it?" the old woman eyed him in concern.

"She's out there still" he grimaced, "Cherry, I left her sitting in the lychgate of the old church!"

The old woman shook her head, "She will be fine"

"Aren't you worried?" Richard asked, frowning.

Ms Sanderson gave a chuckle, head shaking as she studied him across the table, "My granddaughter can take care of herself, trust me on this"

He nodded, "She seems capable"

Across the table, Ms Sanderson gave a nod, "You like her Mr Miles"

It wasn't a question.

"What?" he shook his head, "I don't think that…"

"Please" she shook her head, smiling sadly, "Don't get too attached to her…"

"Oh?" he gave a shake of his head, "What's wrong?"

"Mr Miles, please, respect my wishes"

The author winced, nodding, "OK, sure"

A silence descended upon the room for several minutes as the old woman as she sat drinking her tea, then she raised her eyes to meet his gaze, an eyebrow rising, "Why did your father kill Myra?"

Richard tensed, nausea washing over him as he cast his mind back, able to see it clearly now, the block that his mind had created to protect him gone, "He was beating me…she turned up at our farm looking for me...she threw some stones at his head and he chased her"

The words tumbled from his lips, monotone and quiet, and on the other side of the table, Ms Sanderson nodded, "Were you there when did it?"

"No" he spat the word out defensively, "No...I went to the old barn...I thought she had outrun him...but..."

"He had caught her" it wasn't a question, but Richard nodded in reply anyway, stomach knotting in grief.

"Yes...when I found them, she was dead...I think she had fallen and broken her leg...and...and he had strangled her..."

The sound of the wind and the heavy rain suddenly grew in intensity as it fell upon the greenhouse area built onto the back of the large kitchen and Richard turned towards it, glancing back as she spoke once more, "What did you do?"

"Sorry?" he turned back towards her, "What?"

"You found your father had murdered your best friend...what did you do? Did you tell your mother, or the police, perhaps a teacher?"

He stared down at the cup before him, a wave of guilt rising up within him like a tsunami, and he shook his head, "I did nothing"

"Oh" there was no judgement in that single sound, just confirmation that he had replied, yet the author winced as his shame spiked within him yet again.

Grimacing, he placed his hands upon the table, either side of his cup, hands forming fists once more, nails digging into his palms just as they had that day, "I woke up sometime later in my bed…my father was sitting watching me from a chair…I thought he was going to kill me too, his expression was so dark"

"What did he say?"

"Nothing" Richard shook his head, shrugging as he met her gaze, "He said nothing…he saw me wake and then walked away…I had always seen the woman who watched me but from that moment I began to see more…people all over the place"

"And Myra? Did people not look for her?"

He nodded, "Yes, there were search parties…my father helped…he stood with the family…she was never found. I looked in the barn, but she wasn't there. I don't know what he did with her body"

"But you began to see her?"

He smiled, "She was waiting for me in the woods behind our parents farms one day…"

Across the table Ms Sanderson gave a heavy sigh, her brow furrowing, "And your father…you and he never spoke of her death…at all?"

"No" he grimaced, the muscles clenching in his cheeks as a fresh memory surfaced within him, and he looked down at his fists, "We didn't"

There was silence for a moment and then he gave a shrug, a hand relaxing to gesture towards the front of the house, "Out there...when I saw Myra...I didn't recognise her...I was too busy worrying about Agnes" He rose suddenly, hands patting at his pockets in a panic, his actions drawing a look of curiosity from his housekeeper, "Mr Miles?"

He turned to her, "I had a pouch...like a small bag in my hands...I was holding it when I saw Myra!"

Without a word, she reached into a pocket of her coat and slowly withdrew the object that he was referring to, placing it upon the table and sliding it over to him. Eyes wide, he reached out and collected it, holding it up before him as he studied it intently, seeing now that he was in the light that the sharp protruding object looked like a piece of bleached bone or claw. "What is it?"

He shook his head at her question, "I don't know but it scared Agnes...she was terrified when she saw it" Ms Sanderson gave a grunt of surprise and he glanced back at her, "I found it in the secret room above the bedroom that I went too"

"Secret room?" she eyed him in confusion, and he nodded, staring back at her in utter confusion.

"Didn't you know?"

She shook her head, "It is news to me"

Richard nodded, "Well, whatever it is, maybe we can use it to get the ghosts out of this place"

The laugh from the old woman was bitter, "If only such a thing is possible Mr Miles"

He grimaced at her words, head shaking and then on impulse he turned and crossed the room to push open the door to the greenhouse. It was dark inside, only the rectangle of light from the kitchen door illuminating the overgrown area, his shadow standing in its centre. Taking a deep breath, he stepped out into it, a hand rising before his face to brush back the leaves of plants that were trying to overtake the path, and then paused as he reached the back door, staring out through the pane at the dark shape of the Twins. Even amid the darkness and the heavy rain, the two huge old co-joined oak trees were visible, a darker shape against the night and Richard felt the hairs rise upon his neck as he suddenly pictured bodies hanging from the branches, swaying wildly in the wind like Christmas decorations.

He tensed as something moved behind him, half turning in dread, expecting to see one of The Twelve stalking him through the plants then relaxed as he saw it was just Ms Sanderson. Sighing, he turned back away, glancing out of the window in the door again, then frowned as she moved alongside him, "You told me that there had been over eight hundred people executed on those trees, right?"

She nodded and he raised an eyebrow, "So where are the bodies? That small graveyard in the grounds isn't big enough to hold them all is it"

"It isn't" she replied, grim faced, "The graveyard is for members of my family, they are all there, every single one of them"

"So the executed...The Twelve and the others?"

"Burned" she nodded, her face turning towards the trees, "Cut down once dead and then burned, their bodies cleansed of sin with fire and their spirits bound to the Twins using rites passed down from the time of Larens and Abram"

"Where are their ashes?"

"Spread at the bases of the Twins, scattered by the North wind, washed into the ground by the rain" her voice had taken on a slow, poetic tone, and glancing at her, he saw that her eyes were half closed as if she were suddenly really sleepy, appearing older now.

"Are you OK?"

She nodded, smiling softly at him, "I am as well as one in my position can ever really be Mr Miles"

"One in your position?"

"Quite, I am a mad old woman, destined to spend what little remains of my days alone in a mansion filled with ghosts that would like nothing more than to see me dead" there was a hint mania in her voice

and for the first time since meeting her, Richard saw
what looked like fear present in her bright eyes.
Grimacing, he reached out and placed an arm about
her frail shoulders, ignoring the look of surprise that
she gave him as he nodded grimly, "You aren't alone"
About them the greenhouse creaked as a strong gust
of wind buffeted it and he glanced up, fully expecting
it to begin crashing down about them, then glanced
back down at the old woman as she spoke, her voice
grim, "You lied to me earlier"
He caught his right cheek between his back teeth as
she sent him a knowing smile, "You and your father
did talk about Myra at least once didn't you?"
He nodded, and she smiled and turned to look back
out at the Twins, "Did you make him sorry?"
Throat tight as he pictured the large man, pleading
for him to put down the hammer that he was holding,
Richard nodded, face grim, "Yes"

Chapter Twenty Five

Richard awoke the next morning to the sound of bird call, loud outside the window of the safe bedroom that he had retired to high up on the second floor of Sanderson House, staring up at the open hatch above him until he had finally fallen asleep. Blinking, he lay there beneath the covers, staring up at the hatch once more as he stifled a yawn, and then rolled onto his side, a hand reaching out to press on the spot where he had last seen Myra. He closed his eyes as a wave of emotion ran through him, the sudden memory that he would not see her anymore making his stomach drop away within him into a pit of grief and dread. She was gone. He would never see her face again.

A bitter smile creased his features as he realised that the face that he had been seeing for decades had not actually been her face but his own imagination. The smile slipped as he recalled how Ms Sanderson had suggested that the ghost of his childhood friend had attached itself to him and altered its outer shell to match how he saw her thanks to his *gift.*

"The poor thing probably doesn't know she isn't alive"

He winced as the words of the elderly housekeeper returned to him, guilt touching him as he considered his part in what had happened, both before and after her murder by his father. She had died because she had been defending him. That was the sum of it. She had paid the ultimate price for her courage. After her death there had been countless times that he could have, and should have, told an adult about what he had seen but the fact was that his trust in those who should protect him had been forever ruined by his murderous sire and his mother who loved him too much but not enough.

Not enough to save him from the torture.

And so, he had grown into an angry, but silent young man, taking the beatings from his father and the gaslighting from his mother with stoic grim faced acceptance, but inside he had grown fierce, a wolf awaiting the chance to be free.

The memory of growing that way had always been present in his mind but the core anger and guilt behind it had always been a mystery, just like the memory that had returned to him while he had been sat at the table the previous night.

Ms Sanderson had asked if he and his father had ever discussed the murder of poor young Myra.

Grimacing, Richard closed his eyes as he lay upon the bed, his breathing deepening as he recalled walking his father out to the old barn where he had found him years before with Myra's body, the mans hands cable tied behind his back, his pleas incoherent around the gag that Richard had roughly shoved into his mouth. Rolling onto his back, the author grimaced as he recalled his father suddenly pausing as they had reached the entrance to the barn, eyes wide in terror as he had turned to look back at Richard in fear.

He had known what was going to happen then.

He had to have known.

With a muted mumble he had tried to push past his son but bound as he was, his body filled with alcohol he was no match for his son, who at twenty years of age, and forty years his junior was already as broad and tall as he, and grasping at his fathers clothes, Richard had manhandled him into the derelict old tool barn with ease. His father had screamed in terror as he had seen the tarpaulin laid out on the floor at the back of the barn, head shaking, the gag finally loosening about his mouth as he had pleaded, "Son, you don't have to do this...I won't tell anyone!"

Grim faced Richard had forced him down, and cable tied his ankles together, then crouched beside the older man, features emotionless as he had picked up the heavy lump hammer that he had placed on the barn floor earlier that day.

"Son!" his father had sobbed again, "Look at me!"

For the first time, Richard had done so, looking deep into the tear filled, terrified eyes of his father, seeing for the first time not the violent monster that had beaten him so many times but an old man with grey hair and a tear stained face, his features thin and worn, an outward sign of the cancer that was slowly ravaging his body, "Please…please son…you don't have to do this!"

"Yes, yes I do" Richard had raised the hammer then paused as he father had sobbed aloud once more. "I'm dying…please, let the cancer take me… I have two months…if that…"

Richard had shaken his head, "I can't wait any longer…I've waited too long already"

"God damn you!" his father had found a measure of his former self from some well within him, his top lip curling, "You can't do this…I'm a person!"

Richard had nodded, "So was Myra!"

The first hammer blow had struck his fathers left leg below the kneecap, and despite the fact that his hands were bound behind his back, the old man had sat up like Boris Karloff in the Mummy, his scream of agony torn from his very core. Gritting his teeth, Richard had pushed him down with his free hand and struck once more, this time striking the shin bone full force. There was an audible crack, and the bone had change position beneath the old man's paper-thin skin, his father's eyes bugging out in his face as he screamed, the sound more animal then human.

"Was that how she screamed?" Richard had turned his blank features towards his father, silently angry that he hadn't yet felt any emotion in the acts that he was doing, the hammer raising above his father's face, "Was it?"

"Pleathe" the man had managed to sob, barely coherent through his agony, his words slurred with pain and fear, "Pleathe…pleathe…ah'll give you anytin…pleathe…don…kill…me…"

Blinking, Richard had lowered the hammer, nodding down at his father, "Anything?"

"Yesth" the man had nodded, a spark of light igniting in his eyes as he had seen the hand of hope extend towards him, "Anytin…name it!"

"I want Myra back"

On his back, his father had blinked through his tears, his features twisting in confusion for a moment, then he his mouth had twisted, "Stupid…fuckin…boy…"

The hammer struck him hard on the left cheek, cutting his sentence short, the force of the blow breaking the cheekbone and dislodging the eye to hang upon bloody tendons, the second blow to the same area popping the orb into mush, the third flattening his father's nose flat across his face, smashing the front of the upper jaw loose.

By the time the sixth blow landed, his father was already unconscious. By the eighth he was dead.

Richard continued to hit him twelve more times, one blow for each year of Richards ruined life.

Once that final blow had landed, he had sat there in the near dark of the old barn for what felt an eternity, only glancing up as he had heard someone approach, a heavy sigh leaving him as he had found Myra standing there watching him, confusion on her face.

"Richie?"

"I did it for you" he had nodded, rising to his feet, and she had smiled, stepping forward to embrace him.

Heaving a shuddering sigh, Richard sat up on the bed, his eyes moving to the door of the large bedroom. Beyond that lay the unprotected areas of the vast old house, and The Twelve, eager to see him die.

A cold smile creased his features as he nodded to himself, the fear that he had felt for them no longer as strong, replaced by a burning hatred for the ghosts. It was because of them and their machinations that he had lost Myra a second time. They were going to regret that if it was the last thing he did.

Chapter Twenty Six

"Oh, good morning, Mr Miles" Ms Sanderson paused in the doorway of the kitchen sometime later as she arrived at the house for her daily shift, a curious smile upon her features as she studied him, "How are you after last night?"

The author smiled grimly at her from where he was seated at the large wooden table, a piece of toast in one hand, a cup of tea on the table before him. Gesturing with his free hand to a cup opposite him, he nodded, "OK so far…I think…I made you a tea, its probably cold now, I wasn't sure what time you would be getting here"

She turned her head to look at the clock upon the kitchen wall, and he followed her gaze, before looking back as she spoke, "Nine AM is my usual start time…would you like something cooked?"

He waved his slice of toast in the air and she gave a snort, head shaking, "I mean a real breakfast"

Richard gave a smile, "It sounds great but we need to get to work as quickly as we can"

"Oh, which is?" she removed her coat, and hat, placing the former on the back of a chair, and the latter upon the table beside the cup he had indicated, fingers wrapping about the handle as she picked it up, an eyebrow rising in question as she drank it down.

He chuckled grimly, nodding at her question, "I have been thinking about what you said last night about not having anyway to stop these fuckers…excuse my French, from continuing to ruin our lives…I refuse to have paid half a million pounds for a house and then live in one room!"

She placed her cup down, and seated herself opposite him, "You don't have to just live in that one room, Mr Miles, that is letting them win"

"OK" he nodded at her, "So you are suggesting that I go on about my daily business but try and get used to them trying to scare me to death"

The old woman gave a humourless chuckle, "You do get used to it…trust me"

"But I shouldn't have to" he shrugged, "And you shouldn't have had to live like this…why do you?"

She gave a heavy sigh, rising to her feet as she took her cup to the sink, rinsing it out before returning for his, her expression grim as she met his gaze, "The village of Evenfield pay me very well for remaining connected to this house"

"They fucking should" he grimaced, anger touching him and she turned away, returning to the sink to rinse his cup. Sighing, he forced his anger away, shaking his head at her back as he continued, "From what you said, you and Cherry staying in the village is keeping the ghosts from taking revenge upon them for their ancestors involvement, right?"

She nodded, turning to look back at him, "It is, that and the continued existence of the Twins; were I to leave or the trees to die..."

She let her sentence trail off, the unspoken threat hanging unfinished but it still bore down on the kitchen atmosphere like a ton of steel, and nodding, the author looked down at the table for several moments and then met her gaze again, a grim smile upon his features, "What if we found a way to change that...what if we could get rid of The Twelve for good...what then?"

"What are you proposing?" she paled, her voice shaky, "I'll have no part of anything that will put the people of Evenfield at risk of harm!"

He nodded, "You have friends there"

"Aye" she held his gaze, "Although after your antics last night in the village shop I would advise you from venturing down there for some time"

He winced, head shaking as he leaned back on the chair, "I had no idea that George was a ghost...he spoke to Myra...she replied...how was I to know that ghosts can see ghosts?"

"Alas, as I told you last night, many ghosts simply do not understand that they have passed over and are caught in a loop, repeating actions or going about their business as if they were alive"

Richard nodded, remembering the way that all of the villagers had been watching him and Myra walk about the village, their faces grim, nodding in sudden understanding, "They couldn't see her could they...the villagers?"

"Sorry?" she frowned, moving to sit back down.

"When I went to the village with...Myra, everyone was staring at me and her" he sighed, "Well, I thought they were...Hell, even Myra thought they were...but they were just staring at me...walking alone and talking to myself"

"Don't you worry" she gave a rare grin, "You wouldn't be the first person to have done so"

"You?"

She nodded, "On occasion, I have seen George too, spoken with him, and others...we are alike"

He nodded, smiling softly, then he gave a nod, forcing himself back onto the subject he had waited all morning to speak to her about, "So if there was a way to get rid of The Twelve, without hurting any of the villagers despite them thinking we are a pair of nutjobs, would you help me?"

There was a long drawn out silence as she stared back at him from where she stood beside the sink, her lips pressed tightly together, and then she gave a nod, "You have my interest"

He grinned, "I am going to need to know everything about The Twelve…Cherry has told me about Agnes, and The Fever, The Vessel and The Penitent Man, and you have told me about James Jackman but I need to know about the others, maybe then, we can find a way to stop them!"

She nodded, disappointment in her eyes, "Find a way…as in, you don't have a plan"

"No, I don't…not yet" he admitted, then reaching out he placed the small pouch in the middle of the table, the pouch that he had clasped in his hand and walked through the house with that morning and had received no ghostly visitations whatsoever, "But this is the answer"

Chapter Twenty Seven

"I still don't understand what it is that you want me to do Mr Miles" Ms Sanderson turned from where she was hoovering the carpet in the long basement of the huge old house, the area having been turned into a games room complete with pool table and a small cinema area with seating. Perched upon the edge of the pool table, his right hand clasped tight to the leather pouch, thumb stroking idly over the sharp bone protruding from it, Richard shrugged, "Tell me about the rest of The Twelve"

She sighed, stepping past his legs to hoover under the pool table, head shaking, "I don't see how knowing all about them will help you"

"You are right" he nodded, his free hand rising to scratch at his beard, "Do you think you could talk Cherry in to coming over to tell me instead?"

The old housekeeper turned to meet his gaze, her lips twisting together as if she were trying to stop a wasp from escaping her mouth and then she nodded, a thin hand reaching down to turn off the hoover, her head shaking as she met his gaze once more, "Who would you like to know about?"

The author frowned, catching the inside of his left cheek between his back teeth as he mulled over her question. He had heard the history of Agnes Rand, William Haggerty, James Jackman, Dr Edwin Bennet and Father Ambrose Dewitt. Who else had he seen of The Twelve? Frowning, ignoring the old woman as she raised an eyebrow in question, he tried to picture the other ghosts that he had already encountered, recalling the busty blonde woman, the strange couple that had been in the doorway with the estate agent, and the boy with the blade...the creepy little bastard. Was that it?

He winced as he suddenly recalled that fucking clown and the way that it had careened towards him each time that he had seen it, his stomach knotting as he remembered how it had rushed at him while he had been in the attic room, "Tell me about the clown"

The elderly woman nodded then tensed, her cheeks tightening, and Richard frowned, "What is it?"

The chuckle that escaped her was bitter, "Of them all that one scares me the most"

"The most?" he eyed her in surprise, "I thought you were immune to being scared by The Twelve"

She chuckled again, "I have a good poker face"

"You play poker too?" he gave a laugh, "This day is just full of revelations, isn't it"

For a moment, she stood smiling at him and then she moved to sit on one of the chairs before the small cinema screen and rising he did the same, watching her as she got herself comfortable and then nodded at him, "So, The Great Marlowe"

"Sorry?" he eyed her in confusion, "Who?"

"Your greasepainted guest"

"Oh" he nodded, wincing as he pictured the strange clown, "That was the name he worked under?"

"It was" she settled back into the cushioned blue seat, a grim smile upon her lined features, "He was one of the star attractions of the Shaw Brothers Circus, touring England and Europe. Apparently, he was quite popular for a while"

"For a while?" Richard winced, "What changed?"

She shrugged, her hands folded together upon her lap, "I don't know for certain, but it seems as he aged his act became more and more sinister. People complained, both other members of the circus and punters, and it seems his role in the circus was cut drastically so he was just one of the other clowns, and not the star he had been"

"I bet he wasn't happy about that"

"No" she shook her head, her features grim, "But by all accounts, he was not known for being a happy individual despite his chosen profession"

Richard grimaced and she continued, "It seems that The Great Marlowe, or Jaspar Furlow, his real name, was an alcoholic and a rapist, and that in each town and village that they had stopped at during his time with the circus there had been several rapes, not just

of women but of men and children as well…The Great
Marlowe had something of a voracious appetite"
"How did he end up here?"
The old housekeeper grimaced, "One night, while in
Country Durham in 1862, Jaspar…the Great Marlowe
decided to venture from his caravan and out into the
village where the circus was camping. Using his
contortionist skills, he managed to break into the
home of a woman named Jessica King whose husband
was away serving with the British army in India"
 "Oh God"
Ms Sanderson nodded, "The story has it that the
young woman was in the kitchen of her small home
when he slithered in through a small window,
dislocating his shoulders and popping them back in
again to gain access"
The author blinked, head shaking, "That must have
been agony"
"Apparently he had a peculiar ability to feel no
pain…I mentioned that his act had taken a sinister
turn…it seems that part of his act involved inserting
hooks and blades into his own body more and more
frequently"
"CIP maybe?" Richard muttered to himself, and the
old woman gave him a sudden puzzled look.
"Congenital Insensitivity to pain" he explained,
smiling, "It's a hereditary disease, I only know about

it as I used it in one of my novels, he must have inherited it from one of his parents if so"

"Perhaps" she shrugged, "Either way, by his own admission he crept upstairs and lay beneath the young woman's bed so that when she laid down he was there beneath her, giggling in excitement"

Richard felt his stomach lurch as he pictured the clown hiding in the darkness beneath the bed of the young woman in his black and white costume and greasepaint, "What did he do to her?"

"He ate her"

The author blinked, "Sorry...he what?"

"He ate her" Ms Sanderson's voice was like ice, her expression grim, "He didn't rape her like the others...claiming that she looked too sweet to despoil in such a manner...her innocence so delectable that he wanted to possess it for himself...so he ate her"

Richard felt like he had spiders in his hair, a hand rising to brush over his head as she continued, her voice soft as if telling a child a bedtime story, her eyes locked to his own, "He bit her first when she rolled onto her side, a hand dropping beside the bed, his teeth shearing the flesh from index finger of her right hand. As she had screamed in pain and terror, he had clambered atop the bed, shrieking hysterically, biting each of her fingers in turn before he turned her attentions to her toes...and then her nose...her ears…her eyes…her…chest…her lips…"

"Fucking Hell"

"When her screams finally alerted neighbours, members of the circus were already searching for Jaspar, having sensed something was amiss…they pooled their resources and followed the screams. Upon breaking into the home of poor sweet Jessica King, they found him with his face buried deep in her split open belly, his bloody hands shovelling gobbets of meat into his mouth…"

"I'm going to throw up" Richard rose to his feet, breathing heavily, and Ms Sanderson frowned.

"Mr Miles, I have just hoovered in this room"

He let out a shaky sigh, and sat back down, "I take it this was local…like the others?"

Her chuckle was grim, "One might say that"

"Go on"

Her left arm extended, rising to point at an angle somewhere above them to their right, "It was out there…on the Evenfield village green"

"Holy shit" his swallowed, eyes wide, "Really?"

"Yes" Ms Sanderson nodded, features twisting into a grim smile, "My great grandfather Britt and a group of servants heard the shouts of the villagers and the circus folk, and ventured from this great house to investigate…they found the Great Marlowe barely alive, his wrists, elbows, hips, knees and ankles all broken by the angry mob, yet the man chuckled still, unable to feel it"

"What happened?" Richard breathed heavily.

She shrugged again, "There was no trial for the Great Marlowe…if my great grandfather had not put him on the tree that night, the villagers and circus folk would have killed him there and then"

Letting out a shaky breath, the author stared at the old woman for a moment, then shook his head, "So that was his only murder…I mean don't get me wrong, damn, what he did to that poor woman was awful, but of all the places to commit his only murder, he really chose the wrong place"

She gave a weak smile, "He did…and he's wanted revenge on my family and Evenfield ever since"

Chapter Twenty Eight

Considering the story that he had just heard, Richard sat on the cinema seats in silence, one hand still clasped tight to the small pouch, the fingers of his other hand drumming upon the back of the seat in front and Ms Sanderson rose to her feet, heading back towards the hoover when she stopped and turned towards the stairs that led to the first floor, her cheeks suddenly tightening as she stared ahead. Frowning, the author followed her gaze, "What is it...what are you looking at?"

"Go away" she wasn't talking to him, her voice taking on a tone of authority as she stared at the stairs, "I don't have time for your silliness today"

Gritting his teeth, he rose and moved to stand beside her, grimacing as he saw the ghost of the young boy sitting four steps down from the top, a smirk upon its pale face as it stared back at them in amusement.

"Frances" Ms Sanderson shook her head, taking a quick step towards the stairs but instead of appearing concerned the ghost descended two steps, its chin lifting in defiance as it glared back at her.

"Hey" Richard called out, face grim as he took a step towards the stairs, the fist holding the small pouch held out before him, "Look what I've got"

The ghost gave a sneer, mouth beginning to open but then it suddenly recoiled as if he was holding a weapon, the figure of the young boy fading with a scream of terror that echoed about the cellar of the Sanderson House long after he had vanished.

"What on Earth?" the elderly housekeeper stepped alongside the author, her eyes locked to the small bag for what seemed an eternity before she seemed to remember that he was there too, her head shaking as she met his gaze, "I don't understand...what has just happened?"

He shrugged, lowering the fist and its contents, "I have no idea but that's exactly how Agnes Rand reacted when she saw the bag last night"

The old woman held his gaze for a moment, her eyes drifting over his bearded features as she digested his words and then she turned to look back at the spot where the ghost had been, "He was scared, no, I would go so far as to say young Frances was terrified"

"He was" Richard let his gaze drop to the bag in his right hand, and then met the gaze of the old woman again, "So, what's his story?"

"Frances?"

He nodded, "Aye, what did that malevolent little shit do to warrant getting hung...I mean, he's a kid...how old was he when he got executed?"

"Ten" she gave a nod, her expression grim, "Old enough by far to know that murder is wrong"

Richard grimaced, having already guessed that the boy had killed people but hearing it said aloud made it seem that much worse. Sighing heavily, he moved back to the cinema seats and sat down, "Go on then...tell me"

She smiled at him for a moment, head shaking, and then, "Frances Goodnestone was born into a life of poverty, or so the story goes. Raised by his widowed mother in a village several miles from Evenfield, where she was a maid in the house of a wealthy landowner by the name of Shaw Bishop. When Frances was eight, his mother died after accidently consuming *Conium maculatum*"

Richard shook his head, and she nodded, smiling grimly, "Poison Hemlock, it appears that she had somehow managed to ingest several of the leaves during a hearty meal, paralysis of the respiratory muscles ensued and the poor woman died of asphyxiation later that evening"

The author blinked, "How do you accidently eat poison hemlock? Surely that's not normal?"

"How indeed" the elderly housekeeper nodded, moving closer to where he sat, "Orphaned as he was, Frances was taken in by the landowner, Shaw Bishop, who must have felt in some way responsible for the future of his servants son. To that end, he adopted the child, and took him in, to be raised as his own son alongside his two sons and a daughter"

"This doesn't have a happy ending does it"

"Alas, no" Ms Sanderson shook her head, "Within the year, one of the sons was dead, drowned in the estate's lake while out fishing with Frances"

"He killed him?"

She shrugged, "The boy was allegedly a sickly child, perhaps he fell in as Frances claimed and drowned before he could be rescued..."

"He killed him" Richard grimaced, nodding.

"Who is to say, however, within the next twelve months the remaining boy fell to his death from a window of the huge house, and the young girl went missing while playing in the grounds"

"Did they find her?"

"Not for several weeks" Ms Sanderson stated, her expression grim, "And by that time a travelling salesman had been found guilty of her abduction and murder and hung by a lynch mob. Then they found her body, naked and stuffed under the roots of a great tree that had fallen in the grounds several years before"

"The little bastard" Richard's voice was a growl.

"Indeed" she nodded, "By this time the mother of the family was beside herself with grief, and there were claims made by her at the funeral and in public that the deaths of her children had been perpetrated by the Black Sheep that come into their home, though these claims were disputed angrily by the landowner, himself grieving"

"She knew it was Frances?"

"So it would seem Mr Miles" she nodded, her frail shoulders shrugging, "So loud were her protestations that word reached my ancestors, who were acquaintances of the woman's sister"

"So, they investigated?"

She nodded, "They did…under permission from the wife of Shaw Bishop several of their men took up positions working at the estate. Frances was eventually caught after he had pushed the back of his adoptive mother as she descended the grand stairs, the unfortunate woman tumbling to her death, murdered along with her children"

Richard grimaced, "What then?"

"He was taken into custody by my ancestors, and brought back to Evenfield, to stand trial. Even at the end, the landowner refused to lay the blame for the murders at the hands of Frances, finally admitting that he was the boy's biological father, and that had been the reason for his adoption. It was only when Frances had started laughing while on trial, and admitted that he had seen them together on several occasions and heard of his true heritage and had killed his own mother to gain acceptance into the house as his son"

Shaking his head, Richard grimaced, "Well, he's in my fucking house now…and I want him gone"

"But how" Ms Sanderson shook her head, "Do you think he will return after seeing that bag?"

"Oh" the author gave a grunt of surprise, "I hadn't even considered that…he might already be gone"

She nodded, brow furrowing as she glanced down at the bag in his hand, and he followed her gaze, "I think we need to find out more about the pouch, don't you? But I don't know how"

"I do" he nodded, smiling grimly as he met her gaze again, "But I am going to need a ladder?"

She raised an eyebrow, "A ladder?"

His chuckle was grim, "Yeah, I've played Jenga with a chest of drawers and a bookcase once already…I'm not doing it again"

Chapter Twenty Nine

Stepping from the front door of the Sanderson House, Richard stared up at the sky above, sighing heavily. It was only just past lunchtime and already it was beginning to grow slightly darker, but the sky was filled with low hanging, thick grey clouds, making it seem as though it was even later than it actually was.

"Its going to rain again" Richard muttered, his grey eyes settling upon his housekeeper but she gave a shake of her head, her eyes fixed to the clouds.

"No, we are in for a snowfall

"You think?" he turned his own gaze back upon the clouds, then glanced back as she chuckled softly.

"I think I have lived long enough in this village to know its weather habits, Mr Miles. We are in for snow...a lot of it if I am not mistaken"

"Great" he grimaced, "And we're stuck in the Overlook Hotel...what better place to be"

The corner of her mouth lifted in a half smile, and then she pointed with a hand, past the small graveyard in the distance, "There is a small shed beyond the burial plots...here is the key to it"

He glanced down as she extended a hand towards him, a thick old key clasped in her thin fingers and he took it, "The ladder is in there?"

She nodded, "It should be...I haven't seen it in a number of years if I am honest"

"Well, I'll soon see" Richard shrugged, "If its not there I'll find another way to get easier access to the attic room, if it is then that's easier…what worries me is this snow…do we have enough food in the house to last being snowed in?"

She nodded, "I should think so, but I will head down to the village and get some tins of necessities…and if it would make you feel more at ease I will stay with you at the house"

He turned, nodding at her, "Are you sure?"

She smiled sadly, "I have no family that will miss me Mr Miles, the offer is there"

"Thank you" he nodded at her, "I appreciate that"

"I will fetch my coat and purse" she nodded, stepping back inside the house, and then reappearing with his coat in her hand, "Here"

"Ah" he waved a dismissive hand, "I wont need that, I'm only going to the shed and back…"

His words trailed off as he saw the matronly look that she was giving him, the hand holding his coat jerking as if to encourage him to take it and forcing a smile, he nodded, "OK sure"

Looking like she was fighting the urge to smile, Ms Sanderson nodded, "Good, now do it up"

Fighting the urge to argue, he did as she had instructed, a smile creasing his features, "Do I get a hat and mittens too?"

Ms Sanderson gave a soft laugh, head shaking and he frowned, "Wait…you said you no-one would miss you…what about Cherry? Does she not live with you? She is welcome to stay here t…"

She fixed him with a stare, a finger raising skyward, "I would advise you get the ladder while you can"

Irritated by her change of topic, he raised his eyes and blinked rapidly as a snowflake landed upon his eyelashes, "Oh…oh right"

Without another word he began to move along the front of the huge old property, glancing up at the windows as he passed them by, the gravel crunching beneath his feet. He paused as he drew level with his car and turned, his right hand dragging the small pouch from his coat pocket as he stepped onto the grass, suddenly wondering where Agnes was.

Could she really be gone?

Grimacing, he started walking once more, eyes scanning about for any sign of trouble and then let them settle upon the gravestones ahead off him, his interest piquing as he drew closer. There were more than he had initially thought when he had been standing beside his car with Myra on their first day at the house, his brow furrowing as he moved among them, his stomach lurching as he considered that thought. How long ago had that been?

Two days? Three? A week?

How long had he been in this house?

Frowning, he turned back to look at the huge building, a grey shape amid the falling snow, his eyes drifting over its vast shape for a moment.

Then sighing, he turned back around and began walking once more, brow furrowing as he tried to spot the shed Ms Sanderson had mentioned.

"Where are you?" he blinked away more snowflakes as they fell upon his eyelashes, concern touching him as the flurry suddenly seemed to increase in intensity, each flake the size of a five pence coin, some bigger, and glancing about he saw that it was settling upon the ground despite the heavy downpour of the previous day. Shoving his hand holding the key into a pocket of his coat, the small pouch still grasped tight in his other, Richard stepped among the rows of old gravestones, his grey eyes drifting across the names that were carved into their worn surfaces. He frowned as he read them, familiar names from the stories that Cherry and her grandmother had told him sparking recognition with him, then he followed the wall as it continued northwards, then down a slight incline dotted with trees and bushes. He paused at the top of the bank, brow furrowing as he studied the gravestones that waited blow, newer than those he had left behind.

For a moment, he let his gaze drift over the area, then gave a nod as he spotted a brick building down amid some Holm Oak trees, conifers and holly bushes; the red of their berries bright, the area green amid the winter browns. Frowning, he picked his way carefully down the grassy slope, then began to head through the gravestones towards the building, barely visible amid the undergrowth, a small barred window on its southernmost side. Stepping through the trees, Richard paused before the door, head tilting back to study what looked like a second floor, surprised to find that despite Ms Sanderson's use of the word shed, the building was several metres wide and twice as long, resembling a small house more than a shed. Turning, he glanced back up the rise in the direction on the house, surprised that despite how heavy the snow was falling, the ground almost white already, beneath the trees in the hollow around the shed, there was hardly any snow yet whatsoever.

Shaking his head, he raised his eyes to scan the trees above his head, realising that the canopy provided by the Holm oaks was stopping the snow flurry from touching this area for now. Withdrawing his hand with the key from his pocket, Richard stepped forward through the undergrowth that had grown thick around the door, cursing as a couple of brambles prickled him through his jeans. Wincing, he leaned forwards, placed the key in the lock and then used the same hand to unfasten the brambles from his trousers, not wanting to relinquish his grip upon the small pouch with his right hand. Satisfied that he wasn't about to be prickled once more, Richard stepped closer to the door, and turned the key, wincing as it resisted at first but then turned with a crunch. Worried that he had snapped the key, the author withdrew it, sighing as he saw it whole, then placed it in his pocket and gave the door a hard push. For a moment, it refused to budge, swollen in its frame by lack of use, weathered by the elements, and grimacing, Richard gave it a shove with his right shoulder; once…twice…three times.

With a crunch it swung inward, and Richard winced at the stale smell of mould and damp that rushed out to greet him, his eyes straining as he peered into the dim light of the shed's interior, dust motes dancing lazily in the light from the small window on the southern side and its twin on the northern wall. He had been wrong in his suspicions regarding it being two floors, instead the ceiling rose away high above him into the slanted roof, all manner of tools and boxes being stacked upon shelves which lined the walls in every available space. Cringing as he eyed the numerous spiderwebs hanging with the shed, Richard turned to cast a final look at the area behind him as snow began to drift down through the trees, and then stepped into the building.

Chapter Thirty

Casting a glance back around at the snow as it began to finally filter through the canopy to fall into the hollow behind him, Richard leaned against the doorframe, losing himself for a moment in the picturesque scene before him. The ground was fast becoming white, the green and red of the Holly bushes and their berries a bright contrast amid the flurry and he smiled, letting his eyes drift along the hollow, watching as it seemed to wound to the North. That would take it near the back of the property and the Twins. Those trees and their roots yet again.

They were the key to everything.

They couldn't be destroyed for fear of allowing the ghosts out to harm people yet there had to be a way of removing the threat of The Twelve.

There had to be.

Nodding as he recalled the reason for his trip out to the shed, Richard turned, eyes scanning the dark building for a sign of the ladder he needed.

Shaking his head, he picked his way through the piles of boxes, tools and old fashioned machinery, many of the items that he found confusing him as to their purpose, a smile creasing his features as he chuckled, "Where's the antique roadshow when you need it...I could make my fortune!"

Picking up what looked like some early form of hand drill, Richard gave a smirk, and placed it back down, his brow then furrowing as he turned and glanced back around at the gloomy room, the hairs rising on the back of his neck as recognition washed over him, memories of standing in a similar building returning to him once more. Gritting his teeth, forcing himself not to think of that night, a night that he had only remembered less than twenty four hours ago, he turned back to the task at hand, his pulse rate quicker now as he tried to spot the ladder that Ms Sanderson had told him might be here. Pushing aside a small trestle table at the back of the building, Richard cursed as a couple of boxes upon it fell to the floor, spilling clothes and books out everywhere. Grimacing, he cast the items a scowl, then sighed and dropped to a crouch, his right hand placing the small pouch inside a coat pocket as he began placing the fallen clothes and books back into their former boxes, eyes glancing about as he did so then he froze, his brow furrowing in confusion as he stared ahead. "What the fuck is tha…" his words trailed off as he studied the dark object upon the ground several feet from where he was crouched, its surface reflecting the faint light in the building. Eyes focused to the mysterious object, he leaned forward on his hands, moving from a crouch to all fours, left hand rising to push a tricycle out of the way then gasped in dread, his blood turning to ice as he stared at the tarpaulin on the floor, a shape within secured with rope.

In terror he pushed himself backwards, landing hard upon his rump, legs drawing up to his chest, his back pressed against some shelves as he clasped his hands to his face, "No no no no no!"

It couldn't be Myra. It just couldn't be.

Not here. Not now. Not like this.

He flinched as something black moved in the doorway, a scream escaping him, but then the sound of a birds wings sounded as it took flight, the caw of a crow sounding loud on the trail of his cry, and he cursed, eyes returning to the shape under the tarpaulin, his head shaking slowly once more.

This wasn't possible.

But then what had been since his arrival here?

He wasn't even sure he could gauge normal now.

But no, this couldn't be Myra. It just couldn't.

This was just a trick of his mind. That was all.

He blinked as he realised he couldn't remember the last time that he had taken his pills, relaxing slightly as he pushed himself back to his knees, eyes focusing upon the tarpaulin once more as he leaned forwards. On instinct he raised a hand to his breast pocket, stomach twisting as he recalled that he had stopped placing his bottle of pills in there after Ms Sanderson had told him that he wasn't mad.

That ghosts were indeed real.

But maybe he did still need them.

Sure, ghosts did exist but maybe he still needed the pills to stop him seeing other stuff. Like Myra.

Rising to his feet, he took a step towards the tarpaulin, eyes widening as from this new raised elevation he realised that it was a black dustbin liner, and what he had thought was rope was in fact black bungee cords, secured with hooks. Shaking his head, Richard stepped closer, and crouched, hands taking the strain of the bungee cords as he unfastened them and then prepared to unfold the bin liner to reveal its contents, his hands shaky as he pictured Myra within. "Oh fuck off you tool" he muttered, as he dragged the two sides of the black plastic apart, a chuckle escaping him as he saw what had been making the body shape. Pots of paint, brushes, and a roller tray, stacked atop each other, stored for a day that had obviously never happened. Sighing heavily, he rose and stepped back against the shelving behind him, hands rising to rub at his temples as he tried to make a body shape from the objects but to no avail.

The optical illusion had been ruined.

Rolling his eyes, he chuckled again, then gave a soft curse as he saw the ladder above him, a nail beneath one step holding it high above the floor of the shed.

"There you are!" he grimaced, glancing around for some way to reach it, cursing again, "Great, now I need a ladder to reach the fucking ladder"

Head shaking, he dragged the trestle table over, and leaned it against the shelving he had been standing beside; hands clasping to the shelves as he clambered atop the old furniture. It groaned, swaying slightly to the side and he grimaced, fingers clenching harder to the shelves until the trestle table finally stopped moving. Then, heart in his mouth, he took a deep breath and released his grip on the shelving, his hands reaching above his head for the ladder. For a moment, his fingers stroked air but then with a grunt of triumph, he was grasping the bottom of the ladder's wooden legs, lifting it clear from the nail to let it slide quickly down through his open hands.

"Fuck!" Richard cursed in pain as a splinter lanced into the fleshy join between the thumb and finger of his left hand, and he dropped the ladder to the ground, eyes narrowing as he plucked the offending piece of wood from his skin and cast it aside, "Shit!"

Without warning the trestle table suddenly wobbled violently beneath him as he gasped, arms thrusting out either side like a surfer. For a moment it seemed that he was going to balance himself, his hands fastening to the shelving upon the wall beside him but with a crash, it gave way and fell towards him, knocking him from the table to land atop the ladder. Nearly a minute dragged by as he lay there, eyes closed as he tried to figure out if anything was broken and then cursing, he rose to his feet, hands dusting his jeans and coat as he did so. Sighing heavily, Richard bent, reaching for the ladder that he had dropped, holding it in both hands as he turned and headed for the door. He paused as he did so, eyes travelling over the countless boxes and discarded tools once more, unsurprised that he had made the comparison between the barn where Myra had died. The barn where he had killed his father.

He shuddered suddenly, a hand leaving the ladder to drag the collar of his coat tighter about his neck, and then he strode from the brick shed and out into the hollow once more, head shaking as he turned slowly, staring in shock at the amount of snow before him. Ms Sanderson had been right once again.

Chuckling to himself, he took another step and then froze as he remembered that he hadn't locked the shed behind him, a hand reaching into the pocket of his coat as he turned back around, holding the middle of the ladder as it hung beside him with one hand while his other raised the key. He froze as something moved back within the shed, a dark shape seeming to detach itself from the other dark shapes, and grimacing, he shook his head, placing the key back inside his pocket as he withdrew the small pouch and raised it before him, "Fuck off Agnes"

"Stupid...fuckin...boy" the harsh, guttural curse came from the black shape, and feeling suddenly sick, Richard took a step back away, his feet crunching in the fresh snow, "No...not you!"

Nose flattened across his bloody features, one eye missing, his father took a faltering step into the doorway, the hammer that had ended his life clasped in his right hand, "Stupid...fucking...boy!"

With a sob of terror, head shaking in denial, Richard thrust the pouch back into his pocket, grabbed the ladder with both hands and ran screaming for his life.

Chapter Thirty One

Grimacing, mind dizzy with the realisation of what he had just seen, Richard charged through the hollow, dodging among the gravestones, the ladder swinging ungainly in his shaking arms. He reached the bottom of the incline to the higher level and started to climb, cursing as his feet slid on the snow, and he crashed to his knees then his face, gasping at the sudden cold. Grimacing, he pushed himself to his knees, and glanced back towards the falling snow to the shed, shock swelling his throat with emotion as he saw his father striding towards where he knelt watching, the hammer raised overhead. With a curse of terror, Richard pushed the fallen ladder to lay on the incline, bottom feet pushed onto the snow, and then he was clambering up it, hands hauling at the rungs as he forced himself upwards. Shaking violently, he reached the top and bent, hands dragging the ladder up behind him then froze, head turning as he realised that the figure of his father had vanished from sight. "Where the fuck are you?" he straightened, holding the ladder up vertically before him, hands clasped to the wooden rungs as he looked about in a panic, eyes peering through the flurry that was falling heavier. Yet his father, the man that had murdered his childhood best friend, the man that he himself had violently murdered in cold blood was gone.

Shaking his head, the author bent at the knee slightly, trying to get a better look down into the hollow but with the snowstorm the light was fading, and he could barely make out the shed amid the trees and the falling snow. It had seemed so very real just moments ago but then he had also been certain that he had found the body of Myra wrapped up in its tarpaulin only to discover it had actually been nothing of the sort. Was he going insane?

Shaking his head, Richard sighed heavily.

The ghosts of The Twelve were in the grounds and in the house because their spirits were bound to the Twins, and Myra, God rest her soul, had been at the house because she had, according to Ms Sanderson, attached herself to him, but there was no reason for his father to be here. No reason at all.

Which meant one thing.

It had been just his imagination.

There was no other explanation for his presence.

He winced, blinking away a rising sense of nausea as a sudden need to take his pills surfaced within him, and turning towards the house, moving the ladder to hang horizontally beside him, he began walking towards it, the deep snow crunching beneath him as he trod on its unbroken surface. He passed the small upper graveyard, and smiled grimly as the shape of his car appeared through the flurry, the expression slipping from his features as he heard the faint whisper of a voice somewhere off to his left amid the falling snow, "*Three blind mice. Three blind mice...*"

"Oh fuck me" he shook his head, "Not now!"

Agnes came charging at him out of the snow, hands reaching for his bearded features and he dropped the ladder and screamed in terror, both of his hands rising instinctively to thrust her away, aware as he did so that his hands were going to pass straight through her form just as he himself had passed through the form of the ghost of the overweight priest, Father Ambrose Dewitt. He gasped in dread as his hands touched her clammy flesh, his fingers curling about the bony wrists and mind reeling, he raised his eyes to stare at the face of the ghost, eyes widening as he saw her staring down at her wrists. She blinked, her features slowly raising to meet his gaze, and she gave a chuckle like leaves in the wind, her body tensing as she pushed back at him.

"What the fuck" he managed to curse then gasped in sudden pain as she threw herself at him, the long nailed fingers of her right hand scratching at his left cheek. On impulse he thrust her back, releasing her wrists and she staggered slightly then rushed him once more screaming in pure hatred and anger.

His right fist struck her square in the forehead and she gave a grunt of shock, and fell to the ground, a mournful scream escaping her stick-thin form. Grimacing, Richard bent and grasped at the bottom rung of the ladder with his right hand, his left rising to touch his cheek where she had scratched him as he began to hurry towards the house through the snow, his grey eyes widening as his fingers came away wet. She had somehow scratched him and drawn blood. And he had not only touched but hit her.

What the fuck was going on?

Ms Sanderson had told him there was no way The Twelve could harm anyone unless the Twins were destroyed or the Sanderson bloodline was at an end. He grimaced as he considered those important details, sudden concern for the elderly woman washing over him like a tsunami of raw emotion.

Had something happened to her and Cherry?

He turned his face towards the gateposts that led to the village of Evenfield beyond, his eyes then lifting towards the heavy snow that was falling, covering everything in a thick blanket of white.

Had she fallen in the snow and hurt herself?

No, he shook his head, that couldn't be true.

Even if the worst had happened to the old woman then there was still Cherry alive to carry on the presence of the Sanderson's bloodline.

Had the Twins somehow been damaged?

He frowned at the thought, certain that snow couldn't kill oak trees, at least not this quickly.

So, what the fuck was going on?

He flinched as he suddenly saw movement in the corner of his eye, and turning, he watched as Agnes Rand pushed herself to her feet once more and began to run towards him, her gait unsteady as if she were still stunned by his punch, her long nailed fingers reaching out for his face as she sang, "*See how they run…see how they run!*"

"Will you fuck off!" he shouted in a mixture of confusion, anger and fear, backpedalling towards the house, desperate to get away from her, then cursed as he slipped on the snow and fell heavily to his back.

Before him, the old woman charged onwards, bending as she saw him fall, a cackle of triumph leaving her body and Richard winced, then thrust a hand into the front pocket of his coat as he suddenly remembered the small pouch that he had found.

She was less than six feet away when he threw it at her, a weak under-arm throw, not helped by his prone position lying in the snow and it struck her on the chest with the force of a gentle pat, his action merely an attempt to drive her away once more.

Yet the result was instantaneous.

With a shriek, she staggered back, bony hands frantically brushing at the pouch which seemed to somehow be stuck to her, her lined features contorted in what looked to be complete agony.

Her feet caught fire first, the unnatural looking flames rushing upwards, consuming her legs and waist at an alarming rate, her clothes igniting as if she had been doused in flammable liquids. Mind reeling, the author stayed where he was upon the snow, head shaking in disbelief as he watched the old woman burning, the flames washing up over her chest and finally her head, her long grey hair whipping out like tentacles of fire as she thrashed about, screaming in agony. Without warning, she seemed to come about, her form collapsing in upon itself, turning to ash.

Yet the fire still burnt amid the blackening figure, changing colour to a deep indigo as her charred remains began to separate from her body, lifting up and drifting away like embers upon a bonfire only to change direction and rush towards the pouch, as if drawn by its own powerful gravitational pull.

In a matter of moments there was nothing of the ghost left or any trace that it had ever existed. Agnes Rand; The Cook, was gone, and only the pouch remained, resting on the snow innocently.

Chapter Thirty Two

Grimacing, stunned at what he had just witnessed, Richard rose on shaky legs and stepped over to where the small pouch sat upon the snow, and slowly crouched down beside it. He flinched as he reached out a hand, his fingers recoiling from the bag, the leather as cold as ice, and grimacing, he took a deep breath and picked it up, holding it before his features.

What had it just done?

It looked like Agnes Rand had been burning, and he himself had just witnessed her form come apart.

But could ghosts really die a second time?

Was The Twelve now just numbering eleven?

Shaking his head, he stepped back towards the house, his left hand rising to touch his cheek once more with shaking fingers as he recalled her attack on him, his mind struggling with the facts.

Something had changed.

Somehow the ghosts, or Agnes at least, had been able to physically touch him, someone on the mortal plane or whatever the term for the real world was. That meant either the Twins were dead, something he found unlikely, or something had happened to Ms Sanderson and Cherry.

He grimaced at the thought, moving quickly towards the porch of the huge house, and pushed the door open wide before him, his voice calling out, "Ms

Sanderson...Margaret...are you here?"

There was no reply, the sound of his voice echoing through the downstairs hall and he gave a shake of his head, moving through the pile of boxes and furniture to the bottom of the stairs as he called out once more, "Margaret!"

Still the house was quiet, almost as if it was holding its breath as it watched him, and Richard winced at the thought of the building being sentient, stepping away towards the kitchen, voice rising in volume as he continued to call out, "Margaret...are you back?"

Once more his voice faded away unanswered and he clapped his free hand to his forehead in stress.

Where on Earth could she be?

How long had he been in the hollow at the shed?

Could she still be down in the village getting supplies for the snow that she had predicted?

Cursing, a hand swinging angrily to knock a tea cup that he had left on the table to smash onto the kitchen floor, its meagre contents spilling across the floor, the author hurried towards the door to the greenhouse, and banged it open. Raising the hand holding the pouch before him, he stepped inside, eyes glancing quickly about in concern that one of the remaining Twelve might attack, but the coast was clear.

Would they be able to touch him like Agnes?

He grimaced as he pictured the clown, The Great Marlowe, his stomach knotting as he recalled the words of Ms Sanderson, explaining that he had been a rapist of not just women, but also children and men. No way. Not a chance.

An image of the huge James Jackman entered his mind, unbidden, and he cursed aloud as he imagined trying to get close enough to the ghost to touch him with the mysterious leather pouch in his hand.

He could throw it like he had with Agnes but what if other ghosts were about at the time?

There was no sense in giving up his only weapon. Shaking his head, Richard stepped carefully through the greenhouse until he was standing before the door to the rear garden once more, his stomach knotting in dread as he stared out at the Twins as they stood amidst the blizzard, bare branches heavy with snow.

The grand old trees looked to be no different. Which meant that it wasn't their demise that had allowed Agnes Rand touch him physically.

He closed his eyes as he realised the implications. That meant that both Ms Sanderson and Cherry were dead. But how? How could they both die?

Cursing, he started to turn away from the door then stopped, shaking his head in confusion as he caught sight of his reflection in the windowpane, a hand rising to the cheek Agnes had just scratched.

"How?" his fingers of his free hand traced gently over the smooth unbroken skin above his beard and below his eye, then raised before his face, stomach knotting as he realised there was no blood stains upon them. Yet he had seen blood on his fingers. Hadn't he?

So why was his face now unmarked and his fingers clean of the blood that had been on them?

Shaking his head, he staggered towards the door to the kitchen, passing through it to enter the hallway

Groaning, he raised a hand to his head, eyes closing as he groaned, "I'm going fucking mad..."

Yet with that terrifying thought came solace.

For if it had been his imagination and Agnes hadn't managed to hurt him physically outside the house then that meant that both Cherry and her grandmother might still be alive and well.

"My pills" he muttered, moving on unsteady legs across the kitchen, and exiting it, he moved to the bottom of the stairs, edging past his furniture once more and looked up at the mid-way landing above. There were no ghosts that he could see but he could feel them up there somewhere, waiting for him to climb the stairs so they could scare him to death.

Yet that was it. They couldn't harm him after all.

All he needed to do was remember where he had last seen his bottle of pills, go and retrieve them, and then

take as many as possible without overdosing.
Anything to get his mind back under control.
Then he would search for Ms Sanderson.
But first, the pills.
Shaking his head, he began to climb the stairs, his right hand held ready, the pouch enclosed in a fist as he called out ahead of him, "Right, I'm coming up…and I've got the bag of…well, you know…the bag…so don't fuck with me…OK?"
Just like before when had been calling out for his housekeeper, there was no answer, and wincing, he had continued up the stairs, reaching the halfway landing to the first floor unchallenged, then turned and continued up the second set of stairs, his voice shaky as he spoke again, "I swear to God, any of you mother fuckers try and jump scare me and I am going to stick this leather bag up your…!"
He had barely managed to sound the first syllable of the word arse when Frances Goodnestone appeared on the stairs before him, the features of the boy twisted in hatred as he lunged forwards with small blade that he had been holding before.
Startled, Richard tried to step back, the word arse morphing mid pronunciation into a scream of terror, then one of agony as the blade sank into his left thigh to the handle, the pain like ice. Eyes wide, the author hopped back on his good leg, the corner of the

landing facing the first flight of stairs stopping him from falling, while before him the ghost watched with excited eyes, a giggle escaping it as he stepped closer. "Back off!" Richard thrust the hand holding the pouch out before him, "I'm warning yo…"

He screamed once more as the huge figure of The Butcher; James Jackman, suddenly took shape beside him, a meaty hand fastening about the authors extended arm, his big fingers squeezing powerfully. Driven mad by pain and confusion, acting purely on impulse, Richard reached down with his free hand, his fingers wrapping about the handle of the blade in his leg then with a supreme effort tore it free to raise beside his bearded features, "Get the fuck off of me!" He twisted, nearly falling as his wounded leg touched the floor and pain surged through him, then he was stabbing the huge ghost in the chest again and again, screaming in desperation, his cries changing to one of pain as Frances suddenly rushed in and started punching the knife wound in the back of his left thigh. "Cunt!" Richard changed direction, bringing the knife down into the side of Frances shoulder and the child ghost staggered back, taking the weapon with him as he blinked in disbelief, and then vanished suddenly. As if in slow motion, Richard turned his gaze back on the huge man beside him, watching in dread as the ghost suddenly swung his arm to the side out over the first flight of stairs, his hand still holding on to the authors wrist flicking out. With yet another scream, Richard flew through the air as if thrown from the top rope by a paranormal wrestler, gut lurching as he headed towards the furniture stacked in the hallway.

Chapter Thirty Three

"Richard?"

The author lifted his head from where he lay upon the hallway floor, blinking as he heard the voice of Cherry as she entered via the front door. Grimacing, he pushed himself to his hands and knees, amazing to find that despite having passed out, most likely from his impact with the wooden floor, he seemed to have sustained no broken bones when he had been thrown from the first mid-way landing by James Jackman.

He spoke her name as he rose to stand amid the furniture and boxes, drawing a gasp of shock from her as she turned to see him standing there.

For a moment she began to smile, then she shook her head, the expression slipping, "What have you done?"

"What?" he stepped past the wardrobe, heading towards where she stood beside the front door, a pained look on her features as she shifted her eyes from his face to look up the stairs and then back at him, head shaking as she stepped closer to him.

"What is it?" he repeated, a grim smile creasing his bearded features, "What's the matter?"

"Are you OK?" she fixed him with a concerned look, and he shrugged, unsure exactly what to tell her.

"I've seen my father"

"Your father?" she gave a shake of her head.

He shrugged once more, a hand rising to scratch at

his beard, "I thought it was his ghost but it doesn't make sense, the ghosts in this house are those that have died here, except for Myra, and…"

She winced, nodding, "You know about Myra?"

Richard nodded, suddenly remembering how he had left her the previous night, alone in the lychgate of the small church, "Hey listen, last night…I get that you were trying to tell me about Myra…I…I guess I just didn't want to let her go"

Cherry winced and he shrugged, smiling sadly, "I am hoping that I will still get to see her…but she'll be different…the her that I thought I knew…I guess that's not how she really looked"

"How did you find out?" Cherry asked, a hand rising to brush blue hair from her face, "Tell me"

"She appeared to me as I'd last seen her…as she'd died…I…she was just a kid…I…" his words trailed off and he realised that he was staring down at the floor. Sighing, he raised his eyes once more to find Cherry watching him with an odd expression upon her face, and he winced, "What, what is it?"

"What have you been doing?" she eyed him in curiosity, "Why were you laying upon the floor?"

He grimaced, nodding, "I got knocked out…the big one…James Jackman, he threw me down the stairs from the half way landing to the first floor"

Cherry nodded, letting her gaze drift to that area then frowned, "He touched you?"

"Yeah" Richard confirmed, his voice grim, "First Agnes attacked me outside the house…I was worried that you and your grandmother were dead and that The Twelve were free. But when I got in here, the scratches that she gave me were gone"

He nodded at her, "It doesn't matter now…it's my mind…I'm seeing things…my dad…the injuries…I thought that the ghosts being able to touch me was my mind too when I found that the scratches from Agnes were gone but it cant have been my mind…because first that little prick Frances stabbed me in the leg and then James Jackman threw me through the air!"

Cherry stared back at him in silence for a moment, eyes narrowing as she listened to his words, and then she shook her head, "You got stabbed by Frances?"

The author nodded, then frowned as he realised that his leg wasn't hurting him, grimacing as he glanced down to stare at his leg in disbelief, "I don't understand…he stabbed me in the leg…"

"Richard"

"I can't have imagined it" he shook his head, eyes rising to meet hers, "I can't have…I know what I saw"

"Richard, you need to calm down" she shook her

head, her hands rising before her in a placating manner, "We need to figure out what happened!"

For long moments he stared down at the floor, head shaking, and then he met her gaze once more, his voice breaking, "I don't know what's real anymore Cherry...you have to help me"

She held his gaze for long moments, her features etched with concern and then she glanced in the direction of the kitchen before meeting his gaze once more, "Where is my grandmother?"

He raised a hand, gesturing off towards the front door, "She went to the village to get some supplies while I went down to the shed"

"The shed?" she winced, "In the hollow?"

"Yeah"

"Why?" her voice was soft, "Why go down there?"

"I needed a ladder"

"A ladder?"

"Yeah, I need to get back up into the secret room above the bedroom on the second floor"

The blue haired young woman looked at him in astonishment and he raised an eyebrow, "You didn't know it was there either?"

"No"

He gave a grunt, "I was up there yesterday, before I went looking for Myra...before I met you out in the middle of that storm. It was where I found the bag"

As she sent him another look of confusion, he realised that in his desperation to find Myra the previous night he had failed to tell her about the bag that he had found up in the secret room, and he reached a hand down to his coat pocket only to curse, "It's gone…its fucking gone!"

"What's gone?" she frowned, giving him a look of confusion as he hurried back over to where he had woken upon hearing her voice as she had entered Sanderson House, "I don't understand"

"The bag, the fucking bag" he was nearly hysterical as he dropped to his hands and knees, eyes scanning the floor for the bag he had been holding when James Jackman had thrown him from the mid-way landing.

"Richard, we need to talk" Cherry moved around the furniture to stand beside him as he crawled about on all fours, then gave him a look of confusion as he cried out, and rose to his feet, his right hand clasped about the leather bag that he had been searching for.

"What on Earth is that?"

He shrugged, "I don't know…but The Twelve are scared of it…I touched Agnes with it and she burst into flames…I think she's gone for good…if it was real…I'm not sure anymore to be honest"

Eyes locked to the bag that he was holding, Cherry stepped closer to him, her head shaking as she stared at it in astonishment, "It can't be"

"Can't be what?" he shook his head, "Tell me"

She lifted her eyes from the bag to meet his, the effort of doing so seeming to take considerable willpower, "I might be wrong but I think it's a medicine bag...I think you have found the medicine bag of Chaqit"

Richard nodded at her words, eyes drifting down to study the bag himself for a moment before he met her gaze once more, "I have no idea what the Hell you are talking about"

The young woman groaned softly, "Chaqit, the Patowomeck brave, the friend of Abram, one of the two sons of Haller, the patriarch of the Sanderson family. Family legend claims that not only did Chaqit help Abram on his hunt for the first few of the Twelve but he was instrumental in teaching the other brother Larens about the Patowomeck faith, and in creating the Twins"

Richard raised an eyebrow, "Creating the Twins? You grow trees, you don't create them"

She shook her head at his words, "The Twins were already growing at the Sanderson Estate when this house was built, but Chaqit and Larens linked them in with the soul of everyone that was executed on them...grandmother has told you the story surely?"

He nodded, "Yeah, if the trees are destroyed or you and your grandmother die then The Twelve, and the others are released to take their revenge"

She winced, a strange look on her face as she nodded. "Which is why I was worried that something had happened to you and your grandmother!" he groaned, "I have checked the Twins and they are fine. When James Jackman and Frances attacked me, and I realised that I hadn't imagine Agnes physically attacking me…I thought the worse had happened…I was really worried about you"

"Richard" she winced, head shaking, and he nodded, a heavy sigh escaping him as he smiled awkwardly.

"I know…we barely know each other but I can't help it…I like you…when I thought you might be dead…"

"Richard for God sake!" she shouted, a hand rising to hold her forehead, her eyes wet with the promise of tears as she stared at him, "Stop!"

"Hey!" he gave a shake of his head, about to speak when his eyes drifted from her features, drawn by the sudden realisation that something was very wrong, the breath leaving his body in a rush as he saw the wide slashes in the wrist of the hand on her head, its depth making bone visible amid the muscle.

"No" he gave a shake of his head as he took a step back, stomach knotting in dread as his gaze slipped to her other wrist only to find it hidden by the sleeve of the coat she was wearing, "No!"

She gave a heavy sigh, her features seeming to pale by the second as he stared at her, a look of infinite sadness in her expression as she moved the hand from her face to grasp his free hand, her touch like ice, "Richard...please!"

Without a word, the author turned and ran up the stairs, her bitter laughter after following him.

Chapter Thirty Four

Screaming in confusion and fear, Richard charged headlong up the stairs, swinging his clenched fist holding the pouch before him as he ran, like a deranged soldier clasping a live hand grenade.

Cherry was a ghost. How could that be?

How could he not have known?

Memories of Ms Sanderson asking him politely to not get too attached to her returned to him in a rush, followed by her statement that if he needed to speak to her, her granddaughter was always about somewhere. His stomach knotted in dread as he recalled their first meeting, how he had stood in the hallway outside the kitchen listening as Cherry had begged her grandmother for permission to see Richard and how surprised she had seemed when he had offered to walk her out. Blinking, he froze as he reached the first floor, heart wrenching as he recalled the sincerity in her voice as she had stood under the porch with him, thanking him for seeing her.

Seeing her.

How had he not realised?

Just like with Myra. Was anyone real?

Cursing in dread as he considered the thought, he began to continue on and then froze as he saw the fat priest Father Ambrose Dewitt watching him from the far side of the corridor, his fat features twisted in hatred. With a snort of anger, the portly ghost pushed himself away from the wall, and Richard tensed, glancing at the pouch he was holding, considering touching the ghost to see if it burst into flames like Agnes Rand had. Movement in his peripheral vison caught his eye, and he turned, stomach dropping away as if he was on a rollercoaster as he saw the busty blonde woman striding down the corridor towards, the laughing, scuttling greasepainted figure of the Great Marlowe following excitedly behind. Wincing in terror, the author turned to run, and screamed as he found the couple upon the stairs behind him, Clemence and Elias, The Witch and The Devil. As the square-faced man snarled and reached for him, large hands grasping and Richard gave a howl of terror and thrust his arms forward, ready to fend of the large man's blows. At the last minute the man seemed to notice the pouch that was clasped in Richard's right hand, his own hands starting to recoil, then the pouch bumped gently against the ghost.

His sudden scream of pain and shock was loud, the pale faced ghost taking a step back along the landing, its features turning towards its female companion, as it raised its right hand before it.

Without warning, flames erupted at the feet of the ghost, its scream of terror and confusion rising in pitch and volume as it stared down at the flames that were licking at its old-fashioned clothes but leaving the stair carpet untouched. Eyes wide in its face, the male ghost lurched to the side, hands desperately grasping at the female that it was always with, her scream of terror and concern joining his in an unholy duet as she fought to keep away from the flames as they rose to his waist, and then higher, tongues of flame igniting his sideburns and thick hair.

Maddened beyond belief, the ghost seemed to stumble and with a grimace, his eyes locked to what he had inadvertently done, Richard darted past the burning ghost to stand on the halfway landing to the second floor, staring back in shock.

The ghost, Elias was on its knees now, features split in a wide scream as it howled in pain and misery, one hand extended to the female ghost as it stood with its back to the wall, head shaking. The flames around the ghost turned indigo, and as had Agnes, Elias began to come apart, pieces breaking off and falling to the carpet like charcoal, only for them to turn to a fine dust on impact, which rose on some magical breeze and soared towards where Richard waited watching. As the pieces soared in his direction, the author raised his right fist before him in the air, brow furrowing as he watched them touch the bag and vanish as if melting like a snowflake on skin. With a sob, the female ghost, Clemence, shot him a look of abject horror and vanished, the hand of her dying suitor rising weakly towards her only to break off and smash to pieces upon the stair carpet.

That was enough for the ghosts of the blonde woman and the priest, both vanishing from sight, terror on their faces as Elias Crumb finally came undone.

Grim faced, Richard stared at where the pair had been standing watching the scene in confusion and fear, then winced as he saw the Great Marlowe edge around the corner of the corridor towards the balustrade, fingertips tiptoeing their way along the old wooden banister as it crept towards him, its movements shaky and awkward as it moved.

"Fuck you" the author raised the pouch, shaking it before him in the air as he stared at the slowly approaching clown, "Keep the fuck back!"

The clown paused, eyes widening amid the greasepaint, hands rising to its cheeks as it made a mockery of being shocked, like some starlet of the silent movie era, then it giggled, a finger rising to point at him while its other hand rubbed at its stomach, "Yummy yum yum"

"Fuck off" Richard turned, racing up the final few stairs, screaming like a child as he glanced back over the railing to see the great Marlowe give chase, hands clapping excitedly as it chased him, long legs stepping awkwardly, hooting in delight, hands clapping.

Arms pumping at his sides, Richard reached the second floor and turned to charge towards the bedroom at the end of the hall, any thought he might have had of facing the ghosts head on in combat washed away in an overwhelming wave of terror. Glancing back over his shoulder, he saw the ghost of the clown round the corner and charge towards him, arms extended before him, fingers wiggling, and the author charged onwards, turning his head back to focus upon the far door and his chance of safety. "Let me bleed you!" Dr Edwin Bennet suddenly appeared before the door of the room that Richard had encountered him in earlier, features twisted in a grim smile as he slashed out with his straight razor and the author leaned backwards, the blade sweeping at him in slow motion. Off balance, he fell heavily to his back on the floor of the corridor, the straight razor slashing past where his head had been just moments before. Snarling in a rage, the ghost of the Victorian physician stumbled past and then spun about as the author rose quickly, the razor sweeping out once more and Richard gave a hiss of pain as it sliced into his right bicep, the pouch falling from his nerveless fingers as he staggered and fell back. Instantly, the physician was after him, razor raised once more, and Richard stared up at it in shock, left hand clasped to his slashed arm, blood running through his fingers to drip onto the floor.

With a cruel smile, the ghost of Dr Edwin Bennet nodded down at him, "Let me blee…"

His words turned to a choking gasp as a large figure suddenly appeared behind it, big hands fastening to the ghostly physician's throat as the newcomer turned and threw him back down the corridor several metres, the strength of the attacker obvious. The ghost of the physician blinked as it landed, then stared up in dread as the large figure that had thrown him, stormed in his direction and knelt astride him, one large hand pinning his hand holding the straight razor to the floor, the other rising to hammer a punch into his thin features. Dumbstruck, the author managed to rise to his knees, staring at the figure atop Dr Edwin Bennet in confusion, eyes traveling over the big man's shaven head, his form almost large enough to rival that of James Jackman, then glanced to the side, watching in astonishment as the ghost of the Great Marlowe began to back away, fear upon its features before it too slowly faded away from view like a mirage. As Richard knelt watching, left hand still clasped to his right arm, the ghost of the big man continued to hammer it's large fist into the face of the struggling ghost of the physician until without warning, Dr Edwin Bennet vanished from sight. Slowly, the big ghost rose to its feet, head turning to glare at Richard in a mixture of anger and hatred, nose wrinkling as if it was sniffing the air, a black handlebar moustache framing its mouth,

Then it spoke, it's voice like ice, "Murderer"

Mind numb, Richard watched as it took a step towards him then flinched as a hand touched his shoulder, his eyes widening as he turned to find the child version of Myra standing beside him, her pale features grim, "Run Richie, run!"

Chapter Thirty Five

As if in a dream, Richard rose and allowed the girl to take him by the hand, his eyes locked to the powerful form of the approaching man, realising for the first time that the newcomer was dressed in a pair of grey trousers, a white vest smeared with what looked like blood and dirt, and a pair of braces, his bare arms and shoulders heavy with slabs of corded muscle.

"Come on!" Myra shouted, pulling on his hand and as if waking, he let her drag him back towards the open door of the room that he had been heading towards, stomach knotting as he saw the eyes of the new ghost flick towards it, his features twisting into a snarl.

"Come on Richie!" Myra suddenly released his hand as the big ghost tensed, and with wide eyes, the author turned and watched her sprint for the door, the broken leg not seeming to bother her at all.

"Shit!" the author charged after her, not needing to look over his shoulder to realise that the big ghost was chasing him, fear turning his blood to ice as he imagined how bad it was going to hurt him if it managed to catch him before he reached the door. And he was now without the pouch, a deep sense of loss coursing through him as he recalled dropping it when Dr Bennet had cut him moments earlier.

"In here!" Myra raced through the doorway to the room, turning as she reached the bed to watch as

Richard raced towards her, a grunt of fear escaping him as he almost felt his pursuer right behind him, and glimpsed hands either side of his face, about to grasp and drag him backwards into the hallway. But then he was in the room, his inertia so great that he careened into the bed in the centre of the room, and nearly fell over to the other side of it, the child Myra moving quickly out of his way as he landed. Sprawled sideways upon the bed, Richard turned his head, watching in horror as the man that had been chasing him moved to stand directly in front off the open door, the palms of his large hands rising to press against the air before him, a curious expression creasing his moustached face as he realised he couldn't gain entry to the room to attack them. Blinking, the author rose to his feet and stepped closer to the doorway, just inches separating the two men, the eyes of the ghost slowly travelling about the doorframe as if seeking a way inside to get them. Shaking his head, Richard studied the hard features of the big man, taking in his broken nose and square jaw, then stepped to the side, staring past the ghost to stare with longing at the pouch as it sat some twenty feet from where he stood. So near and yet so far. Sighing heavily, he let his gaze drift back to the ghost, a gasp escaping him as he found it staring at him, its body still as if frozen like a statue where it stood.

"Who are you?" Richard frowned, then cursed and staggered back to sit on the bed in shock as the ghost hammered a punch into the air between them, then another, each stopping at the door frame, blocked by whatever magical power had bound the ghost to the roots of the Twins, features twisted in a mask of rage.

"His name is Britt…Britt Sanderson"

Richard flinched at the voice, head spinning to find Myra standing back against the wall beside the bed, palms pressed against it as she watched him.

He tried to smile and failed, "Are you real?"

"Boys are so dumb" she rolled her eyes in reply.

Turning his gaze from her, Richard studied the man in the doorway once more, wincing as he saw the hatred in his eyes, then shaking his head he rose and moved to the door, shutting it, "God, I need my pills"

"Pills?" Myra asked, drawing his gaze, "Why?"

Ignoring her, he walked away from the ghost of his childhood friend, and entered the large bathroom, relief touching him as he opened the door of the medicine cabinet and saw his pills waiting for him. With a shaking hand, he reached out to collect the bottle, fingers fumbling with the lid and then he poured out three of the small white pills into the palm of his other hand. Holding them before him, he turned the tap on the sink below the medicine cabinet and took a small plastic beaker out of it and then shut the door of it once more. Sighing heavily, he filled the beaker, placed it down and then turned off the tap before letting his gaze drift back to study the three white pills. His doctor had told him to never take more than two at a time, but he needed to think clearly, to let himself level out without for a moment. He needed to know what was and wasn't real.

For a second, he let his gaze drift to meet his own stare, feeling ill as he saw his own reflection.

His beard seemed to have more grey hairs then before and his face was lined and weary, as if he hadn't slept in days. Sighing, he raised the hand holding the pills towards his mouth, his other hand picking up the beaker and then froze as he realised that his arm was no longer hurting him like before. Grimacing, he shifted position, studying his right arm in the mirror, unsurprised to find that it was no longer wounded, and he knew without looking that the blood would be gone from his left hand.

The ghosts were fucking with him.

Somehow, they were still unable to permanently hurt him, but they had progressed from using jump scares, tricking him into thinking that his wounds were real. He cursed as he realised that he had dropped the pouch for a wound that hadn't even existed, eyes closing as he gave another curse then frowned, his thoughts drifting back to the new bald ghost.

He had attacked the Physician Dr Edwin Bennet;
Cherry had called him The Fever, and The Great
Marlowe had looked terrified upon seeing him.
So he was clearly not fond of his ghostly brethren,
and they were very clearly not fond of him either.
Yet he had obviously been hung upon the Twins, the
fact he had been unable to enter the room where
Richard and Myra were hiding was proof of that.
Sighing, he raised the pills back towards his mouth,
then froze as something suddenly occurred to him.
Taking a deep breath, he placed the beaker of water
down, and stepped back towards the door, stomach
tight as he studied the figure of Myra as she stood
against the wall still, her throat badly bruised, her
right eye bloodshot, her clothes dirty and stained.
"It's rude to stare!" she turned to meet his gaze and
he winced, head shaking as he glanced quickly down.
Nearly a minute passed as he fought to ready himself
for the sight of her and then he nodded and raised his
head, surprised to see her now sitting on the edge of
the bed, an eyebrow rising as she studied him,
"What? Cat got your tongue?"
Wincing, he moved around the end of the bed and sat
down several feet away from her, his voice tight as he
gestured towards the door, "You said you knew the
name of that man"

"He's a ghost" she gave him a knowing look, a smile on her face, "You know that don't you?"

The author nodded, "So what's his name again?"

"Britt Sanderson"

"Britt Sanderson" Richard blinked, head shaking as he rose to his feet and stepped away from the bed, his mind racing as he tried to recall where he had heard the name before. It was obvious that he was some descendant of Ms Sanderson but how had he ended up hung upon the Twins?

Suddenly his cloud of confusion cleared, the grim words of Cherry returning to him from the Lychgate the night before as she had explained about the execution of Dr Bennet, *"...my great, great, great grandfather Britt hung him. He was the last executioner"*

The last executioner.

"How did you know his name?" he turned to look at Myra, his fear regarding the appearance of his childhood friend fading in the wake of his sudden curiosity, "I don't understand how you know it?"

The ghost of the girl sat watching him silently for a moment and then grinned, "I listened"

"You listened?"

She nodded proudly, "And I watched, the others, the rest of The Twelve are all scared of him"

"So am I" Richard glanced back at the door before meeting her gaze once more as she gave a laugh.

"You are such a girl"

He laughed then, head nodding as he considered how insane the entire situation was, "Yeah, I am"

For a moment, there was a strange, indescribable comfortable silence and then Richard nodded at the girl, his throat swelling with emotion, "I am so sorry for what happened to you"

She shook her head, wincing, "I can't remember anything about it or before it. I just know you have been here for me ever since"

"What else can I do?" his throat was tight.

The smile of the girl was bright, "Don't cry, it will make your mascara run"

Unable to stop, Richard howled with laughter.

Chapter Thirty Six

"What are you doing now?" Myra asked him several minutes later as he stood upon the double bed, ready to step back onto the chest of drawers that he had dragged back to the foot of the bed like he had the previous day, and turning, Richard frowned at her.

"I'm going up into the attic"

The ghost of the girl frowned, "You need a ladder"

Sighing as he considered the ladder that he had left outside in the snow following the death of Agnes, Richard shook his head, "Why are you like this?"

"What?" she made a face as if he had gone mad.

He chewed the inside of his cheek, wondering how best to word what it was he was about to say, then he sighed, "You know you are a ghost don't you?"

She grimaced, "Yeah, so?"

The author shook his head, "But you didn't"

"Didn't what?"

"Know that you were a ghost" he pointed out, eyeing her curiously, "The older Myra...she had no idea that she was a ghost...Hell, neither did I"

"That wasn't me...not really" she winced, head shaking as his eyes widened in shock, "It was like I was going through the motions...like sleep walking...I don't really remember much of it"

Richard swallowed the dryness in his mouth as he considered the words of the ghost, a strange sense of loss for something that had never been real settling about him, twisting his stomach in a vice grip, "So, what was she?"

"It was me...but it was mainly you...I was like, you know when bugs get caught in tree sap...like that...I kind of had moments where I got to do or say what I wanted but most of it was you"

The author shook his head, blinking slowly as he tried to understand what she was describing, then fixed her with a curious look, "But now...?"

"Its me...she's gone...your Myra"

"You are my Myra" he stated defensively and she gave a soft chuckle, her head shaking up at him.

"Nah, not like her...you wanted to kiss her"

"I did not!"

"Did too!" she nodded, enjoying his discomfort.

"For fuck sake" he groaned, head shaking, "Shit"

"I kind of only really got control of myself back last night" Myra continued, and he turned his head to watch her as the ghost frowned, "It was like waking up...she was gone...and then you were there, in the rain, calling out my name...I didn't know who you were at first...my memory still isn't great"

Richard winced as he recalled the moment that he had found her on the village green amid the storm and how she had revealed her identity to him, "You scared me, Myra!"

"Its never been hard" she gave a chuckle, then a sad expression came over her face, "You got old"

He nodded at her words, smiling grimly, I know"

They held each other's gaze for what seemed minutes, and then he frowned at her, "You said you have been listening and watching the ghosts...you obviously know about The Twelve"

She grimaced, "Everyone here knows about the Twelve...or should I say The Ten"

"The Ten?"

She nodded, "Clever little Richie...you got two of them...and there's no coming back a second time"

The author blinked, "Are you serious...Agnes and that other one on the stairs...Elias?"

"Uh-huh"

"Seriously...they are gone for good?"

Myra nodded once more, her eyes bright as she gave a chuckle, "Yeah, everyone is talking about it..."

"Everyone?"

"Sure, the others"

"Other ghosts?" he winced, feeling ill, "Seriously?"

She nodded once more, "Yeah, this place is a regular hive of activity...like a train station"

"And they discuss stuff that the living do?"

She gave a chuckle, "What do you mean?"

He groaned, "They are talking about the two of The Twelve that I have managed to get rid of?"

"Oh, yeah" she nodded at his words, eyeing him strangely and he gestured with a hand at her.

"Well, go on"

"Go on what?"

"Tell me about these other ghosts…are they angry with me…that's the last thing I need"

"Why would they be angry with you…when The Twelve are gone, they can all move over"

Richard blinked at her words, "If I get rid of the remaining ten then all the ghosts can leave?"

She nodded at him, "Yeah, but there's a lot"

"Of ghosts?"

"Duh" the ghost of his childhood friend studied him for a moment, eyes scanning his bearded face then she continued, voice soft, "There are four different lots of ghosts here…"

"Four?" Richard was incredulous, eyes widening.

"Are you going to let me finish speaking?"

"Sorry" he winced, sitting down upon the edge of the chest of drawers that he had been prepared to climb upon to gain access to the secret room once more, nodding at Myra, "Go on"

"Four…" she held up four fingers, ticking them off as she spoke, "The Twelve…or ten or whatever you want to call them, real bad news…real mean…everyone here is scared of them…then there's the others who were hung out on the trees, they keep to themselves, some of them don't even know they are dead, some do…then there are the ghosts of people who died here…in accidents or suicides…stuff like that"

He frowned, raising an eyebrow, "The fourth?"

"The ones like me, Richard" she shrugged, her smile sad, "The ones that have been brought here"

He winced, the weight of her words settling heavy about his shoulders as he studied her, "I'm sorry…I have no idea how it happened"

She shrugged, her gaze staring down at her shoes as she sighed heavily, "Damn it"

"What?" he followed her gaze as she straightened her legs, trying to avoid looking at the misplaced bone beneath her skin as she lifted her feet from the floor, one clad in the pink and turquoise sock, the other in her baseball boot with the laces hanging down.

Myra shook her head, her voice breaking, "I've fastened that lace about thirty times now…then I stand up and its undone…hanging like that"

Richard grimaced, realising the truth of her words; she was trapped, forever locked in the form in which she had died so many years before. She turned her eyes to meet his as he sat staring at her and he felt his gut knot at the pain in her brown orbs, "I just want to go home and see my mum and dad…that's all I want"

Fuck. Shit. Damn.

Forcing a smile, he nodded, "Then we best get rid of the other ten of The Twelve, right?"

The ghost of the girl smiled, nodding, "Right"

Chapter Thirty Seven

"What is this place?"

Richard turned from where he was standing staring down at the small writing desk before him, shrugging as he studied the ghost that was sitting upon the edge of the hatch that he had just climbed through, "It has to have belonged to one of the Sanderson's, maybe one of the hangmen"

The ghost of the girl grimaced, nose turning up as she studied the shelves lined with old books and pieces of paper, "It looks boring...like a library"

The author grinned, turning away from her to study his surroundings, "It looks amazing"

She gave a grunt and he smiled, enjoying having her back, even if her appearance had changed. Stepping closer to the desk, Richard stared down in fascination as he had previously once more picking up the early pencil, studying it, then turned as Myra moved beside him, her brow furrowing, "What's that?"

"It's an early pencil smiled at her, "It's amazing"

She made a face, a bored expression upon her deathly features, "Really? It just looks like a lump of lead wrapped in string"

He shook his head, "This is graphite, not lead"

"I thought you said it was a pencil"

"I did"

She gave a snort, "Pencils are made with lead"

"No" he placed it back down, "Pencils have never been made with lead…they have always used graphite…people just assume its lead"

She rolled her eyes, his stomach knotting as he saw the red of her damaged eye fill the socket, and he looked away, her words reaching him as she walked off, "You are weird with book stuff"

"I am" he nodded, smiling back at her, "I am"

Glancing back, he found her sat on the edge of the hatch once more, and smiling to himself, he sat down gently upon the old chair, fearing it might break under him, then turned his head to study the attic room, a strange sense of excitement touching him as he let his gaze stop on the shelves full of papers.

Maybe the answers to how the spirits of those executed were bound to the Twins was written there somewhere, or perhaps details on what the bag was and why it was able to kill ghosts again.

Could it really be the medicine bag of the Indian brave that had travelled to live in England with the Sanderson family as Cherry had suggested?

He winced, eyes closing as he pictured the young woman with her blue hair, lip ring and attractive features, then he released a shaky sigh of regret, head shaking once more as he wondered how he hadn't realised that she was a ghost like Myra.

His stomach knotted as he recalled the pain in her eyes as she had shouted at him down in the ground floor hallway, eyes filled with sadness.

She had known all along that she was dead.

He grimaced as he suddenly wondered if she was one of those ghosts that Myra had claimed were forever trapped in the house after dying here, a victim of the Twelve, and their vile machinations.

Shaking his head, he rubbed at his eyes, recalling her story about how Agnes had killed her mother by scaring her suddenly, making her fall over the banister to her death, like the estate agent had.

Cherry had claimed she had been five at the time.

Was she like Myra? Still a child?

Had he only been seeing Cherry as an adult because Ms Sanderson imagined her that way, refusing to give up on her granddaughter, like he had with Myra?

No, if she had died from the fall like her mother then surely she would have bruises, or broken bones.

Instead her wrists were sliced wide open.

So, it had been suicide, most likely at the age she appeared to be now, most likely in the house.

Why else would she be here and the grounds?

He frowned as he realised that she had been further than the grounds of Sanderson House though, as far as the village green and the church.

Blinking, he turned to study Myra as she sat on the edge of the hatch, recalling that she too had been outside the grounds of the large estate. For a moment he studied her silently then frowned, "Ms Sanderson says that you have attached yourself to me"

Glancing up at him, she made a face, "Ugh, that sounds really weird…like, just ugh"

"Myra" he groaned, head shaking, "Please"

"What?"

"How far away from me can you go?"

"What does that mean?"

He shrugged, "I don't know…are there rules to this stuff…how far away from me can you move?"

She shrugged, "A ways"

"A ways?" he sighed in defeat, head shaking as he studied her and then he raised an eyebrow, "If I was to stay here could you leave and head out of the grounds and into the village?"

"Why would I go out there?"

"No" he shook his head again, "I don't want you to, I just want to know if you could…like move away from me…function on your own and stuff"

On the edge of the hatch, Myra frowned, head tilting to one side, "Why all the questions?"

He shrugged, "I am just curious"

The ghost nodded, "Is this about the woman?"

"Woman?" he eyed her in dread, "What woman"

"The ghost" she stated, eyes locked to his, "The ghost
that is always standing near that old lady"

"You've seen her?"

"The old lady?"

"No" he shook his head, "The ghost...the woman"

"Of course, I mentioned her didn't I"

Richard nodded, resisting the urge to argue with a
ghost, "So, I get that you have seen her with Ms
Sanderson but have you seen her on her own?"

The girl nodded, her features grim, "Yeah"

"Where?"

Her eyes drifted to look down the hole and the author
raised an eyebrow, both happiness and dread
coursing through him at the thought of seeing Cherry
again, "What? Is she down there?"

"No"

"So?"

"That's where she did it?" Myra made a face.

Richard felt giddy, "The bathroom?"

"No" she glanced down again, gesturing with a hand
below, "The bed, she sits there staring at it"

The bed. Where he had slept. She'd died there.

"Have you spoken to her?" his voice was soft, as if he
was suddenly unsure who might be listening.

"No, but she's smiled at me" Myra shook her head,
shrugging, "She seems nice for a grown-up"

"Hey" he fixed her with a stare, "I'm a grown-up"

"You wish"

He grinned, turning away from her, and rose, forcing the image of Cherry away as he stepped closer to the shelves and began leaving through the papers, "Let's see what we have here"

He turned as Myra gave a grunt of boredom, frowning in confusion as he found her standing on the edge of the hatch, "What are you doing?"

She shrugged, narrow shoulders shrugging, "This is boring...I'm going to explore"

He grimaced, head shaking, "It's not safe"

Her chuckle was humourless, "I'm already dead Richie...I can't be hurt remember"

"Yeah?" he gave her a sarcastic smile, "I am sure Agnes and that Elias dude thought the same"

She shrugged again, "The bag doesn't bother me, the others, The Twelve seem scared of it but it doesn't bother me or the others who died here"

"Really?" he raised an eyebrow, "That's odd"

"I guess"

Richard sent her a look, "Even if it doesn't hurt you, you have to watch out for the other ghosts, like Britt Sanderson...he tried to kill The Fever"

Myra's chuckle was genuine, "He only goes after those that have murdered people"

Richard winced, nodding at her as she continued talking, "Besides, when he does try and kill them they always come back when they remember they are already dead, that's all it takes. The moment they remember they are dead, their wounds heal"

He frowned, "What if he kills them before they remember...what then?"

Myra winced, head shaking, "The final death, there is no coming back from that...apparently"

He studied her for long moments in silence then sighed, "Promise me you'll be careful"

Her smile was mischievous as winked and faded away, her voice lingering, "Careful as mice"

Chapter Thirty Eight

Time lost all meaning as he sat in the attic room, ankles crossed before him as he slowly began to work his way through a huge pile of handwritten papers, amazed at the swirling scrawl of the authors writing, stunned as he studied dates to discover that many had been written over four hundred years before. It soon became clear that the papers were a form of documenting the hangings throughout the ages, and naturally, as Richard worked his way through them, he saw the writing change, as new people took over the job of recording the trials and then executions of the various criminals that had died on the Twins.

His stomach knotted as he read about the capture and execution of James Jackman; The Butcher, and William Haggerty; The Vessel, the events recorded by Laren's the brother of Abram.

Sighing, his eyes beginning to ache as he studied the old-style writing, Richard stifled a yawn with the back of his left hand and then picked another piece of paper up from the large pile beside him on the desk. Placing it atop those that he had already read upon his lap, the author yawned once more and then let his eyes drift over the writing, searching for familiar names then cursed softly as he recognised several that were written there;

On this day, 23rd of May 1713, the villains; Clemence Stoke and Elias Crumb, didst hangeth upon the Twins, the penalty f'r their crimes. We didst catcheth the villains in the midst of one such crime, as those gents did seek to dispatch one William Brand, b'rn of Copley.

The Wytch, as Clemence beest known, wast taken without struggle, yet the Devil; Elias Crumb, didst striketh two of our men boldly, killing both. We shalt grieve f'r thi'r loss and the loss of their families. At their trial at this house, Clemence didst confesseth h'r crimes, and yond of h'r lov'r, f'r the mute couldst not speaketh f'r hiself. fifteen men, both young and ag'd didst the beldams lure to their dwelling with promises of sinful pleasures, only f'r the Devil to striketh those folk cruelly down, their bodies and innards to beest hath used in h'r spells, their livings to supp'rt their living.

The lady didst pleadeth f'r h'r life, but not the life of h'r partn'r, f'r t wouldst seemeth yond affection wast largely one sid'd. Elias wast the hamm'r to h'r guile, a willing s'rvant to h'r plans, hath caught up in his loveth f'r h'r. W're t not f'r the termagant crimes that gent hast committ'd one might beest inclin'd to feeleth some s'rrow f'r the dull-witt'd sir.

Yet sineth is sineth, and wilt beest did punish acc'rdingly.

The villains w're taken to the Twins, Clemence sobbing while Elias hath walked fain, and nooses did place 'round their throats as wast customary.

Due to the sev'rity of their crimes, t wast hath decided by myself and mine own broth'r yond these two wouldst beest induct'd into the pact, securing those folk f rev'r to the twins, in the desire yond the purity of the oak, shall keepeth those folk lock'd hence, as with James Jackman, and William Hagg'rty bef're those folk. To this endeth, a toenail, a fing'rnail and a tooth wast remove from each and did place inside the medicine pouch of Chaqit, to secureth those folk to the Twins in the aft'rlife, unable to ado the living.

Then, those wretches w're hang upon the branches to danceth their lasteth jig togeth'r.

As is the way, mine own broth'r William hath carried out the executions in his role, inh'rit'd from our fath'r bef're us, Lars Sand'rson, son of the 'riginal execution'r Abram Sand'rson. I, Renauld Sand'rson, as young sibling, shall continueth to rec'rd the dead, and their crimes, so yond the w'rld may not judgeth us too harshly shouldst those gents discov'r what we doth h're. yet i wond'r, art we right to becometh jury, and execution'r? shouldst we not trusteth in the law of this landeth yond our ancest'rs hath chosen f'r us to groweth in? mine own mind is in conflict, and so i writeth high-lone, in this room, mine own thoughts troubl'd.

Renauld Sand'rson

Head shaking, Richard sat back on the old chair, grey eyes staring off into space ahead of him as he considered what he had read on the paper.

They had taken a fingernail, toenail and tooth from each of them before hanging them and placed it in the bag with those of James Jackman and William Haggerty. He grimaced at the sudden realisation that he had been carrying around a small bag full of the body parts of serial killers, stomach tightening as he recalled all the times that he had sat scraping his thumb over the piece sticking out of the small pouch. Was it a tooth? If so, whose had it been?

Fighting nausea as he pictured the tooth inside the mouth of Agnes or the Great Marlowe, he frowned, glancing down at the paper once more, re-reading the section about the pact. Was this their reference to those who would eventually grow in number to become the infamous Twelve?

Sighing, he rubbed at his eyes, realising suddenly how dark it had gotten with the small attic room, the meagre light that was provided by the small window above his head nearly non-existent now. Sighing, he moved the pile of papers from his lap to rest upon the desk beside those he had not yet read, and then rose and stretched his arms above him, eyes travelling up to stare at the dirty window in the sloping roof.

It was almost dark outside; the snow clouds no doubt making it seem even later than it actually was. Yawning once more, he turned and moved back to the hatch, crouching down as he swung his legs through the hole, feet reaching for the bookcase beneath him, cursing as he wished once more that he had thought to bring the ladder in from the grounds. After all, he had gone through so much to get it only to drop it and run in the wake of escaping Agnes, then forget it after Cherry's revelation downstairs in the hallway.

Shaking his head, he climbed down from the crude ladder he had created, stepping on to the mattress and then down to the floor, brow furrowing as he turned back to stare at the bed.

Cherry had died there. In that bed.

How could he sleep in it now, knowing that?

Yet where else was there for him to get rest?

Shaking his head, he rubbed at his eyes, and then cursed as he realised that he didn't know if Ms Sanderson had returned from the village yet.

How long had she been gone?

He had headed for the shed in the hollow, to retrieve the ladder then returned to the house, dispatched Agnes and Elias, and been attacked by others, then sat reading for God knows how long.

Had she returned to the house while he had been in the attic reading about her ancestor's deeds?

Grimacing, he headed for the door, hand grasping at the handle and then froze as he realised he didn't have the bag to protect him anymore, and while it seemed that the wounds the remaining Twelve were inflicting upon him were only illusions, he was still unsure about facing them without the protection the pouch afforded him. Gritting his teeth, he opened the door slowly, relief flooding him as he saw the pouch still sitting in the middle of the corridor, just feet from the door, then cursed as James Jackman appeared in the air a couple of feet beyond it, the overweight priest and the blonde woman appearing further down the hall. Cursing, he slammed the door and moved back to the bed, and laid down upon it, rolling onto his left side, his weary eyes closing.

His stomach tightened as he felt the bed move behind him, the mattress creaking as someone laid down and snuggled in against him, then he heard the soft voice of Cherry in his ear, and felt the cool touch of her hand as she stroked his head, "Sleep now, I will watch over you"

Chapter Thirty Nine

It was dark when he awoke, and for a moment he was unsure where he was, panic surging through him for a moment as he tried to remember what he had been doing just before falling asleep. The sudden memory of Cherry being upon the bed with him made him sigh heavily, his chest hurting with grief, and he rolled over, a heavy blanket of sadness settling about him as he found that the bed was empty apart from him. Had he just imagined Cherry there?

Shaking his head, he rose to sit on the edge of the bed, hands holding his forehead as he sat in the darkness, eyes gradually becoming accustomed to the gloom. Then he rose, walking past the crude ladder that he had made to the bathroom, pushing the door wide. He froze, heart lurching as he saw the two pale figures that turned towards him, his right hand instinctively reaching for the magical pouch only to remember that it was currently lost to him, and wincing he took a step back away from the ghosts. Both were children, the oldest, a boy of perhaps six, dressed in shorts and a blue sleeveless tee shirt with an image of the Thunderbirds emblazoned across the front, the other, a girl of maybe three in a cream summer dress. They stood side by side holding hands as they stared back at him, both dark-haired and smiling and as he blinked, the girl gave a soft excited chuckle, "Hello baby!"

"Shush" the boy gave her hand a gentle but not unkind shake as he held it, a smile on his face as he looked at her, "You'll wake him"

"What?" Richard blinked, dropping down to crouch so that he was facing the pair, "Who are you?"

The girl chuckled at his words, and the boy opened its mouth to speak only to grunt suddenly, eyes growing wide, blood running from his mouth in a torrent and Richard fell back to his rear, staring in horror at the stab wound that had appeared in the middle of the child's tee shirt. As the boy dropped to the ground, the girl sobbed, several stab wounds appearing in her tiny chest, blood soaking the cream dress as she fell alongside the boy, her voice filled with pain and terror as she cried out, "Daddy….where's my daddy"

"No" Richard made it to his hands and knees, not sure what he was going to do but unable to stand the sight of the children being brutalised before his eyes, then cursed as the bathroom door suddenly tight shut. Heart hammering in his chest, the author rose, hands grasping at the handle of the door as he tried to open it, cursing aloud as it appeared stuck then swung inward to reveal an empty blood-free bathroom.

"Fucking Hell" he winced, taking a step backwards away from the door then he jerked to the side, cursing as a voice spoke in the far corner, "Richard"

"Cherry?" he swallowed the tightness in his throat as he saw the shape standing in the corner, dread washing over him as he took a step towards her, "Is that you?"

She stepped forwards at his question, a sad smile on her perfect features, her body clad in the same clothes that she had been wearing downstairs and he winced as he saw the pain in her eyes. They held each other's gaze for a moment then he winced, head shaking, "Did you see them...the children?"

She nodded, the grim look on her features showing the truth of her words, "I did...it was awful"

"Who are they?" he turned to look at her, his guy twisting as he recalled their cries of pain, "And what the Hell just happened to them?"

"I don't know" she shook her head, glancing past him towards the bathroom, "It looked like something..."

"Killed them" he finished, grimacing, and she nodded, stepping closer so that they were almost touching, Almost a minute slipped by as he held the gaze of the attractive ghost, and then he sighed heavily, pain in his voice, "Why didn't you tell me...about you?"

Her lips twisted as she shrugged, "Would you have spoken to me...honestly?"

"Yeah...I guess...I don't know"

She laughed at his words and despite himself he smiled, watching as she moved to stand staring down at the bed in which they had been laying, her expression pained and he sighed, "Why?"

"I just told you" she shrugged once more, eyeing him curiously, "I didn't want you to not speak to me…I have a good feeling about you…I like you"

The seconds ticked by as he held his gaze across the bed and then he sighed, head shaking, "Besides, that wasn't what I mean then I asked why"

"Oh" she nodded, her eyes leaving his to settle back upon the bed and he cursed inwardly, wishing that he hadn't asked her the question regarding her suicide. A heavy silence settled upon the room, she staring at the bed, he staring at her, and then she spoke, her voice little more than a whisper, "I was at a low ebb…missing my mum, shunned by my grandmother who never wanted me to visit her here…and she is always here…and so I let myself in one day while she was at the village and made my way up here with my bags. I had decided to stay at the house whether she liked it or not…the previous owners had been dead for several years and there was no interest from new buyers…what could it hurt right?"

She glanced up at him, and he shook his head in confusion, "But you knew about the ghosts"

Cherry flinched as if struck and he cursed as he recalled that she had been present when Agnes Rand had made her mother fall to her death.

Of course, she knew about the ghosts.

Shaking his head, he opened his mouth to offer an apology then fell silent as she began talking once more, "I knew…I thought I could handle seeing the Twelve despite what gran thought"

He nodded at her words as she cast another glance at the bed then met his gaze once more, not wanting to rush her telling of her last moments of life, "After all, until mum died and granny sent me away to private school, I had spent five years living under this roof with them both. Trust me, I had seen all of the Twelve, and they didn't scare me much at all"

"So, what happened?" his voice was a whisper.

Cherry sighed heavily, "I was ready for all of the ghosts…all of them except hers"

"Hers?" Richard gave another frown, "Agnes?"

Cherry swallowed, "My mum"

Oh fuck.

Richard nodded at her words, trying to form an expression of sympathy but he was too stunned to do much more than wince at her as she continued to speak, "I had only been here an hour, granny still hadn't come back from the village and I decided to go down to the kitchen and make myself something to eat…she always kept the fridge well stocked for herself…"

"Go on"

She swallowed, haunted eyes locked to his, "I opened the door, and there she was, standing there in the hallway...watching me...I closed the door, I didn't know what to do but then she was in here...standing by the bed...watching me"

Richard suppressed a shudder, "What else?"

She shook her head, "Nothing...that was enough"

He blinked at her words, recalling his own similar conversation with Ms Sanderson down in the lounge when he had told her about the dark-haired woman that used to watch him all the time; when he slept and bathed, when he ate and watched television. Nodding in understanding, the hairs rising on the back of his neck at the memory of the woman returned to him in a heady rush, Richard winced at Cherry, "I really don't know what to say"

She gave a soft chuckle, dropping down to sit on the edge of the bed, her face turning to look back at him as he studied her, "I tried to speak to her but she didn't reply...she just stared at me...I couldn't bear the pain in her eyes...so I did it"

Richard turned his gaze to stare at the bed, grimacing as she suddenly lay back upon it, her eyes closed, and without giving it conscious thought his eyes drifted down to study her wrists, shaking his head slightly as he saw again the slits that ran vertically up her arm.

"And you know the worst part" Cherry's voice made him shift his eyes up to meet her gaze as she opened her eyes and turned to look at him.

"What?" he was almost afraid to ask the question.

She was silent for a moment, then, "After I did this, after I took my penknife from my bag and opened my wrists, after I gave it all up to be with her she still doesn't speak to me"

"Your mother?"

Cherry nodded, anger in her voice, "Yeah, she still just stands there, watching me...just watching"

"Oh God" Richard stared at her in shock, then sighed, "I don't want to ask but...when was this?"

"2015" she rolled on to her left side, an arm curling under her head as she held his gaze, "My granny found me several hours later. She didn't know at first, she walked in and saw me standing over by the door to the bathroom and asked what I was doing here...then she turned her head and actually saw me...the physical me on the bed"

"Jesus fucking Christ" Richard was unable to keep from swearing as he imagined the scene and the sheer horror both of the women must have felt.

Cherry gave a chuckle, "It was just a week before my thirty second birthday"

"Oh" he was surprised at how old she had been. "What?"

"Nothing"

"Tell me" she asked and he shrugged, sighing.

"I thought you were younger than that"

Her chuckle was bitter, "Before too long I will be one hundred years old and still look like this"

"Damn" he shook his head, moving over to sit on the edge of the bed, turning to meet her gaze again as he spoke, "Myra...young Myra...I have seen her again...she said you have seen her too"

Cherry nodded, still lying upon her side watching him, and he shrugged, "She seems to think, from having listened to the other ghosts, that if the Twelve are banished...like I did with Elias and Agnes then they will be able to move on"

She blinked, her lips pressing tight together and he tried to smile, "Wouldn't you want that?"

"I don't know" she shook her head, sighing, "I don't know what to think...I know I'm dead...I know I am a ghost...but I feel...so real...I don't want to just give that up and die..."

He winced, "This is all so confusing"

Cherry opened her mouth to speak then shook her head, her features tightening as she looked past him, and he followed her gaze, turning to find a blond haired woman standing against the far wall, her head bent slightly, her features pale.

Shivering in a mixture of shock and fear, he glanced back at Cherry to find that she was now sitting up beside him, his voice tight as he looked back at the woman, "Is that her?"

"Uh-huh" Cherry's voice was pained, "It is...and that's all she does...stands and watches me"

Richard nodded, eyes locked to the silent woman that was standing by far the wall staring at them, memories of his own watcher returning again.

"It's not her fault though" Cherry sighed heavily, and glancing at her, Richard saw her give a sad smile, "Granny says that its often the way with their kind...she says they are so filled with grief and pain all they can do is stand and stare at the children that they will never hold again"

Richard felt suddenly dizzy, his head shaking, his throat tight as he blinked, "Their kind?"

Cherry nodded once more, "Yes, mothers who were murdered in front of their children"

Chapter Forty

"He killed her" Richard rose to his feet on shaky legs, eyes staring down at the floor in shock for several moments before he turned and looked at Cherry, head shaking, "She was my mother"

"What?" the blue haired ghost shook her head, frowning as she stared up at him, "Who?"

He blinked, stepping away from the bed, a hand rising to his forehead as he cast his mind back to his childhood, and the woman that had always been there watching him, then grimaced as he recalled the times he had tried to tell his father and the woman he had thought was his mother. His father had always reacted angrily when he had mentioned the woman with the long dark-hair that stood watching him, exploding into outbursts of rage, and his mother...or the woman that had raised him, had always brushed his claims aside as if hearing them made them real. Yet now sitting there, casting his mind back over the decades Richard was able to picture the faces of the pair with disturbing clarity and for the first time he recognised their fear for what it really was, passed off as nothing more than anger and apathy as they shared quick, knowing glances.

A grim smile creased Richard's bearded features as he wondered how terrified his father must have been, to have killed his wife and then hear his son describing the woman to perfection. He must have been beside himself with terror, and that had become an anger that he had taken out on Richard while the ghost continued to watch him in complete silence. "She wasn't there to scare me" his words were barely audible as he stepped further away from the double bed towards the bathroom, past the woman that was still standing at the wall staring at Cherry, a ghost attached to yet another ghost. Yet with the small sense of satisfaction that he was feeling regarding his father's fear, a deep sense of pain and loss began to seep into him as he considered the woman that he had always just assumed was his mother. She had never once mistreated him in the slightest, if anything she had loved him too much. Agreed she had never tried to physically protect him from the beatings, but she was always there afterwards, tending to his wounds and apologising for his father's actions. Nausea washed over him suddenly as he considered her last days while he was in his late teens, her body all but destroyed by lung cancer, his waking moments dedicated to her care. To think now that she might have in some way been involved with the death of his real mother was a blow to the heart that he was unsure he could bear to handle.

Yet even if she had been involved, did it erase the love she had shown him until she died?

Perhaps her guilty looks had simply been down to the fact that he had been raised as her son, and she feared the truth of their relationship might ruin their bond. Perhaps his father had told her that Richards mother had left the pair of them.

After all, what woman in her right mind would stay with a man who had already killed one wife?

Of course, it was entirely possible that his father was himself innocent of Richards mother's death.

And pigs might fly.

The man had murdered a ten-year old girl.

He had killed Richard's mother without question.

Grimacing, he turned back to explain to Cherry the memories that her words had generated only to grunt in surprise as he realised she was gone.

And so was her mother, her own silent watcher.

Shaking his head, he moved to the door, opening it wide to stare out down the corridor ahead, his gaze instantly searching for the small pouch. It was there, where he had seen it last, untouched, and sighing, he stepped closer to the doorframe.

Eyes narrowing, he stared out at the long corridor ahead off him, turning his head slowly as he studied every inch of the area, searching for the ghosts he knew must be there somewhere.

They had him cornered in the safe bedroom.

They weren't going to let him walk out of here without attempting to hurt him in some way.

Licking his lips, Richard let his gaze drift to the pouch once more then cast another glance at the seemingly empty corridor, brightly lit by the series of lamps set into the ceiling overhead, a stark contrast to the dark bedroom he had awoken in. Grimacing, he glanced behind him, surprised to find that despite his eyes having grown accustomed to the gloom enough to talk with Cherry and see the ghost of her mother, now that he had been staring into the lit corridor the bedroom he had slept in was dark once more.

Night had fallen while he had been sleeping and he hadn't realised the implications until now.

Where the Hell was Ms Sanderson?

More than anything he wanted to rush from the room to go and find her but it wasn't that easy.

Cursing, he stepped back away from the door, his voice grim as he spoke, "Myra, where are you?"

Several minutes drifted past as he stood in the room, eyes scanning about occasionally for some sign that his childhood friend had returned from wherever it was that she had gone before he sighed, repeating her name, louder than before.

Yet still she did not come.

Grimacing, Richard stepped forwards a pace, eyes

locked to the small leather pouch that sat waiting for him in the centre of the hallway.

The medicine pouch of Chaqit.

Filled to the brim with the teeth, fingernails and toenails of the Twelve, whatever spells that bound the dozen spirits to the tree also turning the bag into a weapon capable of killing them.

The real death that nothing could return from.

He had already taken down two of them.

Just ten remained.

Ten.

That was all. Easy as pie.

And for his next trick…

Richard grimaced as he considered what would happen to the house once The Twelve had been banished. Myra had suggested that all the other ghosts would also be able to leave this place too.

But what of her and Cherry?

She was bound to him, and the latter seemed like she didn't want to leave her grandmother.

Her grandmother.

Ms Sanderson.

He grimaced as he considered the old woman, knowing that he was going to do all he could to make sure that she was OK. He owed her that.

Shaking his head, fighting the sudden urge to vomit that rose within him as he considered what it was he was about to do, Richard cursed under his breath and charged from the door.

Chapter Forty One

The moment he crossed the threshold of the door, there was movement to his left side as something materialised and he flinched away from it, angling his run to the right then grunted as something struck him on the right temple. Shocked, his vision blurred by pain, Richard staggered off balance for several steps and then fell to his knees, turning his head as he blinked rapidly, trying to see who had struck him. He grunted in dread as he saw the huge figure of James Jackman there, his right fist still raised in the air from where he had just punched Richard.

Head still ringing from the force of the blow, the author tried to stand, nearly fell and then made it to his feet, only to curse in shock as the ghost of the overweight priest, Father Ambrose Dewitt, charged at him from the left side of the door he had exited. The obese man struck him like a train, body slamming him back to the floor unlike their last encounter where Richard had passed through him, and the author grunted as he landed hard.

A feral snarl beside him made him twist as he tried to rise, his eyes leaving the forms of The Penitent Man and The Butcher to widen as he saw Clemence Stoke; The Witch crawling quickly towards him, her features twisted in raw hatred. In desperation he rolled away from her, then grunted as one of the feet of the priest stamped down on his left arm, his toenails long and twisted out of shape, blackened with dirt and mould, all except for one toe on his right foot where the nail was gone, leaving a bloody furrow in its place. Through his pain, Richard realised that was no doubt where they had taken the toenail for the bag of Chaqit, his eyes leaving the foot of his ghostly assailant to settle upon the pouch as it lay metres from where he was doubled up in pain.

Movement beyond the priest, snatched Richard's attention and he felt terror course through him as James Jackman loomed large behind his attacker, a thick fingered hand grasping at the other as if to move him aside so that he too could attack Richard. With a curse and snarl, the priest vanished, and the author all but screamed as the Butcher reached down for him, legs kicking wildly as he pushed himself away on the carpet. Suddenly Constance was scrambling atop him as he rolled to his side, intent on rising to his feet and he screamed out in raw terror.

"Tooketh him from me thee didst" her voice was near hysterical as her fingers scratched at his face, panic coursing through him as they neared his eyes, *"I'll has't thy eyes as payment!"*

"No!" his scream was filled with fear at the thought, his hands rising to grasp her wrists, desperately trying to stop her from blinding him, then behind him

Constance screamed in pain and surprise and suddenly fell away from his body. Mind reeling, blood running from the gouges she had carved into his features, Richard struggled to his knees and turned, eyes widening in disbelief as he saw Constance on the ground, hands reaching back as she tried to free her long black and iron hair from the tight grip of Cherry, the features of the blue-haired ghost a mask of anger. Richard muttered her name, stunned that she had come back and put herself in danger to save him, then cursed in dread as the busty blonde ghost that was still a mystery to him suddenly appeared behind Cherry, one arm wrapping about her throat while the other stabbed a blade repeatedly into her back, laughing maniacally. With a scream of shock, Cherry released her grip on Constance and turned to face her attacker, a punch soaring up to strike the blonde ghost in the face, the pair tumbling back to the floor. Shouting in anger, concerned for his friend, unknowing if ghosts could really hurt each other, Richard made it to his feet, a cry of warning leaving him as Constance rose and threw herself on the two struggling ghosts, screaming in hate. Unsure what he was intending to do, he hurried towards the pile of arms and legs, wincing as he heard a combination of the three fighting women screaming, and saw the knife rise in someone's hand, stabbing wildly into the back of another. At the last minute he saw the huge figure of James Jackman loom beside him and he cursed, having no more time to do anything flinch in dread before the huge ghost grabbed him and lifted him from the floor with embarrassing ease.

Almost mesmerized by the power of The Butcher as he was hefted high above the floor, Richard turned his head to stare down into the blank, almost serene features of the mass murderer, terrified by how calm the monstrous ghost was. Without warning, James Jackman dropped to one knee, his arms swinging down, and Richard screamed as he realised the ghost intended to break the authors back over his knee. Then without warning, the ghost dropped him to the side to land heavily on the hallway carpet, the authors eyes wide as he stared up as the Butcher rose to his feet, his scream like the bellowing of a bull in pain as he clutched the handle of the knife that was embedded to the hilt in his thick bull-like neck.

"Richie!" he turned at the voice, stunned to see the ghost of Myra standing there, glaring at the huge ghost of James Jackman as he dragged the blade free from his neck before fading quickly from sight.

As the blade fell to the floor, the young ghost turned to throw him a smile and he grimaced, hurrying to snatch the knife up only to grunt in dread as the ghost of the obese priest suddenly reappeared before him, a fat fist smashing down into his features, sending Richard crashing to the carpet. Through blurred vision he saw the pile of female ghosts, Cherry and the blonde woman struggling as they fought for possession of the knife, both sets of hands grasping to it as they swung left and right. With a scream Constance fell away from them as the blade slashed into her abdomen, then his vision was blocked as the ghost of the priest knelt astride him, hands fastening to his throat as it began to choke him. "*Foul miscreant...vile deviant...*" spittle flicked from the fat lips of the ghost as it leered down at him, its features almost red with rage, the pain of its thumbs digging into Richards throat almost more than he could bear. Blinking through tears, he stared up at his attacker, hands fastening to its wrists as he fought to free himself but leaning forward as it was, the weight of the ghost was too much for him to dislodge. He flicked his eyes to the side as he saw Myra rush in, knife raised above her head just as she must have stabbed James Jackman, and snarling, the priest swung an arm about, an open handed slap throwing the girl to the floor, "*Filthy dram cunt!*"

"You mother fucker!" Richard managed to snarl, a sudden rage coursing through him, his hands reaching for the face of the priest only to grunt in pain as the ghost hammered the hand that it had struck Myra with down into his unprotected face. Barely conscious, he lay there, his head turned to the side as he stared at Myra, surprised that she was already trying to rise once more, then his heart leaped as he saw what he was lying beside.

"*You are an abomination!*" the ghost of the priest snarled, his voice more a growl than actual words.

"After you!" Richard managed to mutter, his right hand rising from beside him to push the small black pouch against the bloated face of the priest.

With a scream of unbridled terror, the priest fell back away from him as if he had struck it with a sledgehammer, the ghosts legs kicking high as it landed upon its back. Grim faced, Richard made it to his hands and knees, watching in grim fascination as the ghost tried unsuccessfully to remove the pouch from its face but as with Agnes, it seemed stuck to him as if with magnets. The fire ignited with a rush, long tongues of flame quickly licking their way up the body of the ghostly priest, igniting his vestments as it went, until he was completely ablaze, and screaming. Rising to his feet, Richard turned his head, surprised to find a smile upon the face of Myra as she nodded at him, "Just nine to go Richie!"

He winced, nodding back at her and then turned to find Cherry kneeling on her own, the blonde ghost having vanished from sight. Concerned, he moved to her side, "Are you OK? Where is she?"

"Gone" the blue-haired ghost nodded, her voice weary, "As soon as that fire started, she fled"

He nodded, turning to watch as the flames shrouding the priest began to turn indigo, and inside the pyre the ghost started to come apart, pieces of him breaking off to fall to the hallway carpet.

"Is she OK?" Cherry asked, a hand gesturing and following it, Richard watched Myra standing before the flames, watching as the ghost burned wildly.

"She's OK I think" he nodded, rising to his feet and extending a hand down towards Cherry, "Can you stand? Are you hurt?"

"No more than you" she smiled grimly, taking his hand as she rose, and he raised an eyebrow.

"Eh?"

"Your wounds" she gestured and he raised a hand to his face, touching in the places where he knew that Clemence had torn at his cheeks, surprised to find his injuries had gone, like those inflicted on him by Frances, Dr Bennet and Agnes had done before.

They were still unable to hurt him completely.

Surely that meant that Ms Sanderson still lived.

Within the flames, the overweight ghost finally came completely undone, his body turning to ash, which began to rise, and drift towards the pouch that sat at the centre of the black mess until nothing remained of Father Ambrose Dewitt but bad memories.

"You did it" Myra gave a grin, and he turned to nod, gesturing at her and then Cherry beside him.

"We did it"

Myra gave a smile, flicked her gaze at Cherry and then shrugged, "She didn't do much but sure, whatever makes you look good in front of her"

Cherry gave a soft chuckle and shaking his head, Richard moved to where the pouch sat on the floor, bending as he scooped it up into his hand.

He tensed as there came a gasp from Cherry, and fearing the return of James Jackman or the arrival of the Great Marlowe, Richard rose and turned, brow furrowing as he saw she was fine.

"Cherry?" he began, stomach lurching as he saw the fear in her eyes as she stared past him, and as if in slow motion he turned, the ground seeming to drop out from under him as he saw the figure standing behind Myra, one hand clasping her mouth shut as it held her struggling form to his body, crushed features twisted in hatred as it snarled at Richard,

""Stupid...fucking...boy!"

Then the ghost of his father vanished, taking the terrified struggling figure of Myra along with it.

Chapter Forty Two

"No!" Richard rushed forwards to where the two ghosts had just been standing, concern for his childhood friend coursing through him as he turned to look back at Cherry, "He's taken her...oh my God, he's taken her from me again!"

The blue-haired ghost shook her head, her voice thick with dread, "Richard, who was that man?"

"My father" the words felt like poison in his mouth as he voiced them, his free hand forming a fist beside him, the right clenching tight to the small pouch he had regained, "He's the one who killed her"

"Oh God no" she shook her head, eyeing him in complete horror as she moved to stand before him. For a moment they held each other's gaze without speaking then he frowned, his head shaking, "I don't understand how he can be here"

She shrugged, "It must have been you"

"What?"

"He must be attached to you"

"Me?" he was aghast, head shaking at the thought of the violent, bitter man being permanently connected to him, "No, that cant be possible"

Cherry frowned, her eyes narrowing as she held his gaze, "There's no other way...unless he died here. For some reason he has attached himself to you"

Richard raised his free hand to rub at his forehead,

sighing heavily, "I don't see why"

"Was there any divining moments between the pair of you? Were you there at his death?"

"What?"

She gave a shake of her head, "How did he die Richard...he looks like he'd been beaten badly"

He grimaced, head shaking and she raised an eyebrow, taking a step back from him, "What did you do to him, Richard?"

"He killed Myra" his words were grim, his head shaking slowly as he held her gaze, "He strangled her with his bare hands...and now it looks like he murdered my birth mother as well"

She cringed at his words, her head turning partially away as she eyed him grimly, "You...you killed him?"

"He killed Myra" he stated, "She was ten"

"Richard" Cherry shook her head, "Richard"

"Ten years old" he repeated and before him, Cherry gave a sigh, smiling sadly as she nodded.

"Well, you killed him...that's reason enough for a spirit to attach itself to someone. Lots of spirits attach themselves to murderers"

Richard winced, "I'm not a murderer!"

She blinked, "Did you murder him?"

"He deserved it!" he was suddenly angry, his words spoken slowly, and Cherry nodded back.

"So, you murdered him...you are a murderer"

He shook his head, a hand gesturing at the house about him, "Maybe but I'm not like these…not like The Twelve…he deserved what he got!"

She nodded, "But still a murderer"

He winced, "You sound like him"

"Him?" the blue-haired ghost raised an eyebrow.

"Yeah, your ancestor" Richard grimaced, brow furrowed as he tried to remember the name that Myra had told him earlier that day, then nodded at Cherry, "Britt…Britt Sanderson"

She flinched at his words, fear in her eyes as she shook her head in disbelief, "You've seen him?"

Richard took a step towards her, nodding, "Huge, bald, handlebar moustache…yeah, I've seen him"

Cherry swallowed, nodding at him for a moment and then licked her lips, "What happened?"

"He attacked Dr Bennet; The Fever, he chased him away…then he called me a murderer"

The ghost winced, "What then?"

Richard hesitated for a moment, still angry that she had called him a murderer, however right she was, and then turned to walk away, "I haven't got time for this…I need to find Myra"

"Richard please, you don't know where he has taken her!" she moved to step alongside him as he walked down the long corridor towards the stairs, "We need to come up with a plan!"

"We?" he cast her a sideways glance, "You want to help me still...even though I'm a murderer?"

Cherry took the dig without biting, nodding as she met his gaze, "Of course, why wouldn't I?"

Richard smiled, relieved to have her support and then cursed, the pair of them pausing as in the distance the blonde-woman that had been fighting with Cherry suddenly appeared but she kept her distance, her eyes dropping fearfully to the pouch Richard held. Grimacing, the author began moving once more, eyes casting about for any sign of the other members of what was left of The Twelve, his free hand gesturing towards the blonde ghost, "Tell me about her, Cherry, who is she?"

"Lydia Tanner; better known in her day as The Widow's Wail" the voice of the blue-haired ghost was thick with what sounded like disgust," She was the seventh to become one of The Twelve"

Casting her a glance filled with confusion, Richard angled his walk, taking them further near the wall on the wide of the corridor that the stairs touched, his eyes drifting back to rest upon the voluptuous blonde woman, "Widow's Wail?"

"She got the name from the sound she perfected at funerals...twelve times to be exact"

The author frowned, casting the blonde ghost a final glance as they reached the top of the stairs and turned to moved down them, "She had twelve husbands?"

"That we know of" Cherry confirmed with a grimace, her voice cold, "Like Clemence Stoke nearly a hundred years before her, Lydia used her charms...well, her tits, to seduce men into having affairs with her and leave their wives, naming her in their wills"

"OK" he nodded at her, turning as they reached the mid-way landing to the first floor, "And?"

"And then she would kill her new husbands, some with poison, some with a blade. She did the latter five times and each time claimed that her husband had been attacked while travelling home and had arrived at the door near death, or feigned break-ins at their home in which her brave husband had died protecting her virtue"

She gave a bitter chuckle as she finished talking and Richard sent her a puzzled look, "Tell me"

"What?" the blue-haired ghost shook her head, trying unsuccessfully to hide the anger in her brown eyes.

"Tell me what she did" the author persisted, "Please"

She paused as they reached the first floor landing, her head shaking slowly, "My mother fell to her death because of Agnes Rand; The Cook"

"OK" he nodded, brow furrowing, "Go on"

"The Widow's Wail is responsible for the death of my

father several years before that...I was only about three but I have these vague memories of my father and mother shouting at each other, she is angry about something and keeps saying that he has betrayed us both...I think...I don't know. Gran was there...she was angry...she is shouting at my father...accusing him of touching *her*...I think he has had an affair...then mother carries me downstairs...father and gran are still arguing up on the second floor...then he screams..."

Cherry fell silent, head shaking and Richard grimaced, "What...what happened?"

The blue-haired ghost shrugged, "We heard the bumps as he fell down the stairs, father broke his neck...gran told us that Lydia; The Widow's Wail had rushed at him as he was starting to follow us down, and he got startled and fell to his death"

"Holy shit" Richard grimaced as Cherry nodded before him, the pair of them continuing on down the stairs towards the second floor, the author unable to stop picturing the grim smile upon the face of the old housekeeper the night before as she had asked if he had made his father pay for what he had done to Myra so many years before.

Suddenly, unsure if he was the only living murderer within the walls of Sanderson House.

Chapter Forty Three

"So where do you think your father has taken poor Myra?" Cherry asked as they reached the ground floor, edging their way among the boxes and furniture and shaking his head, Richard turned.

"I have no idea; he shouldn't be here...can you sense them within the house anywhere?"

She gave a soft chuckle at his words, her head shaking, "It's not like that...I don't have a radar for other ghosts...this place is solid for me...I don't have special powers"

"I've seen you vanish...well, I've turned and you have been gone" he pointed out, and she shook her head, a strange smile upon her features as she studied him. "When?"

"Upstairs...just after you told me about your mother still not talking to you...I mentioned my mother then turned around and you were gone"

"No" she shook her head, "I was still there, you opened the door...stared into space...stepped back, called for Myra, then ran out...I moved to the door to see what you were doing and that's when I saw the ghosts attacking you so I pulled Clemence from your back..."

Richard blinked, "I couldn't see you there"

"Layers" she nodded, gesturing about them with her hands, "There are layers all around us"

"Layers?" he shook his head, "I don't understand"

She nodded once more, "Imagine that I did a big drawing of this house on a piece of card"

"OK" he nodded, unsure what she was getting at.

"Right, after that initial drawing, I am going to get a piece of tracing paper and draw a circle for each one of The Twelve and the others ghosts that were executed on the Twins OK?"

Again he nodded and she continued, her eyes locked to his face, "On another piece of tracing paper I am going to draw the house again but then I am going to draw a circle on that to represent each ghost that is here because it died here...then on another piece I will draw the house again and draw a circle for each ghost here because they are attached to someone"

"Like Myra and my father?"

She nodded, "Yeah, then on one more piece I am going to draw the house one more time and add a circle for the living people that live here or visit"

Richard gave a shake of his head, "I am confused"

"Bear with me" she smiled, hands gesturing as she continued, "Imagine now I lay the drawing on card down on the floor then I am going to place the pieces of tracing paper on it one at a time"

"OK" he raised an eyebrow, trying to picture what she was talking about, "Then what?"

She gave a smile, "We would be able to see the house and it would look like all of the people and ghosts were together...but in reality, each set of ghosts and people is on their own layer...some, like The Twelve, myself and Myra are able to move sideways through layers into the layers of others...others stay in their own layer...unseen"

Richard blinked, surprised to find that he actually understood what she meant then frowned, "So when I thought you'd vanished in the bedroom...when The Twelve vanish...they are actually still in that place?"

Cherry nodded, "Yeah, just in their own layer where you can't see them"

"Holy fuck"

She eyed him curiously, "That's how the world is. Layers upon layers. Most people are oblivious to it. Yet every now and then there are those, like you and my gran, who can see through layers"

"What about sightings of ghosts by others?"

She shrugged, "In some places the layers are paper thin, allowing people with no psychic to see ghosts and for ghosts to travel through"

He winced, head shaking as something occurred to him and she stepped forwards, "What is it?"

He studied her in silence for a moment, eyes

travelling over the features of the blue-haired ghost and then he spoke, his voice thick with dread, "And if a ghost didn't want to be found?"

She winced, no doubt realising what he was hinting at, "They would stay in their own layer"

"How are we going to save Myra?"

She shook her head at his words, obviously having no better idea than he and he grimaced, spinning away to stare at the front door, "I first saw him out there in the hollow…he was in the shed…could he have taken her there?"

"Why would he?" she shook her head at him.

He paused before answering, stomach knotting as he recalled the day that he had found his father kneeling over the dead body of his young friend, then he spoke, his voice shaky, "The shed…it looks like the place where he killed her…the place where I…well…you know"

"Murdered him" her voice was barely audible.

He nodded, shrugging, "Yeah, I'm a murderer, we established that…your ancestor called it right"

"Britt" she breathed his name as if in fear and he shook his head as he studied her, brow furrowed.

"You need to tell me about him. He is the last of The Twelve I don't know anything about…no, wait…" he frowned, counting through names in his head, "That still only makes eleven I've seen"

Cherry winced, glancing about the hallway as if she expected her ancestor to suddenly appear beside them both, then she met his gaze once more, her features grim, "The one that you haven't seen yet is Edward Albright...the former best friend of Britt Sanderson and the last of the executed to become one of The Twelve before Britt became the final one"

"His best friend?" Richard shook his head, mind racing as he tried to imagine how someone could execute their best friend, then he nodded, "Then we find Myra and get her back"

The blue-haired ghost stayed silent as she nodded back at him in agreement, her smile sad.

Chapter Forty Four

"Edward Albright used to be the owner of the Hangman's Rest" Cherry stated several minutes later as she stood close to Richard under the porch beyond the front door of Sanderson House, the blue-haired ghost insisting they leave the building before she began talking about her ancestor Britt Sanderson. "The Hangman's Rest?" Richard gave a confused shake of his head, "Where was that? A local pub?" She turned, gesturing with an arm out into the darkness, and he followed the gesture, his eyes staring out through the snow that was still falling heavily, the blanket it had laid now two feet deep. Blinking as a gust of wind blew snow in at him, Richard sighed, wondering just what had become of Ms Sanderson during her trip to the village earlier. Before heading out under the porch, they had briefly searched the downstairs of the property, and discovered that Ms Sanderson was nowhere to be seen at all. Panic stricken, Richard had suggested to Cherry that her grandmother might have gone upstairs to sleep, but the ghost had disputed it, pointing out that whenever she was at Sanderson House the housekeeper would always leave her coat resting upon the back of one of the kitchen chairs. However both she and her coat were absent.

"The Hangman's Rest was the Inn at the bottom of the

village green, the large empty building" the voice of
Cherry had him forcing himself from his thoughts to
study her, an eyebrow rising slightly in surprise.
"Me and Myra were looking at that the other day"
She nodded at his words, "It hasn't been open since
November 1870...following the execution of Edward
Albright for his crimes"
"What did he do?"
She smiled but it didn't reach her eyes, "Do you
remember me telling you last night that the church
was built after the Sanderson family, my family, had
lost their sway over the village"
Richard nodded, recalling sitting with her beneath
the lychgate of the church during the bad storm.
God that seemed so long ago now.
Had that really only been a day ago?
Before him, Cherry turned and stepped to the edge of
the porch, her gaze tilting as she stared up at the dark
sky overhead, a sad smile creasing her features as she
studied the falling snow in silence, then turned to
look back at him, "Britt Sanderson became the family
hangman back in 1847 at the age of thirty one,
inheriting the position from his father Thomas.
Unlike a lot of the other hangmen, Britt had been an
only child, and so it had been left to him to not only
hang those that were deemed a threat but to also
record the deeds that he had done, like the family

scribes before him. Once done, Britt would often seek solace at the Hangman's Rest, where over the course of the next thirty years he built up a powerful friendship with its owner Edward"

"But Edward was a murderer" Richard stated, and she nodded, her features grim as she replied.

"Oh, if only he had been a murderer…alas the foul deeds of Edward Albright earned him the name the Collector, and the enmity of Britt"

"The Collector?"

She nodded, "Edward had rooms for rent at The Hangman's Rest, a name he had chosen in tribute of his friendship with Britt, and for the most part he was a hospitable and fair host. Yet every now and again, a traveller would arrive at Evenfield with no companions, and Edward would make it his business to ply them with drink to find out where they had come from and where they were headed to. If they had no-one expecting them or no general destination, then Edward would drug their drinks, and sneak into their room in the night to abduct them while they were in a stupor.

"Where did he take them?" Richard frowned, stepping to the edge of the porch alongside the ghost, staring into her eyes as he gave a frown of confusion. Her smile was cold, "Beneath the Inn, in a backroom adjoining the store, Edward had built an area capable of holding four people at a time"

"Like a prison?" the author shook his head and Cherry gave another humourless chuckle, her head shaking slightly as she held Richard's confused gaze.

"No, in a prison you get food and water, and you don't get tortured...however those that Edward decided were worthy to be a part of his people zoo as he called it were tortured daily"

"God" he shook his head, "That's insane"

She nodded, "Yes, common tortures were the removal of eyes, fingers, toes, ears and noses, but Edward was not afraid of sexually assaulting his prisoners either, no matter the gender, and seemed to take great delight in forcing them to torture and rape each other at his command, perhaps hoping that to do so would win them their freedom...it never did...anyone who entered the people zoo of Edward Albright died...but none of them died as quickly as they might wish"

Richard let out a low whistle, head shaking as he considered her words, imagining how desperate and terrified the poor prisoners must have been.

Grimacing, he met the gaze of Cherry once more, his voice grim, "And all of this went on right under the nose of Britt Sanderson?"

"For thirty years"

"Fucking Hell" the author winced, "That's mad, he knew what the village did to killers...he knew that his best friend was the current hangman but still he did it...that's utterly insane"

"It is...three of The Twelve were executed while he was in charge of the Hangman's Rest and secretly murdering unfortunates; Father Dewitt; The Penitent Man, Dr Edwin Bennet; The Fever, and The Great Marlowe were all captured and hung from the Twins while he was killing in secret, in fact he even helped with the capture of the Great Marlowe after the clown had eaten poor Jessica King"

"Fucking Hell"

"And each time, following the executions, Britt Sanderson would come to the Hangman's Rest and sit in the corner of the Inn, sharing a drink with his best friend, opening up about what he had done and how it made him feel inside"

Richard raised an eyebrow, "You make it sound like old Britt wasn't fond of his lifestyle"

Her smile was sad in the darkness, illuminated only by the light shining through the small pane of glass set into the front door, "He hated it, Britt was at heart a gentle soul...he hated killing"

Richard frowned, "He looks like a madman"

She nodded at him, gaze drifting up and down him for a moment before she shrugged, "And you don't look like a murderer"

"Touché"

They held each other's gaze in silence for a moment and then she shrugged, "When Britt found out by pure chance what his friend had been doing, he lost control of his rational thought. This was a man who he had confided in about everything. A man who he would have died to protect. To find out that the man had been killing under his nose for so long…in such a manner was too much for him to bear. After executing Edward upon the Twins, he ordered the Inn closed down, as a shrine to those that had died there though it may also have been because the building held so many memories for him"

"How many people did he kill?" Richard asked.

"The Collector?"

He nodded, and she shrugged, "Over fifty, many of them he kept alive for months at a time, and by his own admission, one prisoner was at his mercy for nine years before she finally died"

"Nine years!" Richard was incredulous, "Fuck"

Cherry nodded, "Imagine nine years of torture"

"What happened next…you said that the Inn was forced to close…but how did the Sanderson family lose their sway over the village? Was it because Britt hadn't known about Edward?"

"Oh no" she smiled sadly, "Apparently, the village had been as equally shocked as he, and they held no-one responsible for The Collectors long reign of terror but the killer himself"

"So?" Richard shrugged, "What went wrong?"

"Britt" she winced, "After discovering that his best friend, a man that he had trusted above all others had been killing people, Britt lost his ability to trust anyone…as if caught up in some form of zeal to make amends and catch killers, he saw villains at every turn, and over the next two years he sent over fifteen people to the Twins, many of whom were believed to be innocent of the charges against them"

"Fucking Hell" the author grimaced as he recalled the mania that he had seen in the eyes of the big ghost as it had stormed towards him, "Shit!"

Another silence descended upon the pair of them then Cherry sighed, "In November 1872, the villagers of Evenfield had endured enough, and fuelled by the fear that the authorities might discover what the village had been a party to for centuries due to the growing carelessness and mania of Britt Sanderson, they lured him from Sanderson House with a tale of a man in the next village who had murdered his lover, and set about him in a mob of thirty men or more"

Richard blinked, head shaking and she nodded at him, "I know right…even then, mania increased by this fresh betrayal, Britt managed to kill seven of the men before he was finally subdued, and brought to the Twins"

"To be executed?" he nodded, his voice grim.

"Yes, they had seen enough of the other executions to know what needed to be done. So a fingernail, a toenail and a tooth was removed from him, and placed within the bag, that bag in your hand" she gestured to the pouch he still held, "And then he was hung until he was dead"

For several seconds, Richard studied her in silence, head shaking and then he raised an eyebrow, "What happened to the rest of your ancestors at that time?"

She smiled grimly, "They were left untouched, and allowed to continue living within the house. By that time the ghosts of the previous members of The Twelve had been sighted by villagers who had visited the house. None of them wanted to take the house on and live there. Besides, they had all heard the stories by then about how when the last of the Sanderson bloodline was gone The Twelve would be free to take their revenge. The people of the village knew the part they and their own ancestors had played in all the executions and the thought of The Twelve coming for revenge terrified them. So, they let my family remain in the house, though over the past century they have taken control of its ownership and reduced my family's role to that of housekeepers or watchmen"

"And now your gran is the last" Richard turned to stare out into the snowy darkness, a grim smile creasing his bearded features, "The villagers must be shitting themselves"

"Good" Cherry gave a soft chuckle, eyes sparkling.

"We need to find her though" Richard met her gaze once more, "I need to make sure she is OK"

For a moment, Cherry stared at him in silence and then she frowned, "What about Myra?"

Richard sighed heavily, shrugging, "She's already dead, I need to put the living first for a change"

Chapter Forty Five

Grim faced, Richard strode onward through the deep snow covering the path from the house, his right hand clasped tightly to the pouch that was within the pocket of the coat that he wore, his left aiming the torch that Cherry had directed him to find in the kitchen, ahead of him, the thin light cutting through the darkness, illuminating the snow that continued to fall in heavy sheets. When he had been retrieving the torch from its hiding place in a cupboard under the sink, he had noticed the kitchen clock, surprise touching him as he realised that it was only seven PM and not the middle of the night as he had assumed when he had awoken in the bedroom with Cherry. Which meant that the elderly Ms Sanderson, while still missing, had actually not been missing for as long as Richard had feared she had been.

He winced as he walked, wishing that the blue-haired ghost had accepted his request to come, but she had declined, wanting to stay back at the house in case Myra somehow managed to escape his father. Grimacing at the thought of how the ghost of the vile man had abducted Myra once again, Richard cursed, and shook his head, trying to concentrate on his task. Ahead of him, the torchlight shone upon the stone gateposts, and he aimed the light on the snow between them, and continued onwards, pausing as he left the grounds of the Sanderson estate to swing the torch beam left and right along the road that cut through the village. As he had expected there was no vehicles in sight, the snow upon the road deep and unbroken, and as he stood staring at the area Richard found it impossible to tell where the path he was standing on, the road itself and the actual village green connected to each other. Shaking his head, casting another quick glance in each direction, he took a step forwards, cursing as his foot dropped down further than it would to the road surface buried beneath the deep snow, and off balance he fell forwards, gasping in shock as his bearded features landed on the cold surface. Grimacing, he released his hold on the pouch as he struggled to rise, hands pushing into the snow as he fought to get his legs under him, the torch clasped in the ice cold fingers of his left hand, stomach tight as he imagined what would happen if by some miracle a car or lorry came around the curve of the country road right then. Driven by the fear of being crushed by some out of control vehicle, the author pushed himself forwards, practically crawling onto the higher area that he knew was the village green and rolled to his back, staring up into the snow as it fell upon his face. Sighing, his hand holding the torch resting down by his side he reached into his pocket with the other, making sure he hadn't inadvertently lost the pouch. Satisfied that it was there, the author rolled to his side and then his knees, forcing himself up to his feet to stare through the falling snow at the lights in the windows of the village beyond the green.

Nearly a minute drifted by as he let his gaze drift over the village, his brow furrowing as his eyes settled upon the large shape of the abandoned Inn, head shaking as he pictured what had gone on beneath it, then he was walking once more, striding through the snow, his passage slow. Angling his path towards the houses on the side of the Post Office, Richard crossed the village green, slipping several times as it began to slope downwards, and then fell once more as he reached the road that curved around the village in an arc before re-joining the main road again.

Cursing, he struggled to his feet, shivering as the chill from where the snow had made his jeans and coat damp starting to spread throughout his body.

Head shaking, he reached the first of the houses, and knocked upon the door, his brow furrowing as the light within turned suddenly off as if the people inside were trying to pretend they weren't home. Shaking his head, anger touching him, Richard knocked again, calling through the letterbox, "I saw the light…I know you are there!"

Yet still there came no reply and cursing once more, Richard stepped to the door of the house beside it, hands knocking first upon the window of the property and then the front door, "Hello!"

He took a step back in surprise as the front door wrenched open, a large man with short silver hair and a black and silver beard filling it as he stepped outside, "Who the fuck are you?"

"Woah easy" Richard raised his hands, his left pointing the torch skyward, "I'm looking for Ms Sanderson...the housekeeper at the big house"

He gestured with his right hand as he spoke, watching as the big man glanced in the direction of the house and then met his gaze again, "What do you want with her, like?"

"She's my housekeeper" the author slowly lowered his hands, nodding as he spoke, "My names Richard, I have just moved in up there"

Once more the big man glanced at the house and then met his gaze once more, head shaking, "She's not here...I don't know why you thought she would be"

"No" Richard sighed, realising the man's error, "I didn't think she would be here...I'm just trying to find her...she told me she was coming to the village earlier...but she hasn't returned yet"

The big man frowned, "Maybe she's gone home?"

"Yeah" Richard nodded, sighing as he spoke, "See that makes sense but she made a point of saying that she was coming back to the house…I fully get that maybe by the time she got down here the snow was too bad and she went home, but I don't want to risk her having had an accident…does that make any sense?" The big man frowned, lips pressing together as he studied Richard as if he was trying to decipher what the author had said and then he gave a nod, a hand reaching back inside the front door to return with a thick black donkey jacket which he slid his arms into. Confused, Richard watched as the man turned and shouted back in through the door, "Jayne, where are you woman?"

"Don't you woman me, Ian" a busty woman appeared in the doorframe as the door opened wider, giving Richard a brief view inside their home, a smile creasing his features as he spotted several horror movie posters. He blinked as he saw the woman studying him curiously, her attention flicking to the big man, "Who is this, and where are you going at this time of night?"

The large man, Ian, gave a nod of submission despite being almost twice the size of his wife, a hand gesturing towards Richard, "Old Margaret Sanderson has gone missing from the big house, I'm gonna help…what's your name again mate?"

"Richard" the author nodded at the big man, turning to do the same to the woman, "Richard Miles...I've just moved in at the big house"

"Right" the woman nodded, her gaze flicking between the men, "What's this about Margaret?"

"She's gone missing" the big man sent Richard a weary look before shaking his head at his wife, "I swear you don't listen to me! If it was Woody Allen you'd be paying attention wouldn't you"

"Oh fuck off" the woman gave a laugh, "Twat"

"Right, come on, I'll help you" Ian nodded at Richard, "We'll have a quick scan about the village and if we cant find her, we'll stop by her cottage...Jayne, you phone round and ask if anyone has seen her alright?"

The blonde woman nodded, stepping back inside the house and closing the door, and sighing, Ian gestured for Richard to start walking with him, "Right where have you looked?"

"Just the green" the author winced, "I came from the house and yours was the second house I tried, your neighbours turned their light of when I knocked"

"No-one's lived there since old Maude died a few months back" Ian cast a glance back at the house as they walked down the slope towards the village hall, his brow furrowed, a sad chuckle escaping him, "Mind you, that's what she'd do if anyone knocked after dark, switch her light off and pretend she wasn't there, funny old bird she was...come on, let's try the village hall"

Nodding at his new companion, Richard cast a glance back at the house beside Ian and Jayne's himself, a deep sense of sadness coursing through him as he saw the old lady standing in the upstairs window watching them walk away, yet another ghost.

"Woody Allen?" he asked suddenly, quickening his pace to keep up with the big man and Ian chuckled, his head shaking as he met the authors gaze.

"Jayne's obsessed, she can't get enough of Woody" Richard laughed, head shaking and beside him, Ian sent him a mischievous grin, "There's no understanding lasses, Richard my old mate, it's like my Catholic priest friend always says...women, you cant live with them...and you can't live with them"

Unable to stop the grin creasing his face, Richard gave a laugh and followed his large companion on through the snow, his humour fading as he began to worry about the elderly Ms Sanderson once more.

Chapter Forty Six

Wincing as they stepped out of the darkness of the village into the brightly lit reception of the village hall, Richard thumbed off the torch, and followed Ian as the big man headed through the main set of doors into the large hall beyond.

As they entered, the doors clattering back either side of them, a thin, bearded man that was sweeping the floor at the end of the room glanced up, frowning at Richard before he realised who he was with, and chuckled, "Ian!"

"Neil" the big man strode up to him, nodding as he glanced about, "You ain't seen old Margaret on your travels this evening, have you?"

"Maggie?" the thin man stroked his pointed beard, eyes narrowing in concentration behind his glasses and Richard realised with amusement how much the man bore an almost uncanny resemblance to the comedian David Baddiel. After several moments the man shook his head, frowning as he saw Richard studying him, "No, I haven't seen her since Tuesday, she was in here asking me about the next Huffs and Buffs event"

"Huffs and Buffs?" the author raised an eyebrow. Beside him, Ian gave a chuckle, "It's a local thing, the old folks get together a few times a year for a dance and a bit of dinner, I cant remember where the name came from…Neil?"

"I've got no idea" the younger man shook his head, then fixed Richard with a stare, "Who are you, then?"

"This is Richard Miles" Ian answered for the author before he could even move his lips, "He's just moved in to the big house up on the hill"

"Oh" Neil gave him that look that everyone had seemed to do so far, a mixture of surprise that someone had moved in there and a village's natural distrust of strangers, "And you are trying to find old Maggie? What's she done now?"

Richard winced, head shaking, "Done? Nothing. She was headed down into the village earlier to get some supplies…then this snow came down, I just want to make sure that she's OK"

"Ah" Neil waved a hand, "She's a tough one is old Maggie, tougher than us three put together"

"He's not wrong" Ian gave a throaty chuckle.

For a moment, Richard nodded, smiling, and then he shrugged, "Still, I'd like to make sure she's OK"

The man named Neil fixed him with a curious look, as if stunned that his words hadn't been enough to convince the author, and then he gave a shrug, "Well, as I say, she's not been in here"

Richard winced, and Ian nodded, clapping a hand on the shoulder of his fellow villager, "No harm done,

Neil, we'll keep looking, give my love to the family"
The younger man nodded, glancing at Richard, "Nice
to meet you, Mr Miles"
"Yeah, likewise" Richard began, but then the man
named Neil was hurrying off across the large hall as a
telephone began to ring in the distance, his voice
calling back to them, "I better get this"
Chuckling, the large man named Ian gave Richard a
nudge, "Come on, let's keep looking for her"
As one they turned, heading out through the double
doors to the reception and then stepped back out
under the heavy snow, Richard thumbing his torch
back on while Ian gave a shake of his head, "It hasn't
come down like this decades, a proper bad one this
and no mistake"
Richard nodded, the pair of them falling into step
beside each other, only to turn back as the man
named Neil suddenly called out to them both.
"Hey, hold up"
"What's up?" Ian gave him a grin as Neil stopped
under the edge of the village halls porch, hands
rubbing at his arms, teeth chattering together.
"That were your missus on the phone" Neil explained,
jerking a thumb back into the hall, his features grim.
"Oh?" Ian raised an eyebrow, "What's up?"
Neil winced, glancing from Ian to Richard and back
again, "She's phoned round and found Maggie"

"Is she OK?" Richard took a quick step back towards the village hall and Neil, Ian moving alongside him. Neil winced, hands raising before him, "Calm yourself, the vicar has her in the church, it seems she took a bit of a tumble there earlier today"

"Oh fuck me" Richard felt sick, his head turning to stare out across the snowbound village green.

"How is she?" the deep voice of Ian asked, etched with concern, drawing Richards attention back on the pair, "Is she going to be OK, Neil?"

The bearded man gave a shrug, head shaking, "I don't know, Dr Chapplow is over with them now apparently, do you want me to come with you?"

"No" Ian began walking towards the green, Richard falling back in beside him as the big man called back to the younger man, "We'll let you know how she is"

Head aching, mind racing, Richard fought the urge to charge headlong across the snowy green, knowing that if he were to attempt it he was going to end up falling and possibly hurting himself badly.

That was the last thing he needed to do.

So instead, he kept pace with the larger man as best as he could, trying not to let his emotions show on his face as Ian glanced back at him, "I hope its nothing too serious, no way the ambulances are going to be able to get to the village any time soon"

Oh God. And if she dies, the village is fucked.

Richard frowned as he considered his thoughts, glancing up at the side of the large man's features, seeing his jaw muscles clenched tight in his cheeks.

Did he know the legends?

Did he know that if Margaret died The Twelve would be unleashed on the village of Evenfield?

Or was it genuine concern for Ms Sanderson.

Shaking his head, trying to keep from voicing his thoughts, realising how mad he would sound if the big man had no knowledge of the Sanderson legends, Richard walked on beside him in silence.

Ahead of the church loomed out of the falling snow, the old wooden lychgate already bearing more than it looked able to stand atop it, and wincing, fearing it might collapse upon him at any moment, Richard followed Ian through it and left, following a winding path amid the graves until they found themselves at a small side door. Without hesitating, Ian knocked and entered, the door swinging open before him with a creak, and feeling sick with concern for the old woman, Richard followed, stepping inside the church. For a moment, he stood there alongside Ian, turning off the torch and placing it in a pocket, his brow furrowing as he let his gaze drift quickly over the rows of wooden pews, set at certain intervals by metal stands topped with wrought iron candelabra, his eyes moving past them to settle upon the altar and the pulpit at the front of the church, then he saw the group of people crouched near the front aisle.

"Ian?" a man in a vicar's robes rose to his feet, taking a step in their direction, the thin face beneath the silver hair etched with concern as he watched them.

"Vicar" Ian nodded as he and Richard reached the group, a large hand gesturing to the author, "This is Richard Miles, owner of the big house, he's been out in the snow looking for Maggie"

"Richard" the vicar nodded, smiling grimly as he extended a hand, taking the authors in his own for a moment before gesturing to the small group that was crouching on the floor, "I am afraid Margaret has taken a tumble while placing flowers in the graveyard earlier, she has hit her head on the ground…"

"Oh God" Richard cursed, then winced as he realised his location, but the vicar seemed not to notice as he gestured for the author to join the small group.

Taking a deep breath, Richard stepped forwards, nodding at the three faces that turned to glance up at him, a middle-aged woman in a coat and glasses, and a young couple, then cursed beneath his breath as he saw the figure of Ms Sanderson lying upon the ground, a pillow under her head and blankets atop her frail form. Without giving it conscious thought, he rounded the trio, crouching down beside the old woman as he took her right hand in his own, wincing as he felt how cold her skin was, concern growing as he saw the large plaster on her right temple.

Releasing a shaky breath, Richard glanced up as the woman with the glasses spoke, "I am Dr Chapplow…Margaret has taken quite a fall and we need to get her to hospital ASAP"

He winced, head shaking, "Ian said that the roads are too blocked with snow for the ambulances"

The doctor nodded, "I am afraid he's right"

Richard blinked, feeling as if the ground had dropped out from beneath him, "So, she'll die?"

Time dragged as the doctor held his gaze in silence and then she winced, "We have to prepare ourselves for the worst I am afraid"

The worst. The Twelve.

God have mercy on us all.

Chapter Forty Seven

As if on some unspoken cue, the young couple rose and moved to stand speaking with the vicar and Ian, and Richard watched them for a moment before meeting the gaze of the doctor as she gestured towards them with a nod, "Nathaniel and Layla live in the house beside the church, they heard Margaret's cries and alerted the vicar"

"Why is she in here and not a house?" Richard asked, trying to keep the sudden anger from his voice.

"That was their intention however each time that Nathaniel lifted her, she cried out in pain. The vicar thought it best to bring her inside the church, and Layla brought blankets and the pillow from their home. If they hadn't heard her crying out for help she would have frozen to death out there"

He nodded at her words, eyes drifting to the long haired young man with the glasses and the young woman with the bobbed hair, neither looking to be older than twenty, then glanced back at the doctor as she spoke again, "They saved her life"

For now, Richard thought, but he stayed silent, refusing to voice his fears and seem ungrateful.

The doctor was right. If the young couple hadn't found her, she would now be buried under the snow, and the entire village would pay the price.

Sighing heavily, he turned his face to stare down at the still figure of his housekeeper, the barely perceptible rise and fall of her chest beneath the blankets the only indication that she still lived. There was so much resting on her shoulders.

"Are you OK?" the voice of the doctor made him glance up from the face of Ms Sanderson, and he forced a smile, knowing that it was unconvincing.

"Yeah" he nodded, then shrugged, "She shouldn't have been out...she was going to get supplies and then stay up at the house with me until the snow had gone...I shouldn't have let her go alone"

The sad chuckle of the doctor made him raise an eyebrow, watching as she shook her head, her eyes upon the unconscious old woman, "I have known Margaret here for thirty years...believe me when I say that when she has decided to do something there is no stopping her"

He gave a soft laugh, "I've learned that"

For a moment the two shared a smile, and then she reached across the old woman, a hand gently squeezing his that was holding Margaret's, "I'll give you some time together"

Richard nodded in thanks, and she rose, moving away to stand with the others, now at the far end of the church. Shaking his head, he studied each of them in turn, thankful for what they had done, fearful of what they would suffer at the hands of the remaining Twelve if Ms Sanderson died here in the church. Paying the price for their ancestor's actions.

"Richard" he turned at the barely audible sound of Ms Sanderson's voice, the movement so quick that he got momentarily dizzy, a smile creasing his bearded face as he found her watching him, her eyes bright.

"Hey" he nodded, crouching down closer beside her, his voice soft, "How are you feeling?"

She scowled, her free hand rising towards the plaster on her head and he winced, stopping her from doing so, "Hey, come on, you need to rest"

She blinked, her tongue wetting her lips, her voice croaky, "Why am I on the damn floor?"

He winced, "You've had a fall, Margaret"

The elderly woman studied him for a moment then her eyes drifted about at her surroundings before she met his again, "This is the church"

"It is" he confirmed, once more stopping her hand as she tried to touch the plaster, "Please, you need to keep still, the doctor is worried about you…I'm worried about you!"

"Bah" she gave a huff, her free hand giving a weak wave of dismissal at his words, "I'm fine"

"No" he shook his head, "You really aren't"

She stared up at him for several moments, her eyes seeming to peer right into his soul, and she gave a weak shake of her head, "Is it bad?"

"Bad?"

"Dying am I?" she gave a soft chuckle, eyes closing for way longer than Richard was happy with and then she opened them once more, "It's about time...I have lived too long as it is"

"Don't say that" his voice was thick with emotion. She smiled, eyes sparkling, "Miss me would you?"

"Of course" he gave a nod, his throat tight with the effort of stopping from breaking down, the fact that he felt so emotional about her a surprise to him.

She studied him for a moment, then placed her free hand atop the one of his holding her other, patting gently, "You are a good boy Richard"

He nearly broke then, his eyes growing wet, and Ms Sanderson gave a sigh which seemed to shake her body to the core, "It will be good to see my daughter once again"

He winced, "And Cherry"

The old woman sighed once more, eyes leaving his to stare at the ceiling high above them for a moment before meeting his again, "So you know then"

Richard nodded and she gave a smile, "She told you herself didn't she"

"She did"

"She never could keep a secret" Ms Sanderson smiled, rolling her eyes, "Still, the truth is out now, you know that I am a mad lonely old lady"

"No madder than me" he pointed out, giving her hand a gentle squeeze, "We are a team"

"Yes" she nodded, "I suppose that we are"

She closed her eyes once more, her face muscles seeming to relax and he felt the stab of terror lance through his chest, then relaxed as she met his gaze once more, "You know what will happen if I die don't you Richard?"

"The Twelve?"

She nodded, her features grim, "The Twelve"

"They are already changing" he stated, his voice dropping to a whisper as the Vicar glanced over at them, "I have been stabbed, hit, scratched and more…but each time the injuries fade as if they have never existed"

Ms Sanderson grimaced, "They can sense I am weak, and nearly at an end, they are growing stronger by the moment. When I die those injuries will be real enough to kill. And that is what they will do, Richard, they will kill and kill"

He nodded at her words, then gave a shrug, "At least there are only nine of them now"

"Nine?"

Reaching into the pocket of his coat, he withdrew the small bag, keeping it out of sight as he showed it to her, "This…it doesn't only scare them…if I touch them with it they die for good"

She studied the bag for what seemed an eternity, then met his gaze once more, "And you have killed three of them...really?"

"Yes"

"Which three?"

"Father Ambrose; The Penitent Man, Elias Crumb; The Devil...and Agnes Rand; The Cook"

As he knew it would, the features of the old woman split into a smile at the last, her bright eyes filling with tears, "She killed my daughter"

"Well, she's gone now" he smiled down at the old woman, "Now, I just need to get rid of the other nine"

She smiled up at him, nodding, "You will, I know it"

He gave a chuckle, "You have too much faith"

The old woman smiled, head shaking and he grinned for a moment, then frowned, "I saw some new ghosts earlier...up in the bathroom attached to the room where Cherry took...well, you know"

"Oh?" she raised an eyebrow, "I know of no ghosts that linger in that bathroom"

Richard winced, "They were children, a boy and girl, as I watched them they died...before my eyes"

The old woman made a face, head shaking, "I fear they are caught up in their deaths, repeating it over and again...but I have no idea who they are"

He shrugged, sighing heavily, "Right then, I just need to get rid of the remaining members off The Twelve, save Myra and everything will be fine"

"Save Myra?" Ms Sanderson raised an eyebrow.

Richard took a deep breath, nodding slowly as he spoke, "My father...the ghost of my father is in the house...Cherry thinks he has attached himself to me years ago...when I...killed him"

Ms Sanderson grimaced, "He has taken Myra?"

"He has" the author nodded, feeling sick with dread, "Cherry says that he could be hiding anywhere in the house, and that I won't be able to find them because I can't go to their plane"

She grimaced, "Even were you to go to their plane it would mean that the remaining Twelve and any other ghosts that choose to try and hurt you, your father included, would be able to do so as you would be physically solid to each other"

Richard nodded at her words and then blinked, eyeing the old woman in confusion, "Wait, you didn't say that I couldn't go their plane...you just told me that I would be open to attack"

The old housekeeper nodded, "That is right"

"Oh my God" he said a little too loudly, eyes wide as he stared down at Ms Sanderson, "So if I can get to the same plane as them I can stop him from hurting her again?"

Once more she nodded, and Richard leaned closer, "You have to tell me how to do it, how do I find my way into the other planes of the house?"
Nearly a minute dragged by as she held his gaze, and then a sad smile crept onto her features, a frail hand rising to hold his right cheek as she held his gaze, "Why that's simply my dear, You have to die"

Chapter Forty Eight

"Please, tell me that you are joking"

Richard turned from where he was bent over the bathtub in the bathroom that was attached to the safe bedroom that he had returned to after leaving Ms Sanderson in the care of Dr Chapplow. The elderly housekeeper had passed out once more, moments after telling him he could travel to the different planes of Sanderson House if he were dead, and grimacing he had risen to his feet, and made his excuses with all of those present. Then he had returned through the snow to Sanderson House to find Cherry waiting for him, her features concerned. Straightening beside the bathtub, he nodded as he met the gaze of Cherry, "I don't have a choice"

"Richard!"

The author shook his head, smiling sadly, "Look, I know you don't think this is a good idea but it's the only way I can think of getting Myra back"

"Its too dangerous" the blue-haired ghost shook her head, taking a step closer to him, "Please don't do it"

Wincing, he turned away from her, his eyes staring back down into the bath of water, bending slightly as he ran a hand through it, shivering at how cold it was. Frowning, he turned back to stare at the taps, wondering if perhaps he should run some warm water with it but then changed his mind, and straightened once more, fighting the heavy, almost smothering weight of fear that settled about him, tightening his throat as he considered just what he was about to do. He turned slightly, glancing at Cherry as she moved to sit on the edge of the bath, her brown eyes staring up into his, her voice thick with emotion, "Richard, please do not kill yourself"

He tried to chuckle, but it came out sounding forced, and he shook his head, "I'm not going to die"

"That's what suicide is Richard" she grimaced, suddenly angry, "You do understand that right?"

"I know what suicide is" he sent her a smile.

"I don't think you do" she thrust her arms towards him, palms upturned and he grimaced as he saw the wide slashes that ran from her wrists towards her forearms, "This is what it looks like Richard...its not a game...you cant do this"

"I have to" he met her gaze again then moved away to stand in front of the medicine cabinet once more.

"It's not safe" she was back beside him, "Besides this might not even work...it's a huge risk"

He glanced at her, "Your gran says it will"

"Ah right" Cherry gave a nod, her jaw setting. When he had returned to Sanderson House, the blue-haired ghost had been overjoyed to hear that her beloved grandmother was still alive, though she had obviously worried that she had hurt herself so badly.

Now though there was sarcasm in her tone, "My grandmother isn't known for being the voice of reason...was this before or after she suffered a serious head injury?"

He winced, nodding, "After, but she seemed convinced...I think she might be right"

The ghost nodded, smirking, "So earlier you had no idea about ghosts and how they travel about this house and now you are a Parapsychologist?"

"I didn't say I was a parapsychologist" he fought the urge to snap, understanding she was only angry because she cared about him in some small way.

Grimacing, Cherry turned quickly away, her gaze drifting towards the bath before she turned back to him, her head shaking, "I won't let you die"

"Good" he nodded, giving her a smile before he moved over to the bath and switched the tap off.

He winced as he found Cherry close to him, arms folded across her chest, her expression one of barely controlled anger, and he shrugged, "You don't even know what I am going to do"

"You are going to kill yourself" her gaze flicked to the bathtub, "In there presumably"

He nodded, "I am"

"How?" there was fear in her eyes, "Razors?"

"What?" he flinched, head shaking, "No, I am going to drown myself under the water"

"Richard!"

"Calm down!"

"Calm down?" she eyed him as if he was insane, her head shaking, "Do you seriously expect me to just stand here and watch you drown yourself?"

"No, I need you to help me"

"What?"

"I need you to hold me under the water"

Cherry took a step back away from him, a look of horror upon her features, "I can't do that!"

"You can" he insisted, "You have touched me...I have felt your hand on me...you can make yourself solid...I am going to lay in the bath and you are going to hold me under the water"

"I am not!"

"Oh" he gave a nod of understanding, "You don't mean you can't...you mean you won't"

"Of course I won't" she nearly shouted back at him, anger in her eyes, "You can't ask me to kill you!"

"But I am" he shrugged, eyes locked to hers, "And then I want you to bring me back"

"You are insane"

"Probably" he nodded, glancing down at the bath filled with cold water before meeting her gaze again, "I can't think of a better way of doing it though...if I can rescue Myra, I will find some way to let you know and then you let out the plug so that the water drains away and then you give me CPR"

She grimaced, eyeing him in dread and he looked away as he reached into a pocket of his trousers and withdrew the leather pouch, studying it for a moment then met her gaze again, "If I have this with me when I die will it move with me?"

She grimaced, eyes narrowing and he sighed, "Please, Myra is somewhere in this house with the man who killed her...my father...I couldn't save her back then...I have to try now...I owe it to her"

Cherry started to speak, head shaking and he interrupted her, "Please...please help me"

She studied him for a moment and then nodded, her voice grim, "If you pass over with the pouch it will travel with you as if it were part of your clothing"

"Will it still work on The Twelve?"

She shrugged, "I don't know...I really don't"

He grimaced, reaching down to place the pouch in his right pocket, "Then I'll have to risk it"

"Richard" she gave him a grim look, and he avoided her gaze, hands unfastening his coat, placing it on the lid of the toilet before he returned to stand beside the bathtub, still dressed in shoes, jeans and a tee shirt.

"Well, here goes nothing" he raised his right leg, stepping into the water, a gasp of shock escaping him as the cold water wrapped about him, making his jeans feel like a heavy second skin. Knowing that if he paused too long he might change his mind, he stepped in with his other leg, then quickly sat down, cursing aloud as the ice cold touch of the water reached his skin through his clothes, making his chest ache and his penis shrivel, "Fucking Hell, its cold!"

"Richard, please stop now" Cherry crouched beside the bath, her eyes wet as he met her gaze once more. He smiled, touched by her emotion, then he winced as he spoke, "When I lay down I am going to put my arms under my back, I need you to hold me down no matter how much I struggle OK"

"Don't make me do this"

"You have to" he nodded at her, "Please, help me" The blue-haired ghost grimaced, then reached out to place a hand in the centre of his tee shirt, her voice grim, "Take a deep breath"

"That kind of defeats the point doesn't it?" he managed to smile, and she gave a pained laugh.

"You are such a dick"

"I'll see you soon" Richard threw her a wink starting to lay back in the water, then froze as she winced.

"Don't leave me here alone Richard…you have to come back…I can't keep being on my own"

He nodded, stunned by the depth of emotion in her brown eyes, "I promise you, I'll be back"

"I love you" she winced as she spoke, and he blushed,

realising that she meant it as a friend, yet he was suddenly unable to meet her gaze as he nodded.

"I love you too"

As he glanced up, she smiled awkwardly and he winced then he placed his hands behind his body and laid back, staring up at her through the water. Almost instantly, panic surged through him and he tried to sit up, his eyes widening as he felt the hand of Cherry pushing down on the centre of his chest, trapping his arms behind his broad body. Desperately fighting the urge to breathe, his legs thrashed wildly as he tried to sit up, his lungs burning with the sudden need to inhale, years of poor living having reduced his ability to hold his breath to the point that it was barely existent. Above him the face of Cherry danced and shimmered before his eyes, her attractive features distorted by the splashing water, and then as his vision began to waver, Richard realised he was losing consciousness. As if acting on its own accord, his body took an involuntary gasp, a spasmodic breath drawing water into his mouth and windpipe. His throat tightened as the water rushed through his throat and into his lungs, and on instinct he tried to breathe out, the effort making the pressure with him intensify. With pure, unbridled terror, his chest and throat on fire with pain, Richard realised this was it.

Game over. He was about to die.
Then the darkness took him.

Chapter Forty Nine

With a gasp, Richard sat up in the empty bathtub, hands dragging their way from beneath him as he grasped at the sides. For a moment he sat there in the gloom, blinking and coughing, fighting to clear the blockage from his airways, tears streaming from his eyes and then as if it had never existed, the pain was suddenly gone, its absence as much of a shock to him. Nearly a minute drifted by as Richard sat in the bathtub, confusion coursing through as he stared down at his body, trying to remember what he was doing there, then it returned in an overwhelming rush of images and emotions. He had been under the water, hands behind his body and Cherry had been drowning him, pushing on his chest, killing him.

No, he shook his head, realising the truth.

He had asked her to do so.

It was what he had wanted her to do.

He grimaced as the implications suddenly dawned on him, and as if the bathtub were full of deadly snakes, he scrambled from within it, head shaking as he rapidly stepped away to the wall. It had worked.

He was dead. Holy fuck, he was dead.

Without warning, his legs buckled, and he dropped to his knees, hands resting on the floor either side of him as he forced himself to focus on his situation.

This was what he had wanted.

No point complaining about it all now.

He rose on shaky legs, and took several steps back towards the bathtub, brow furrowing as he leaned forwards and peered inside its depths once more. There was no water within it, just a thick layer of dust that his frantic efforts to escape the tub had turned into some fantastically strange mural.

An author in life, a fingerpainter in death. Great. Shaking his head, he turned slowly, studying the bathroom about him carefully for the first time. When he had first awoken it had seemed exactly the same as the one that he had just left behind with the exception of the light being off and the fact that both the water in the bath and Cherry had been missing. But it was deeper than that.

There was a level of grime to the room that Ms Sanderson would never allow on her worst day. Not dirt as such, but there was a layer of dust on both the edges and the sink, and within, like that which he had disturbed and atop the seat and back of the toilet. Like a show home left that had been abandoned.

Turning his gaze, he stepped over to the medicine cabinet, a hand rising to wipe the dust from the mirror only to pause, an inch from the grimy surface, suddenly afraid to see his face. What would he see? Would his face be distorted in terror and pain? Cherry didn't look that way, but she had died through blood loss. Myra and his father both bore the signs of their deaths upon their new ghostly forms.

Raising a hand, let his fingers trace his features, relaxing as he felt nothing amiss. Shaking his head, he turned his hand from his face, wiping it across the surface of the mirror, cleaning a smeary path in the grime, insufficient to see himself properly but enough to tell that he looked to be no different to normal.

He flinched as a noise suddenly sounded beyond the door of the bathroom, a distant thud as if something heavy had been dropped within the house, and he grimaced, his eyes narrowing as if he expected the door to fly open at any moment to reveal the culprit.

For long moments he stood, staring at the door in silence, ears straining, then he stepped to the side to open it, peering into the bedroom beyond.

Like the bathroom in which he was standing, the bedroom looked forgotten, a thick layer of dust coating the chest of drawers and bookcase that sat at the foot of the large double bed in exactly the same place as he had left them back on his own plane.

His old plane, he corrected himself, grimacing.

He needed to find Myra and get back there.

Myra.

Cursing, he crossed the room quickly, and opened the door to the long hallway beyond, his hand instinctively reaching for the pouch that he had placed in his right pocket, sighing as his fingers curled around it and pulled it clear once more.

The medicine bag of Chaqit.

Would it still work here in the afterlife?

Grimacing, he held it before him, fingers wrapped tightly about its shape, revulsion coursing through him as he felt the sharp touch of the jagged piece.

The tooth of one of The Twelve.

Shaking his head, Richard stared at the bag, hoping against hope that it would work just as well in this plane as it had for him back in the real world.

Gritting his teeth, he stepped from the door, one pace, then another, head turning quickly as he tried to predict where the remaining Twelve might attack from, dread touching him as he recalled the words of Ms Sanderson, telling him that now The Twelve would be able to hurt him and possibly kill him.

Yet he was already dead.

What more could they do to him?

Unless if he died here and now, he would die again, a second time, just like the three members of The Twelve that he had already dispatched.

That would mean he would never get back to the mortal plane. He would be trapped here forever.

Of course, if he took to long dwelling on 'what if's' Cherry might not be able to revive him at all.

Grimacing at the thought, he took another step forward then another, his eyes focusing upon the distant balustrade where the stairs waited.

From there it would be a mad rush downstairs and back out into the grounds of the estate as he raced towards the hollow and the old tool shed.

That was where his father had to have taken her.

The very fact that it had resembled the murder site of both his father and Myra had been what had spooked Richard so much when he had been down in the shed, that similarity having no doubt released the angry and mutilated ghost of his father from wherever it had been hiding in him. Shaking his head at the thought, he picked up his pace, hurrying onwards towards the stairs then cursed as the door to his immediate right burst open, the familiar figure of Dr Edwin Bennet charged from within, straight razor raised over head as the ghost snarled, *"Let me bleed you!"*

Chapter Fifty

Cursing, Richard spun towards the man in the old fashioned suit, left arm reaching up to grasp the physician by the wrist holding his weapon, turning the blow aside, while his right thrust forward, a grunt of triumph escaping the author as he touched the ghost's chest with the pouch. And nothing happened. Blinking, both Richard and the ghost lowered their gaze to stare at the bag that the author was grasping tight in his right hand, then with a bitter snarl, Dr Edwin Bennet swung his right fist up, striking the author hard in the face, snapping his head back. Thrown off guard by the sudden pain that was coursing through his face, his eyes stinging as he blinked away the tears of pain that always seemed to accompany a blow to the nose, Richard stumbled back several feet, releasing his grip on the weapon hand of the doctor, then cursed as the ghost swept at him with the straight razor. Mind numb, Richard watched as a small pink oblong sailed up to his face, bouncing off his left cheek before falling out of sight, then screamed in agony as pain lanced through his left hand. In desperation, he watched as the ghost raised the straight razor once more, its edge wet with blood, and cursing he dropped the pouch and lashed out with his right hand, his fist cracking hard into the left cheek of his snarling foe, drawing a grunt from it.

The ghost, physically thinner than he, staggered to the side as the blow landed, its intended slice with the straight razor cutting noting but air and grimacing, Richard took a step back, his eyes glancing down to stare at the pain in his left hand, feeling sick as he saw that his ring finger was missing down to the first knuckle, blood running freely from the severed stump. Stunned, he raised his eyes to see the ghost physician had righted itself and was staring back at him in hatred, the straight razor ready, its other hand clasped to its face, holding its cheek. Shaking his head, Richard raised his hand before his face, his voice thick with disbelief and anger as he realised the thing that had struck him in the face was his fingertip, his eyes locked to the ghost, "Mother fucker...you cut my finger off!"

"*You have a fever*" the ghost nodded, once more repeating its litany, "*Let me bleed you*!"

Without another word it rushed him, covering the ground between them quicker than Richard had expected and it was all that the author could do to block the hand sweeping in at him from the left, the blade missing his face by a fraction of an inch.

With a grunt, he bent slightly, dipping his right shoulder as he slammed into the ghost's chest, the force of his impact, lifting the man from the floor of the hallway, carrying him back several feet to collide heavily with the wall beside the door that the ghost had earlier emerged from. Richard cried out as he felt the razor slash into his back as the ghostly physician lashed out in anger and pain, and releasing his grip on his foe, he stepped back and swung his right arm up, punching the doctor hard in the side of his face. Once more, the ghost went with the impact, sliding along the wall for several feet before he tripped and fell to his side, then rolled to his hands and knees, gasping and groaning in pain. Without pausing, the author moved to his side, a boot lashing out to kick the ghost in the ribs, throwing it to the wall hard. "Wait!" the ghost blinked as it rolled to its back, staring up at Richard in disbelief as if it couldn't believe what was happening, the glass in one lens of his round glasses broken, the other missing.

Gritting his teeth, the author paused, staring down at the ghost then cursed as it snaked out a hand, reaching for the straight razor that it had dropped. "Bastard!" Richard stamped down on the wrist of the ghost, drawing a gasp of pain from it, then kicked out with his other leg as it rolled to the side and reached for its weapon with its other hand, his boot catching it hard under the chin. Grimacing, he dropped down to kneel atop the well-dressed ghost's chest, his legs pinning its arms to its sides as he raised his right fist and brought it down hard into the others face.

The glasses broke completely under the first blow, the wire across his snapping apart, and as they fell either side of his head, Richard struck him again, a deep sense of satisfaction surging through his as he felt the nose of Dr Edwin Bennet break under his knuckles. Grim faced he raised his fist for a third time, then paused as he saw the eyes of the ghost flicker to his hand, fear within those pale deathly orbs and Richard followed his gaze, nodding in understanding as he saw the fresh blood upon his knuckles.

"That's yours!" Richard grimaced, watching as the ghost met his gaze again, "How does it feel?"

"You have a fever" the ghost snarled, suddenly dragging its left arm free from beneath the right knee of the author, its hand grasping hold of Richards severed finger and squeezing hard. With a cry of pure agony, Richard grasped at the hand squeezing his finger with his right hand, all thoughts of anything but stopping the pain gone. Through eyes filled with pain, he glimpsed the ghost reach for its straight razor and he leaned back out of instinct, rolling from atop the other to land heavily on the dusty old carpet. Mind numb, he rolled to his back, watching in shock as the ghost rose to its feet before him, one hand placing its broken glasses back upon its face as it took a step towards him, its split lips creasing into a cold smile as it nodded at him in triumph, *"You have a fever...let me bleed..."*

Its words trailed off as it suddenly lifted its gaze to stare beyond where he lay, the head of the ghost tilting to one side, voice confused, *"You have a fever?"* Blinking, Richard rolled to his side, head turning as he stare back in the direction the Dr Edwin Bennet was staring in confusion, a whimper escaping the author as he saw the familiar figure standing there in silence, a figure he hadn't seen since his early teenage years. Shaking his head, he pushed himself back until he was seated against the wall, legs out before him as he stared in disbelief at the figure in long dirty nightgown, its long hanging hair obscuring its features as it stood facing the confused Dr Edwin Bennet, the voice of the ghost dragging Richards attention as it spoke once more, *"Let me bleed..."*

He never got to finish the sentence he favoured so much, for with a scream like a banshee, hands rising before it, fingers arching, Richards mother attacked.

Chapter Fifty One

Mind reeling, Richard sat back against the wall, hands holding his knees up before him like a child who has been allowed to sit up late and watch a horror film, fear coursing through him, his grey eyes wide as he watched the pair of ghosts fight with each other.

No.

That was an inaccurate description.

There was no fight; such a wording would imply a trading of blows, an almost equal challenge.

In the case of the ghost of Richards mother and Dr Edwin Bennet the scales were nowhere near level. As the female ghost had neared him, the physician had raised his straight razor, intent on slashing at her with it but she was too quick by far, slipping under his clumsy attack and within his reach before he had even realised the danger. She took his eyes first, her left-hand clasping the back of his head while her right scraped at his features, fingers hooking behind his eyes one at a time as she tore them from the sockets. Richard flinched at the mournful screams of woe escaping the physician, stunned by the level of violence that his mother was capable of as she suddenly leaped back then rushed forwards again, darting nimbly under the screaming ghosts blind futile sweeps from the straight razor, her long nailed hands slashing quickly at his face, ripping his lips away from him mouth with ease. He tried to flee then, hands desperately trying to push her away, only for her to grasp his left hand with her own and drag into within the hair that still hung about her features like a curtain, the body of the physician tensing as it screamed once more and jerked its arm back away from her, raw stumps where his middle three fingers had been. With a sob of terror, Dr Edwin Bennet faded from view, and Richards mother followed suite, only for the pair of them to reappear several feet down the corridor from where they had vanished, he on his hands and knees while she knelt behind him, fingers hooked in his mouth, pulling on his cheeks. "No" Richard muttered as he rose on shaky legs to his feet, his head shaking, and his mother glanced up to meet his gaze, the hair falling aside to reveal the face that been hidden from him during his childhood, the newfound knowledge that she was his mother doing little to quell his fear in the face of his memories and the violence that she was now currently committing. She's doing it for you, Richard reminded himself as he watched, his bearded features twisting in disgust as the long fingernails off his mother began to tear through the cheeks of her victim, splitting him from mouth to ear, her right hand reaching in his mouth to tear his tongue loose with a sickeningly wet sound.

Feeling giddy, Richard closed his eyes, reminding himself that this was the ghost of a man who had brutally murdered twenty-three woman in his care, stealing their dignity and their lives from them when they should have been receiving help or sympathy. Opening his eyes once more, forcing himself to be brave, Richard cursed aloud as he found the ghost of his mother standing over the bloody, ruined remains of Dr Edwin Bennet, the body of the physician bursting into flames as he watched. Feeling sick with dread, Richard watched as the fire licked along the remains of the ghost yet left his mother untouched, black flakes of skin rising into the air as the flames turned purple, and the body of Dr Edwin Bennet finally came undone. Stunned, Richard watched as the black flakes drifted lazily through the air, circling aimlessly and he turned his gaze to where he had dropped the pouch, expecting them to head there as they had before only to frown as they began to drift lazily towards the ghost of his mother instead. Pushing himself away from the wall, he moved to where the pouch lay, and bent to collect it, placing it back inside his front pocket before moving to where the fight between his mother and Dr Bennet had begun, bending once more as he picked up the straight razor he had dropped during his fight.

Frowning, the author turned it over in his right hand, surprised that it hadn't faded away with its owner, then winced as the stump of his ring finger bumped the handle, drawing a moan of pain from his lips as he studied the raw wound, concern touching him as he realised that unlike before when the ghosts had hurt him, the wound wasn't fading away this time around. When he made it back to the mortal world would he be missing the finger too? Was Cherry even now staring down at him in the bathtub in shock, wondering why his ring finger had come loose? Grimacing at the thought, he raised his eyes once more then cursed again as he found his mother watching him from just a matter of feet away, her pale features blank as she stared back at him, her black eyes holding his own without blinking.

"Thank you" he nodded, his voice childlike and weak, and before him the ghost of his mother continued to stare, hands down by its sides, fingers tensing.

He winced, "I know who you are"

If his mothers ghost had heard his words she didn't acknowledge them, her black eyes locked to his.

Time seemed to drift away into nothing as he stared back at her, eyes travelling across what he could see of the nightgown that she wore and then her face and neck, searching for the wound that had stolen her life, another victim of his father but there was nothing that he could see. Wincing, he sighed, head shaking once more as he took a single step towards her, continuing his thread of conversation, "I didn't know who you were at first...back when I was a kid I mean...I have only known for a couple of hours. To be honest you used to terrify me...the way you'd just stand there staring at me...if I'd known...if I had realised what he had done to you..."

He flinched as her features twisted into a snarl at the mention of his father, and suddenly she was there before him, a gasp of dread escaping him as she moved with a speed that he hadn't expected.

For long moments she stood there before him, her features a mask of rage, he too afraid to move, and then he gave a nod, "He's here"

She tensed, her body seeming to vibrate in the air before him at his words and Richard nodded, "Yeah, he is here on the grounds of this house or in it somewhere, he has my friend...her ghost...he killed her when she was just a child"

His bowels almost turned to water as the ghost of his mother suddenly gave a small smile, her thin lips drawing back to show her surprisingly perfect teeth, the sound of her amusement like leaves in the wind, and Richard nodded at her, somehow finding the ability to match her smile with his own, "Let's finish him once and for all"

She studied him for an eternity, that smile still etched upon her features and then she raised a hand to stroke across his head, and Richard shuddered at the chill of her touch, her voice like escaping steam as she nodded, "*My precious boy*"

Chapter Fifty Two

Straight razor clenched tight in his right hand, the now useless medicine bag of Chaqit stuffed into a pocket of his jeans, and his left hand throbbing, Richard moved to stand at the top of the stairs, staring down as he grimaced, "There are another eight of those bastards down there somewhere…and then him…the wanker"

He tensed as the ghost of his mother moved alongside him, her head tilting as she stared down the stairs and he turned to study her profile, his eyes drifting over her features, recognition coursing through him as he saw his nose, and eyes, her features a mirror of his own. How had he not realised this when he was a child and she had stood watching him constantly? Yet why would he have done?

His overriding emotion upon finding the woman that no-one else could see standing watching him had always been outright terror not sudden curiosity. Richard flinched as she turned to study him, her lips pressed tightly together and he gave a shake of his head, "How old was I?"

She stayed silent, her eyes locked to his and he winced, refusing to give up, "How did he do it?"

His mother tensed, her eyes narrowing as she took a step towards him, and he shook his head, his childhood fear of her returning momentarily, then he nodded in understanding as she brushed her hair back out of the way to reveal heavy bruising on the sides of her neck, dark against her pale skin.

"His hands" Richard nodded in understanding, grimacing as he spoke, "Just like he killed Myra"

His mother gave a grim chuckle, and turned away from him, slowly descending the stairs and he moved after her, "Wait for me"

He caught up with her at the midway landing to the first floor, shaking his head as he considered his father and the crimes that he had committed.

He had killed his own wife and successfully covered her death up and then gone on to successfully kill a young girl and almost escape justice once again.

Almost.

Richard had stopped that.

He might not have been arrested but Richard had made him pay, for the murder of Myra at least.

Was that why he had taken Myra now?

To punish Richard for murdering him?

Murdering him.

Maybe it was in his blood to kill.

The author grimaced, pushing the thought away as they turned to walk down the second set of the stairs which led to the first floor then cried out as a burning pain lanced into his left thigh. Stunned by the pain coursing through him, he staggered forwards, dropping the straight razor as he fell to his knees, the back of his leg burning with pain. Before him, his mother turned, screeching at whoever had attacked Richard from behind, and taking his weight upon his right hand, he turned, cursing as he saw Frances Goodnestone crouched there, knife in hand.

"You little cunt!" Richard managed to mutter through clenched teeth, his right hand reaching for the dropped straight razor as the ghost of the murderous boy took a quick step towards him. Without warning his mother surged towards the child, nightgown trailing behind her, the long fingernails that had torn the un-life from Dr Edwin Bennet reaching for the ghostly youngster, and with a grimace, Frances vanished from sight. Just as when The Fever had tried to flee her, his mother also vanished from sight, the pair of ghosts instantly reappearing at the top of the stairs on the second floor, she slashing wildly with her nails while the child snarled and swung its blade. Grimacing, Richard pushed himself to his feet, overjoyed to find that the injury to his leg hadn't done any damage to his nerves, and began to climb the stairs back towards the fighting pair.

He was halfway there when they vanished again, the boy first, chased by Richards mother, the pair reappearing almost instantly in the centre of the hallway, the female hissing in pain as Frances materialised behind her and stabbed her in the right shoulder two times in quick succession.

"Mum!" the word escaped Richard before he had given it thought, his voice thick with concern, but then both ghosts vanished from sight once more. Cursing, the author reached the second floor, hurrying out into the centre of the hallway where the pair had just been fighting, then turned his head as a gasp of pain sounded from the entrance to the attic stairwell opposite where he was now standing. Teeth clenched as a fresh wave of pain seemed to surge from his stabbed leg and his severed ring finger at the same time, the author grimaced and headed into the stairwell, straight razor held before him as he slowly climbed up to the attic. He turned as he reached the top, realising that this was the first time that he had been up here since his day of arrival at Sanderson House, and he, Myra and Jonty had all been here together. Turning, he glanced along towards his left, seeing the wall in the distance that separated the secret study room from the rest of the attic then turned back to his right as he took several steps forward, grimacing as he saw the figure of his mother kneeling atop the struggling figure of Frances. She glanced at him as he stepped closer, her lips pressed tight together in a grim smile, her fingers locked tight around the throat of the boy, thumbs pressing hard together, his left hand clasped to one of her wrists, his right trying desperately to reach her face only to be several inches too short. As she turned her gaze back upon Frances, the author let his gaze drop to that of the ghostly boy, his stomach knotting in horror as he saw his eyes filled with tears, several running down the sides of his face as he opened his mouth in a large 'O', tongue poking out as he choked. Richard blinked, his head shaking as an image suddenly came back to him from the depths of his memories, of Myra lying upon her back in the old gloomy tool barn, her fingers clawing at the hands that were choking the life from her, her eyes wide, her legs kicking frantically as she fought to live, her baseball boot coming free in her desperate struggle. Had he been there to see her actual death and blocked that from his mind as well or was it an image conjured up by seeing the ghost of Frances dying? Grimacing, he shook his head, stepping forward as he addressed his mother, "You have to stop!"

She turned to meet his gaze, her features twisted in a grimace, and he stepped closer, "Stop!"

Beneath her body, Frances gave a choking rasp, both hands now grasping to her wrists but there was no real fight left within him; it was almost over for him. "Please!" the author raised his voice, "Let him go"

He took a faltering step back as she hissed at him, her pale features twisting and he shook his head, his voice grim, "I know he's one of them…I know the things he's done but…he's a kid…this is what he did to Myra…I cant be a part of it!"

His mother laughed at his words, the sound making his skin crawl and he grimaced, "Let hi…"

Richard flinched as something moved in his peripheral vision, and he span towards the threat, his straight razor sweeping out before him in a wide deadly arc. The figure gave a scream of pain, and fell back to the attic floor, hands leaping to clutch at its face, blood seeping through its fingers. Stunned, Richard glanced back at his mother, their eyes meeting and then she was hissing in pain as Frances Goodnestone suddenly broke free of her grip around his throat, and vanished again, laughing hysterically. Snarling, his mother tensed as if ready to follow the boy but then stepped closer to Richard as the figure upon the floor removed a hand from its face, holding it up before it as it gave another sob, "Please, no more…I'm on your side!"

With a snarl, his mother made to rush the figure, but Richard stopped her with an outstretched arm, his bearded features twisted in confusion as the figure removed its other hand, revealing its face. For a moment, the author studied the athletic young blonde man in the suit in confusion, the sobbing man pressing a hand back against the slash on its forehead as it nodded at Richard, "It's me…Jonty…Jonty Beaumont!"

Chapter Fifty Three

Richard blinked, nodding slowly as he suddenly realised who the man was, "The estate agent"

"Yes!" the blonde man sat forwards, an eager expression upon his features, "Yes, that's me!"

Grimacing, Richard glanced at his mother, making sure that she wasn't about to rush forwards and dispatch the ghost of the young man, then glanced back as the other spoke, "You have to get me out of here...please"

"You're dead" the author stated, grimacing as he spoke, "You understand that don't you?"

Jonty Beaumont winced, head nodding slightly, his eyes growing wide, "I...they...Clemence...the woman...she makes me..."

His words trailed off, a haunted look on his handsome features and Richard fought a wave of nausea as he recalled the story that he had read in the diary about how Clemence had seduced her victims before her accomplice had murdered them, then remembered seeing the ghost of Jonty several days before when Frances had first attacked him on the second floor. The young man had been standing against the doorframe of one of the bedrooms, his features etched in terror as Clemence had leaned against his body, sexual hunger in her eyes as she had stroked him through his trousers, while Elias stood guard.

Had she been forcing him to have sex with her in the afterlife? The thought of having the bone thin ghost doing such a thing to the young man making Richard suddenly wince in a mixture of dread and disgust. Shaking his head, he studied the man as he knelt before him, noticing the bruises on his face for the first time, recalling how he had fallen to his death, then he nodded, "How did you escape?"

"From Clemence?"

The author nodded, and Jonty Beaumont cringed, head shaking, "She was off, looking at the young girl"

Richard tensed, glancing at his mother before meeting the gaze of the young man once more, his voice shaky as he spoke, "Young girl?"

Jonty nodded, his lips looking like they were going to twist into an arrogant smirk but holding back as he held Richards gaze, a measure of confidence seeming to have returned to the estate agent, "Yes, a young girl...pretty little thing...only one shoe...a friend of yours if I am not mistaken. Clemence was off seeing her, and the new one, oh...how he hates you"

Richard closed his eyes, his dislike of the man from their one meeting returning to him in a rush, "So you escaped...why come to me?"

Jonty Beaumont nodded, "I told you, I want you to help me escape...I want out of this fucking house before I go mad…I cant spend any more years here…with her…doing…"

Richard shook his head, watching the other intently for a moment before continuing, "Years? You only died a couple of days ago"

Before him, the almost-smirk vanished from the features of the blonde man, a look of devastation creeping onto his face as he blinked, a confused laugh escaping him as he shook his head in denial, "No…it's been…you're lying"

"Why would I" Richard shrugged, "I'm sorry"

With a low moan, Jonty Beaumont took several unsteady steps to the side, hands rising to grab at his blonde hair as he shook his head, "No, no, no"

Richard glanced at his mother as she shifted position, and then he took a step closer to the broken ghost of the young estate agent, suddenly curious, "Was it them that killed you…Elias and Clemence? Did they throw you over the stairs?"

It seemed for a moment as if the other had not heard him, his head shaking as he stared down at the floorboards of the attic and then he glanced up at the author, his eyes struggling to focus for a moment before he shook his head, "No…they chased me…I was at the top of the stairs…then the priest…he rushed at me and I…I fell"

"Father Ambrose Dewitt; The Penitent Man" the

author gave a nod of understanding, and then sent the man a grim smile, "He's dead now…I killed him…I sent him over to the final death. I did the same with Elias too…they are both gone"

Jonty nodded, a haunted expression on his features as he stared back at Richard, "You have to get me out of here…I'll do anything"

"There is no getting out of here, Jonty" Richard winced, head shaking slowly, "The only way to get out now is to move over…to pass on"

"Pass on…where…Heaven and Hell?" there was bitterness in the voice of the estate agent, so much so that it seemed evident that he didn't believe in the former but feared ending up in the latter, "I don't think so…I want out of this house and grounds…"

Richard shook his head, "It's not possible"

"Damn you" the ghost of the estate agent spat angrily, taking a step towards the author only to back quickly away once more as Richards mother suddenly tensed as if she intended to rush at him.

"I'm sorry" Richard shook his head, stepping after his mother's ghost as she moved away towards the stairs back down to the second floor hallway, "I really wish I could help you"

"You cant leave me here…not with her" there was terror in Jonty Beaumont's eyes, "You can't!"

The author winced, turning away as he placed his right foot upon the top step of the attic stairs, his mothers ghost already half way down them, then froze as the voice of the estate agents spoke once more, "I'll take you to her"

"What?" Richard blinked, turning back to him.

"You heard me" the ghost of Jonty Beaumont took a step towards Richard, the smug grin back upon his pale features, "If you get me out of here I will take you to Myra!"

Richard held his gaze for a moment, brow furrowing and then he stepped back towards Jonty, "You know where he is holding her?"

"I know where Clemence went to see her" the other replied, lips twisting into a cocky smile.

"Why would she tell you anything?" Richard raised an eyebrow, another step taking him so close that just inches separated their chests.

The chuckle that escaped Jonty made the authors skin crawl, "She has a thing for me…"

Richard held his gaze in silence, the fingers of his right hand flexing slightly around the grip of the straight razor that he was holding, fighting the sudden almost inexplicable urge to use it, then he nodded at the larger young man, "Tell me where"

"Oh no" Jonty took a step backwards, his smirk growing wide across his face, "I don't think I will"

"She could make you tell me" Richard gestured
towards the ghost of his mother with a nod of his
head, enjoying the sudden flicker of fear that passed
over the pale features of Jonty Beaumont.
"I...I just want to get out of here"
Richard nodded as he considered his options.
There was no way to let Jonty leave the house.
He was dead, and while Cherry seemed able to travel
as far as the village in her ghost form, he had a feeling
that the estate agent wanted more than that.
Yet he claimed to know exactly where Myra was.
Admittedly given time, Richard and his mother could
conceivably search the entire house and grounds,
after all, until Jonty had mentioned his knowledge of
Myra's location that had been the plan.
Now, possibly, they could go straight there.
And time was of the essence.
Grimacing as he pictured his body, still laid within the
bath up on the second floor of the huge house,
wondering how long had passed, Richard glanced up
to find the ghost of the estate agent smirking, "Well,
do we have a deal?"
"Sure" Richard nodded, lying through his teeth, a
grim smile creasing his bearded features, "Deal"

Chapter Fifty Four

"So, who is she?"

Richard turned at the question from Jonty, pausing as he stepped from the attic stairs onto the second floor, realising that the ghost was gesturing towards the figure of his mother. The author hesitated before answering, certain that he couldn't trust the smug, well dressed man in the slightest but then he shrugged, realising that the knowledge of her identity couldn't give him any power, "She's my mother"

"Oh?" Jonty Beaumont raised an eyebrow as he moved alongside Richard in the hallway, the pair of them turning to study the female ghost as she began to descend the next set of stairs to the first floor. Then the estate agent met his gaze again, "Why would you buy a house where your mother had died?"

"I didn't" the author began walking once more, the blonde Jonty falling in step alongside him.

"Then how is she here?"

"She just is" Richard sent him a grim look, the pair of them starting to descend the stairs, the author wishing that his mother would wait for them. She hadn't spoken since touching his face earlier and calling him her precious boy, apart from the few times that she had laughed at him, and he was beginning to worry that when they encountered his father the ghost off his mother would kill him before they had managed to rescue Myra from him.

Just like she had nearly killed Frances.

Richard grimaced at the thought, knowing that as one of The Twelve, the ghost of the boy had to die once more for the rest of the ghosts trapped within the house to finally be free, and that the evil little monster had tried to kill him already on three separate occasions. Yet as he had seen the child choking to death, and had pictured Myra dying the same way he had suddenly felt sympathy for the boy. Now the ghost was free once and he couldn't help but feel that he was going to regret his mercy.

"Who killed you...one of The Twelve?" Jonty asked, turning to look at Richard and the author grimaced. "Suicide"

"Really?" the other gaze an amused laugh.

"What?"

"Nothing?" Jonty shrugged, a smile on his hand some features, "You just don't seem the type"

"What does the type look like?" Richard was surprised at how angry he was, an image of Cherry suddenly entering his mind, "Go on"

The ghost of the estate agent gave a chuckle as it shrugged again, "You know, the type who are all...oh...hello...what's wrong with mother dear?"

"What?" Richard turned to follow his gaze.

Ahead of them, his mother had stopped on the first floor, her head tilting to one side as she stared at something out of sight and reaching the midway landing between the second and first floor, Richard tensed, "Is everything OK?"

"What's she doing?" Jonty gave a snort, moving ahead of Richard, starting to descend the steps to the first floor then froze, "Oh shit"

Grim faced, the author hurried forwards, wincing as pain flared up through his left leg then froze as he drew level with the ghost of the estate agent, his eyes fixing upon the figure standing fifteen feet away from the ghost of his mother, "Fuck"

"Who the fuck is that...one of The Twelve?" there was sudden fear in Jonty's voice and Richard grimaced. "Haven't you seen them all?"

"No" there was sarcasm in the others voice, "I've seen Clemence...Elias...the priest, the boy, the old woman I saw on the first day, and the blonde woman...that's it...they don't all socialise!"

Nodding, Richard stayed silent, his eyes locked to the powerfully built man that was standing facing his mother, the ghosts features twisted into a mask of rage as it stared out from amid the tangle of long dirty hair, blackened teeth snarling amid the dirty unkempt beard that hung down to its chest.

With a growl like a rabid dog, Walter Haggerty; the
Vessel took a step forward, swinging the long
handled axe up from its side to hold across its broad
chest with both its hands, lips drawing back as it
snarled, *"Heathens"*

Both The Vessel and his mother suddenly charged at
each other, the former swinging the axe back and
releasing it, the latter sliding beneath the blow that
would have taken her head from her shoulders,
twisting as she darted past, the nails of her right hand
slashing at the Vessels stomach. With grunt of pain,
he reversed the weapon in his hands as she came at
him from behind, striking the haft of the axe hard
across her face, and Richard cried out in alarm as she
flew across the hallway as if she weighed nothing.
Without thinking, Richard was running forwards,
shouting in anger as he leaped astride the back of the
Vessel, left arm wrapping about the thick neck of the
ghost while his right raised the razor. Even as he
began to bring it down towards the head of his foe,
the bearded ghost was dropping to one knee as it
bent forwards, a hand reaching back to grasp at
Richard and pull. Already thrown of balance, the
author tumbled forwards over the head of the
enraged ghost, the razor slipping from his fingers as
he tried to rise again, only to grunt in shock as the
ghost brought a boot down hard upon his chest

without warning. Groaning, he managed to roll to the side, fingers feebly reaching for the straight razor that lay several feet between him and his mother. As his eyes flicked to her, she pushed her head up from the floor, her eyes meeting his and then lifted higher, and grimacing, Richard raised his gaze to watched as The Vessel raised the axe high above his head, snarling down at him in pure, unbridled hatred. Then the unthinkable happened.

Jonty struck the bearded ghost about the waist, arms encircling him in a rugby tackle, the pair of them falling back out of sight, and unable to believe what he had seen, Richard forced himself up to his hands and knees, then finally his feet, forcing himself towards where Jonty was now on his back, doing his best to ward of powerful punches from The Vessel.

"Hey Rasputin" Richard grimaced as he stepped alongside the pair, the axe that he had collected from the floor held back over his shoulder in his hands. Eyes wide, The Vessel started to rise, lips drawn back in a curse, "*Heathen*!"

"Oh fuck off!" Richard swung the axe forward, the weight of the weapon and the fact that he had never swung one before sending the blade of it sinking deep into the chest of its intended target instead of taking its head from off its shoulders. Gritting his teeth, he tried to draw the weapon clear, his stomach lurching as he found it was stuck, the head caught in the chest of the Vessel and Richard grimaced as he stared through the wound, realised it was stuck in his ribs.

"*Heathen!*" the voice of William Haggerty was thick with pain and anger as the ghost suddenly reached forward, hands grasping at the arms of Richard as he held the axe, strong arms dragging the author's body closer until they were almost touching each other.

"Get off me!" Richard brought his right fist about, hammering it into the side of The Vessel's head only for it to take the blow and snarl, snapping its forehead forward to strike the author in the face. His nose broke under the impact, blood splashing down over his mouth, and in desperation, he swung another punch, cursing as his arm got caught on the haft of the axe between them, deflecting his blow.

"Fucking kill it!" Jonty was suddenly there beside him, hands trying to grasp the handle of the axe, the pair of them kicking and hammering punches at the ghost as it screamed and snarled at them. Suddenly Richard's mother was there behind it, hands fastening to either side of the long hair, twisting quickly to the side, breaking its neck with a crack. Without a sound, William Haggerty dropped to the ground, the axe still protruding from its chest, and as the supernatural fire ignited at its feet and began to course through its body, Richard stepped away, glancing first at his mother and then at a bloody faced Jonty, his voice grim, "Five down...seven to go"

Chapter Fifty Five

"We showed him, eh" Jonty gave a grim chuckle as they reached the ground floor hallway, edging their way among the boxes and furniture that Richard still hadn't moved. Grimacing, Richard glanced sideways at the estate agent, somehow resisting the urge to point out how close they had both just come to dying a second time. Instead, he nodded, wincing as his broken nose sent a wave of pain through his face, his right hand tightening about the axe that he was now carrying in his hands, being sure not to let his wounded left ring finger touch it. Ahead of them, the ghost of his mother had reached the front door, her pale fingers reaching out to open it, and Richard watched her intently as she stepped outside. Shaking his head, the author turned to give his companion a grim stare, "Are you certain that Clemence said she had seen the girl by the shed?"

"That is what she said to me" Jonty nodded, a hand rising to cross himself, and Richard expected him to burst into flames for doing so yet of course he didn't. "Come on" the author began walking again, gesturing for Jonty to keep pace, then grunted as his severed stump bumped against the axe haft once more. "Don't suppose you fancy swapping weapons do you, old boy?" the voice of Jonty had Richard glancing sideways at him once more, grimacing as he saw the ghost of the estate agent raised the straight razor that the author had given him in his right hand, "I'll take the axe...you take this?"

"No" Richard shook his head, "I'm keeping it"

"Bit unfair" Jonty continued, and despite not looking back at him, Richard could hear by the tone of the others voice that he was pouting like a schoolboy.

"I killed him" Richard gave a shrug, hating the fact that he felt inclined to explain himself, "So I am getting the axe...its not open for discussion"

"Technically not true" Jonty gave a bitter laugh, "She killed him...you tried and failed"

"I still hit him with the axe" the author snapped.

"Only because I knocked it out of his hands when I charged him!" Jonty was incredulous, "If I hadn't come rushing in then you'd be dead now!

"Yeah" Richard nodded, "And you'd be stuck with Clemence...I am in charge of this not you"

"Really?" the other ghost gave a sneer, a thumb jerking towards the now open front door, "If you ask me, mummy is running the show!!"

"What the fuck is that supposed to mean?"

Jonty shrugged, "When I found you in the attic she was killing that little prick Frances, then she killed the guy with the beard just now!"

"So?" Richard shook his head, pausing in the doorway as the pair reached it, "Your point?"

The blonde ghost gave a smile, free hand raising before it in a calming manner, "Relax old boy, I am just saying it looks like she is in charge"

"Well she's not"

"Good" Jonty nodded, the pair of them leaving the house, Richard shutting the door behind them.

Side by side they stood staring out at the heavy snow for a moment, the author grimacing as he realised that even on this plane, the weather seemed to hate him. Shaking his head, he watched as his mother moved past his car parked up on the driveway, heading for the small graveyard, and then Jonty turned to look at him again, "Does *she* know you are in charge and she is just here to kill things for you?"

Sighing, Richard turned to throw his companion a grim look, "Are you going to shut up?"

"Sorry" Jonty gave a smirk as the pair of them walked side by side across the front of the property, "She is good at it though isn't she"

"What?" Richard stopped walking, "What now?"

"Eh?" Jonty Beaumont suddenly seemed to remember what it was he had said, his blue eyes seeming to sparkle as he nodded, "Ah yes, killing things...she's rather superb at it isn't she...in an utterly horrifying brutal sort of way"

Shaking his head slowly, Richard stared into the eyes of the other ghost, "I have no idea what you are talking about...are you mad...is that it?"

Jonty raised an eyebrow, bending a fraction as he made a show of peering deep into Richards eyes and then he pointed with a finger, "Oh, there it is"

"What?" Richard blinked, suddenly defensive.

Chuckling, Jonty began to walk once more and cursing, Richard hurried to keep pace, "Where what is...what are you talking about?"

"You know the truth" the estate agent gave another chuckle, "I can see it in your eyes. She scares you as much as she scares me...maybe a bit more"

"Shut up" Richard snapped, suddenly angry as he glared at the ghost beside him, "You have no fucking idea what you are talking about"

"OK" Jonty nodded, free hand raising defensively between them as if to ward of a blow, "Whatever"

Grimacing, Richard picked up the pace, flinching as the wind blew a flurry of snowflakes at him only for them to not touch him, a quick glance at himself and Jonty revealing that despite the heavy snow neither of them had any on them. Lifting his gaze from their snow-free clothes to the side profile of Jonty, Richard fought the almost overwhelming urge to bury his axe in the ghosts head, mostly because everything that he had said about Richards mother was true.

She was good at killing.

Very, very good.

But it went beyond being capable.

The problem was that she seemed to enjoy it.

For fuck sake. Were both his parents mad?

Grimacing, he turned his gaze to settle upon his mother as she walked ahead of them through the snow and then cursed, stopping dead on the spot.

"What?" the voice of Jonty was etched with a high-pitched tone as if he were about to scream, his head twisting about, straight razor raised, "What is it?"

"It's my mother" Richard's voice was grim.

"What?" the blonde ghost spun back to the direction that they had been facing, a grunt of surprise escaping him as he glanced back at Richard, "Where the fuck has she gone?"

The author grimaced, eyes studying the snowy night before them in silence for a moment, and then he nodded, "Where indeed"

As if frozen in a plateau, the pair stood for an age, eyes peering through the snow, their weapons raised ready for trouble, and then Jonty shook his head again, "Do you think something got her?"

"Something?"

"One of The Twelve" Jonty hissed, "Or Seven"

Grimacing, the author shook his head, his stomach knotted in dread, "I have no idea"

"Fuck"

Feeling the curse of the estate agent with every fibre of his being, Richard nodded and began to walk forwards once more, only to pause as Jonty reached out to grasp at his arm, making him turn.

"What?"

"Are you utterly insane?" the blonde ghost almost screamed, his blue eyes flicking towards where Richards mother had last been standing, before meeting the authors gaze once more, "If there was something over there capable of taking her out without making a noise, we don't want to go in that direction!"

"You told me that Clemence had seen Myra at the shed" Richard's voice was grim, "Right"

Jonty gave a nod, eyes still casting about as if he expected to be attacked at any moment, "That is what she told me...I promise"

The author nodded at his words, shrugging off the restraining arm of his companion as he began to walk through the snow once more, and with a groan, Jonty moved to walk beside him, "We don't need to do this...Richard...come on, there has to be another way of finding your friend?"

"Like what?"

"I don't know" Jonty was almost hysterical, "But this feels like a really bad fucking idea!"

Sighing heavily, Richard stopped walking, his expression grim as he met the gaze of the estate agent, "If something has somehow managed to take my mother down then it was one of the Twelve...I have already got rid of five of them, even if I did have help with a couple. That means that we can take whatever is out there"

"We?" Jonty grimaced, head shaking slowly.

Richard nodded, "The choice is yours, you can either come with me or stay here and be the sex slave of Clemence for the rest of time, your call"

"You utter cunt" Jonty nodded at him, sighing heavily, and it was all Richard could do to not burst out laughing as he nodded back, smiling bitterly.

"You have no idea"

Chapter Fifty Six

Grim faced, the two moved past the small graveyard, and stopped at the top of the slope to the hollow, the brick shed visible amid its depths. With shock Richard realised that he could see perfectly well, despite it being night and the sky being thick with snow clouds which had obscured the moon, the area before him appearing as though it was only just dusk and the remaining light of the day was refusing to go.

"Is that the shed?" Jonty's question had the author turning to look at him, wincing as he saw the fear etched upon the face of his younger companion.

He was scared. No, scared didn't cover it.

Jonty Beaumont was terrified.

But he was still there with Richard, that fact making the author cringe with shame as he considered the fact that he had shamelessly tricked the ghost of the blonde estate agent into helping him find Myra.

There was no way for him to escape this place.

"What is it?"

Richard forced himself to focus as Jonty stepped closer to him, concern on his features as he glanced about, "What's the matter? What are you thinking?"

"Nothing" Richard lied, shaking his head as he began to edge down the slope only to stop as the other placed a hand on his arm, brow furrowed slightly.

"Something is wrong...the look on your face!"

"I told you I'm fine" Richard shrugged Jonty's arm off, almost slipping as he made his way down the snow-covered slope, arms wind milling wildly beside him. Somehow, he made it on two feet, though the exertion of the descent had made the pain in the back of his thigh flare up even more than before. Turning, he glanced back up to the top of the small rise, his eyes meeting those of Jonty and he shrugged, "Are you coming with me or not?"

The blonde ghost shook his head, "Are you going to tell me the truth or not?"

"I told you, there is nothing wrong"

Jonty gave a humourless laugh, his head shaking as he stood atop the rise staring down at the author, "I have spent my entire life lying to people...I know how to do it exceedingly well...you however are shit at it"

Richard grimaced at his words, embarrassed that Jonty had realised there was something wrong, and turning away, he began walking away across the hollow, eyes fixed to the shed then suddenly stopped. For long moments, he stared down at the snow beneath his feet, brow furrowing as he looked behind him and realised that he hadn't left any footprints. Then he sighed, eyes lifting to meet those of Jonty as he turned to face him atop the rise, "I lied"

"I know" came the reply, "I told you thi..."

"I lied about being able to get you out of this fucking place" Richard interrupted, shaking his head as he held the gaze of the blonde ghost, his broad shoulders shrugging, "It was wrong...but I needed you to tell me where Myra was!"

"And now you know" there was bitterness in the voice of Jonty Beaumont as he took a step back, head shaking, "I fucking trusted you...well, that's great"

"I know" Richard nodded, wincing as he gave an apologetic smile, "I'm sorry"

Without another word he turned once more, continuing on towards the large brick building, his steps more cautious as he drew closer to it, his eyes scanning about for any sign of one of the remaining Twelve or his missing mother, his gut tightening as he considered her unexpected disappearance.

Had she really fallen prey to one of The Twelve?

It was obvious from the words of Myra earlier and of Jonty that The Twelve were aware of other ghosts within the house and there was some form of hierarchy, with them all apparently being scared of Britt Sanderson, even The Great Marlowe having fled when the ghost off the last executioner had attacked Dr Edwin Bennet. Myra had claimed that the ghosts in the house were talking about the fact that he had dispatched Agnes Rand; The Cook and Elias Crumb; The Devil. They were bound to be aware that there was a new female ghost within the house that was helping him dispatch the others of The Twelve.

Had several of them teamed up to take her out?

It was entirely possible but which ones?

Grimacing, he stopped walking just ten feet from the shed, eyes narrowing as he peered through the doorway that he had left wide open when fleeing the ghost of his father earlier that day, his enhanced vision revealing nothing untoward. Yet that didn't mean that his father wasn't in there waiting for him to come inside the door. Grimacing, Richard tightened his grip on the handle of the axe, hoping that he was better with it this time around than when he had tried to kill William Haggerty, The Vessel.

He flinched as a shape moved alongside him, a curse of dread leaving his lips as he took a quick step back, raising the axe over his right shoulder to strike.

"Wait, it's me, you mad bastard!" the voice of Jonty screamed, his hands raising before him, the straight razor falling from the fingers of his right hand.

Eyes wide, Richard glanced about, peering into the near darkness behind the blonde ghost, head shaking, in confusion, "Is this some sort of a trick?"

"What?"

"You heard me!" the author snarled, giving the axe in his hands a shake as if intending to bring it swinging down into the unarmed ghost, and Jonty actually gave a yelp of unbridled terror and took a step backwards. "Stop, for fuck sake!" the ghost's voice was near falsetto, blue eyes large in his bruised but handsome features, "Put the axe down!"

"Oh, you'd like that wouldn't you!"

"Yes!" Jonty nodded frantically, "That is exactly what I am saying...put the axe down!"

Trying to keep the axe steady, Richard eyed the ghost before him in confusion, his head shaking, "Why are you here?"

"To help you find the girl!"

"Why are you really here?" the author grimaced.

"I already told you...to find the girl!" Jonty attempted a sneer then cursed and flinched as Richard took a quick step towards him, "OK, OK, I am too scared to walk back on my own!"

"For fuck sake!" the author relaxed, head shaking as he gave the other ghost a grim smile, "Really?"

Before him, Jonty nodded, a sarcastic smile on his features, his voice raising as he mock-bowed to an invisible audience, "Yes, it is all very funny...let's all laugh as the coward...what a hoot!"

Shaking his head, Richard nodded down at the straight razor, "Pick that up, and hope you don't need to use it...and I promise, if you help me find Myra, I will do all I can to help you...I don't know how but I will do my best"

Before him, Jonty Beaumont made a face as if he wasn't sure how to take Richards words, finally settling for a nod, and a smug grin, "Well, I suppose it's better than nothing...oh shit"

"What?" Richard raised an eyebrow, turning to follow the gaze of the other ghost, his features twisting into a grimace as he saw the familiar figure of Clemence Stoke standing in the trees off to the side of the shed, her long-nailed fingers twitching as she stared back at them, "Fuck"

Behind him, Jonty gave a gurgling choke, and feeling sick, Richard spun about, cursing as he saw ghost of Lydia Tanner standing behind the ghost of the estate agent, the blade of her knife slipping off the side of his neck, leaving a wide gash across the front of his throat, blood spurting from the grisly wound. Eyes wide, Jonty gurgled once more, then grunted as Lydia reached lower, stabbing him repeatedly in the chest and gut, and with a final groan, Richard's companion dropped to his knees and then his face in the snow. Taking a step back away, moving so that both the female ghosts were in sight at the same time, Richard shook his head, axe held ready, "Come on then you crazy fucking bitches!"

With a howl of excitement, they attacked.

Chapter Fifty Seven

With a roar, Richard swung the axe as the pair neared him, realising almost as soon as he had committed himself to the swing that it was going to miss them by an almost embarrassing amount. Cursing he moved his feet, turning his body in a circle so that the axe was headed round once more, trying to move closer to the women. Snarling in anger, Clemence darted to the left, Lydia going right, a smile upon her attractive features, and swearing like a sailor, Richard backed away, trying to make sure that he could see them both. He tensed as Lydia took a step towards him, his axe swinging once more only to feel his stomach knot as he realised it had been a ruse, as she stepped back. Grimacing, he released his grip on the axe, and spun about, hands rising before him to catch Clemence as she leapt astride his chest, legs wrapping about his waist as if she were trying to climb a tree, her features twisted in excitement as she clung on. "Fuck off!" Richard spun, pushing at the snarling ghost with his hands, sending her crashing back down to the ground, then spun, eyes widening as he saw Lydia Tanner just a matter of feet behind him. In desperation, he lashed out with his right fist, but she easily ducked the blow and stepped back away from him, the rising Clemence joining her.

Cursing, Richard searched for his axe, grimacing as he saw it some distance off beside the large shed, then flicked his eyes back on the two women as they struck him at the same time, neither actually of them attempting to actually fight him but instead throwing themselves upon him like a pair of rabid cats.

He cursed in shock as he felt the blade in the hands of Lydia Tanner, his right wrist grasping at her arm, desperately trying to keep it away, then grunted in shock as Clemence bit his right ear. With a scream, he tripped, falling backwards onto the snow, the sudden impact dislodging Clemence but Lydia stayed atop him, straddling his chest as she freed her arms from his and pressed the point of her blade against his throat. Richard winced, eyes closing for a moment, expecting her to stab him then and there, only to open her eyes as he heard her give a cold laugh. Grimacing, he stared up at her as she knelt atop him, realising this was the closest he had been to the ghost, despite having seen her several times.

For a moment, he considered grabbing her and rolling to the sides, throwing her from his body, but as the thought occurred to him, she gave a soft chuckle and leaned forwards, a gasp of pain escaping Richard as the point of the knife broke his skin. Hands forming fists either side of his head as he lay on the snow, staring up at the busty blonde ghost, her large breasts threatening to spill from her top. Sudden movement made him flick his eyes to the side, his skin crawling as Clemence crawled into view on her hands and knees through the snow, snarling like a feral cat as she loomed beside his features.

"Tooketh him from me thee didst" her voice was cold as she stared down at him, her features twisted into a snarl, and Richard frowned in confusion, realising after a moment that she was referring to Elias Crumb, not Jonty Beaumont, as she reached up with a hand, stroking his bearded features almost sexually, *"Thee oweth me sir, and I wanteth paying anon!"*

"Where's Myra" Richard grimaced then winced as the two women exchanged amused smiles, Clemence rising to curtsey to her fellow ghost companion.

"I toldeth thee the knave wouldst leadeth this gent h're if 't I did pretend the wench wast h're!"

The author tensed at her words, realising that both he and Jonty had been led into a trap, then cursed as atop him Lydia shook her head, pressing with her knife as she gave a chuckle, and then Clemence gave a strange moan as she moved her face down near his, rubbing her angular features against him like a cat nuzzling another. Grimacing, Richard kept as still as he could, ignoring the stroking hands of Clemence, his eyes locked to those of Lydia as she knelt astride his chest, seemingly amused by his plight, her eyes occasionally moving to study her fellow female ghost as she sniffed at Richards hair and beard, her moans becoming coarser. He cringed as she suddenly licked his face, her mouth pressing hard against his, her tongue fighting its way into his mouth for a moment before she leaned back, rising on shaky legs as she cast Lydia a look of triumph, "Holdeth the villain still sist'r, I intendeth to has't mine own way with him" Atop Richard, Lydia gave a grin, her eyes turning back to meet his, and the author grimaced, then cursed as Clemence ducked down out of sight behind her companion, his body tensing as he felt her weight upon his ankles and the fumble of her eager fingers upon the front of his trousers, his zipper sliding. "No!" he started to shake his head, only to freeze as Lydia Tanner raised a finger to her lips, hushing him. Swallowing the tightness in his throat, Richard laid back, eyes staring up at the trees that towered over them, blinking out of instinct each time that it seemed as if a snowflake was going to land on his eyelashes, even though none ever did. Anything to take his mind of the feel of the probing fingers of Clemence as she spread the front of his trousers wide and dragged down his underwear. He tensed as he felt Clemence take him in her hand, her fingers working away at him, and as the ghost gave a lustful chuckle, Lydia turned to look down behind her, muttering something before turning back to grin down at him once more, a different look in her bright eyes now. "Tis liketh wet clay in mine own hands!" the voice of Clemence was disgruntled, her hands working harder at him, only to pause as Lydia gave a chuckle, turning to look at her once more, her voice coarse with lust.

"Thou hast a mouth in thy head"

Richard cursed, his stomach turning over as he heard the fresh chuckle from Clemence, then he winced as he felt himself sucked into a tight 'O', his mind reeling as it drew him in deeper then slid back off, long nailed fingers holding him as she worked her mouth. Time lost all meaning as he lay in the slow, the blade of Lydia Tanner; The Widow's Wail held against his throat while Clemence Stoke; The Witch, worked away at him with her hungry mouth, mind reeling as his body betrayed him, responding to her attention. He was vaguely aware of Lydia Tanner turning to stare down at her companion as she worked, one of the ghosts hands rising to cup one of her large breasts through her clothes but the knife stayed pressed against his throat, ready to kill him should he even attempt to fight back against the evil pair.

So, he lay there, a prisoner to their attentions, a victim of the two of The Twelve who had used their sexual dominance over their many victims.

He was just another to add to their list.

Was he to replace Jonty and Elias when this was done, or would he be killed a second, final time. If that was the case, no-one would rescue Myra. Cringing as he heard a hungry moan from Clemence, Richard turned his head to the side, blinking as he saw Jonty laying in the snow, his throat torn wide open, his blank eyes staring blankly into the night. The author had put his own needs, and the rescue of Myra above all else and tricked the ghost into joining him, even when he had admitted the truth, Jonty had stayed and died; a victim of Richards ego.

Ego.

Of course.

Turning his head back to stare up at Lydia, Richard raised his hands from where they had been fists beside his head and placed them on her legs. As he had expected, she snapped her face back to stare down at him, knife pressing, an eyebrow raised in question, and he winked at her, his hands gently stroking her bare legs where her long skirt had rucked up about him, exposing her to the thighs.

"I wish it was you" his words felt like poison in his mouth as he spoke, trying his best to sound convincing, and atop him Lydia Tanner gave him a quizzical look, her top lip curling in suspicion.

"What art thee up to?"

"Nothing!" he shook his head slowly, wincing as the point of the knife jabbed him again, "I just wish it was you...down there...you are so much prettier than she is...a real beauty..."

Lydia gave a sneer, her head shaking slightly, clearly wise to his game but at his groin, the mouth of Clemence was slowing down, the grip of her fingers upon the base of his cock loosening suddenly, her mouth leaving him completely along with her hand.

"Yeah" Richard continued, raising his voice, making sure that the other could hear, "No wonder all the men love you...look at you...I cant believe hot fucking gorgeous you are...not like her...not like that ugly whore sucking me!"

Atop him, Lydia grimaced, "*What trickery?*"

"Trickery?" Richard sounded surprised, "I don't understand...you told me that I was going to be yours...like you had Elias and Jonty...they all preferred you...they all loved you the most...but not like I do...you are the best...the prettiest!"

With a roar, Clemence suddenly surged to her feet beside Lydia, her right hand sweeping out at the blonde ghost, and with a cry of shock and pain, The Widow's Wail fell backwards from Richard. Snarling like a woman possessed, Clemence went with her, right hand raised once more and sitting up quickly,

Richard saw the straight razor that Jonty had dropped in her fingers. Rolling to his knees, he put himself away, stomach turning as he felt the slick wetness of her saliva upon him, and then rose, watching in disbelief as Clemence knelt astride a struggling Lydia, slashing her repeatedly across the face with the razor, "*Behold at thy visage wh're! I am the prettiest not thee!*"

Grunting in shock and pain, her features a criss-cross of deep slashes, Lydia suddenly snaked up a hand, fingers feeling for the face of Clemence, only to scream in agony, as The Witch sank her teeth into the reaching fingers, biting two free and spitting them away into the snow. Blind and dying, Lydia tried to sit up, but was pinned back down with ease, the straight razor opening her throat wide like a mouth. As blood gushed from the wound, The Widows Wail thrust her own blade up under her chin of Clemence, twisting viscously as she did, blood cascading down over her. Stunned by the level of violence from the two ghosts that had only just moments ago been companions, Richard stood amid the heavy snow, watching as Clemence slumped forward over Lydia, the sudden rush of flames from The Widow's Wail signalling that she had died, a second sudden conflagration showing that The Witch had gone with her, the flames consuming them both, leaving the snow untouched.

Richard stayed long enough to watch until they began to turn to ash, and only then did he turn away.

Chapter Fifty Eight

It had been a waste of time.

A waste of time that had resulted in Jonty's death.
Richard hadn't known the man personally and in his
brief encounter with him when they had both been
alive and also in their ghostly reunion, the author
hadn't seen any redeeming qualities in the man at all.
Yet he was dead, and Richard couldn't help but shake
the feeling that he was to blame for his second death.
His mother was also gone without a trace, most likely
another victim of Lydia Tanner and Clemence Stoke.
The Widow's Wail and The Witch.

Two more members of The Twelve beaten.

Shaking his head as he stood in the Hollow, Richard
turned his gaze to study the large brick built shed,
briefly considering going inside it to check for any
sign of his father and Myra but then changed his
mind. Clemence had already told him that it had all
been a ruse to get him down to the isolated shed.
Revenge for him dispatching her lover, Elias.

Grimacing, he turned slowly, glancing about the
hollow, searching one final time for a sign of his
mother but there was nothing to be found at all.
Even the body of Jonty had finally faded away.
At first the fact that the body of the estate agents
ghost had remained long after it had died while each
of The Twelve had burst into flames almost at once

had bothered Richard until he had realised Jonty hadn't been bound to the Twins like they had.

It was only The Twelve who burst into flames as their connection to the ancient oaks was broken.

Shaking his head, he released the handle of the axe that he had retrieved from the snow with his right hand and reached into the pocket of his jeans to withdraw the medicine bag of Chaqit, scowling at it as he raised it up before his face, head shaking angrily.

Back on the material plane it had managed to dispatch Agnes Rand; The Cook, Father Ambrose Dewitt; The Penitent Man, and Elias Crumb; The Devil, yet here, it seemed to have no effect at all.

What was wrong with it? Was it broken?

Sighing, he shoved the pouch back into his pocket and tried to work out where he should search for Myra.

Where would his father have taken her?

He grimaced as he wondered how much time had past already since he had drowned in the bathtub on the second floor. Was it already too late for him?

It felt like hours but then Jonty had said it felt like he had been here for years when it had only been days.

Did time move differently for ghosts?

Shaking his head, he cast another look around the hollow, his right-hand fastening to the haft of the axe.

He didn't want to be taken by surprise, not when he was so unskilled with the axe and the pouch was a shadow of its former self. Satisfied that he wasn't about to be attacked any time soon, Richard turned and began to walk back towards the slope that led up to the small graveyard, then paused as he sensed something large move among the trees just off to his left. Grimacing, he turned, his brow furrowing as he studied the area, unable to see anything wrong.

Then he cursed, taking a backward step as the huge figure of James Jackman stepped from out of the darkness to stand amid the falling snow, a sledgehammer held across his body, large fingers shifting on the handle as if getting a better grip.

"Oh, not you" Richard winced, remembering how the huge ghost had thrown him from the first-floor landing as if he had weighed nothing at all, the sheer strength of James Jackman utterly terrifying him.

Features devoid of emotion, The Butcher stepped forwards several paces and stopped, huge chest rising and falling as if trying to calm its anger, and Richard shook his head slowly, "Stay there"

Without a word, the huge ghost began to walk towards him, long strides carrying him quickly across the snowy ground of the hollow despite the fact that he appeared to be moving slowly, and with a curse, Richard backed hurried away through the trees.

Reaching the slope, he tried to climb it, cursed and fell to his knees, head shaking as he recalled fleeing

from his father and his inability to climb up the snowy rise. Then he had used the ladder that he had come to find, the ladder that he had dumped outside the huge house in the wake of Agnes Rand's final attack upon him earlier. Cursing, Richard forced himself back to his feet, a quick glance over his shoulder showing him that James Jackman was less than five feet away now. Grimacing, forcing himself into a run, the author careened headlong through the falling snow, following the hollow as it wound along the side of the property, then turned to the right to find that the incline was less pronounced. Sighing in relief, Richard followed it, climbing to higher ground to find himself stood at the rear of the huge house, his head turning to find the Twins towering over him, covered with snow. Flicking his head back to the hollow, Richard watched in dread as James Jackman emerged from the falling snow, stepping up onto the higher ground, blank eyes locked upon the author. Then as if in a dream, the huge man blinked slowly and turned to stare at the conjoined old oaks, a troubled look creeping onto his features as if he were remembering something awful. Richard cringed as the huge man released his sledgehammer with one hand, his large fingers rising to his thick throat. He's remembering being hung.
Richard grimaced, taking several steps away from the

ghost of the huge man as it stood staring up at the trees, trying his best not to distract him, then he turned and ran through the snow, his eyes locked on the large greenhouse built onto the back of Sanderson House. He reached it in moments and let go of the axe with his right hand, turning the handle and opening the door to step inside, his eyes turning back to his pursuer only to find the ghost of James Jackman gone. Grimacing, Richard stepped inside the greenhouse, and closed the door behind him, his free hand rising to press against the glass of the back door as he stared out into the snowy night beyond.

"Where did you go, you big bastard" his words were a coarse whisper, his head shaking as he peered out from his hiding place, then froze, his nerves jangling as he heard a soft chuckle from somewhere off to his left amid the overgrown plants and bushes, another following at once. Grasping to the axe with shaky hands, Richard made his way down the centre aisle towards the door that led to the kitchen, his eyes scanning the area where the chuckle had come from, mind racing as he tried to work out who it might be.

Frances. It had to be. The little fucking shit.

He should have let his mother kill him earlier.

Hefting the axe, Richard gave a nod, trying to keep his voice calm, "OK you little prick, I know its you..."

"*Peek-a-boo....I-see-you!*" the Great Marlowe popped

his head out from behind a bush several metres away from where Richard had been staring, and screaming in terror, the author dropped the axe and fell back towards the kitchen, eyes wide as he landed hard. Mind reeling in dread, bowels threatening to loosen, Richard began to scoot back across the path of the greenhouse, his skin crawling as the ghost of the cannibal clown stepped into view, a pleasant smile plastered across its oil-painted features, feet high stepping at it walked slowly towards him, fingers wiggling in the air before it, the sing-song voice of the ghost almost hysterical with excitement, "*I'm-coming-to-get-you*"

Chapter Fifty Nine

Filled with horror, Richard pushed himself to his feet, a quick glance at the axe he had dropped showing that it was too close to the ghost clown and therefore lost to him, and backing hurriedly he turned and raced for the kitchen, pushing the door open wide. He cursed as he caught his feet upon the step and fell heavily to his knees, but he was up instantly, charging headlong across the kitchen, a hand spinning chairs behind him to slow his pursuer down. He reached the door that led to the main ground floor hallway and turned to look back across the kitchen, a gasp of terror escaping him as he saw the Great Marlowe leap atop the large table in its centre, avoiding the chairs he had placed behind him, the ghost freezing in place atop the large table as it saw him looking back. Long moments dragged by as it stood staring at him, that broad smile plastered across its grease painted features, and then slowly the expression faded to be replaced by blank indifference, the voice of the clown no long squeaky but deep, slow and emotionless, "*We are going to have so much fun together...I am going to fuck you...bite you...cut you...you are going to ask me to kill you but I am going to make it last forever*"

Richard didn't wait to hear more, pushing open the door he charged out, slamming it behind him, then winced as the pain in his left thigh flared once more and he stumbled, crashing forwards upon the hallway floor. Blinking in dread as he heard the door open behind him, the author pushed himself to his hands and knees, and then his feet, turning towards the stairwell, intent on getting upstairs back to his body. This had been a mistake. A huge mistake.

He cursed as the diminutive figure of Frances lurched wildly from behind the large wardrobe at the foot of the stairs, the child's blade missing his chest by inches and cursing he began to back away, then swore as he found the Great Marlowe standing in front of the kitchen door, that mocking smile back in place, "*Going somewhere sweetheart?*"

"You!" Richard raised his left hand, wincing as he pointed at the clown and the stump of his ring finger bumped against his palm, "Stay away!"

"*Oh*" the Great Marlowe gave a pout, head tilting comically to one side and Richard tensed as Frances stepped into view to his left, the child ghost grinning. Shaking his head as he realised that he was in dire trouble, Richard took several steps backwards, glancing at the wall to his left, trying to discern how close he was to the front door. The stairs were no longer an option for him, which meant that he was going to have to go back outside into the snow once again. But to where? Where could he go?

Gritting his teeth, he took several more steps back and turned his head towards the stairs, cupping his right hand to his mouth, "Cherry! Revive me!"

There was no answer as he had half expected, but he glanced down at himself nevertheless, hoping that something was going to change, that somehow, some way his friend had heard him and was reviving him. Yet nothing happened, and he glanced up as The Great Marlowe gave a chuckle, head shaking slowly, a mock sad expression upon its white features, *"I don't think the lass heard you...don't worry though...I'll find her once I've tasted your fruits, and bring her along to our little party"*

"Leave her the fuck alone!" Richard took a step forwards, surprised at his sudden anger and the clown clasped both hands to its cheeks in mock terror, knees bending and wobbling together.

"Let us kill him!" the voice of Frances sounded, the pale face of the ghost boy etched with hatred as it took a step forwards, knife raised ready.

"Are you proposing a team effort young lad" the Great Marlowe did an elaborate turn, dropping to a crouch before the boy, hands on his hips, an eyebrow raised. Frances Goodnestone turned to his fellow Twelve member, a cruel smile on his face as he nodded, *"Aye, let's share the kill!"*

Richard felt his bowels knot as the clown gave a chuckle, and turned to look over at him, its voice thick with amusement, "*Why not*"

Snarling, Frances turned back to glare at Richard, dropping into a crouch as if about to charge him, then grunted and looked back at the Great Marlowe as the clown gave a gasp and tapped a long finger against its lips, *"I have a better idea!"*

"*Oh?*"

The clown nodded almost wisely, "*How about I eat your face and then I have him for myself?*"

Frances Goodnestone gave a confused chuckle, head shaking, "*What are you ta...*"

His words turned to a scream of terror and pain as the clown threw itself upon the boy, one long arm pinning his knife hand to the floor, while it buried its teeth into his features like a rabid dog, head shaking. Feeling sick, Richard backed away to the door, one hand reaching up to open it, but he found himself unable to move, his eyes locked to the grisly scene in the middle of the hallway floor, nausea rising in him. The Great Marlowe was crouched atop the body of Frances Goodnestone like a spindly legged black and white spider upon a fly, his head shaking as he worked his teeth into his bloody face like a dog killing a rat, the authors stomach knotting as he heard the hungry moans coming from the clown as it ate the

433

face of the child ghost, the struggles of its victim growing weaker. With a gasp like a drowning man surfacing, the irony of that not lost of Richard, the Great Marlowe suddenly raised its head and turned towards Richard, an almost sleepy expression upon its painted features as it chewed slowly, blood and gore coating his nose, mouth, chin and throat. Shaking his head, Richard opened the door wider as the Great Marlowe took a step towards him, then stopped and turned around, bending as it picked up the knife that Frances had dropped. Turning back to face Richard, it raised a hand, wiping the gore from its mouth across its cheek with the back of its free hand as it continued chewing, its eyes rolling as it moaned in appreciation like a food critic, then threw the knife across the floor to land at the authors feet. As the small body of Frances Goodnestone burst into flames, Richard bent and picked up the weapon in his right hand, staring at the Great Marlowe as it finished chewing what was in its mouth and made a show of swallowing it down, the mouth of the cannibal clown opening to show its tongue like a child proving to its mother it had eaten its Brussel sprouts completely. "You mad mother fucker" Richard took another step backwards, out under the porch and then the snow beyond, head shaking as the clown moved into view, a frown on its face as he sighed almost sadly, "That's

the trouble with child portions...I'm already hungry
again!"

Chapter Sixty

Turning, Richard began to run, the pain in his left thigh coming more frequently now, making him draw up into a loping trot, cursing as he glanced behind to see the Great Marlowe gaining on him. Grimacing, he raced past his car, and angled his run towards the gateposts, knowing that if he could get through them and of the Sanderson property, the clown might not be able to follow. The author gasped as the tall, skinny figure of the Great Marlowe suddenly ran past him, all arms and legs, the cannibal clown putting itself between Richard and his planned escape route. Grimacing, the author turned left, running around the side of the house, cursing aloud as he charged through the snow, the laughter of the clown following him. He stumbled and fell suddenly, his left leg finally giving out, and cursing, he rolled to his back, the knife that the clown had given him held ready, "Come on!" Ten feet behind him, the Great Marlowe stood smiling as he watched him, head tilted to the side, but then, just as it had on the kitchen table, the smile faded and the clown stared at him blankly, the sudden lack of emotion upon his features even more terrifying. "Stay back!" Richard pushed himself to his feet, wincing as he took several steps back, eyes locked to the features of the clown standing there before him, an almost vacant expression on his face for a moment before it blinked, as though suddenly remembering the author was there before him, quaking in fear. "*Where were we?*" his voice was almost bored.

"I'm warning you!" Richard waved the blade before him, head shaking, "I'll kill you!"

The Great Marlowe stopped walking at the author's threat, brow furrowing as he stared back at Richard for a moment before staring up into the falling snow, his narrow shoulders slumping as he gave a heavy sigh and met his gaze once more, "*My life wasn't supposed to end up like this...I was famous...I was adored by the masses...I used to make people laugh!*" Stunned by the Great Marlowe's words, Richard took another two steps away, his right hand keeping the knife between them, his features twisted in confusion as the other began to talk once more, a hand gesturing about him, "*I am not like these others...these Twelve...if you were to ask each of them why they did what they did you would get a different answer...the Butcher was beaten and abused by his parents so he killed them and took over their farm...the Black Sheep was shunned by his real father...the Cook was taking revenge on those who had mocked her son...the Witch and the Devil were in love...and so on and so on...a constant stream of excuses, a veritable litany of half-truths and delusions, all created to give validation to their*

437

heinous crimes…but not me…I am nothing like them"
Richard tensed, not wanting the ghost to continue
talking but suddenly in that moment he needed the
Great Marlowe to finish his speech more than he had
ever need anything in his life. As if sensing his morbid
interest, the clown shook its head, that wistful look
still upon its features as it turned and stared back out
into the night for a moment, the authors gut knotting
as it continued speaking, "*No, not me…I did what I did
because I enjoyed it…it is as simple as that…no
excuses…no lies…no violent parents…no poverty or
hardship to blame it on. I was loved as a child, born to
a caring family, fed and watered, and made to feel
special…I do what I do because it excites me…to see
fear in the eyes…to hear their begs and cries…*"
He smacked his lips together as if he had just tasted a
fine wine, then turned back to look at Richard, "Is
there anything that tastes so sweet?"
"You are insane" the author shook his head.
"*I'm honest*"the Great Marlowe shrugged, then
clicked the fingers of his right hand, his arms rising
either side of his head, his huge fake smile
reappearing on his face as he did so, "*Now, back to
the show…are you ready for some fun, lover?*"
Grimacing, Richard turned to run, charging around
the rear of the house only to grunt in shock as
something heavy struck him across the chest,

throwing him heavily back to the ground, the small knife flying from his hand as he landed on his back. Blinking rapidly, tears filling his eyes as pain surged through his upper body, Richard stared up from where he lay, watching as the Great Marlowe winced in sudden genuine terror and took a step away, black and white form fading away quickly from sight.

Since his arrival at Sanderson house and his baptism in the history of the village and The Twelve, there had only been one time that Richard had ever seen the Great Marlowe react with such raw palpable fear.

Oh fuck.

Britt Sanderson.

Pushing himself to his knees upon the snow, Richard looked up at the large ghost stepped into view around the side of the house, still dressed in grey trousers, a white vest smeared with what looked like blood and dirt, and a pair of braces. As Richard stared up at Britt Sanderson from where he was kneeling, the ghost moved to stand before him, a large hand rising to smooth back over his bald head, his pencil thin moustache twitching as he grimaced, his voice thick with disgust and hatred, "*Murderer!*"

"No!" the author shook his head weakly, his hands raising either side of his head, "It wasn't murder...it was revenge...I was punishing him!"

Britt Sanderson studied him for a moment, eyes narrowing, and then with a speed that belied his size he sent a right hook cannoning into Richards face, throwing him back heavily to the ground once more. Barely conscious, the author stared up at the snow as it fell towards him, agony washing through him like a tsunami, flooding every nerve. The headbutt from the Vessel had already broken his nose but the powerful right hook from Britt Sanderson had made it worse, blood running from it to coat his beard, the taste and smell of copper filling his senses as he moaned aloud. Through blurred vision, Richard watched as the ghost moved to stand over him, big fists clenched, *"You are a vile murderer"*

"No" the author's voice was a whisper through his split lips, his head shaking weakly, "The one you say...I murdered...he is here..."

"I know" Britt Sanderson dropped down to a crouch, eyes staring down into those of Richard angrily.

"He...he has taken a girl...a ghost...he is a killer...he killed her when he was alive...he..."

Britt Sanderson grimaced, head shaking, "Lies!"

Richard blinked, confusion vying with pain for control of his thoughts, "No...he killed her!"

"Don't judge Britt too harshly" a strange voice suddenly sounded, *"He never was too good at spotting who was a murderer and who wasn't"*

As Richard tensed, Britt Sanderson lurched to his feet and spun about to face the newcomer, a growl of anger escaping the large ghost, "*You!*"

Fighting his way past the pain, Richard turned his head, staring up in astonishment at the man who stood some fifteen feet away, dressed in brown trousers and a white shirt, the sleeves rolled up, an apron covering his stomach and the top of his legs. Blinking, the author let his gaze rise higher, drifting over the red cheeked face of the man that had laughed, the centre of his head bald, an island amid the silver hair that ringed the sides and joined his large sideburns. With shock, the author realised that he had never seen the man before, confusion coursing through him until Britt Sanderson snarled, "*Albright!*"

"*Come now Britt*" the other sighed, *"There was a time you called me Edward!"*

Richard frowned as he realised he had now seen all of The Twelve, his voice weak, "The Collector!"

Both ghosts turned to study him as he lay there, a thing of pain, too dizzy to even attempt to stand.

"Murderer!" Britt Sanderson turned from the author to step towards the ghost of the innkeeper, his former best friend, his large fists raised before him, his face a mask of unbridled fury, yet Edward Albright seemed unconcerned, his deep voice thick with amusement.

"For someone who relies upon their brawn as much as you, my old friend, you should realise that there is always someone bigger than you!"

Richard tensed as a huge shadow fell across him, his stomach knotting as he glanced at the cause. Too late, the ghost of Britt Sanderson seemed to realise the implied threat and sense that there was someone behind him, and he spun, that powerful right hook swinging out, the force behind it staggering. James Jackman turned the blow aside with his own right arm as if it were nothing, his left snaking out to hammer a punch into the stomach of the former executioner, doubling him at the waist and then stepped in closer, the same fist smashing down upon the back of Britt Sanderson's bald head, sending the ghost crashing to the snowy ground with ease.

As Richard blinked in disbelief, the ghost of Edward Albright stepped alongside Britt Sanderson, nudging his prone form with a foot, then turned to smile down at the author, his tone conversational, *"Are you having fun yet?"*

Chapter Sixty One

Blinking through his pain, Richard watched as the huge figure of James Jackman bent at the waist and grasped the right ankle of Britt Sanderson with one hand and then his with the other, then straightened up once more. Without warning, the huge man began to walk backwards, dragging them back through the snow towards the front of the house, dragging both men as if they weighed nothing at all and Richard let it happen, too weak to even think about staging any form of resistance. And so he lay there, trying to stay calm as he turned his head, watching the face of Britt Sanderson as he was dragged alongside the author, the face of the bald man was almost serene, his eyes moving beneath his eyelids as if he were dreaming. Richard grimaced as he imagined the ghost snapping its eyes open, roaring in a rage, and rolling over to kill him with those large hands. Yet it didn't happen. Their bodies shifted position suddenly, sliding in the snow which still never seemed to stick to their bodies, and with vague awareness Richard realised that they were passing along the front of the house towards the porch and the porch and the main door. They slid past the authors car, covered in heavy snow, and then the grip about Richards ankle went away suddenly, and his leg dropped to the ground. "Bastard!" Britt Sanderson grumbled beside him, and turning his head, Richard watched as the large ghost tried to sit himself up, only to drop back down as a punch from James Jackman smashed into him. Richard cringed as the hands of the giant ghost grasped at him suddenly, lifting him from the floor and then he was turning in the air, a grunt escaping him as his head bumped off the door frame, and then he was unceremoniously thrown across the hallway floor. He landed hard, cursing in pain, and rolling to his side, he watched as the Butcher, reappeared back through the front door, carrying Britt Sanderson under the arms before dropping him down as he had Richard, the ghost's face striking the hallway floor. Suddenly Edward Albright was there once more, striding across the hallway to mutter something to the huge James Jackman before walking back the way he had come towards the kitchen, a broad smile creasing his ruddy features as he noticed Richard watching him from the floor. The author gasped as he suddenly felt the Butcher grasp at his ankle once more, the left leg this time and he nearly passed out as pain from the stab wound inflicted by Frances coursed through the limb. Grimacing past the pain, still hurting too much from the attack by Britt Sanderson to try and fight back, Richard let himself get dragged through the hallway, turning before the kitchen towards the top of the basement stairs.

Too late Richard realised the implication and then he was sliding forwards as the Butcher swung his arm, through the open door and down the stairs. He cried out as his forehead came down upon the edge of a step, the scream followed by another as his wounded leg, severed finger and broken nose all found a way to strike the stairs on his ungraceful descent of them. Richard grunted as the floor of the basement stopped him hard, senses reeling, and through blurry tear-filled eyes, he glanced up to see James Jackman about to throw Britt Sanderson down to land on top of him. His concern was short-lived however as he began suddenly sliding across the basement floor, his head rising to see Edward Albright holding him by both ankles, the ghost backpedalling towards the pool table and the seating area before the cinema screen where two wooden chairs waited. Drunk on pain, Richard watched as Edward Albright released his ankles and stepped back, directing James Jackman as the ghost dragged over the body of Britt Sanderson. With one powerful lift, The Butcher placed the last of the Sanderson hangmen in one of the chairs, and Richard watched as Edward Albright quickly bound him to it around the ankles, wrists, and chest with thick rope, excitement registering in his eyes.

Then they turned to him, The Butcher lifting him onto the remaining wooden chair with embarrassing ease, and still dizzy, the author turned to watch as Edward Albright appeared beside him, tying his hands to the arms of the chair, before dropping to secure his legs. He had survived all of the other attacks just to become a prisoner of Edward Albright, The Collector. A man who in life had killed over fifty people during a thirty year reign of torture and murder, a man who had taken people as exhibits in his own twisted and perverse people zoo, torturing and abusing them before ending their lives. The sudden realisation of exactly who was tying him to a chair dawned on the author and he shook his head, arms straining against the rope around his wrists, his legs starting to kick only for him to realise that he had been too late.

"Let me go!" he snarled, trying to sound threatening, straining against his bonds until a hand dragged back on his forehead, and he felt a blade at his throat, the voice of Edward Albright whispering in his ear.

"Now, now, let's have a measure of decorum shall we...this is going to be a long night...let's not start of by playing silly buggers eh?"

Teeth clenched together, muscles tight in his cheeks, Richard stopped struggling, then winced as the ghost gave him an almost affectionate kiss upon the cheek and released him, a hand ruffling over the top of his head, "*There's a good lad*"

"I'll kill you" Richard grimaced, glaring at the ghost as

it moved to stand before him, "I swear"

"*You will?*"Edward Albright gave a chuckle, glancing at the large silent figure of James Jackman before meeting the gaze of the author once more, *"And how pray tell will you do that?"*

Richard snarled, unsure how to reply then blinked, heart racing as The Collector reached into a pocket of his apron and withdrew the small medicine pouch of Chaqit, "*With this? It fell from your pocket while James was dragging you*"

Licking his split lips, Richard shook his head and Edward Albright took a step towards him, holding the bag on his palm, "*This is what I think it is, isn't it?*"

Again, Richard stayed quiet, eyes locked to the bag and the Collector clicked his fingers of his free hand in front of the authors face, drawing his gaze, "*I believe I asked you a question…is this the item you used to kill Agnes, Father Dewitt and that fool Elias?*"

"Yes" Richard grimaced, nodding slightly, "It is"

The Collector raised an eyebrow, his gaze drifting from Richard to study the pouch intently before drifting back to the author once more, "*Why isn't it killing me? Why do I feel no pain?*"

The author grimaced and stayed silent, unsure himself but not wanting to let his potential killer know that he had lost control of the only thing that had given him any power over The Twelve.

"Answer me" Edward Albright took a quick step towards him, suddenly holding the knife that the author had dropped outside, the point hovering just an inch from Richard's right eye, "*Tell me"*

"I don't know" he grimaced, trying to act tough, knowing that the faint tremor in his voice had betrayed him, and The Collector gave a snarl.

"*Murderer"* the deep voice of Britt Sanderson suddenly slurred from the chair beside the author, and with a chuckle, Edward Albright straightened up and took a step back, one hand sliding the knife back into the front pocket of his apron along with the small leather medicine bag. Blinking, amazed that he could still see with both of his eyes, Richard turned his head, wincing as he saw the face of Britt Sanderson glance back at him, his nose broken from James Jackman's earlier punch, blood congealing amid his pencil thin moustache. He held the author's gaze for a moment and then grimaced, "*Murderer!"*

Richard gave a grim nod, turning to study the smug expression upon the face of Edward Albright and the blank features of the Butcher, then he met the gaze of the last hangman again, "We should start a club"

"*Murderer!"* the big man tensed, muscular arms straining against the rope holding him, and James Jackman took a step away from the wall where he had been watching silently, large hands forming fists, only to step back at The Collector raised a hand, gesturing for him to be calm. Then the ruddy-faced man in the apron took a step forwards, alternating his gaze between Richard and Britt Sanderson, a warm smile upon his features as he gave a business-like nod, "*Right then gentlemen, shall we begin?*"

Chapter Sixty Two

Grimacing, suddenly feared with a terror the likes of which he had never known before, Richard clamped his lips together, watching as the Collector moved to stand before the snarling figure of Britt Sanderson, a smile on his features as he nodded, *"I think we will start with you, my old friend"*

"Do not call me friend" the last of the Sanderson hangmen grimaced, head shaking slightly as Richard turned to study him, *"I will see you dead"*

"No" Edward Albright gave a weary chuckle, *"You have done that and yet here we still are...bound together in a strange new world...and this time you are mine to toy with"*

"Bastard"

"Perhaps" the ghost of the innkeeper shrugged, eyes studying the features of Britt Sanderson carefully, then he sighed, *"Do you know how many times I considered placing you in my zoo?"*

Richard frowned, glancing between the two men, the tension of the moment heavy in the air as Britt Sanderson stared back silently, the muscles bunching his cheeks until with a heavy sigh, Edward Albright nodded, *"All those times you fell asleep at a table in my Inn, drunken and sobbing, remorseful that you had taken another life even though the life you had taken was that of a villain, and each time, I would* cover you with a blanket and make sure that you were safe and well...because you were my friend..."

"*You are a murderer*" Britt Sanderson growled.

"*I am, yes*" Edward Albright gave a nod, his body straightening from where he had bent to look into the eyes of his former friend, "*And so are you...regardless of your reasons...so is big James over there in the corner...and so is our host Mr Miles*"

Richard winced as the Collector turned to study him, and he shook his head, surprising himself as he snarled, "I killed my father for his crimes, that's not murder...it is revenge"

The Collector chuckled, glancing back at Britt Sanderson but the ghost was staring off at the huge figure of James Jackman in raw hatred. For a moment, the Collector followed his gaze then he turned back around and stepped closer to Richard, "*I think perhaps I was wrong...we will start with you*"

"Fuck you" the words left the author's mouth before he could stop them, as if uttering a verbal ward to prevent him from being harmed and a flicker of irritation flashed over his captors ruddy features.

"*When I had my zoo my attractions treated me with respect at all times or they paid dearly*"

Trying to keep the fear from his voice, Richard shook his head, holding the gaze of Edward Albright, "Two things Eddy...for one, that wasn't respect, it was fear…and secondly, this isn't your zoo…it's my fucking house!"

He finished his sentence shouting, hands straining at the bonds about his wrists and Edward Albright grimaced, the words of the author having clearly touched a nerve in him. Without warning he stepped forwards, eyes staring down at the left hand of the author, a smile spreading across his features as he clasped in in his own left hand, *"I see you have lost the tip of your ring finger Mr Miles"*

The author grimaced, fighting the wave of pain that surged through him as the ghost of Edward Albright fastened his fingers about the end of the stump and squeezed, his eyes watching Richard. Eyes closed, teeth clenched together so tight that he thought the muscles in his jaw would snap, the author tried to focus past the pain, refusing to allow his captor the pleasure of his discomfort only to suddenly gasp as it grew too painful. Opening his eyes, he felt his penis shrivel as he saw that the Collector was holding the knife once more in his free hand, the tip hovering above where the stump of his finger joined the hand. "Please…you don't need to do this!" Richard shook his head, both surprised and ashamed at how quickly he had resorted to begging, "Don't!"

"Hush now" the conversational, almost pleasant tone of Edward Albright's voice only served to intensify

Richard's fear and he opened his mouth to ask him to stop once more only to scream in agony as the Collector pushed with the knife. Blinking in shock, screaming at the intense burning that was coming from his hand, Richard watched as his captor picked up the small section of meat that had once been a part of him and raised it before his features, smiling broadly as he studied it a moment then cast it away.

"There, don't you feel better now that we have tidied you up a little bit?"

"Maniac!" Richard roared, his pain giving birth to anger that he had never felt before, his arms, legs and chest straining at the ropes securing him to the chair as he glared at his captor, "I'll kill you!"

"There he is" Edward Albright nodded, turning to glance at Britt Sanderson before meeting the gaze of Richard once more, *"Did you see it, old friend, the real face of Mr Miles"*

Shaking his head, dislodging tears of pain from his eyes, the author turned to look at the ghost bound to the chair beside him, grimacing in anger as he saw the look upon its bloody face. Their eyes met, and Britt Sanderson grimaced, then turned to watch as the ghost of the innkeeper stepped in front of him, nodding as he spoke, *"I think we shall keep this fair...everything that I do to one of you, I will do to the other too"*

Britt Sanderson's face was devoid of emotion but his muscular chest rose and fell beneath his vest, the need to breathe for him long since gone, but the habit of doing so remaining within the ghost. Grim faced, Richard watched as the Collector placed the blade against the base of the ring finger on the ghosts left hand, the eyes of the two former friends meeting, and then with a flick of his hand, the finger was cut away. Yet unlike the author, the ghost of the former hangman stayed silent though the pain showed in his eyes, and his right hand clenched the chair tightly. Before him, the ghost of Edward Albright gave a sneer, head shaking in dissatisfaction, "*Oh I think we can do a little better than that don't you?*"

Britt Sanderson grimaced, lips moving as if he were about to speak only for the Collector to suddenly slash at his face in rapid succession with the blade that he was holding, and wincing, a ragged gasp of pain escaping the large ghost, it twisted its bald head towards Richard once more. The author grimaced as he saw the deep slash that ran across the face of the bald man from his left eyebrow, across his nose to end up beside the right side of his mouth, the bone of his nose visible through the wound, then winced as he saw the second slash starting above the right eyebrow of the large ghost and ended up on his right cheek, somehow managing to miss the eye itself.

He blinked as he realised that The Collector was now standing back before him, a smile upon his features as he raised the blade, "*Now Mr Miles, I just told Britt here that I would be treating you both the same, do try and keep your head still!*"

The author screamed in anger, straining against his bonds once more, hope taking flight within him as he felt the rope around his right wrist give slightly, and licking his dry lips he glanced down then snapped his head back up as he saw movement. Too late he saw the knife slashing forwards, and he cried out in dread, then nearly passed out as pain coursed through his face, the scream torn from him raw and animalistic. Awash with pain, he twisted and writhed on the chair, eyes clamped tight together, every nerve ending jangling with agony. Without warning, his perception shifted as the chair toppled to the side, rocked off balance by the ferocity of his struggles and he grunted as his head struck the floor. The laugh of Edward Albright was rich as he spoke, "*James...please stand his chair up*"

Heavy footsteps crossed the floor, and the world seemed to tilt once more as Richard was hauled back into a vertical position on the wooden chair.

A thing of pain, the author tried to calm himself, doing his best to focus past the pain in his face, and gritting his teeth, he opened his eyes, only to scream once more as pain tore through the left side of his face, panic surging through him as he suddenly realised that he could only see with his right eye.

"I did tell you to keep still' the voice of Edward Albright was amused as he shook his head, the knife rising to point at Richard's face, "*You have made me cut too deep and take your eye!"*

Sobbing, maddened beyond rational thought, Richard began to rock in the chair once more, teeth clenched as he watched the Collector move closer to him, "*So, what shall we do next? I am open to suggestions if you have some"*

Richard shook his head, his one-eyed gaze lowering to his lap as his shoulders shook with emotion, each sob seeming to make the pain in his destroyed eye hurt even more than before. Once more he wondered if he would carry these injuries back to his moral body if he somehow managed to survive this whole experience, a bitter, insane chuckle escaping him as he pictured how his photo would look on the back of his novels now; one eyed with a broken nose and a face of scars, not to mention an entire missing finger. If only these injuries would fade like the one's he had received from The Twelve before had when the ghosts had been testing the boundaries between planes after Ms Sanderson's unfortunate fall.

Yet that was not going to happen.

He had been human then and those wounds just illusion, now he was a ghost on the same plane as they and the wounds he suffered were for good.

He raised his head as he realised the truth of his thoughts, his good eye staring past his captor as the conversation he had shared with Myra following his initial escape from Britt Sanderson suddenly returned to him in a dizzying rush of images.

He was a ghost.

"Anything but my hands" he glanced up at the Collector with his one remaining eye, "Please"

"*Oh?*" Edward Albright gave a smile, nodding as if he were actually interested in the authors pleas.

Richard nodded, sobbing, "Please...I write...my hands, they are my life...don't take them"

"*I see*" the ghost of the innkeeper seemed to supress a shudder of excitement as he stepped closer, head shaking as he placed the blade of the knife against Richard's right wrist, "*This may hurt...usually I'd have the right tools for the job*"

Mind reeling, the author watched in grim horror as the ghost began to saw through the flesh of his arm, a scream of agony escaping his split lips despite his best efforts to the contrary. He choked back a sob of disbelief as the blade touched bone and The Collector began to pivot the weapon, sawing through the flesh all around the wound, before snapping the bone.

As Richard howled in terror and pain, the ghost of the innkeeper turned to his left wrist, the author shaking his head slowly as it began to repeat the process until he was finally handless. Barely conscious, Richard slumped in the chair, his arms dragging back from the ropes about his bloody, ragged wrists, the bonds no longer keeping him secured with his hands missing.

At the far side of the room, James Jackman took a step forwards, eyes narrowing but The Collector shook his head, casting the hands of Richard to the basement floor, *"Leave the wretch be, James, he can do no harm in his current condition"*

As the huge ghost stepped back against the wall, the Collector moved to stand in front of Britt Sanderson, nodding as he spoke, *"Are you ready to lose your hands my old friend?"*

Slumped in the chair beside the ghost of the last hangman, Richard blinked, watching as the Collector took a step forwards, knife heading for the wrists of Britt Sanderson, and then the author grimaced, "You forgot one thing, Eddy"

The Collector grimaced, then forced a smile back into place as he stepped back towards the author, *"Oh, what might that be, Mr Miles?"*

"Closer" Richards voice was a whisper, his lips barely moving as the ghost moved to lean towards him, an amused look on its ruddy face, enjoying his game. *"And?"*

"I'm a ghost" Richard stated, nodding as he spoke, his left eye closed, his arms hanging down either side of the wooden chair, "*I'm a ghost*"

"*I know*" Edward Albright gave a chuckle, glancing sideways at Britt Sanderson before meeting the one-eyed gaze of the author once more, "*We are all ghosts here Mr Miles*"

Richard nodded slowly, a smile lifting one side of his mouth, "Aye, and you know what that means"

The Collector gave him a smile, no doubt an old hand at having his prisoners try to talk their way out of his clutches, "*Why don't you tell me*"

The author nodded, excitement coursing through him as he felt the familiar tingle of his fingers and an itch in his left eye, "If we remember that we are ghosts before we die we heal our wounds"

"*Whuh?*" the Collector gave a grunt of shock, his features twisting into a mask of dread as Richard suddenly opened his left eye and raised his arms back into view, all of his hands and fingers back in place.

"Abra-ca-dabra mother fucker!" the author grasped at the blade the Collector was holding with one hand, turning it upwards, while his other wrapped the back of his captors head, dragging him down onto the point of the knife, punching it deep into his heart.

459

Chapter Sixty Three

As Richard pushed him away, Edward Albright fell back chocking in pain, a hand rising to clasp to the bloody hole in his chest, blood running through his fingers. Without warning his feet erupted into flames, signalling his death, and without another word, he fell back to the floor, blank eyes staring at the ceiling as the fire began to quickly spread through him.

With a roar like a wounded beast, James Jackman began to stride towards Richard, his usually blank features registering anger and cursing, the author turned and reached out to cut through the ropes restraining the right wrist off Britt Sanderson, "Don't make me regret this"

With a snarl, the hangman jerked his arm loose from the cut rope, snatching the blade from the author to quickly cut his chest and both of his legs free. Sensing the danger that Britt Sanderson posed him compared to Richard, James Jackman swung towards him, then grunted as the ghost of the last hangman rose quickly and swung the chair he was still attached to by his left hand against him. The furniture broke apart with the heavy impact, freeing Britt from his last bond, and as James Jackman brushed aside the wood that was crashing around him, the moustached ghost threw itself at the Butcher, knife hand stabbing. With a roar of pain, James Jackman threw his assailant back, large hands sending powerful punches towards Britt Sanderson, but he was ready this time, his bloody features fierce.

 Without a word, they charged each other in the centre of the room, The Butcher taking a half a dozen hard punches from Britt Sanderson as if they were nothing, before hammering a large fist into the gut of his opponent, bending him double at the waist. Instantly his hands went about the throat of Britt, lifting him from the floor with ease, the legs of the big man kicking wildly, and leaning forwards, trying to untie his legs, Richard cried out in concern, "Kill that big bastard Britt, kill him!"

With a snarl, the smaller ghost lashed out with a foot, catching the other in the groin with his boot, seemingly to no effect, and choking, he raised the knife, stabbing James Jackman hard in the chest.

With a grimace, the larger ghost spun, releasing Britt to crash across the top of the pool table, then turned towards Richard as he sat working on the last knot on his remaining bound ankle, large hands reaching out.

"Oh fuck" the author grimaced as the huge ghost loomed large over him, big hands reaching, only to suddenly straighten and spin about as Britt Sanderson suddenly leaped upon its broad back. Grimacing in dread, hands fumbling with the knot, Richard watched as the two ghosts spun, the larger desperately trying to reach back to grab the smaller one upon its back, before finally grasping one of Britt Sanderson's arms and biting deep, drawing an agonised curse from his foe. As The Butcher worked his teeth in the forearm of the ghost on its back, Britt Sanderson reached down, dragged the knife from his chest and drew it across the throat of James Jackman. Richard cursed, gagging as the arterial blood rushed from the wide wound, coating him as he sat there, one hand rising to clear his eyes as he coughed and spluttered, head shaking in disgust. With a choking gurgle, James Jackman dropped backwards towards the basement floor, a last ditch, dying attempt to kill the ghost that had cut his throat by crushing him, the pair crashing down to lay still, the large figure of Britt Sanderson hidden by even large body of The Butcher. Unable to tear his eyes away from the bodies, Richard continued trying to escape, a curse escaping him as the huge body of James Jackman; the Butcher suddenly caught alight, the flames rushing up from his large feet over his bulk. Grimacing, Richard nodded in satisfaction, then gave a murmur of triumph as the knot came loose and he freed his leg from the ropes, to stand staring at the burning figure of James Jackman, watching intently as the flames turned purple, and the Butcher came undone.

Shaking his head, he shifted his gaze, studying the blackened flakes that littered the floor where Edward Albright had been burning, black flakes and ash all that remained of the man that had killed over fifty.

How many of the Twelve were left now?

He frowned, trying to recall all those that he had managed to send to the other side already; Agnes Rand; The Cook, Elias Crumb; The Devil, Father Ambrose Dewitt; The Penitent Man, Dr Edwin Bennet; The Fever, William Haggerty; the Vessel, Clemence Stoke; The Witch, Lydia Tanner; The Widow's Wail, Frances Goodnestone; The Black Sheep, Edward Albright; The Collector, James Jackman; The Butcher and Bri...

He flinched as the blackened body of The Butcher came apart, large pieces falling to the basement floor, and within the mess, untouched by the purple fire, Britt Sanderson; The Last Hangman, rose to his feet, a large hand rising to wipe at his square features.

So, he was still alive. Or still a ghost.

The Twelve weren't all gone just yet.

Wincing, Richard watched as the large ghost took several steps to the side, a hand reaching out to lean on the back of one of the chairs in the rear row of the cinema seating, his eyes moving to study the still smouldering remains of James Jackman, The Butcher.

"He was a big one eh?" Richard nodded, calming

slightly as Britt Sanderson turned to look at him, bald head nodding, before glancing back as James Jackman's body turned to black flakes then dust. Sighing heavily, Richard glanced down at his body, then his left hand, wiggling the finger that he had lost, shaking his head as he considered the pain that he had suffered at the hands of The Collector, a grimace creasing his features again, "What a pair of cunts" Britt Sanderson glanced at him once more, then straightened and strode over to where the knife was lying upon the floor, bending to collect it, before stepping over to where Edward Albright had died.

"He's gone" Richard nodded, taking a step closer to the bald ghost, "I expect you have wanted that for a long time right...some closure?"

Britt Sanderson half turned his head, nodding slowly and then he sighed heavily and rose up to his feet, turning about to stand facing Richard in silence.

"So" the author forced a smile, nodding, "These two are gone...really gone...and I freed you...I guess that kind of makes us Ok right?"

For a long moment, Britt Sanderson studied him intently, the muscles of his body seeming to relax as he held Richard's gaze in silence. Then without warning, he hammered a punch into Richard's face, throwing him to the basement floor, the bald ghosts features grim as he moved to crouch alongside him, his voice thick with anger as he spoke, *"Murderer!"*

Chapter Sixty Four

Staring up at the large ghost in pain and confusion, Richard tried to focus, his voice weak, "What are you doing...I helped you"

"Murdering scum" the ghost of Britt Sanderson suddenly bent, hands grasping at the clothes of the author, dragging him almost effortlessly to his feet.

"Wait!" Richard shook his head, trying to meet the gaze of the other as it turned him roughly about, large hands pushing him towards the stairs, "I am not a murderer...how many times do I have to say this!"

Britt Sanderson moved quickly alongside him, the fingers of his right hand wrapping about the throat of the author, his face a mask of hatred as he loomed closer, "*Until it is true!*"

Choking, Richard blinked, trying to speak then gasped as Britt released him and pushed him towards the stairs once more, "*Go, climb!*"

Wanting more than anything to point out that his claims were true, of a sort at least, Richard gave a nod, slowly climbing the stairs to the ground floor, the large ghost following up close behind.

As he reached the top, Richard half-turned, an overwhelming desire to push Britt Sanderson back down the stairs and then turn and run coursing through him, but then the large ghost was off the stairs and in the hallway beside him, a muscular arm

pointing towards the kitchen, "*Walk...that way now!*"
Grimacing, Richard nodded, his eyes drifting to
glance at the wide staircase, wondering if he would
be able to get up the stairs to the safety of the far
rooms before Britt Sanderson caught him, realisation
reaching him that he didn't need to go that far. If he
managed to get past the last of the Sanderson
hangmen and into the living room with the red
leather sofa's he should still be safe.
Yet what would he do once there?
He would be trapped and running out of time.
If he was going to make a break for it he needed to go
as quickly as he could to the second floor where
Cherry was waiting for the signal to bring him back.
Wincing, he glanced at Britt Sanderson, realising that
despite the fact that the ghost was covered in muscle
and weighed possibly twice as much as he did, he was
so far out of shape it was unreal.
He'd be caught before he reached the first floor.
"*I said move!*"he staggered off balance as Britt
Sanderson suddenly shoved him towards the kitchen
door, his bulk moving between the author and the
staircase and Richard felt his stomach lurch at the
second missed opportunity. Mind racing, he opened
the door to the kitchen and entered, the large ghost
following behind him, and as one they crossed the
room, Richard following the directions of his captor

as he ordered him to enter the greenhouse beyond.
"Where are we going?" Richard slowed, turning to
glance back at the large ghost, his stomach knotting
as he saw the grim look on the others face, his square
jaw clenched, his narrowed eyes filled with hate.
"*Keep walking murderer*!" the reply came, and
shaking his head, Richard grimaced and began to
walk through the greenhouse, his eyes on the path
before him as he came to a decision. The moment that
he got outside the greenhouse he was going to make a
break for it. A quick run around the side of the house
to the front door, up the stairs and into the bathroom
where Cherry waited to revive him. There was a
chance that the moment he ran, Britt Sanderson
would go back through the house to cut him off but if
that looked like the case, Richard would double back.
He had already wasted two chances to escape.
Nothing was going to stop him this time.
Nothing.
As they worked their way through the overgrown
plants, they turned, Richard nodding to himself as he
saw the door to the outside ahead, its pane of glass
coated with steam, the heat from the plants making
them all foggy. He paused as he reached the door, a
hand grasping the handle, steadying himself for the
chase that he knew was about to take place and

behind him, the voice of Britt Sanderson gave a snarl, shoving him roughly, "*Go now, outside murderer!*" Smiling grimly to himself, Richard wrenched open the door, and stepped outside into the falling snow, the smug expression slipping from his bearded features as he stared in disbelief at the Twins ahead of him, his head shaking slowly. "No...you can't!"

"Move!" Britt Sanderson grasped him by the back of his neck with a large hand as he stepped outside the greenhouse, and the author cried out in pain as the big fingers dug into him with a grip like iron, "*Get walking now, murderer!*"

Feeling sick, Richard let himself be steered forwards, his legs picking up pace to stop himself from falling as his captor forced him onwards towards the two conjoined oak trees, the mind of the author tilting in mania as he stared at the two nooses hanging down from one of the lower but thickest branches.

"You can't hang me!" Richard's resolve broke as they were less than ten feet from the tree, a fear unlike any he had ever known growing inside him, fists clenched as he spun about, "I wont le..."

He grunted in shock as the right hand of Britt Sanderson snaked out, grasping at his right arm, dragging it under his left armpit as he turned away, Richard's chest being pulled tight against his back, his left arm pushing frantically at it. Panic touched him as he felt Britt Sanderson's grip on his right wrist tighten, his right hand being turned over and then he grunted as he felt something touch the tip of his index finger, the grunt turning to a startled sob of agony as pain coursed through the digit. Without warning, Britt Sanderson released him, and he snatched his hand back towards his face, staring in disbelief at the raw wound where the fingernail of his index finger had once been. Shaking his head, mind numb, he raised his eyes to watch as the large ghost placed his fingernail in a pocket of his trousers and stepped towards him once more, the knife that had killed James Jackman clutched in his left hand. Richard cried out as the large ghost grasped his right leg, dragging it high, the movement dropping the author to crash down on his back, his cries of denial loud as he watched his shoe and sock dragged from his foot. "No!" he begged, then howled as the large ghost pushed the point of the blade under the toenail of his big toe, the left hand of Britt Sanderson flicking suddenly, and the author gagged as he watched the toenail come loose, small strands of skin feebly attempting to retain possession if it. Releasing his foot to drop to the ground, Britt Sanderson placed the toenail in the same pocket as he had placed the fingernail, and from his prone position upon the floor, Richard stared up in horror, suddenly remembering what else the Sanderson hangmen had always taken from those that they were about to hang. Grimacing, Britt Sanderson reached for him, and he cursed, hands desperately trying to ward him off only to cry out as the large ghost broke both his arms.

A thing of pain, he lay upon the snow, staring up into the suddenly business-like features of Britt Sanderson as the ghost knelt beside him, large fingers reaching into the authors mouth to grasp his two front teeth at the top, hand wiggling hard.

Richard sobbed at the pressure, legs kicking wildly, desperately acknowledging in his mind that he was a ghost, praying for his arms to heal so that he might attempt to fight the ghost off. Without warning, Britt Sanderson dragged his hand away from the mouth of Richard, pain flaring like fire through the authors gums, as he stared up through tear filled eyes at the ghost. As if he were doing the most mundane of tasks, the ghost of the last Sanderson hangman rose to its feet, studying the pair of teeth in its fingers and then cast one aside to the snow like so much waste, that act of apathy seeming to break the author more than the removal of his teeth. Sobbing like a child, his arms still not healed yet, he watched as Britt Sanderson placed the tooth in the same pocket of his trousers as the toenail and fingernail, then placed the knife away once more, humming softly as he worked.

Stepping to the closest of the Twins, the large ghost bent to pick two squat logs up from where they had been resting, previously unnoticed by Richard, and placed it under the nooses, then returned to drag the author over to where he had placed the pair.

"Get on one!" the large ghost snarled, gesturing with a hand, and grimacing, Richard did as he had been instructed, a childlike whine escaping him as Britt Sanderson placed the noose over his head, and drew it tight, his large hands moving the large knot of the noose so that it was over the side of his neck.

"Don't do this" Richard begged, blood running from his mouth as he tried to get the attention of his would-be executioner, wincing as he almost lost his balance on the log, "Please...don't do this"

Britt Sanderson ignored his words, moving out of sight behind the Twins, only to return a moment later pushing a familiar figure before him, its hands tied before it. Blinking, Richard shook his head in disbelief as he stared at the other, then turned to watch as Britt Sanderson snarled, voice thick with hatred as he pointed at the second log, *"You, get up on that now!"*

Without a word, the figure did as instructed, standing still as Britt Sanderson placed the noose about their thin neck and tightened it securely. Richard let out a shaky sigh as they met his fellow captive's gaze, his mind reeling with questions he was in too much pain to ask them, head shaking as they stared back at him. As Britt Sanderson took a step back, the author gave a nod of defiance, trying to sound brave as he forced a bloody smile at his fellow captive then met the gaze of their hangman, voice breaking with emotion, "We will get out of this then I am going to kill you"

As the ghost of Britt Sanderson snarled in anger at his bold claim, the figure upon the Twins beside Richard gave a soft chuckle, their voice filled with mania, *"My precious boy"*

Chapter Sixty Five

Nearly a minute dragged by as Richard stood on the log, trying his best not to lose his balance, his broken arms now healed, gaze locked to that of the ghost of his mother as she stared back at him. He glanced up as the ghost of Britt Sanderson suddenly stepped towards him, one large hand dragging a length of rope from a pocket of his trousers, taken from the basement where he and Richard had been bound.

"Put your hands before you" the snarl of the ghost was coarse, and the author shook his head grimly. "Fuck you"

"Do you want me to break them again and then do it?" the ghost arched an eyebrow, *"Or just push you off now...your choice"*

"You are going to kill us anyway" Richard spat out, head shaking, the noose itching his throat.

"As you wish" Britt Sanderson raised a hand as if intending to push Richard's chest and the author's bravery faded like dew under the morning sun, hands raising together before him as he extended his arms. To his credit, Britt Sanderson didn't gloat as he began to bind the wrists of the author together, then stepped back to study his captives quietly.

Balanced precariously atop the log, Richard blinked as he stared past the large form of the ghost, his eyes taking in the huge shape of Sanderson House amid the snow that still fell heavily, a sudden sense of realisation settling over him as he felt the noose about his throat. Ms Sanderson had said over eight hundred people had been executed upon the Twins. Over eight hundred people that had stood here and seen the view that he was seeing now, perhaps without the snow, eight hundred people who had stood atop a log and faced certain death.

How had they felt?

Had there been any remorse in any of them?

By the law of averages there must have been some of that number who that had regretted their actions, and others still who had perhaps only committed their crimes in defence of themselves or others. Surely he couldn't be the first innocent man to face death upon the broad branches of the Twins, hadn't Cherry told him that Britt himself had been hung by the villagers after going delusional and executing people who had not committed serious crimes.

He blinked, eyes focusing upon the blunt features of the large ghost as it began to speak, its deep voice sounding uncertain for the first time, "*The sentence of this court is that you have been found guilty of the crime of murder afoul, and you have therefore been brought to the Twins, your designated place of execution to be hanged by the neck until you are dead. Do either of you have any last words?*"

"Wait!" Richard grimaced, staring into the eyes of the ghost as it turned its face to meet his gaze, "This is wrong…I shouldn't be here…neither of us should" Britt Sanderson grimaced, mouth opening to snarl and the author winced, head shaking, "I know what you think but you are wrong…I only killed my father as revenge for what he did!"

The ghost of the last hangman grimaced, its moustache twitching for a moment and then it shook its head, "*You are not the law of the land!*"

"Neither are you!" Richard shouted, surprised at the wave of anger that coursed through him, his face twisting in rage, "You and your family, your descendants…you might have thought what you were doing was right but you weren't the law!"

"*Shut up!*" if Richard's anger had flared like a furnace, that of Britt Sanderson was an exploding sun, his large hands forming fists as he stepped closer to the author and his mother, "*Don't you think I know that! Do you think me blind?*"

For a moment, Richard knew that the large ghost was about to push him from the log and that he was dead and gone, killed for a second final time.

Yet suddenly the large ghost spun away to stand staring out into the falling snow, his bald head shaking, his voice think with emotion as he spoke, "*I didn't want this…any of this*"

Stunned by the sudden change, Richard cast a quick look at the ghost of his mother, finding her staring down at her feet, her hair hanging about her features and frowning, the author turned back to Britt Sanderson, his voice imploring, "I can see that...this isn't fair on you...that you have to do this...all the death...all the killing"

The large ghost seemed to tense but stayed quiet, his head nodding slowly, "*It has to end*"

Richard winced, realising that he was getting through to the large ghost, head nodding as he spoke, "Then cut us down and let us both go...we are innocent...this isn't needed"

"*You are a murderer*" Britt grimaced, turning fully to face the author, "*You are a murderer!*"

Richard winced, nodding, gesturing to his mother with his bound hands, "Then let her go...apart from killing one of The Twelve she's innocent"

Britt Sanderson blinked at his words, head tilting to one side as he studied the author for a moment in silence and then turned to the ghost standing upon the log beside him, moustache twitching as he gave a grim smile and shook his head, "*Your son does not know you*"

Grimacing, Richard glanced at his mothers ghost, her head still down, hands bound before her as she sobbed, and with a snarl, Richard turned back to Britt

Sanderson, "She was a victim of murder not a murderer herself you fucking prick...she was killed by my father when I was a baby...find him...ask him...he is behind this!"

"I don't need to find him" the voice of Britt Sanderson was grim, eyes flicking to the left as he spoke, and following the gesture, Richard turned his head, anger and shock flooding him as he saw the figure of his father standing several feet beyond the ghost of the hangman, Myra standing half hidden behind him.

"Bastard!" Richard snarled, then tensed as the log wobbled beneath his feet, his stomach lurching.

At his side, his mothers sobs began to grow in intensity, her head shaking back and forth and wincing, the author dragged his eyes away from the ghostly trio watching him, and stared at her in concern, his voice thick with grief, "It will be OK, I promise you mum...we will get out..."

His words trailed off as she lifted her head, turning to face him, his mind reeling as he recognised her sobs for the chuckles that they were, her features twisted with amusement as she met his gaze, her stick thin body shaking as her laughs grew in intensity, *"Weak child...I should have stabbed you first, and then killed your brother and sister"*

Chapter Sixty Six

"What?" his voice sounded alien to his own ears as he found the ability to talk, staring at the ghost of his mother in confusion, "I don't understand!"

"Children" she spat, the word sounding like acid in her mouth, her nose crinkling in disgust as she stared back at him, *"Bastards, every one...but you...you were the worst of the bunch...always shitting...stinking up the house...always screaming!"*

The author shook his head, "I don't understand, you used to watch me...Cherry told me ghosts who stand watching their children are women who were murdered in front of them!"

She gave a sneer, *"I watched you because I hated you...I always did...if I'd had five more minutes you would be dead like the other cunts!"*

"No" Richard blinked, his eyes filled with tears, head shaking, "Dad killed you...he killed you!"

"That man?" at the mention of his father, the ghost of Richard's mother turned her head to stare through the snow at his ghost, her pale features twisting in hatred, *"He was weaker than you!"*

The author stared blankly at her, his mind a turmoil of grief and emotion, "But..."

"Gah" his mother snapped her face around to stare at Britt Sanderson, *"Hang me and be done with it, before this one starts to cry and scream!"*

"Do you acknowledge your crimes?" the large ghost took a step towards her, broad brow furrowed.

"Acknowledge them?" she gave a chuckle, her face turning to smile at Richard, *"I relish in them"*

He shook his head, then turned to stare at the ghost of his father as the man stepped forwards, his features the ruin that Richard had left them in, *"My babies...you bitch...you took my babies!"*

"Weak little man" she turned back to send him a broad smile, her voice almost hysterical, *"If only I had the time, I would have taken this one too!"*

His fathers ghost flicked its attention towards him, a grimaced passing over its features and then he was staring back at his former wife, *"I should never have left you alone with them"*

"But you did...you left them with me and I killed them both..." she laughed, the sound like broken glass and then suddenly she fell silent, a pained look creeping onto her wide-eyed pale features as she nodded solemnly, *"Michael...he died straight away but Molly...the blade missed her heart...she sat there, not knowing what was going on...sobbing for her daddy she was...but you weren't there"*

Richard shook his head, mind reeling at the sudden knowledge that he had once had an older brother and sister, Michael and Molly, both brutally murdered by their mother, while he had been just a little baby.

Suddenly he realised the identity of the two ghosts that he had seen in the bathroom where he had committed suicide becoming clear to him, grief coursing through him as he recalled the little girl, Molly, his big sister, looking at him and talking to him as if he were a baby only for her brother...his brother, Michael to stop her. Had they seen him as the baby that they had known? Why were they at the house? Were they attached to him like the others?

He grimaced, anger flooding him as he recalled them dying before his eyes, killed by an invisible assailant. His mother.

"Whore!" the ghost of Richard's father made as if to surge forwards, leaving the figure of Myra standing alone behind him and as Britt Sanderson moved to block his path, Richard gestured with his head to his childhood friend, mouthing for her to run, only for her to wince and look down at the floor. Grimacing, realising that she was too scared to run in case he chased and caught her once more, Richard turned his gaze back upon the scene before him, watching as the ghost of his father stepped away and Britt Sanderson turned to face the authors mother who was now laughing softly once more, *"Molly Miles aged three years...Michael Miles aged five years...you admit your guilt in their deaths?"*

"I killed them" she nodded, smiling coldly, *"I am*

death...I am God's right hand...and the children will always suffer...you can't kill me..."

"Yet you stand here a ghost" Britt Sanderson gave a shrug, "Killed by fellow prisoners, held down and strangled while awaiting sentencing"

"Cunts" she snarled, turning to look at Richard, her features twisting in hatred, "I was coming back for you boy...my precious boy"

Had his cries pushed her over the edge?

Had she been suffering from mental illness?

Or was there something else, something darker?

He grimaced as he recalled her choking the un-life from the ghost of Frances Goodnestone, and the look of excitement that he had seen on her face, and the violent way that she had killed the ghosts of Dr Edwin Bennet; The Fever and William Haggerty; The Vessel. All those times that he had seen her watching him as a child, and he had felt fear, he had been one hundred per cent right after all. He hadn't been mistaken. She hadn't come to watch him out of grief like the ghost of Cherry's mother but out of raw hatred. Grimacing, Richard turned away from her to stare at the ghost of his father, the sudden realisation that both of his parents were killers hitting home with the force of a runaway train. Stepping into his line of sight, Britt Sanderson grimaced, "And you...do you accept your crimes?"

"I told you my murder was one of revenge" the author shook his head slowly, weary now, as he raised his bound hands to gesture towards the ghost of his father, "He should be here not me"

The ghost of the last hangman shook his head slowly, his voice grim, "*This man is innocent*"

"What?" Richard blinked, head shaking in confusion as he stared back, "That's bullshit...he killed Myra!"

"*Silence!*" Britt Sanderson took a step forward.

"Tell him!" the author twisted his face towards the ghost of the young girl, "Tell him the truth!"

She winced as he shouted, taking a step back, and then suddenly the ghost of his father was standing before her once more, his broken and bloodied features twisted in anger, "*Leave the girl be...don't you think you've done enough!*"

"What?" Richard blinked, head shaking, "I..."

"*Enough!*" Britt Sanderson shouted, his voice loud enough to silence them both, hands forming fists as he stepped up to stand before Richard and the ghost of his mother, "*The time is now, prepare yourselves and your unclean soul...*"

His words turned to a gasping choke, his eyes widening as a torrent of blood ran from his mouth and stunned, Richard lowered his own eyes to stare in disbelief at the knife that had suddenly seemed to grow from the throat of the large ghost, the blade slicing left and right, opening the hole even wider before vanishing. Blinking, one hand trying to stop the blood from pouring from the ragged, mortal wound in its throat, Britt Sanderson dropped to his knees, then his face, flames erupting from his shoes. As the ghost of his mother started shrieking in amusement, the author slowly raised his gaze up the black and white costume of the figure that stood behind the rapidly burning ghost, its grease-painted features fixed with a faint smile as it raised an eyebrow, and winked at him, "*Did you miss me?*"

Chapter Sixty Seven

Shaking his head, unable to believe that he had forgotten all about that fucking clown, Richard stood atop the log, watching as the clown took a step back, studying each of them in turn, *"So what is this...a family reunion...how sweet"*

"You mad bastard!" the word's left Richards mouth before he realised he was speaking and the Great Marlowe turned to flash him a black-toothed smile. The ghost of the clown shook its head slowly, *"Not mad...I can assure you I am one hundred per cent sane...I am however bored, I always have been...and so I seek out my own pleasures...something to pass the time!"*

"Rape and murder" the author shook his head, the rope of the noose itching his neck once more. *"I only killed the one person"* the Great Marlowe wagged a long finger at him, then gestured to the blackened form of Britt Sanderson as it began to flake apart, *"Two if you count this one...oh, and that delightful child in the hallway...so three"*

Richard grimaced, remembering how it had killed the ghost of Frances Goodnestone by eating its face while savouring every moment. Grinning, the ghostly clown studied him in silence then with a chuckle, it turned to survey the trio of ghosts, *"So, what to do with you"*

"Stay away" the ghost of Richard's father took a step back towards Myra, one hand reaching out to the side as if to keep her back the other rising to point at the Great Marlowe, *"I'll kill you!"*

"Oh?" the clown gave him a broad smile, stepping quickly to one side, its right hand rising to wave at Myra, long fingers wiggling in the air, *"I see you there little girl...do you like clowns?"*

"I told you to stay the fuck away!" Richard's father repeated his threat, his deep voice rising angrily.

"Or what?" the Great Marlowe fixed him with a look of genuine curiosity, taking a step towards him, the knife he had killed Britt with clasped in his hand, his tone conversational, *"What exactly do you think you can do to me?"*

Grimacing, the ghost of Richards father took a step away, eyes lowering to study the blade, and standing upon the log beside him, the authors murderous mother gave a sudden chuckle of excitement, *"Do it...kill him!"*

The Great Marlowe turned at her words, a broad grin creasing its features as it did a strange little spinning skip back over towards where she stood with the noose about her neck, *"Well, hello you"*

Grimacing, Richard turned to watch the pair, his skin crawling as he saw his mother lick at her lips with a pale tongue, *"Kill him...do it for me"*

"For you?" the Great Marlowe shook his head, irritation registering upon his painted features, *"I don't think so...if I do it then I'll do it for me"*

"Spoilsport" she gave a soft chuckle, her voice growing husky, and the author cringed inwardly.

Oh God, was she flirting with him?

The cannibal clown and the murdering mother.

What a pair they made.

"How about you cut me down so I can help you kill the cunt" his mother gave the clown a broad smile.

"Maybe I should kill you instead" the Great Marlowe raised his blade, pointing it at her right eye, *"How do you feel about that, woman?"*

She shrugged, *"Don't talk to me about it...either do it or shut the fuck up"*

The ghost of the cannibal clown suddenly leaned back at her words, his laugh loud in the night, eyes wide as he hooted and hollered, turning to throw Richard a wink as he calmed down, *"I like your mothers wit...maybe I should marry her, what do you think?"*

Looking away from the pair as the clown laughed at his own words, Richard's mother joining in, the author turned to study his father, unsure how he felt about the man for the first time in his life.

Or death. Or whatever he was experiencing now.

He had spent his entire lifetime hating the man for beating him as a child whenever he had mentioned seeing the woman with the long black hair; the woman who he had learned was his mother; the woman who had killed his older siblings.

Richard grimaced, hating the fact he suddenly felt a vague sense of understanding for his father's actions, imagining the grief he must have felt at the mention of the woman who had killed his children.

Had it been wrong to beat him? Yes.

Could Richard understand why his father had acted so at the mention of his mother? Also, yes.

The author grimaced, fighting the tightness in his throat as he recalled how he had killed the man so many years before, revenge for his murder of Myra, an act that if Britt Sanderson was to be believed his father had actually been innocent of.

Richard winced, head shaking as he considered the memories that had returned to him the other day, stomach knotting as he recalled staring down from the barn loft at his father as the large man had knelt beside the lifeless broken body of the young girl.

He had not imagined it. He knew what he'd seen.

No, the ghost of the last hangman must have been incorrect in his claims his father was innocent.

But what if he *was* innocent?

The suggestion pushed forwards from the back of Richard's mind, scattering all his other thoughts.

What if his father had not been responsible for Myra's death, and he had killed an innocent man?

Wincing at the thought, he cast his gaze over to where the young girl stood, half hidden behind the ghost of his father, her eyes peering up at him as he stood balanced precariously upon the log.

If his father had been responsible for her death then why hadn't she taken the opportunity to say so when Richard had claimed that he had been?

Had she been too scared to speak up?

Just like she had been too scared to run when he had silently pleaded with her to do so while the ghost of his father had been distracted earlier.

Richard turned his head to watch as the Great Marlowe moved to stand before him, casually tossing the knife he had killed Britt Sanderson with from hand to hand, a broad smile upon his features, *"I was going to save you for last but I think I'll have the girl instead...no offence"*

The author grimaced, "Fuck you"

Before him, the Great Marlowe shook its head, chuckling, "*No, I just said, I am having the girl*"

"Bastard"

"Let me do it!" the ghost of Richard's mother suddenly begged, her eyes wide, "*Please, I will do whatever you want...let me kill the little cunt*"

The ghost of the clown gave a smile, glancing at her, *"I don't know...what is it worth?"*

"Let me kill him and then you can do what you want to me...rape me...bite me...kill me" there was almost a pleading tone in her voice, *"I wont fight back...unless you want me too...but the death of this runt should be my doing!"*

"Oh?" the clown stepped before her, tapping the blade onto the palm of his other hand, *"Go on"*

"He's mine to kill" she gave a defensive snarl.

Unable to keep quiet any longer, Richard glared at her, "You stopped Dr Edwin Bennet killing me...you saved me from William Haggerty"

Her chuckle was mocking, *"I saved you for myself boy...and if that hangman hadn't captured me before the hollow, I'd have killed you before those two whores even tried to"*

Lydia Tanner and Clemence Stoke.

He shook his head, recalling how she had vanished, and he had feared she had been killed by the pair.

"Why?" he gave a shrug, "My brother and my sister...tell me why?"

"Because I could" her eyes seemed to sparkle with amusement as she smiled back at him, *"I just couldn't stand the sight of your ugly little faces a moment longer. It was all I..."*

Her words turned to a choking gurgle as without

warning the Great Marlowe stepped forwards, a long leg kicking the log from beneath her feet, dropping the ghost of Richard's mother to hang upon the rope, bound hands tensing before her, her legs kicking wildly as she sought to gain purchase on something. Grimacing, the author kept his eyes upon her as she died, a cold hollow opening up inside him, a deep void of emotion, as he watched the woman who had given birth to him die in excruciating pain.

After what seemed an eternity, she stopped struggling, her tongue poking from between her lips as she swung on the rope, moved by the wind, and Richard blinked, then turned to study the Great Marlowe as the ghostly clown gave a chuckle, "*Was it just me or did she seem like she was never going to stop talking?*"

Chapter Sixty Eight

Grimacing, fully expecting for his log to be kicked way at any moment, Richard stared into the excited eyes of the ghost clown, trying his best to appear unafraid.

"Are you ready to go?" the Great Marlowe asked, his left foot rising, a big grin on his features, *"I have got a busy evening ahead killing your father and then giving the girl my undivided attention"*

Richard winced, seeing sudden movement as the ghost of his father crept towards the clown from behind, the hammer that Richard had killed him with clasped in his right hand, his left gesturing for Myra to stay back, and the author shook his head, hoping to distract the Great Marlowe, "You are the last of the Twelve...if you kill yourself you will be free...you can pass over, you will be free and so will all the other ghosts in this house"

The clown blinked, head shaking slowly, *"And why would I want to do that...I am the top dog now...imagine the fun I am going to have...first with the girl over there and then with your bitch in the bathroom...like I told you earlier..."*

The clown grunted as the ghost of Richard's father rushed forwards and struck it over the back of the head, the Great Marlowe staggering forward to drop to one knee, a hand rising to clasp the back of its head, eyes blinking rapidly.

"Hit him again!" Richard shouted urgently, eyes flickering to his father's ghost, "Hit him again!"

The other hesitated, brow furrowing as the author addressed it and then it was stepping forwards once more, raising the hammer high. Yet the fraction of a second's hesitation had been all the ghost of the cannibal clown had needed. With a snarl, it rolled to the side and came to its feet cat-like, its right hand thrusting out towards the off-balance ghost of Richard's father, the knife that it held plunging deep between his ribs. Gasping in pain and shock, the ghost staggered to the side away from the knife, bending at the waist as it clasped a hand to its wound. With a chuckle, the Great Marlowe surged to its feet and pursued its wounded victim, knife raised overhead only to grunt and stagger back as the ghost of Richards father swung the hammer up, catching the clown hard underneath his chin. Eyes wide, bound hands forming fists before him, Richard watched in disbelief as both of the ghosts took several steps in opposite directions, the Great Marlowe shaking its head as if trying to regain its senses and his father, raising the hammer before him, his other hand clamped to the deep wound in his side.

"Remember that you are a ghost!" Richard found himself shouting out to his father, cursing as the log suddenly titled slightly beneath him then righted itself. Wincing, he glanced back up from the log, calling out once more, "If you remember and acknowledge you are a ghost your wounds will heal! You have to listen to me!"

The ghost of his father turned its head towards him, his broken and bloodied features etched with confusion as it met Richard's gaze, and then a soft chuckle from the Great Marlowe had the author glancing towards it, his stomach knotting as the ghost of the clown straightened up, a smirk upon its features, "*Thank you for the tip*"

"No" Richard shook his head, then cursed as the two ghosts charged each other amid the heavily falling snow, their weapons raised before them.

Eyes wide, the author watched as the two ghosts clashed and passed each other then instantly swung about to close on each other again, the hammer of his father swinging but wounded as he was, the blows were wild and off-target. Side-stepping the clumsy attacks of the larger man, the skinny clown, jabbed and slashed with the knife it held, each attack seeming to draw a grunt of shock or gasp of pain from the other, until with a curse, the latter bent at the waist and stayed there, hammer dropping from its hand. Feeling sick, Richard watched as the Great Marlowe stepped closer to the wounded ghost, a long leg kicking the hammer away before it stabbed the ghost of Richard's father in the back twice, dropping the large man down to his knees. Shaking his head, the author watched as the ghost of the clown gripped at the hair of its badly wounded victim and dragged its hair back, the blade of its knife ready to open him from ear to ear, only for the ghost of Richards father to turn its head, voice grim, "*Run...run to the house!*" Blinking, the author snapped his gaze to the ghost of his childhood friend, watching as she backed into the snow then turned and charged in the direction of the house, arms pumping at her sides as she ran away.

"*Damn it!*"the Great Marlowe scowled as it turned to watch the girl vanish into the snowstorm, then leaned closer to the ghost of Richard's father, "*You shouldn't have done that*"

The large ghost smiled wearily, closing its eyes as if in acceptance of the death that was coming, and sneering, the Great Marlowe drew its blade back from the throat of its victim, then bent to collect the hammer from the ground, studying it for a moment before striking him hard over the back of the head, throwing him forward to lie in the snow, his feet twitching wildly in a spasm. Richard flinched at the sudden cry of concern, stunned to discover that it was coming from him, and grinning, the Great Marlowe gave a little bow, "*Thank you thank you...I appreciate your enjoyment of the show"*

"I'll fucking kill you!" Richard grimaced angrily.

"I'm sure you'll try" the Great Marlowe gave a nod, chuckling as he began to walk backwards into the snow, a finger pointing at the author, *"I have changed my mind about killing you first...I will be back for you...just hang around here!"*

Then he was gone, long arms and legs flapping wildly as he turned and ran off into the snow towards the house in pursuit of young Myra, and balanced upon the log, noose tight about his neck, Richard had no choice but to watch him go.

Chapter Sixty Nine

In moments, the ghost of the clown was gone, lost amid the heavy snow, and wincing, Richard turned his head to the left, studying the noose that had previously held his mother's ghost. She had faded quietly away after her death like Jonty had earlier that day, instead of bursting into flames like The Twelve, and devoid of an occupant, the noose swayed wildly upon the branch, buffeted by the wind.

She was gone.

The mother that he had never known.

The mother he wished he still knew nothing of.

Grimacing, the author turned his gaze back on the falling snow, eyes narrowing as he tried to see into its depths, hoping to see sign of Myra but it was no use.

Sighing, he raised his bound hands up to the side of the noose where the large knot rested tight against his neck, his fingers probing. If he could loosen the noose, he could escape and save Myra from the horror the Great Marlowe had in store for her.

If he hadn't caught her already.

He winced as he considered the possibility, the fact that there was no way the clown was going to kill her immediately giving him any solace.

Sometimes death was better than suffering.

Gritting his teeth, he pushed a finger into what felt like a gap in the knot and pushed, then lurched to the side as he wobbled upon the log, his arms thrusting out in front of his body as he tried to regain his balance. For a moment it looked like he had done so, the log beneath him slowly settling and he sighed heavily, shifting his feet beneath him only to curse as his left shoe slid from its surface. Desperately, he kicked with the dangling leg, catching the side of the log as it toppled over, leg muscles bunching so that he lowered himself to the end of the noose rather than dropped. Instantly, the knot on the noose slid as his weight pulled down, the rope quickly tightening about his throat and eyes wide, he began to choke, legs kicking wildly, just as the ghost of his mother had done minutes before. His vision blurred, the pain in his neck almost more than he could bear, and yet somehow an almost calm and tranquil part of his mind wondered how many of those hanged upon the Twins over the centuries had choked this way and how many had died from a broken neck.

Gasping, bound hands raised before him, his fingers trying unsuccessfully to loosen the noose about his throat, Richard felt his body failing to the side.

It was over. For a second time.

Then unbelievably he was lifted from the ground, his eyes blinking open to stare down into the broken and bloody features of his father as the large ghost lifted him up with one arm about his waist, the other cutting at the ropes binding the hands of Richard with what looked like Britt Sanderson's knife. In moment's his hands were free, and he stared in disbelief as his father pushed the handle of the blade into his fingers, the voice of the ghost coarse as it met his gaze again, *"Cut the damn rope"*

Without hesitating, the author raised his hands above him, one hand holding to the rope while the other sawed at it with the blade, just three strokes being enough to free him the noose. Without warning they fell, the legs of his father seeming to give out, the pair crashing down to lay in the snow upon their backs. Fearing a trick, Richard forced himself to his knees, the blade held before him as he stared down at the body of his father's ghost, his face screwing up in dread as he saw the deep wounds that lined his sides and his overweight stomach, what appeared to be muscle and internal organs showing through the deep wide knife wounds the clown had inflicted.

"Going to kill me again are you?" the bitter chuckle from his father had Richard shifting his gaze to stare down at the bloody face of the ghost, his stomach knotting as he saw the damage that he had done. Suddenly unable to speak, the author grimaced, head shaking and the other gave another laugh, this one causing blood to run from its mouth, *"I only ever wanted what was best for you boy"*

Suddenly, Richard could speak again, his head shaking as he stared down at the ghost of his father, mouth twisting in anger, "You beat me...how is that wanting what was best for me?"

To his surprise there was sudden grief in the eyes of the ghost, its head shaking weakly as it lay on its back, eyes turning from Richard to stare up into the falling snow, "*You look so much like her...I...couldn't see past her likeness*"

The author winced, head shaking, "That wasn't my fault, I didn't choose to look like her!"

The ghost of his father grimaced, "*It wasn't just that...I was trying to stop you becoming her!*"

"What?" Richard shook his head, sitting back on his heels, suddenly angry again, "Meaning what?"

The large ghost was silent, his eyes drifting over Richards features, head shaking as he grimaced once more, "*You look so much like her, boy*"

"What did you mean?" the author leaned closer, stomach knotting, "I need to know, tell me"

The ghost of his father gave a low moan, eyes rolling and for a second, the author thought he was gone, dead for a second time while Richard knelt beside him, but then he opened his eyes once more. He struggled to focus for a moment, head shaking as he stared about, and then he blinked once more, eyes settling upon the face of Richard, "*Rebecca?*"

"What?" the author blinked, thrown by his fathers sudden use of his stepmothers name.

"Where is my boy?" his father's voice was filled with concern, hands suddenly grasping Richards forearm's, *"Where is he, Rebecca?"*

"I..." Richard stammered, unsure what to say and on the ground beside him, his father gave an almost haunted moan, his head shaking in dread.

"She was here Rebecca...I saw her...Richard...he saw her too but she's dead now...he knows about Molly and Michael...she told him it all"

The author winced, staring down into the terror filled eyes of his father as the ghost began to ramble, *"I did my best for him Rebecca...I tried...I wasn't the best father but I was so scared he was going to be like her what with the farm animals"*

"The farm animals?" Richard repeated his words, eyes narrowing as he stared down at the ghost.

"All those little lambs...the kittens of the farm cats...and then the dog..." there was another long silence and then his father's ghost shook his head once more, *"That was the day..."*

"What happened?" Richard leaned closer, his voice barely more than a whisper, "Remind me"

The ghost blinked, brow furrowing as if it were thinking back, its voice grim, *"I came home from the field...the timing belt had broken on the tractor...I walked into the yard and he...the boy, had Dusty upon the table...a knife in his hands"*

"Dusty" Richard blinked, a vague memory of a small black dog returning to him from the past, his brow furrowing as he glanced back at his father as the ghost began to speak once more, his voice weak.

"That poor dog...he was whining...still alive some how though I cant figure it...I was so mad with the boy Rebecca...I turned over the table and broke the neck of the poor dog...and God help me, I began to beat him...I was so angry"

"Wait" Richard shook his head, "No, that's wrong"

"That's when the girl from the next farm appeared...the dark-haired little thing that the boy was obsessed with...she saw the dog...she saw me beating the boy, and he saw her...God Rebecca...he snarled at her... snarled like an animal!"

"No, no no!" Richard rose to his feet, blinking as he shook his head, "Not true...not true!"

On the ground, the ghost of his father was staring back up at the falling snow once more, tears in his eyes, *"I tried to tell her to run...but she was too scared too move...I even threw stones at her and then...finally the little thing ran...but he got away from me...Oh sweet God, he chased her!"*

"Lies!" Richard pointed down at the ghost with the knife in his hand, his free hand gently slapping himself on the side of the head, "No, no, Myra was my friend...Myra is my friend!"

"Oh Rebecca, you know she was scared of him...its why we would only let her come to the farm when he was at school or in his room!"

"Shut up shut up!" Richard was shouting at the top of his voice now, muscles tensed, "You are a liar!"

"That poor little lass" there was misery in the voice of the ghost, a sob of horror escaping him as he turned back to look at Richard, *"If you had seen the state of her when I found her...she must have fallen and broken her leg...and he's beaten and strangled her...that poor little thing"*

With a roar like a demon, Richard spun away, staring out into the blizzard, his brain feeling like it was five times too large for his head, his vision blurry with rage and tears. Time lost all meaning to him as he stood there, the sudden memory returning to him of Myra choking, desperately trying to fight off the hands tight about her neck, then he turned, glancing back as he heard the ghost speak once more, weaker now, almost at an end, *"It wasn't his fault...it was his mother's...she had passed on her darkness...I took the girl from him and carried her to the old tool barn, wrapped her in an old tarpaulin...then I heard him screaming up in the old hay loft where he had gone to hide. I think he'd been watching me"*

Swallowing the tightness in his throat, Richard stared down at the ghost, watching as it turned to meet his gaze, *"I tried to love him...in my own way I did...he didn't seem to remember what he had done, and for my sins I never told anyone...not even you Rebecca..."*

"You are lying" Richard gave a sob, dropping back down beside the ghost of his father, a hand grabbing at him, "Stop lying...it wasn't me!"

"Richard?" his father's eyes suddenly widened in recognition, his large hands grasping at the authors arms, *"You stupid fucking boy!"*

"Get off me!" Richard struggled to free himself, cursing as one of the hands rising to grasp at his throat, and instinctively he raised the knife above him, ready to stab the ghost only to relax as the large hands suddenly dropped down to rest on the snow.

"Lies" Richard grimaced, rising to his feet, head shaking as he waited for a confirmation that he knew would never come, "Tell me I didn't do it!"

Yet his father was dead once more.

Chapter Seventy

Partially blinded by the tears in his eyes, a storm of emotions coursing through his broad frame, Richard stood staring down at the body of his father for what seemed an eternity, a deep rooted sense of loss that he hadn't expected to experience settling in the pit of his stomach when the body of the ghost faded away.

Grief for a man he himself had murdered.

He grimaced as he considered that thought, realising for the very first time it was exactly the right word.

His father would had been innocent of murdering Myra all those years ago, just as he had been innocent of murdering Richard's mother, the most recent of his theories regarding the man he had grown to hate.

All he had been guilty of was beating him.

That was all.

He winced, remembering the deep fear of the man that he had carried around like some form of cancer, eating away at his confidence and spirit, realising his father had broken him emotionally and physically.

It was still not worthy of being murdered but he had been far from a decent father to Richard growing up.

The author winced as his father's voice returned to him, and he pictured the fear that had been in the eyes of the ghost as it mistakenly assumed he was his step-mother, "*I did my best for him Rebecca...I*

tried...I wasn't the best father but I was so scared he was going to be like her what with the farm animals"
The animals. God sake.
The author shook his head as he recalled his fathers claims that on the day that Myra had died, he had returned home to find Richard calmly mutilating the family dog upon a table in the yard of the farm.
No, he had been sat writing, he could remember it clearly, he had been writing and his father had returned to the farmyard, his features twisting into a mask of anger as he had stared in shock at Richard.
Grimacing, Richard closed his eyes, casting his mind back to that moment, drawing on the memory that had resurfaced just the other day, locked away for so long amid his childhood grief. Once again, he saw his father stride into the yard, the square features of the man twisting with anger as he had turned to stare at Richard, and wincing, the boy version of him raised his hands before him in a defensive gesture, only this time his hands were thick with blood, one clasped tight to a silver metal handled Stanley knife.
"No!" the author spun away from where the body of his father's ghost had been lying, his free hand clasping to his eyes, his other gripping the knife that he was still holding in a white knuckled grip.
Richard blinked, his eyes filled with tears, several running down the sides of his face as the image

suddenly came back to him of Myra lying upon her back in the old gloomy tool barn, her fingers clawing at the hands that were choking the life from her, her brown eyes wide in fear and shock, her legs kicking frantically as she fought to free herself, her left baseball boot falling from her as she struggled.

Had he really done it as his father had claimed?

Had he really murdered his childhood friend?

No, for if his father was correct then he and Myra had never been friends, and everything since had been just a lie, forged from just his guilt and denial.

She had told him up in the bedroom that she could not remember her death, but she could remember Richard being there since. She must have brought into his false memories regarding their friendship.

The author winced, suddenly remembering the face of his father after he had awoken in his bed following seeing the man in the old barn with Myra's body, the author wincing as he recalled the haunted look in the eyes of the large man as he had sat watching him.

His son was a murderer, just like his mother.

Yet instead of handing him in to the authorities he had kept his silence, concealing the murder of the young girl from everyone, and Richard had mistakenly blamed him for her untimely death.

Myra.

Richard turned his head slowly, staring through the

falling snow towards the huge old Sanderson house, dread coursing through him like a flood as he remembered how the ghost of the girl had ran in the direction of the building, pursued by the ghost of the Great Marlowe; the cannibal clown.

As if in a dream he began walking towards the building, head down, eyes staring at the snow beneath his feet that he knew he was leaving no trace in, his feet leaving footprints that would be gone the moment he took another step forward. With shock he suddenly realised that his right foot was bare from where the ghost of Britt Sanderson had stripped off his shoe and sock to removed his toenail, the author grimacing as he stared down at the bloody furrow where it had been, nausea washing over him as he recalled the pain, of that and having his teeth and fingernail torn from his body, ivory from a rhino.

"I'm a ghost" he muttered, repeating the words as he strode onwards through the blizzard, blinking in surprise as he noticed that his toenail was back, the fingers of his right hand rising to probe his top row of teeth, sighing as he felt the front two in place, his wounds healing themselves. Casting a quick glance at the index finger of his right hand, noting that the nail was back there too, Richard strode onwards, brow furrowing as he considered why Britt Sanderson had bothered going through the process of taking the items from him before placing him on the noose. Back when he had been alive, it had no doubt been the way that they had bound the most dangerous of murderers to the Twins, but that had always been done to them while they were still alive, and then placed in the medicine pouch of Chaqit.

Had the ghost of the last hangman simply been carrying out his former habits?

Grimacing, Richard hurried onwards through the swirling snow, and then the house suddenly seemed to appear large ahead of him, like some ancient monster lurching out of the darkness, and he angled his run towards the overgrown greenhouse.

Crashing the door open, he hurried inside, pace quickening as he moved down the path between the rows of heavily overgrown plants, then paused as he noticed something on the ground by some bushes.

Grimacing, the author bent at the waist, hands fastening to the handle of the axe that he had dropped in terror when the Great Marlowe had surprised him earlier, and turned, heading through the greenhouse and onwards into the kitchen.

He paused in its doorway, eyes narrowing as he scanned the room for any sign of Myra or the clown, then crossed it quickly, pushing open the door to the hallway beyond with his booted foot.

"Myra?" he called out as he strode to the bottom of the wide staircase, head tilting back as he climbed them quickly, staring at the landing above, his voice calling out once more, "Myra!"

From somewhere in the upper regions of the house came a scream, short and childlike, followed by a whoop of sudden delight, and cursing, Richard began to run up the stairs, his former fear of venturing around the huge house gone with the passing of eleven of The Twelve. He reached the landing of the first floor in moments and stepped out into the main corridor, head turning as he glanced in both directions, calling out once more, "Myra?"

Once more the scream sounded, longer this time, drawn out before rising falsetto at the end.

The scream of someone in pain.

With a snarl, Richard, clasped the axe tighter in his hands and hurried along the landing, taking the stairs up to the second floor in no time at all.

"Myra!" he charged up on to the landing and through into the main length of the second floor hallway, turning towards the far end almost instinctively.

"Bastard!" the word left his mouth in a hiss, eyes narrowing as he saw the ghost of Myra lying face down upon the floor of the hallway down near its far end, the Great Marlowe kneeling atop her, one hand holding her down, knife raised in the other.

As if in slow motion, the ghost of the cannibal clown turned to face him, its features splitting into a mischievous smile as it rose to its feet like a jack-in-the-box unfolding, *"Well, well, well...look who it is"*

Chapter Seventy One

Head banging with anger, Richard clenched his fingers tighter about the haft of the axe that he was holding, the one that they had taken from the ghost of William Haggerty, and began to walk purposefully down the corridor, "I'll kill you"

"*Oh?*" the ghost of the clown gave a heavy, almost mournful sigh, head shaking as it stepped into the centre of the wide hallway, *"We've spoken about this...I am going to kill you!"*

Richard grimaced, shaking with the sudden overwhelming feeling of rage that coursed through him, temples aching, spittle flecking his lips as he began to run forwards, snarling like a mad dog. Before him, the Great Marlowe spread his arms wide as if to extend him the offer of a hug, the knife that it had killed his father and Britt Sanderson with clasped in the fingers of the left. In no time at all, Richard had closed the gap between them, his fingers sliding along the axe to hold it by the base with both hands, hips twisting as he swung it in a wide, waist high sweep. Somehow, the ghost of the cannibal clown leaned backwards as if limbo dancing, its back brushing the floor, the axe sailing over its face harmlessly. Off balance, carried by his own inertia, Richard stepped past the twisting form of the ghost, suddenly recalling how the clown had allegedly been a contortionist.

With a coarse chuckle, the Great Marlowe twisted to the side and rose quickly, knife thrusting towards the unprotected back of the author, but Richard was spinning once more with the axe, turning a full three hundred and sixty degrees. The ghost of the clown screamed in shock as the blade took his right arm off several inches above the wrist, the knife and detached limb flying to hit the wall to their left, leaving a blood stain. As the Great Marlowe took a hurried step back, eyes wide in its face, its features twisted in agony and disbelief as it clasped its bleeding stump to its chest with its left hand, blood coating its black and white costume, Richard raised the axe and stepped forwards, "I told you I'd kill you" Shaking its head, the effort of not screaming aloud showing upon its oil-painted features, the Great Marlowe forced a grim smile, *"It's just a flesh wound...besides...I'm a ghost"*

Richard grimaced at the words of the other, head shaking in anger as he watched the ghost of the clown drag its right arm from beneath its left, the hand once more back in place, fingers wiggling as it waved at the author. Shaking his head, Richard glanced behind him, eyes settling upon the figure of Myra as she lay on the floor staring back at the pair of them in silence, face etched with fear as she stared up at him in dread.

In that moment, he knew.

As if the words of his father hadn't been enough.

She was terrified of him. And rightly so.

It had been he who had taken her life.

She could remember it now.

He had murdered her and his father.

But that wasn't who he was now. Not anymore.

Shaking his head, he blinked, "I am so sorry"

Turning back towards the ghost of the clown, the author grimaced, "You've got your hand, big fucking deal, you don't have the knife"

As the ghost of the clown gave a grimace of dread, Richard rushed forwards, the axe sweeping out once more in a decapitating blow only for the Great Marlowe to throw itself into a forward roll beneath the killing blow. Cursing, Richard turned towards the ghost, grimacing as he saw it snatch up the blade it had lost moments before, a boot kicking away his own severed hand with almost casual disdain, and then met his gaze, chuckling, "*Now I do*"

Without another word, they charged at each other, weapons slashing out, the ghost of the clown managing to duck beneath the sweep of the axe to thrust his knife deep into Richards side under the arm pit. Grunting in shock as the blade plunged into him, the author swept his arms about, the handle of the axe smashing the nose of the Great Marlowe flat, rocking him off balance. As the clown took a step away, Richard leaned heavily back against the wall, his strength suddenly seeming to fail him as the pain of his wound spread throughout his broad frame. Cursing in pain, Richard dropped to one knee, eyes half closing as he gritted his teeth, the axe falling from his hands to the hallway carpet before him. *"Done already?"* the Great Marlowe raised an eyebrow, smirking as it stared down at the author, head shaking as if in confusion as it dropped down to crouch facing him, "*You know for a moment there you had me worried, there was something there, something dark, something wild and dangerous...it reminded me of me*"

Richard winced, staring at the ghost of the clown through half closed eyes, his left hand reaching across to press against the wound in his side, and with an almost disappointed sigh, the Great Marlowe rose to its feet, turning to cast a smile at the kneeling figure of Myra before it took a step that brought him feet away from the author, "*It looks like I was wrong, you're not a killer*"

The chuckle that escaped Richard was ice cold, and before him the ghost of the cannibal clown winced in dread as it realised it had been fooled. With a snarl, the author rushed forwards, bent at the waist, the blade that he had been given by the ghost of his father, the blade that he had placed in his coat pocket upon finding the axe, now clasped back in his hands. He caught the Great Marlowe about the waist, lifting him from the floor in a powerful tackle as he punched his blade in under its right armpit, just as he had been stabbed moments before and then they were crashing back heavily to the floor of the hallway.

As the ghost of the clown writhed in agony, Richard released his grip on the blade, his right fist hammering a powerful punch down into the features of the Great Marlowe and then gasped as the knife of his foe thrust out to stab him in the upper left side of his chest, under his collar bone. Roaring in agony, he knocked the knife arm of the ghost clown aside to the carpet, the weapon staying stuck in his body, and then he began to hammer down with both clenched fists onto the face of the Great Marlowe, snarling like an animal. Beneath him, the clown tried to fight back, split lips moving weakly, panic in its eyes, but Richard was beyond stopping, his fists repeatedly pummelling down upon his victim, satisfaction coursing through him as he felt bones break.

Without giving it conscious thought, the author dragged the knife from the side of the ghost, his other yanking the blade from his own chest, and then he was stabbing with both of them, blood spraying up as finally the clown began to scream in pain and terror.

Yet Richard didn't stop, blood running from his nose, eyes wide in his head as he laughed aloud, knives stabbing repeatedly down into the body of the Great Marlowe, so caught up in his attack that when the ghost began to burn he didn't notice until the fire began to pass him, the flames not harming the author as it flowed quickly through the last of The Twelve. Richard winced as a hand suddenly grasped at his shoulder and he spun, the blade in his right hand sweeping out, blood splattering his features as the figure gasped and fell back, and snarling the author went with it, blades rising and falling, spittle flying from his bearded features as he stabbed repeatedly, refusing to lose the fight when he was so close to surviving this nightmare, so close to living again. Beneath him, the body was almost limp, one hand vainly rising to ward off the blows and grimacing, the author raised his blades once more, brow furrowing grimly as he saw the countless stab wounds already covering the Care Bear tee shirt they were wearing. *Care Bear tee shirt.*

With a choking gasp, he cried out, head shaking as he rose on shaky legs, hands casting aside the blood-stained blades as if their touch burned, his eyes blurring with tears as he stared down at the mutilated figure in shorts, her face a bloody ruin, her body an island in a growing sea of dark blood.

Chapter Seventy Two

Stepping back from the body of the young girl, head shaking as he fought back a wave of guilt, tears streaming from his eyes, Richard dropped to his knees, a scream of agonised denial escaping him.

He had done it yet again, he had killed Myra. Blinking, he leaned forwards, hands resting on the floor as he lowered his forehead to the carpet, his broad frame shaking as he sobbed uncontrollably. Without warning the memories came to him, images of him chasing Myra through the farm of his father, the young girl glancing back over her shoulder in terror, her voice begging for him to leave her be. She had tripped as she had tried to climb over a wall, and fallen, her right foot catching amid some rocks as she did so, snapping her femur and he had been upon her, fists punching, then his hands encircling her throat. Blinking past the tears, the author tried to force the memories away but it was no good, the intensity of them making him scream in shame, hands covering his eyes as he curled into the foetal position, and began to rock back and forth, his cries animalistic. Without warning the images faded, their sudden absence making his head spin, and Richard opened his eyes in shock, lurching to his hands and knees. The first thing he noticed was that the body of Myra's ghost and the blood that she had been lying in was gone, the carpet clean and unspoiled. Forcing himself to his feet, Richard turned his head, brow furrowing in confusion as he realised the house felt different, the hallway seeming lighter than moments before. Blinking, he turned his head, stomach knotting as he heard the sudden laughter of a young girl downstairs. "Myra? Is that you? I'm sorry!" he began to walk quickly, his voice rising as he hurried down the stairs to the first floor, peering along the landing before turning and descending towards the ground floor. He froze as he reached the mid-way landing, eyes widening as he stared down at the hallway below, devoid of all of the boxes and furniture that he had brought with him upon moving in, then turned and stared at the kitchen door as the laughter of the girl suddenly sounded once more. On leaden legs, Richard slowly reached the ground floor, eyes locked to the kitchen door as he moved towards it, the flat of his right hand reaching out to push it wide open before him as the girl within laughed once more, "Myra?" He had a fraction of a second to stand staring in at the kitchen, brightly lit by the warm sunshine beaming through the large window, his head shaking in confusion as he stared at the young boy and girl that were seated at the dinner table, then he flinched in shock as a smash suddenly sounded loud to his left.

Turning his head, he found himself staring into the eyes of Ms Sanderson as she stood beside the kitchen side, one hand clasped to her chest as she held his gaze, a broken pot of sugar lying beside her feet.

"Ms Sanderson?" the girl, no older than eight, rose from her chair and moved to stand beside the old woman, concern on her young face, "Are you OK? Can I help you clean it up?"

"I am quite alright, Emily dear" the voice of the old woman was tight with barely controlled emotion as she nodded down at the youngster, a tight smile on her features as she brushed the girls blonde hair from her face, "Don't worry your little head"

"That's the man" Richard turned at the voice, meeting the gaze of the dark-haired little boy who sat at the table, paper and crayons spread before him, "That's the man in the bath"

"What man?" the blonde girl turned her head, eyes wide in fear as she looked at Richard and looked away, "Frankie stop being a weirdo!"

The boy blinked at her words, nose and mouth twisting in confusion as he pointed, "There!"

"Now, children" Ms Sanderson shook her head, voice rising a fraction, "Why don't you run and play, enjoy the summer holidays while you still can"

"Can we play outside?" the girl asked, hands clapping together, and the old woman gave a warm smile, nodding, "Of course, don't get too dirty, your parents will not be best pleased"

With a hoot of delight, the girl rushed to the door, pausing beside Richard as she glanced back, a hand gesturing, "Come on Frankie, let's go play"

The little boy frowned, not having looked away from Richard since his arrival, "Uh-huh, I want to stay with Ms Sandlestone and the man"

Beside Richard, the girl gave a groan, eyes rolling in her head, "It's Ms Sanderson...I told you...and stop talking about the man...or I'll tell mum!"

"Frankie" Ms Sanderson moved to stand beside the boy, throwing the blonde girl a wink before bending, her voice lowering but enough that the girl could still hear her words, "Why don't you go and play, the man and I need to talk about grown up things"

"Uh" the little boy sighed heavily, but nodded, sliding from his chair as he moved to join his waiting sister, only to pause and look back at the elderly woman in triumph, "I told you he was real"

"Yes you did, Frankie" she nodded, "Yes, you did"

Grinning, the boy followed his sister, the door closing behind them, and only then, did Ms Sanderson meet the gaze of Richard, nodding as she spoke, "Mr Miles"

He winced, his eyes flickering to the brightly lit window, then met her gaze again, about to speak only to turn as a voice spoke his name, the single word thick with emotion, "Richard?"

The author turned, heart swelling as he saw Cherry standing just feet away, eyes filled with tears, then suddenly they were hugging, her arms about his broad shoulders, "I am so sorry"

"Sorry?" he shook his head in confusion, studying her features as she took a step back from him.

The blue-haired young woman nodded, grief upon her face, "I tried...I tried to bring you back"

"I don't understand" he shook his head, a heavy sensation settling about his gut, "I'm here!"

"No" she shook her head at him, "I did as you told me, I let the plug out of the bath, I pushed on your chest but Richard...I had no breath, I couldn't breathe into you to give you CPR"

"What?" he gave a laugh that turned to a wince as he took a step towards the door, "My body"

"Gone" she shook her head, a single tear leaving her left eye to trail down over her cheek, an arm rising to brush across her eyes, "Granny found you when the Vicar and the others brought her home after she had left hospital"

"Hospital" he blinked, glancing at the old woman.

She nodded back at him, smiling sadly "They landed a helicopter on the village green for me, would you believe, I was in for nearly a week"

"A week" he shook his head, glancing at Cherry and she winced, reaching out to take hold of his hand.
"I stayed with you the entire time"
He winced, head shaking, "Famous author found dead in empty bath in mansion...I bet the press loved that"
Ms Sanderson smiled sadly, "It was ruled death by misadventure...from what I read in the papers all of your books are now bestsellers"
"Great" he gave a chuckle, "That's something eh"
The old woman and the blue-haired ghost exchanged glances and closing his eyes, Richard placed his hands on his head, trying to calm himself then he opened them once more, glancing at the sunshine that was illuminating the kitchen, "How long has it been?"
"Ten months" the voice of Ms Sanderson replied.
"Ten months" Richard winced, head shaking then he met her gaze again, "The children?"
"Emily and Frankie, they live here with their parents, I have taken on the role of nanny as well as housekeeper it would seem"
The author nodded, glancing back at the table where the boy had been sitting, "He can see me"
"He can" the old housekeeper nodded, "He is like us, Mr Miles...he has the sight"
Richard gave a sad smile, then raised an eyebrow, "I thought the house couldn't be sold to people with children or wives?"

"That was then" Ms Sanderson gave a shrug, her eyes locked to his, "Things have changed"

"The Twelve are gone Richard" the author glanced back at Cherry as she gave his hand a squeeze, "You did it...you got rid of them all, and every other ghost in this house has gone too"

"But not you" he stated, frowning, "Why?"

She sighed, glancing down before meeting his gaze once more, "I was waiting for you"

Richard nodded at her, squeezing her hand in thanks, then winced as she frowned, "Did you manage to save Myra from your father?"

"I..." he shook his head, images of her under the knives as he had stabbed her rushing back, her blood coating her fingers as she had feebly raised a hand to fend him off, "I...no...she's gone"

As the blue-haired ghost pulled him into another embrace, her arms encircling him once more, Richard closed his eyes, realising the farce of his death. He had committed suicide to rescue the ghost of Myra only to kill her himself yet again.

"Its OK" the words of Cherry coaxed him, "It is just you and me here now...all of the other ghosts have left...all of the killers are gone"

He opened his eyes at her words, stomach twisting in guilt as he met the gaze of Ms Sanderson over her shoulder, the head of the elderly woman tilted to once side as she studied him intently as if seeing him for the first time, his voice sounding hollow as he nodded, "Yes, all the killers have gone"

About the Authors

Kelvin V.A Allison
Born in Portsmouth, England in 1973, Kelvin V.A Allison has somehow found his way to the hill strewn paradise that is County Durham, where he lives a life of calm and insanity in equal measure in the village home that he shares with his fiancée, three children and a neurotic dog. An author of 32 novels, including the ten book World of Sorrow series, he is also an avid board gamer, and a lifetime fan of fruit filled sugared pastries. He would prefer it if you didn't judge him.

Lisa Hutchinson
Much younger than her co-author, Lisa Hutchinson, a born and bred native of the rolling hills and endless countryside of County Durham, enjoys the quiet life in the small village of her birth where she resides along with her son, and has put her past-experience as a carer along with her love for horror movies and her vast knowledge of crime and serial killers, into co-creating this, her debut novel, the first of many to come.

Also by Kelvin V.A Allison

PHINEAS LUCK SERIES
Highgate
Desmotarian

THE BLIGHTED
Kraken
Ascentia

WORLD OF SORROW SERIES
Demons
Wonderland
Angelous
Rebirth

HOPE CHRONICLES
Hope & Glory
False Hope

STAND ALONE NOVELS
Skin Shifters
Thorns
Renascentia
Pariah
The Trouble with Rabbits Fluid
Bad Seed
Shuft
Ubasute
Witch Rock; Ubasute 2
Ghost Line
Pandemonium
Juggernaut
Unfinished Tales

Printed in Great Britain
by Amazon

52455962R00314